THE OFFICER'S WIFE

CATHERINE LAW

Boldwood

First published in Great Britain in 2023 by Boldwood Books Ltd.

Copyright © Catherine Law, 2023

Cover Design by Head Design Ltd

Cover Photography: Shutterstock

A CIP catalogue record for this book is available from the British Library.

Paperback ISBN 978-1-83751-563-9

Large Print ISBN 978-1-83751-559-2

Hardback ISBN 978-1-83751-558-5

Ebook ISBN 978-1-83751-556-1

Kindle ISBN 978-1-83751-557-8

Audio CD ISBN 978-1-83751-564-6

MP3 CD ISBN 978-1-83751-561-5

Digital audio download ISBN 978-1-83751-555-4

Boldwood Books Ltd
23 Bowerdean Street
London SW6 3TN
www.boldwoodbooks.com

PROLOGUE
ELISE, AUGUST 1932

The beach was hers: the water, blue and wide, waves cresting in the salty air. Her ankles sank into the sand and, all around her, she could hear the sound of the sea. Sitting down, she unbuckled her sandals, bare toes massaging the granular surface, ears filled by the wisps of the breeze.

Not a day for sitting on the beach, yet a family had erected a stripey wind break under the chalk cliff and were huddling together; she could see their tea dress, newspaper and straw hat flinching in the wind. The man wore a bowler. A boy squatted with his back to his parents, bashing the bottom of an upended bucket, hopeful for a sandcastle.

The chalk stack stood to Elise's right, beyond it, the rockpools. But she'd have to walk past the family.

The boy lifted his bucket and the castle collapsed. He shrugged. His whoop of laughter, the mock outrage on his face made Elise smile and as she hurried past, her joy joined in with his.

A passage of wet sand lay between cliff and stack, guarded by the tide. Elise waited, watching the rhythm of the water. When one of the crashing waves, brimming with seaweed, retreated, she made a dash for it, running, but her summer dress became soaked as another wave, as slick as mercury, caught her and made her yelp.

On the other side, in the little horseshoe cove enclosed by pearly-white cliffs, the air fell still. She set her sandals down in a safe spot and started to pick her way over the pavement of rocks, bare feet settling in crevices, finding a path, gathering the harvest of seaweed her mother required for her kitchen and medicine cabinet. Little sandpipers danced delicately over colonies of limpets and the winking sun made the pools iridescent. Below the surface, tiny crabs scuttled, and crimson urchins basked.

Elise squatted down, carefully tugged at specimens of bladderwrack and Irish moss and began to fill her basket. Sea lettuce floated like green hair, a miniature underwater forest. A mermaid's purse drifted past her fingertips. She plucked it from the water. The leathery pod glistened, the fronds curling over her fingers.

'Isn't that stealing?' came a voice. 'Isn't there a law against that?'

Elise looked up, peeled her hair from over her face and tucked it behind her ear. The boy stood where spent waves foamed on the sand, his bare feet wriggling. One of his braces dangled.

'I'm doing errands for my ma,' she called back. 'I'm not stealing any wreckage.'

A tiny white lie. She often presented her mother with sea-polished shards of ships' crockery, rusted pennies and pieces of old rope spilled from the hundreds of vessels that lay in the graveyard of the Goodwin Sands.

The boy gave a shrug of his shoulders and turned as if to go, and yet he dawdled, hands in pockets, his attention drawn to her. She bent to the rockpool, keeping him at the tail of her eye.

'The sand further up the beach is no good for sandcastles,' she said. 'You need to be closer to the sea. Good damp sand is needed.'

'I should know better.'

She spotted his rolled-up trousers, wet at the bottom.

'You got caught running through the gap.'

'Yep. Not quick enough.'

'Same here.'

He took tentative steps into the water, his dark hair lifting in the breeze.

'Ouch. It's colder than it looks,' he said. 'Mother keeps complaining about the wind and the sand, wants us to leave. She says it is even getting into her teeth. Father keeps saying it's supposed to be summer. We're supposed to be on holiday. Are you on holiday?'

'No, I live here.'

He glanced around at the beach.

'Here?'

Elise laughed, perched her basket on a rock. 'No, at Margate. A mile or so that-a-way,' She pointed over her shoulder. 'I'm here nearly every day in the holidays. But I like the beach best in wintertime.' She gazed at the pale horizon and back at the cliff face. She knew the sea to be as beautiful as it could be dangerous, and, close up, the pristine white chalk complex and dirty. 'Do you like it?'

He shrugged. 'Mother didn't want to go to Margate. She thought it wasn't our sort of place. We're at the Grand at Ramsgate, overlooking the Royal Harbour.'

'How posh.'

At her laugh, his cheeks went red. He dug his toes into the wet sand, lifted chunks, scattered them. He turned to walk away. Seagulls rose like white flags above the cliffs and the waves raced in, licking Elise's ankles. A sharp wave swamped the rock where she perched, the thrilling coldness fizzing over her legs. She stood, dripping, grabbed her basket and picked her way back. He turned back, stopped to watch her progress, gave her an amused smile.

'The tide is turning; that's why it's so wild,' she called out.

She paused to choose the best route, but her foot slipped, and her knee slammed down on to a jagged rock. Her palms grazed, water to her elbows. A scream hissed through her teeth.

'Are you all right?' The boy waded towards her, hopping over pools, 'You're bleeding.'

A stream of red coursed down her shin and over her ankle bone. She lifted the hem of her dress. The cut was raw and curved like a smile.

'Quickly, come on.' He grabbed her arm, his fingers firm at her elbow, pinning her with clear, earnest eyes.

She sat down on the sand, panting lightly from shock and embarrassment. He pulled out a handkerchief. She held it to her knee. Crimson blossomed through the white cotton.

'Does it hurt?'

'No, but it will later.'

Later, she thought, at home, with a cup of tea with her mother in the dark little cottage on King Street, Ma would know what to do. She would make her better. She always did.

'You're being terribly brave.'

'I'm trying to be.'

Her knee smarted. Blood seeped around the embroidered initials in the corner of the handkerchief.

'N.C.?'

'That's me,' he said. 'No, don't lift it. You need to keep the pressure up.'

He pressed his palm over the top. Elise winced. She hauled her gaze away from him to study the blue horizon.

'Stop the blood, must stop it bleeding,' he said. 'I've learnt that in the naval cadets.'

Up close, his face appeared sharper, cheek bones prominent, a kindness latent beneath blushing shyness. 'It runs in the family. My grandfather was a captain in the Navy, although Father never joined up. He prefers dry land and making money. Trouble is, I get seasick. Not much of a sailor.'

She giggled.

'That's better,' he said. 'You looked a bit queasy.'

'You're here on holiday?' She resumed their earlier conversation, trying not to think about the blood.

'Yes, we've come down from Farthing, near Canterbury. You won't know it. It's a little place in the middle of nowhere. We're almost swallowed by the woods.'

She glanced at his shirt, the fine stitching, the good linen. The buttons on his braces were imprinted with a miniature coat of arms.

'A big house?'

'Depends on what you mean by big.'

She thought of his parents, sheltering behind their windbreak. Their fine, wind-ruffled clothes. The man's smart bowler.

'How long will you be here?'

'We'll leave this afternoon if Mother gets her way.'

Elise pulled her basket over to check her spoils.

'Let's have a look.' He leaned in closer, his hand still pressing on her knee.

'It's okay,' she said, moving away. 'I think my leg is better now.'

He sat back, folded his arms, an unconscious barrier.

'Oh, dirty old seaweed,' he said, looking into her basket. 'Thought you might have caught fish or crabs, or lobsters. What's that?'

'A mermaid's purse. Brings sailors good luck, Ma says.' She handed it to him. 'You better keep it.'

He cradled it in his palm, fascinated.

'But what is this thing?'

'If I tell you, it will lose its charm.'

He drew out another handkerchief and wrapped the mermaid's purse, slipped it into his pocket.

'Two handkerchiefs?'

'Mother insists.' He smiled.

They fell quiet. Elise dabbed gingerly at her knee. The boy examined the contents of her basket. The waves quietened, expending themselves in gentle lines of froth. Even the seagulls shut up for a moment. They both started to speak at the same time.

'You only live down the road?'

'You live in a big old country house?'

'Nathaniel! Hey, Nathaniel!'

The man in the bowler hat stood on the other side of the chalk stack, fixed to the spot, his burly frame dark against the white rock. On this wild, beautiful beach, he looked ridiculous in his suit and hat. A fierceness set his jaw.

'What on earth do you think you're doing! Get back here. Your mother wants to go. Right now.'

Elise turned to the boy in time to see pain travel swiftly around his face. His dismay was touching, crushed a tiny part of her. She shivered.

'Who's that?' she asked, knowing immediately.

'Time to go.' He sighed, standing.

'I best get home, too.' But she stayed sitting on the sand.

The man bellowed, furious, gesturing. He turned and limped back the way he'd come, with no question that his son would not follow.

'What's wrong with his leg?' Elise asked.

'War wound.' The boy's face sharpened. 'You'll be all right if I leave you here?'

'Of course, I will.' She peeled the handkerchief off her knee and held it out to him.

Laughter brightened his face.

'Keep it. It's yours,' he said. 'I have plenty of handkerchiefs.'

Elise felt her cheeks scorch. 'Of course, how silly of me. You won't want it back. It's ruined.'

Folding the handkerchief, she watched him walk away, realising with a furious tapping in her heart that he did not know her name.

They called their goodbyes to each other across the sand. The breeze picked up, found its way into her little cove and their voices faded into the sound of the waves.

BOOK ONE

1939–1941

1

VIVI, APRIL 1939

Vivi had already travelled three thousand miles and, yet, in the back seat of the chauffeur-driven car cruising through the English countryside, she felt surprisingly fresh and settled into her skin. She kicked off her shoes and wriggled her toes. Pure giddy excitement. Being here, at last, and on her way to London.

Her mother, next to her, glanced at her stockinged feet with an indulgent smile, opened her compact and set to work on her lipstick. Due to the outrageously sharp angle of her hat, only one of her dark-lashed eyes was visible.

'Say, I love your hat, Mama,' Vivi said. 'But isn't it a bit too kicky for a car ride?'

Isobel Miles shook her head and the peacock feathers trembled. 'We have to make an impression, don't we, Vivienne, even disembarking at grotty ol' Southampton Docks. You never know who you're going to run into. Always be prepared.' Her mother flicked her gaze downward. 'And I see that you are. That jacket suits you. And your hair. Too darling for words.' She winked and returned to studying her own reflection, a sharp critical line between her painted brows.

Chanel wins every time, Vivi thought as she rested her chin in her hand and watched the hills and fields pass by, ludicrously green as everyone said they would be; mesmerising, after a week of flat grey Atlantic Ocean. She leaned forward to look for her father, who was fast asleep as usual, head against the other window, hands crossed on his waistcoat, watch chain swinging. At the Docks, as soon as he had ducked into the car, he'd berated it for being small 'like everything British', put his head back and began to snore. But Vivi found the English smallness reassuring: cottages tucked into hills, lanes snaking away, secret woods and storybook meadows. The car, driven by Davies – she always liked to ask the servants' names – felt cosy, contained. Even the sky looked prettier over here.

'He'll never make it through tonight,' Vivi's mother said, nodding at her husband. She rummaged in her handbag for her leather diary, plucking the pencil from its slot. Born and bred on the Upper East Side, her mother worked her diary hard. 'Now, let me see. Ah, yes. It's fine, we're not dining with the Calloways until tomorrow. Perhaps we'll give Daddy a night off. What do you say?'

'I say amen to that.'

Her mother reached her fingertips to rake through the smooth lock of Vivi's fair hair that lay over her shoulder.

'Are you nervous, darling? Or excited?'

'A bit of both, Mama. I can't wait to see the house, see London, and Genna, of course. But don't you think it's all kinda scary?'

Even though she was too young to remember the Miles' mansion on Grosvenor Street, the idea of returning gave her a tender little thrill. For a New York girl on Park Avenue, she could show her face at a party or soiree every day of the week if she wished to, and yet the Miles family were, frustratingly, on the periphery of New York society, pressing their noses against the windows of the Astors and the Guggenheims. But now that her best friend Genna had married an English lord, Vivi could make London her own. Or so her mother said.

'Perhaps a quiet night in, to rest, Vivi,' she said, 'and we can face the Season refreshed?'

For Vivi, the Season sounded like something glorious, terrifying and old fashioned. The ship had been a confinement; the same decks tramped along, every day the same: the same tight little cabin, but First Class of course.

'I'd like to go and see Genna tonight, Mama, even for a short while. Will Daddy let me, do you think?' She sent a wary glance at her snoozing father, sensing her freedom tantalisingly out of reach. 'May I telephone Genna as soon as I arrive? I assume she is in the book.'

'Of course, she is. Anyone who is anyone is. But listen, save yourself.' She turned a page in her diary. 'Let's ask Genna and Lord Dornford to dine with us tomorrow along with the Calloways. That will be fun. You and Genna have the whole summer ahead of you, after all.'

Vivi watched her write a note in her diary. Her mother's hands fascinated her: such pale skin, like her own, but with all manner of tanned patches. Hot sunny days at their summer home, the Colonial saltbox upstate on the Hudson, golfing and riding horses, had played havoc with her mother's skin. Freckles lay beneath thick foundation, and moles sprang like stars over her shoulders.

Vivi, they said, was the image of her mother. And yes, her hair, face and figure were a carbon copy. But her own complexion remained light, almost translucent, thanks to the series of ridiculous bonnets her governesses made her wear.

The suburbs pulled closer, and the car crossed the Thames at Hampton Court. Isobel nudged her husband awake. Edwin sat up, blinked, and gave them both the benefit of his humorous scowl.

'Never wake a sleeping bear,' he said and beamed, teeth shining white against his tanned, handsome face, which was framed by silver hair.

'You didn't want to miss it, Edwin. The palace. Look it's over there.'

'Thank you, honey. So considerate,' he said, his Boston twang more pronounced on waking. He gave Hampton Court a cursory glance and settled back into his seat. 'It looks so goddam magnificent, it has to be a fake,' he said. 'Give me another nudge when we reach grand ol' Mayfair.'

For Vivi, the view of fabled London had started out disappointingly cramped and grey. But the sights of the grubby outskirts faded, and grand streets and wide parks began to open up before her. She caught glimpses of splendid squares, bursting shop windows and yet another palace with high gilded gates. People hurried head-down and funnelled into underground stations, like the subway back home.

The car rumbled over the cobbles of Grosvenor Street as the gas lamps came on, one by one, and the white stucco mansions, plane trees and railings of Vivi's childhood imagination greeted her. She smelt coal smoke and car exhaust, noticed exquisite plasterwork spoiled by chimney soot; the established, aloof elegance held together by the delicate threads of an old society. She whispered a tentative hello to this new chapter in her life.

Pots of hyacinth and narcissi, ordered in by her mother that morning, filled the panelled dining room with fragrance, the promise of spring. Candles glowed, adding to the last of the daylight, accompanied by gas lights hissing above the picture rail. Vivi stood at the door to watch her mother check the places at the table, plucking up name cards and setting them down, drifting her own perfume around the space. Vivi knew her mother thought this evening important for she had put on her new Elsa Schiaparelli gown and wore a circle of diamonds around her throat.

And yet Vivi, in her pale icy blue, felt no nerves. She wondered at this, pleased with herself, concluding that she must be beyond excitement at seeing Genna. She had no idea what to expect from the Calloways, so there seemed no reason to get silly about it. She glanced out the window at the people clipping right past the railings, cars rumbling by, so close, she could touch them. They'd packed up and left their apartment on Park Avenue, on the sixteenth floor of a great geometric slab, one of many monuments of wealth that blocked out the sky around Central Park. They had electric light. From their vertigo-inducing balcony they had views of the Empire State and the Chrysler, and far below, the dirty littered Manhattan streets cut off, out of reach.

'Here's a cab,' said her mother, craning her neck. 'Now, where is Daddy? He'll need help with his cufflinks.' She headed up the staircase as the doorbell chimed.

Vivi caught a glimpse of familiar red hair through the side window and, in a burst of giggles, swooped to open the door before the butler stirred.

'Honey, don't you know, you're supposed to let the staff do that,' cried Genna as she leaned in with a fierce, scented embrace. In her heels, she towered over Vivi, all broad shouldered and glorious.

'Oh, I will never get used to it.'

'But you must have,' said Genna. 'Look at you. Magnificently at home in this splendid house.'

Genna slipped off her sable stole and held it out for the butler to take, looking like a polished penny with her copper hair rolled and intricately pinned, her eyes ablaze, her bias-cut emerald gown in precise contrast to her hair.

'You look wonderful. Always the same, Miss Firecracker,' said Vivi, her eyes prickling with joy.

The tall man with a thin patrician face who stood behind Genna moved forward to greet her, and her nerves bloomed like a rash. Vivi's New York life had become empty last year when Genna had sailed the Atlantic and met this real-life landed English lord. They'd married immediately and she hadn't come home.

'May I introduce Michael, Lord Dornford,' said Genna, her New York accent softened with pride. 'Dornie to his friends. Dornie, darling, this is Miss Vivienne Miles. My best friend. My soul companion. Fresh off the boat like I was when we met.'

His handshake felt firm and warm, not the limp, damp fish that Vivi had been warned she might encounter here in upper-class English society. His eyes radiated kindness.

'So wonderful to have gotten to meet you at last, Michael, Lord, Dornie.' Vivi laughed as she tumbled out her words. 'Genna's letters are full to the brim with you.'

'The pleasure is mine.' Dornie clicked his heels and kissed her hand.

Vivi linked her friend's arm and swept her into the drawing room where a small fire burned in the enormous marble fireplace and oil paintings glimmered darkly around the walls. She loved the way the plump cushions on the armchairs awaited her, her heels sinking into thick carpet.

'Drinks first. My parents will be down shortly.'

Vivi remembered she must sit back and let the butler serve the Champagne. Curled up either end of the chaise, her conversation with Genna sparkled and rebounded between sips: the crossing, the Season already in full swing, the theatre and concerts and parties to go to. How she had missed her. Her excitement matched the bubbles in her glass, while Genna's husband sat by the fireplace and quietly admired proceedings.

'Dornie is going to get his wings,' said Genna. 'His papers will be arriving any minute now. You think it better to choose, don't you, Dornie? To volunteer now, rather than be put somewhere you don't want to be.'

'That's the way I want to play it.'

'Haven't the British already got an army? An air force?' Vivi asked. 'Sorry for asking dumb questions, but I don't know the half of it.'

'Things are hotting up, Vivienne,' Dornie said. 'Each day the news doesn't get any better. None of us trust the mad man of Europe. Better to prepare. Be one step ahead. We need to fill the ranks. The more of us, the better.'

'In the newspaper yesterday, they said the British Museum is being emptied of its treasures,' Genna said.

'I saw soldiers digging in one of the big parks we drove past,' said Vivi. 'What is going on there?'

'That'll be trenches, for some sort of air defence.'

The room fell quiet. Vivi shivered a quiet chill of fear.

Genna roused herself. 'If things get as bad as they say they might, honey, you can come and live with me in Sussex. Dornie will be based at Biggin Hill and we decided I would stay in London at first, but...'

Dornie indicated to the butler to refresh their glasses, while his wife continued, lowering her voice.

'The RAF are fast-tracking him. Pilot officer before he knows it. But he doesn't want his crew to know.' Genna looked intensely proud, if not a little sad. 'He wants to be part of the gang.'

'What is it about you, Genna?' Vivi asked. 'You're either deeply in love with your husband or you're wearing a new dress. But something tells me, it's both.'

Genna laughed. 'Of course I'm wearing a new dress. I'm seeing my best friend for the first time in a year. I must take you to my atelier on Bond Street. As for dear Dornie...' She threw an adoring glance at her husband before turning back to Vivi. 'But I've missed this face.' She reached for her cheek. 'You look luminous, Vivienne Miles. You've grown up since I last clapped eyes on you. Must have been all that fresh ocean air you've been drinking in. Walking the decks, round and round.'

'Don't remind me.'

They were laughing as Vivi's father announced himself, striding into the room in an immaculate dinner suit, his wife on his arm.

'What's all this? What are we having? Still on the Champagne, I see. Time for a proper sundowner. Welcome, Lord and Genevieve, Lady Dornford,' He took both of Genna's hands and bowed low. 'Well, I'll be jiggered. Last time I saw you, Genna, you were in a school uniform.'

He ordered cocktails and engaged in conversation with Dornie. Her mother, Vivi noticed, had changed her gown – her favourite Chanel in the creamy peach satin to flatter her honey-flecked skin. She'd pinned on her new diamond brooch rather too high on her shoulder: a sure sign of nerves. But surely not because of the Calloways? Mr Calloway was some old associate of her father's. It struck Vivi: this was the first time her mother, or indeed any one of them, had been in the presence of a lord.

Sipping her Martini, she watched as her mother's unease melted away when Dornie engaged with her. Vivi exchanged smiles with Genna, who held court with her father across the room, and felt anticipation blossoming, the talk of war fading as the sun set over Mayfair. The doorbell chimed once more, and the room filled with unfamiliar voices.

Digby Calloway commanded his way into the drawing room with a neat moustache, slicked back greying hair, a pronounced limp, and a single Great War medal pinned to his dinner jacket. He shook hands with everyone, with one eye, Vivi noticed, scouting his surroundings, as if scrutinising the value of the silverware. His wife, Freda, seemed to Vivi to be overdressed. It was as if she was wearing all her jewellery. She bobbed her way around the room, telling each person the same thing: 'How wonderful to be here.' And in her wake, their son Nathaniel, recently made a naval officer, as her mother had mentioned earlier to her, rather pointedly, 'A *lieutenant*, Vivi.' Despite the firm set of his shoulders and his long stride, he had a tightness about him, a hesitancy, as if he'd found himself in the wrong place, at the wrong time. Vivi, feeling a nugget of sympathy, wanted to take his arm, lead him into a corner and reassure him: we're not to be feared, we're ordinary underneath.

Freda Calloway grabbed her hand.

'Ah, but dear you *are* beautiful,' she said, her rings, loose on her knuckles, pressing into Vivi's fingers.

Vivi smiled, wondering how on earth to respond. She noticed that close-up, Freda, who must be around the same age as her mother, seemed older, her dark hair severe against her wan complexion. Her necklace looked Edwardian, her lipstick leaching into the lines around her mouth. Freda's shoes seemed too tight and from the expression on her face, Vivi wondered if she was in pain.

'How do you do, Mrs Calloway,' Vivi said. 'Are you staying in town?'

'We have our usual rooms at Browns. We've been looking forward to your family's visit for a long time. This is our son Nathaniel.' She tugged on his arm to pull him over. 'Nathaniel, Miss Vivienne Miles.'

With this, she moved on to collar Vivi's mother, leaving the two alone.

Nathaniel glanced swiftly to one side, and back again, as if catching Vivi's eye might hurt. She noticed an unexpected wave in his dark hair, a boyish air, a hesitation in his eyes.

'You must tell me all about your ship, Lieutenant Calloway,' she said, wanting to lend him some of her budding confidence. 'I know, it's a strange request, as you might think I have had enough of them for the last week or so. But perhaps that is something we will have in common.'

The butler's tray moved between them, proffering Nathaniel his Gin and It. Before answering, he took a sip, ice clinking, then paused, took another.

'I'm sorry, Miss Miles,' he said, with an unexpectedly bright smile. 'Social events seem to stall me momentarily. I've either been stuck in the country, stuck in Dartmouth or stuck on the ship, and I'm worried that I've become a dullard. And I don't suppose for a moment you have this worry, but I am always wondering what my parents are going to do and say next.'

He glanced over his shoulder, and Vivi laughed as her own father's guffaw boomed across the room.

'Daddy does come out with some gems,' she said. 'However, Mama, I can trust. But the night is young, and you'll have to make allowances for us Americans, for we're not entirely sure how to behave.' She sipped her Martini, dipped her finger in to bob the olive. 'This is *London*, remember.'

'I think you are all behaving impeccably.'

She caught his eye and finished her Martini.

'Well, I know some of the rules,' she said. 'I certainly know I shouldn't have another one of these and should stick to water at dinner.'

He laughed. His frame seemed to soften, and she watched as he appraised her, drawing her in. Vivi recognised when men were being gentlemen, and when they were not, and she liked the way it felt when Nathaniel looked at her. Thrilled, and safe.

'I expect you are excited to be here?' he asked. 'You lived here as a child, Mother mentioned.'

'Briefly, when I was about eight or nine. But you know what it is with childhood memories. It's more the *feeling*, isn't it. I don't remember too much about this house.' She gazed up at the stupendous chandelier, the plasterwork on the ceiling. 'But I remember how gloomy things seemed, with the Crash and all. Daddy came here, he says, to mend the roof when it wasn't raining, or something.'

'And I believe that's when our fathers met.'

She spotted her father and Digby sitting either end of the chaise, their arms resting casually along the back, chewing the financial fat, no doubt. Her mother chatted with Genna and Freda in a little group of armchairs by the fireplace.

As Dornie crossed the room to talk to the ladies, her father leapt up.

'Lord Dornford, you need to settle a matter for me.' He took him to one side.

Vivi realised that Nathaniel was waiting for her to continue. 'All that talk from Daddy about the rain and the roof, and all; whenever I imagined London, I saw grey sky and endless black umbrellas.'

He laughed. 'You've got it about right. There's nothing quite like English rain. Seems to get you wetter than any other kind.'

The butler appeared with another gin for him.

'And I had such a formidable English governess here,' she added. 'Whereas the ones back home were a breeze – young girls who wanted to play in the sun as much as I did. I'll never forget being fascinated that this house had five floors, climbing endless staircases up and up. In New York, we only have a duplex.'

Nathaniel listened intently, studying her face. 'You remember more than you think.'

'I like New York, but I love being in the country. Our farmhouse upstate has two storeys at the front and one at the back, with a long sloping catslide roof right down to the ground. Daddy likes to act as if he were a country gent. Goodness me,' she said, 'how I rattle on.'

'Please keep rattling. It is far more fascinating than my dull life.'

'I don't believe that,' she laughed.

Their eyes met with a spark of understanding.

'Everyone has their own story, Nathaniel.'

'Please, call me Nathan.'

'And I'm Vivi. Forget the *Miss Vivienne Miles*,' she laughed, and they shook hands on it, raised their glasses to one another, starting again.

In a sudden hush of conversation, Freda's voice carried across the room as she adjusted her husband's tie.

'...Yes, Digby, a Park Avenue princess...'

Vivi saw her mother's shoulders stiffen and she caught Genna's startled eye. Her friend had warned in her letters of possible prejudice, or misguided jealousy. And here it was in her own drawing room. Freda, oblivious, looked around and signalled the butler, tapping the side of her glass with her fingernail.

Nathan, his face grim, turned his back on his parents and asked Vivi about Vassar.

'Oh no, I'm through talking about myself,' she said, stumbling through shock. 'You must tell me all about the Navy.'

'Must I?' His grin seemed forced. He threw a narrow glance towards his parents. 'Well, it runs in the family: grandfather, missed out my father, who saw brief army action in France, then me. They sent me down to Dartmouth naval college as soon as they possibly could.' He spoke quickly, sounding stifled, once more in the wrong place. 'I'm now a fully fledged naval officer. Believe it or not, I wanted to be an artist.'

The gong for dinner went, and voices raised in chattering relief.

In the dining room, Vivi felt mildly thwarted when she saw where her mother had placed her. But, as she took her seat, she realised her foresight, for Nathan sat directly opposite her, and he could look straight at her through a gap in the flower arrangement. She leant forward to ask him about his art when Digby plumped himself down next to her.

'A pleasure to see you again, my dear,' he said. 'Do you remember me? Last time I saw you, you were this high. Good to have you back this side of the Pond.'

She noticed the gleam in his eye, the hair sprouting from his ears, and had absolutely no recollection of ever meeting him before.

'Is that the plan? For you American girls?' he went on. 'Lady Dornford has certainly landed on her feet. What a smashing chap he is.' Vivi opened her mouth to beg his pardon, but he countered himself swiftly. 'All in good humour, my dear. It's good to have you over here, on our side – hopefully, that is. The way things are going in Europe.'

He patted her arm, resting his hand there, and told the butler he wanted the Chablis, and that Miss Miles would have it too.

Her mother, who was sitting at the foot of the table, tapped the crystal with her spoon. 'May I make an announcement... Dear friends: you are all so very welcome here in our London home. Oh my, it has been far too long, hasn't it, Edwin? Old friends and new acquaintances. And there's to be no talk of politics or impending doom, or anything unsavoury tonight around this table. We're here to enjoy ourselves, you hear?'

Everyone raised their glasses.

Her father laughed. 'Noted, Digby?'

Freda, beaming widely, gazed around the room. 'Isobel, let me start by saying, you must be so proud of your beautiful house.'

'I can't take credit for any of it,' she replied. 'I sent cables ahead to my interior designer, giving him carte blanche.'

'Can we gentleman veto house decorating too?' asked Digby.

Freda threw her husband a dark look. 'Did you hear that? Carte blanche.'

'Whatever that means,' he mumbled.

Freda turned her shoulder. 'Isobel, we have a frightfully ugly Victorian pile in the country.'

'My father built that house,' Digby muttered, lazily outraged.

'But at least these Mayfair mansions are so classic,' Freda continued, ignoring him. 'So much light and space—'

'It doesn't matter what sort of house you have, dear,' interrupted Edwin, 'if Hitler is going to flatten it.'

'Edwin, what did I say?' Isobel laughed.

Vivi spooned at her soup and watched as Genna chatted with Nathan. She couldn't catch their words, but as he listened to her, he looked as if he was taking down an important message.

She asked Dornie, on her right, about his estate in the country.

'It is a glorious spot, down in Sussex,' he said. 'We're fortunate. And Genna has settled in so well. As if she was born to it.'

Even for a Park Avenue princess.

She watched Freda Calloway, sitting at her father's elbow, leaning into him, laughing heartily at his banter, and wondered what murky quagmire of English class had made her slip up like she did. Did Nathan feel that way about her too?

'Genna and I were thinking of going dancing after this, at the Velvet Rose, this little club in Bloomsbury,' said Dornie. 'Would you like to come along?'

'Sounds wonderful, but I'll have to ask Daddy.'

Hearing their conversation, her father looked up. 'There's nothing for it, honey. You kids must buzz off and do whatever it is you want to do.'

'Splendid idea,' said Freda. 'It is Nathaniel's last night, after all.'

Nathan gave his mother a look. 'Second from last.' He addressed the table. 'I join my ship the day after tomorrow.'

'All the more reason to step out tonight,' said her mother. 'I'll ring for Davies. He can drive you.'

'Oh no, we'll take a taxi,' said Dornie. 'We don't want to keep the poor fellow up all night.'

'*All night*?' Vivi exclaimed, feeling her cheeks brighten. 'Mama, are you sure?'

'Oh, I'm sure. You are being chaperoned by a respectable married couple, after all. And I always take my lead from your Daddy.'

At this, he raised his glass to Vivi and gave her one of his ludicrous winks.

'Just look at us,' giggled Genna, as the taxi swung around the darkened Grosvenor Square where shuttered windows offered an intriguing slither of light from within. 'Two tall dark handsome men, a blonde and a redhead. Out on the town.'

'Gracious me,' said Dornie. 'And I bet Nathan thought shore leave at Portsmouth was bad enough.'

'Believe me, this is much more fragrant,' said Nathan.

They headed north up Bond Street, passing glowing shop windows. Vivi, pressed against Nathan as the cab rounded a corner, gazed out the window, mesmerised. In Manhattan it would have been a long haul down noisy filthy Fifth Avenue, battling with the cross-town traffic at every block, stepping over cracked sidewalks to scuttle into a, hopefully, air-conditioned club. Worse in the summer when the city resembled a steaming hot animal. But here, they trundled through sedate streets of an old world where the poised grandeur of mansions, cobbles and plane trees made her feel secure. She was melting with excitement, with possibility.

She saw the evening unfolding before her, unexpectedly, like a silken ribbon. Perhaps she should have said no to the Chablis that Digby had ordered for her, but it had proved hard to counter him. Warmed by the confidence the wine had given her, her head deliciously light, she turned to Nathan and whispered, 'You don't suppose this is a set-up, do you?'

In the dark of the taxi, she saw his eyes go luminous in surprise.

For a moment he fell quiet, and she held her breath, wondering if she had stumbled too far.

But Nathan laughed. 'Well, I for one don't think my parents have it in them.'

Vivi shifted with discomfort, feeling doubtful of that.

'And I think Lieutenant Calloway is too much of a gentleman to have it even cross his mind,' said Dornie.

They drew up outside railings of a long Bloomsbury terrace and clattered down the steps that led to the swaying embrace of the nightclub. The Velvet Rose's maître d' greeted Dornie like an old friend and ushered them through the smoky, dim-lit room to a circular booth. The parquet dance floor sat like an inviting pool of water and people conversed in the light of rose-red lamps. Low intimate murmurings, punctuated by tinkling laughter. Smooth pearls and gold cufflinks shone out like beacons.

'It's like a speakeasy,' said Vivi, settling onto the plush cushioned seat. 'At least, how I imagine one to be.'

The waiter hovered and Dornie ordered Champagne.

'Lemonade for me,' said Vivi. She wanted a clear head. She wanted to talk to Nathan, who squeezed up next to her, and remember everything in the morning.

'Lady Dornford tells me you have horses,' he said.

'*Had* horses,' she corrected. 'Daddy sold them last winter when he planned this trip. It made me rather sad to see them go, but it was all part of some financial plan of his. I don't want to say "harebrained" plan, but you know what I mean.'

'We have stables and a wonderful steward down at Farthing Hall. If you ever want to ride out, you must come down. You will be so very welcome. I am not sure how long you are going to be here in England...?'

'Daddy's is a two-year plan,' she said.

The band, who had returned to the stage, finished tuning up and started with a swing number. Dornie and Genna leapt up to dance.

Alone with Nathan, Vivi felt a rush of shyness.

'This is a treat,' he said and raised his glass to her.

'My my, *what* a treat for an American gal, just landed in town,' she declared, rather energetically. She took a sip of the ice-cold lemonade. 'And isn't it magical in here?'

'You have such a soft accent,' said Nathan.

'You mean, hardly Yankie at all.' She laughed.

'You could say that. I mean it has a lovely flow.'

'Perhaps because Daddy could afford to send me to a good school and decided he didn't want me to have a *Noo York* drawl. I can't say that for his accent, though. It is very Bostonian, don't you think?'

'An honest, hard-working accent.'

She looked at him and could tell that there was nothing wrong with that. How different he appeared to the college boys and would-be Wall Street brokers she had mixed with back home. Boys and young men who thought they ought to impress her with money, bragging about their sports and their jobs and their cars. And yet, she noticed, Nathan barely talked about himself, and seemed to give more of himself to her.

'Please tell me about your art,' she asked him. 'Do you paint? Oils or watercolour?'

'Ah, that's more of a conversation for a quiet private afternoon over tea, don't you think? Here, I must raise my voice and compete with the band. It won't help when I'm trying to impress you with the subtle nuances of my creativity. Sorry, does that sound ridiculous? Pompous even?'

'Not at all. It shows sensitivity. Your modesty,' Vivi said, with a stab of delight at the prospect of a quiet afternoon with Nathan. She saw his eyes grow tender with gratitude. 'So, let's stick to practicalities. You return to your ship the day after tomorrow? Where are you based?'

'Chatham. It is on the Medway, east of London.' He looked at his watch. 'And now, I see, it *is* tomorrow and so I think we should dance, while we can.'

He stood and offered his hand and within two beats of music, Vivi was in his arms. The music swung and rocked around them, as other couples moved close by in the half-dark. She felt light on her feet, her hand on his broad shoulder, his hand cradling hers. Nathan had an easy supple grace, a steady quietness, and an innate confidence slowly revealing itself as he led her around the floor.

He spoke close to her ear. 'The way things are going, I may be away for quite a while.'

'Are you frightened?' She knew it sounded silly even to ask.

'Aren't we all?'

His hand on her waist held her tight. Their faces were close, ear to ear; she felt his cheek brush her hair, his head resting lightly against hers. They seemed to have stopped dancing. She pulled back to look at his face and thought that he might kiss her. He looked as if he wanted to and somewhere inside her, everything felt right. Frighteningly right. And she knew that he didn't have to kiss her to let her know he felt the same.

Back at the table, as Nathan fell into conversation with Dornie, Genna leant over to her.

'You two. It's as if you already know each other. It's like you have had a head start.'

Vivi hushed her, shook her head, but could not stop the huge smile from splitting her face.

'Yes, but he must go back to his ship tomorrow. So that's that.'

'Oh honey, yes,' Genna said. 'That is that. But it doesn't have to be. Oh no, Dornie's ordering more Champagne.' She raised her voice as the ice bucket was placed by the table. 'Darling, you realise it is past our bedtimes.'

'Desperate times, desperate measures,' said Dornie, opening the bottle himself. 'Let's drink to us. The four of us. And more lemonade for Miss Vivi, please, waiter.'

'I'm going to get hiccups.'

They raised their brimming glasses.

'Just think,' Nathan said, 'last year, we were popping Champagne corks because Chamberlain said it was peace in our time. And look where we are now.'

'Yes,' said Genna. 'Just look where we are now. The best of times, the worst of times.'

'Peace in our time?' said Dornie. 'What did we know?'

Under the tablecloth, Nathan reached for Vivi's hand and folded it in his. Joy sent bright sparks through her like the Fourth of July.

But later, as she lay in bed in her twilit room at the front of the white stucco mansion, the first milk van rumbling past, fear, something small and grating worked its way over her. And a chorus of questions began to beat in her sleepy mind, narrowing down to *What did we know?* as she drifted to sleep.

2

VIVI, AUGUST 1939

Genna's laugh rang down the telephone wire. 'My, it's something to tell your grandchildren, isn't it? That you were proposed to by your husband while you were sitting in the bath.'

'*Grand*children? One thing at a time,' Vivi giggled. 'And *really*, Genna! But it puts it all in a nutshell, doesn't it? Everything hurtling at such speed and the war, and all, like a little tornado, and all rather bizarre...'

'Honey, you make it sound like a bad thing. You and Nathan, I mean. Not the war.'

Genna's laugh sounded hollow.

'No, no,' Vivi said. 'With Nathan, it feels natural, and easy and wonderful, but...'

But yesterday, the late-summer morning had dawned humid and grey, the barrage balloons could be spotted through Vivi's bathroom window, beyond the chimney pots, ominous and silvery against the blank sheet of the sky.

The city, or at least Mayfair – so benign and calm compared to the seething mess of New York – had seemed primed, holding its breath. Every day, they listened to the gentlemanly voice on the radio giving instructions of what to do in an air raid. Her mother had announced that they should pack their bags right away and go home; her father said it was ludicrous to try to leave along with all the masses. People were saying, somehow knowing, 'it'll be war tomorrow'. And yet it never was and so they lurched on into the next perplexing day, everything happening far too quickly, but not happening at all.

Vivi had relished a moment alone in the bath, a chance to read Nathan's letter in peace. Whenever one came through the letter box and scooted across the hallway floor, her mother became far too excitable and curious, begging to know the latest. And Vivi had to bat her away, trying to keep a sense of calm, of reality. She had not seen Nathan for months, not since they'd danced at the Velvet Rose, and yet, that whirlwind of delight and trepidation seemed so normal compared to the strange, uncanny hours she lived through now.

He'd held her hand in the pale darkness of that spring dawn, kissed her goodbye in the back of the taxi and promised to write. And Vivi had wondered if he would, for a day or two, and resolved to put him from her mind.

A week later, the first of his letters arrived on HMS *Fair Isle* notepaper, tentative and enquiring. She remembered staring at the envelope in a sort of baffled wonder. He'd kept his promise, and the simplicity of his words, his honesty, his attention, wound its gentle way into her. He wrote every day, and Vivi replied, their conversations crossing and recrossing in a frenzy of laughter and joy, sobering promises, and shy declarations; each describing their worlds and building their own together.

'But what, Vivi?' Genna's voice prompted her in the earpiece.

'No buts. Believe me. Everything is so difficult, and what-all. I mean, it's Nathan, and he is so far away. But everything is also simply, right.'

Vivi smiled to herself as the pips went and Genna said goodbye. She knew why it felt that way: Nathan. He littered her with shards of gold.

Even so, sitting in the bath, and reading his, what must be, forty-fourth letter, his proposal of marriage – tucked in at the end of the fifth page – had astonished her, making her drop the pages in the bathwater.

And, as she fished out the paper, the ink running, his words lost, she found it hard to conjure his face. Am I a fool, she thought, to let my life turn on the outcome of one evening? And a little attention from an English gentleman?

The sodden letter disintegrated in her hands.

* * *

'Don't you think she looks magnificent, Genevieve?'

'Magnificent?' Genna laughed, coming in to Vivi's bedroom, shutting the door behind her. 'Why, Mrs Miles, that's what they call ships, or steam trains, or...'

'Or full-blood mares,' Vivi chipped in, perched on the edge of the slipper chair in her wedding dress. Taxis and cars and buses rumbled on the cobbles along Grosvenor Street as if nothing untoward was happening. As if the British prime minister had not declared war on Germany; as if she was not marrying a man she'd only just met.

'I don't think we can compare Vivi to the occupants of a New England stud stable, Mrs Miles,' Genna offered. She bent to kiss Vivi's cheek, catching her eye with knowing humour. 'Don't worry, honey,' she whispered, 'I'm not going to muss you.'

The duchess satin, designed by Worth and sent over from Paris in miraculous time, possibly on a ferry packed with refugees, encased Vivi in ripples of white. With her blonde hair in a fashionable roll over her forehead, demure long sleeves, and a high neck. This, then, constituted magnificence.

'As always, you are right, Lady Dornford.' Her mother, sitting head to toe in purple, her dress nipped in, relished Genna's title and addressed her by it as often as she could. 'Vivienne's beauty should pass without comment.'

'Mama, please,' she said, catching sight of herself again in the mirror. Her lips glowed red; her mother's diamonds dripped icily around her throat. She smoothed her damp palms down over the satin.

'But there's something else there don't you think, Genevieve?' Isobel said, her eyes travelling over Vivi as if she were a young filly she was about to buy. 'A quality? A potency? Ah, what am I saying? What baloney. Can't believe that I am this nervous, but, after all, my only child is getting married. I think I'm allowed the jitters. Edwin has warned me not to go over the edge... but this could be Mayfair's *wedding of the year*!'

'It's almost shot-gun,' said Vivi. 'What will people think?'

'Oh, how I hate that expression.'

'They'll think there's a war on, Vivi,' Genna chided. 'Thousands of couples are getting hitched quickly.'

'Pity it's not the New York society wedding I had dreamed of for you, Vivi darling,' her mother drawled.

'That's not helping, Mama,' she said, though she felt secretly pleased: her parents trying to outdo the Rockefellers and failing miserably. 'I want to get to the church, to see Nathan. For him to be my husband. Because after that, he will be gone again so quickly.'

'That's the spirit, honey,' Genna said, leaning in to apply another layer of red to her lips.

Vivi pictured Nathan waiting patiently at the altar of St George's of Mayfair. Then the image cut to the steam rising in the bath, how his letter disintegrated in her hands.

She hadn't come to London to find a husband. She'd come because she wanted to take a trip, to see Genna, because she had grown bored of flashy New York. She had not expected to fall in love. The thought of how quickly, and how thoroughly it had happened halted her in her stride, as if her clothes had got caught on a thorny bush.

Genna took the veil from its hanger and carried it over to her.

'Not yet! Don't put it on yet,' cried her mother, laughingly shielding her eyes, 'I want to see you in all your glory as you enter the church. See you as Nathan will see you. Then I shall die a happy woman.'

The butler knocked on the door to remind them that the car was outside.

'That's my cue.' Her mother rose to kiss the air around Vivi's hair, her fingertip circling Vivi's face. She whispered, her eyes youthful against aging skin, 'Are you all right, my darling? You look as though your mind is trying to make itself up.'

Vivi squeezed her hand. 'Mama, stop it, or I will cry, and you don't want me with a red nose, do you? Not for Mayfair's wedding of the year.'

Her mother gave a brief shake of her head, and teary-eyed, left the room, her perfume trailing in the air behind her.

'Do you think it is too soon?' Vivi asked as Genna began to pin and adjust the veil.

'Not at all,' she said, standing so close that Vivi could not see her face. 'Just look at Dornie and I.'

'It is silly I know. I think my parents and his parents... did they plan this? I mean, none of them are surprised at how well it has worked out. You'd think there'd be some resistance, some objection on the grounds of indecent haste. And remember, Daddy has known Digby for years.'

'Ah, but only in a formal business sense,' Genna mumbled,

hairpins in her mouth. 'And I can't believe you are thinking this, Miss Miles.'

'The special licence was gotten in no time. The dress here, double-quick. And this God-dam war. Mama beside herself, and Freda is practically fizzing with anticipation. Did you see her the other evening, when we had drinks?'

'Vivi, now hush. Stop thinking what you're thinking.' Genna stood back to admire her work. 'This is Nathan we are talking about. Dornie and I both said the other day how much we trust and like him. An honourable man. Happiness has landed in your lap and I can feel it radiating out of you. And everyone else is happy about it. Let them make a fuss. Let them have this snippet of joy, when things could turn for the worse at any moment.'

'Perhaps they think I might change my mind at any minute...'

'Will you?'

Genna caught the look on her face.

'Listen, you could hitch yourself to any titled sop you liked. And some of those gentlemen you said you had on your dance card that last winter in New York – Lord so-and-so and the Marquis of who-knew-where, on the prowl down Park Avenue – were as poor as church mice. They would only want you because you're not also poor.' She reached forward to do something to the veil. 'Whereas Nathan...'

Vivi flinched as a hairpin caught her scalp.

'Nathan is going to have a fine naval career,' Vivi said, hearing pride in her voice. 'He does not need my fortune.'

'Exactly. I bet you he has never given it a second thought.'

'Whereas his mother...' She broke into laughter.

'That's better.' Genna stepped back and looked at her, on the edge of happy tears. 'Your mother was right: you *do* look magnificent.'

But what else had her mother said? Something about potency?

Vivi had expected excited butterflies but felt none. Instead, she stood on the edge of something, and a heaviness lowered itself over her. Not fear or anxiety, for those emotions were far too simple.

On the telephone the day before, Nathan had asked her how she felt, and she'd told him she couldn't wait to see him. That's how she'd felt yesterday. But how would she feel tomorrow? And the day after that? After the two-day honeymoon they would take in a seaside town, Nathan was to leave for Chatham to join his ship. There was not much time for her to be a bride; she must get straight on with being a naval wife. Separated, and alone in wartime.

Despite the pricking ache under her collarbone, Vivi gave Genna her best smile, as her friend pressed her bouquet into her hands, the scent of roses and orange blossom settling around her like a spell.

'I am glad you are here,' she said.

'Me too, honey. And your father is waiting in the hallway. It's time to go.'

* * *

Vivi stopped at the top of the stairs and called down, 'Daddy, I'm ready.'

Her father, pacing the chequered tiles, his silver hair pomaded, his morning suit immaculate, cufflinks gleaming, looked up and grinned.

What a handsome, admirable man he is, she thought, as she made her slow, careful way down towards him. Edwin Miles, burnished from New England summer sports and his energy – the drive that had taken him from Boston to Wall Street – sparked as he shot her the same wide blue stare she saw in her own reflection.

Vivi had her mother's face, she had concluded, but her father's eyes.

He met her halfway down the stairs, offered her his arm, and led her to the hall settle.

'We have a little time,' he said. 'Here, sit a while.'

Genna scuttled past them and out the door, blowing Vivi a kiss for luck.

The hall felt cold and echoey, a place for departures only. They sat quietly for some moments.

'Anything you want to tell me, Vivienne?' her father asked as he peered at her through her veil. 'This is what the ol' father of the bride is meant to ask, isn't it? Anything to confess to your Daddy?'

He chuckled as he made the joke, like he always did.

Vivi stared at the wedding ring on his finger and imagined her mother, perched on the front pew at Saint George's, bright-eyed with nerves, exchanging good wishes with the congregation. Her parents' marriage had travelled down its own happy adventurous road. But she wanted to ask him, did he ever think he had made a mistake? Taken the wrong turn? Vivi tried to swallow the chunk of ice in her throat. Her fingers wound themselves around each other.

'No? Nothing? Well, I have something I want to tell you. Mama and I are incredibly happy for you. Our little girl.' His eyes gleamed. Lowering his voice so that the hovering butler could not hear, he said, 'And everything I have done, all these live-long years, has been for you and your mother. We can see how much Nathan loves you.'

'Can you?'

'Sure! And that's why we feel satisfied that you will be safe right here, with the Calloways. Old Digby may be an odd fish, but I feel he is pretty sound, business wise. A lot of people don't like him; a lot of people don't trust him. But I do.'

'What do you mean, Daddy?'

'I wouldn't have been in on this long-winded finance deal with him if I didn't trust him. He and I go back years. You will be fine.'

Vivi glanced at him, still not understanding. She didn't want business talk on her wedding day. And anyway, she was marrying Nathan, not Digby.

Watching her, her father's bravado fell away. He exhaled as if it hurt him.

'But now... because it's war, and because my work with Digby is finalised, Mama and I have decided to return to New York next week.'

The shock hit her, a blow to the chest. Even though she had considered the possibility, like a quiet whisper, her own events had engulfed her, her attention circling around Nathan, and herself.

'Why, if it is what you both want.' She sounded hoarse. 'Of course, you must go home.'

'It's my finances, the war, the uncertainty... things have been turned on their head. When we got here, we only intended this to be a finite trip. You knew that, right? We can't take you away from your husband.'

Vivi shuffled on the seat, the satin folds of her dress re-draping themselves around her knees.

'Just one question, Daddy.' The ice in her throat again. She swallowed hard. 'Do you think that all this has happened too quickly?'

She meant: should she pack her trunk and sail back with him?

The twinkling in her father's eye returned: his ambition and lust for security, his kindness, his vigorous championing of her, the freedom he'd allowed her, the future he wanted for her.

'Vivienne, let me tell you about your mother. I met her in the revolving door at Bloomingdales – you knew that – and she bowled me over. This uptown gal. I was in awe of her. I mean, would you look at her. We said the same things at the same time. She found that kinda romantic. I teased her. And neither of us would ever shut up. Like we'd entered some sort of talking competition, or something... but I knew. I did not want to be without her. And she agreed to come along with me. And yes, it was quick. But it works. Within six months, we were married.'

'But Daddy, this is only...' She faltered.

The night they met came back to her like a clear-as-day newsreel: dancing in the smoky darkness of the Velvet Rose, light on her feet, being cradled and feeling cared for. And in turn wanting to care back and to hold on forever. Laughing with joy as they moved around the floor. Six short tumultuous months ago.

Her smile lifted behind the lace. Only Nathan, and Nathan only.

And in less than fifteen minutes, she would see him again.

'But Daddy, this is only what?' her father teased, repeating her words back at her.

'Nothing. Absolutely nothing.'

He glanced at his watch. He stood and offered her his hand, his smile dazzling against his tan.

'Make haste,' he said. 'To the church, young lady.'

The butler had already opened the front door.

Vivi linked her father's arm and stepped out into the September sunshine, holding her bouquet so tightly that a rose thorn pierced her finger.

3

From their table by the picture windows of the Sands Hotel, Vivi could see the golden curve of Margate beach, the low tide shimmering. If she leaned a little to the left, she could count the fishing boats bobbing along the harbour arm.

'The seaweed is not so smelly today,' said the waitress as she set down their teapot, cups and milk jug. 'You're lucky. Some hot days in summer, it really kicks up.'

'That's good news,' Nathan said, catching Vivi's eye.

Vivi poured, picked up a teaspoon.

'Do you take sugar?' she asked.

The couple on the adjacent table looked their way, perhaps attracted by Vivi's accent. The lady gave Vivi a sympathetic, encouraging smile.

'Two please.' Nathan leaned forward to whisper. 'It must be obvious we're newly-weds. But, Mrs Calloway, I have already taken note that you take your tea without.'

Nathan rested his hand over Vivi's for a moment before withdrawing when the waitress returned with their toast. Vivi felt a prickly burr of unease. There were so many things she didn't know about him. She hadn't had enough time to find out whether he took sugar or not, and each second that passed brought them closer to the moment he had to leave.

The wedding had been over in a flash of chattering voices and congratulations. They had waved goodbye to their parents and Nathan had driven them away from the reception, through the London streets and all the way down to Margate. But, alone together at last, they'd both been too tired, too pensive, to speak. They arrived late, the soft September evening bursting with showers, the water a sheet of glass, reflecting the last of the light.

Soon enough the night fell through the still air. They'd kept their bedroom windows open; Nathan liked to hear the seagulls. It reminded him of a childhood summer holiday. And in the dark, they attempted to make love: quick, uncomfortable, and not like anything Vivi had imagined. Her mother, as gregarious as she was, had failed to fill her in, although Genna had once said candidly, one evening at dinner, 'You love him, so you will enjoy it.'

'We will get there,' Nathan had whispered, falling asleep and leaving Vivi to the darkness, the huge presence of the sea, and the gulls.

Now at the breakfast table, she followed his gaze out to the hazy blue horizon. Even though she did not know whether he took sugar, she knew she loved him. And so, she thought, they must get there, eventually.

'There's a beautiful, wild beach further along the coast,' he said as he scraped butter over toast. 'I can't remember the name, but there's a chalk stack and rock pools. And no people. Or hardly any. At least, that was the case when we were there, on one of our holidays, back in thirty-two. Shall we go today, see if we can find it?'

'It will be lovely to see somewhere you went as a child,' said Vivi. It would be another step into his world.

He called the waitress over, asked if she knew it.

'Botany Bay. Not much more than a mile or so away, along the cliff tops,' she said.

'That's walkable,' said Nathan. 'Don't you think?'

Vivi nodded, her eye caught by the men working on Margate beach, rolling out great loops of barbed wire and pegging them down into the sand. The war had reached this seaside town, and their own precious moments ticked away while they sat at the breakfast table eating tea and toast. Anxiety flashed, bringing treacherous tears to her eyes. She glanced at Nathan, hoping he wouldn't notice.

'Let's get going,' she said.

Nathan looked at her. 'Time and tide?'

She nodded and set down her cup, crushing her napkin.

* * *

They walked up the cliff road heading out of town, passing white Victorian terraces perched along the sea front. The wind picked up, worrying the surface of the water. Huge planes rumbled overhead in perfect diamond formation.

'Troop carriers,' said Nathan, 'heading for France, no doubt.'

Vivi's mouth clotted. 'Do you know where you will be heading?' she asked, irritated by the tremoring sound her voice made.

'Ah, that I cannot tell you. I don't even know yet but as soon as I report to the ship, I will get my detail.' He glanced at his watch. 'About this time, in two days, I will know.'

Vivi couldn't trust herself to find the supportive and brave words a naval wife might say.

Nathan took her hand. 'Vivi, are you all right? Will you be all right once I've gone?'

She forced a laugh. 'Of course, I will. I have Genna if needs be.

And I will be with your parents. They'll help me see it through, won't they?'

'My parents...' he said. 'I'm constantly trying not to disappoint them. By doing so, I am always going against the grain. I wanted to be an artist; did I tell you that?'

'Yes, yes you did.' She wondered how he could not remember their conversation from the half-darkness of the Velvet Rose. She felt confused. 'And your father, he was not in the Navy, I remember?'

'Yes, he served in the army briefly during the last lot. You've seen he wears the one medal. My grandfather was the one with the illustrious naval career. Became Rear Admiral. Quite the old sea dog. He built Farthing Hall complete with a Widow's Watch on the roof, even though we're miles from the coast.'

'A what?'

'A Widow's Watch. The little room built on top with windows all around. Traditionally for sailors' wives to watch for the ships coming home. You'll see them on some of the houses round here.'

Vivi glanced along the terrace of guest houses and hotels, and let her eyes wander out to sea. The planes had gone but a heavy grey cloud billowed in the sky, blotting the sun.

'And I believe because my own father wriggled out of the Navy, the pressure was on me. What luck!' Nathan's laugh sounded hollow. He looked up at the sky. 'Damn, we didn't think to bring an umbrella. The beach will have to wait for another time.'

She felt the first spot of rain on her cheek.

As they dipped and ducked their way back down to the hotel through the drenching shower, sheltering under porches and shop awnings, Vivi squealed and giggled in Nathan's solid embrace, her head tucked under his chin.

Back in their room, she felt him watching her as she flung her sodden hat into the bin and peeled off her ruined stockings, tossing them in on top.

'I'm longing for a hot bath,' she said. 'Now which is my towel, I wonder?'

Nathan stopped her on her way out of the room, making her catch her breath, his fingertips teasing her wet hair.

'Your bath can wait, Mrs Calloway,' he said, tugging at the buttons on her blouse.

Joy lifted through her in a sort of daze as her feet left the floor and he pulled her on to the bed.

* * *

'Happy, darling?' Nathan asked the next morning as he drove them away from the coast, the Thanet plain stretching either side of the road, marshes glittering with standing water.

'I am,' she said. Her bubble of happiness made her want to reach for his hand, to show him, but his grip on the steering wheel, encased in driving gloves, remained unmoving. She felt a quiver of shyness. 'Do you think we are getting there?'

Nathan laughed. 'I think we are too. It's funny...'

Is it? thought Vivi, stung a little when he fell quiet.

On they motored, towards Farthing Hall, Nathan's boyhood home, and soon to be hers, the flat horizon giving way to rolling wooded hills, a scene from a picture book.

'But I've never talked about such things.' He changed gear to negotiate the gradient.

'Things?'

'Marriage things. Growing up, I took my cue from my parents, unfortunately, and what happens between husband and wife has always been something unmentionable in my house. Shameful. Not to be discussed. My parents, you probably noticed, they're not warm people. Not with me, not with each other particularly. Or anyone, really.'

Vivi's mind flashed back to the dinner at Grosvenor Street, the evening she met Nathan.

'Your mother seems friendly,' she conceded, but she remembered the way Digby's cold eyes had glittered at her, his hand resting rather too long on her bare arm.

'Of course, I learnt a great deal about that sort of thing, you know, marriage bed stuff, from the Navy cadet lads.' He took his eyes off the road for a moment to throw her a look. 'And after yesterday, I wonder, how can it ever be bad?'

Vivi let out a relieved giggle. 'When I think about it, my parents were like young lovers all the time. They used to disappear to their bedroom for a nap after Sunday dinner. And I was to go with my governess for a walk around Central Park, or if we were at the farm-house, out riding. I didn't know anything about it. But now, of course, I realise.'

'Perhaps we can take a leaf out of their book,' he said.

But, when? Vivi thought.

The lane grew tighter, steeper, the towering hedges creating a tunnel of turning leaves, scattering chips of sunlight. She spotted a signpost that pointed to Canterbury, ten miles away, and the last village they'd driven through was a good while behind them. They had not passed another house in ages.

They drove along the edge of a deep, rambling mass of trees. 'Nearly there,' Nathan said. 'This is Blean Woods; they go on forever. It's ancient woodland, hasn't been touched in centuries. And my father owns some of this land.'

Vivi's stomach flipped in a mess of dread and nerves, at the thought of her parents-in-law: odd-fish Digby and jittery Freda, who had dismissed her as a spoilt princess.

Around the corner, she spotted a church spire and a cluster of houses and guessed that they'd arrived at Farthing. And through a stand of oaks on Nathan's side of the car, she spied the Hall itself: tall chimneys, a grand gable, the little glass room on top. What had Nathan called it? The Widow's Watch? She pressed her hands together between her knees until her knuckles grew white. Nathan turned between gates set in towering hedges. Freda had been right about her new home resembling an old church, with its perching gargoyles and monumental gothic windows, criss-crossed with tape to protect from bombs.

The tyres scattered gravel as they came to a stop in front of the porch and Nathan leapt out to unstrap the cases. Digby and Freda emerged onto the steps, but Vivi sat still for a breath or two, trying to prepare herself, wondering how to conceal the terror that was beating around her body. Freda's smile was wild and fixed, her hands clasped under her chin, while Digby, casual in tweed jacket with patches on the elbows, raised a solitary hand in greeting.

Vivi's parents were at that moment in Southampton waiting to board their ship back to New York, and she longed more than anything to hear their frivolous snippets of advice; their cheerful boosts to her confidence; the rhythm and rhymes she'd heard ever since she had been a little girl. For this place, lost in the middle of the Kent countryside, was to be her home.

And her husband's ship, also, awaited him.

* * *

'Come through, my dears, we'll have sherry and then lunch will be ready,' said Freda, leading them across the wide hallway, heels clipping on a floor of miniature terracotta tiles.

Vivi smelt furniture polish, a hint of damp and a faint whiff of mouse. Terracotta tiles were scattered loose and crumbling against the scuffed wainscot, little nicks in the door jamb. But the wide stairway with deep-red, albeit worn, carpet anchored by brass rods rose to meet a soaring stained-glass window on the landing, adorned with sweeping green brocade curtains that had seen better days. Sunlight streamed through, sending down patches of colour onto the oak-panelled walls, Nathan's forehead and the backs of Vivi's hands.

'Look, how charming,' she said.

'The hallway is the only place in this house you seem to get any natural light,' Freda said, opening the door to the sitting room. 'Apart from the Widow's Watch.'

Within the room lay a jumble of old-fashioned furniture on a threadbare Turkish carpet; an enormous empty marble fireplace. Ferns in pots curled in corners, and flowers in vases dropped browning petals onto tabletops.

'We can sit here for a bit and you can tell me all about Margate. How was the Sands Hotel?' she asked. 'Personally, I always thought that hotel overlooking the Royal Harbour at Ramsgate a better bet. Remember our summer holidays there?'

'Bloody blistering cold place as I remember.' Digby scowled, slumping down into an armchair. 'Bad for my leg.'

'Don't listen to him, Vivienne; I'm sure it was perfectly wonderful,' Freda said. 'Nathaniel, dear, Cook has prepared your favourite pudding.'

'Ah, good old Mrs Scott,' Nathan said. 'But we've been driving for an hour or more and before we sit down, I want to stretch my legs. I will show Vivi the stables.'

'I must say, the sea air seems to have given both of you some colour,' Freda said, her face, pale against the severe darkness of her hair, lifting in a smile that did not warm her eyes.

'That's right,' Digby said. 'Let the newly-weds have more time alone together, Freda. Because Nathaniel will be away before we know it, and Vivi will be left alone.'

He winked, and Vivi felt a blush burn her cheeks. Freda's thin mouth compressed, almost disappearing into the soft skin of her jawline. Vivi felt sorry for her. She looked momentarily crushed, standing there with her carefully done hair and baggy tweed skirt, all ready to organise the sherry.

Nathan took Vivi's hand and led her across the hall and through a back vestibule. She heard the clattering from the kitchen along the corridor and caught the smell of lunch cooking, before stepping out into the garden where mounds of box surrounded a pristine lawn, a hundred shades of green.

'Mother can be a little hard work, and Father an oaf sometimes,' Nathan said cheerfully, 'but you will get used to them.'

Vivi said nothing. A slow dropping sensation drove through her middle.

'Come on,' he continued, 'the stables are around here.'

'Did you say your grandfather built this house?' she asked, falling into step with him, trying to summon excitement at the prospect of seeing the horses.

'Yes, the sailor Calloway, if you will, built the house last century on the bones of a ruined medieval manor. Which didn't go down too well with the locals, as you can imagine. Someone apparently at the time, I think it was the vicar, described it as a "pompous monstrosity". Someone else, an "ostentation". I like that. We're new money, you see, Vivi.'

'Same here,' she said, and held his hand a little tighter.

'But the way things have been since the last war, we don't have the army of servants here that my father would have enjoyed as a boy. Just Mrs Scott – the cook – Ruby – the "maid of all work", as Mother likes to refer to her – a gardener, and Mr Buckley, who we'll meet any moment now.'

The clock on the stable roof chimed the quarter hour as they stepped into the sheltered yard, fragrant with hay and earthy dung.

A cat, as black as shadows, trotted across the swept-clean cobbles and curled up on a bale of straw, turning its yellow eyes on Vivi. The long dark face of a horse watched her over a half-door and a chestnut mount stomped around in his stall to present his flicking tail.

'This is Sea Captain. He's mine,' Nathan said, running his hand down the black horse's nose, 'and that there is a rather frisky Marmaduke, my father's horse. Mother doesn't ride.'

Vivi brought her face close to Sea Captain's, breathed in the warm scent of leather and horses, and felt herself perking up, a sudden sense of being home, of purpose. She rested her hand on the horse's solid neck and her earlier discomfort, the memory of the look on Freda's face and that wink from Digby, faded. Riding would be her freedom, the way to be herself, by herself, as it had always been.

The sound of light footsteps brought a small tawny-haired boy, no more than six years old, scooting around the corner, calling, 'Mister, sorry Lieutenant Calloway, hello! Did you know, she's not here yet and look! Marmaduke is the wrong way round again.'

'Now, now, Robin, lad, calm down, won't you,' said a man, emerging from the stable office, his beard clipped close, his watchchain shining across his russet waistcoat. 'What will Lieutenant Calloway think of you? Think of us? We have special company, can't you see?'

The boy halted, blushed and ground the heel of his boot into the cobbles.

'Mr Buckley, I'd like you to meet Mrs Calloway,' said Nathan. He turned to Vivi, his eyes wide and beaming, 'Vivienne, this is Mr Buckley, our steward and head groom and all-round saint.'

'And this urchin here is Robin, my son,' Mr Buckley said, shaking Vivi's hand. 'And I apologise in advance, for you will have noticed he is a bit of a loose cannon.'

'Hello, Robin,' said Vivi, squatting down so her face was level with the boy's. He fixed her with pale-grey earnest eyes. 'You said, "she is not here yet", but I am. I am Mrs Calloway, Lieutenant Calloway's wife, and I am pleased to meet you.'

'Oh no,' Robin said. 'I meant the—'

Laughing, Mr Buckley bent down to cover his son's mouth with his hand.

'That's enough, lad. Go and find Mrs Scott. She must surely have some lunch for you.'

'Sorry, Pa,' the boy chimed. 'It's just that I can't wait!'

He darted off in the direction of the house. Mr Buckley wished them good afternoon and stepped back into his office.

'Who did the boy mean, Nathan?' she asked.

'I suppose the cat is half out of the bag, and half a secret is a secret no more,' Nathan said. 'I had hoped she'd be here for when we arrived, but there has been a delay. My dear, I found a beautiful grey mare for you. And this here will be her stall. You shall name her of course and I wanted to see you ride her before I go, but she is not expected until the day after tomorrow. I'm sorry.'

Vivi put her arms around Nathan's neck, perched on tiptoes to kiss him on the lips.

'Thank you,' she said, struggling through joy to find the words she wanted to say. 'What a wonderful surprise.'

Close to him, she felt the same as she'd done in her damp clothes in the hotel room: the sensation that made her want to be immediately alone with him.

Nathan pushed her back gently by the shoulders and looked down at her face. 'Now we better quickly go and have some of Mother's sherry.'

* * *

After lunch, during which they enjoyed Mrs Scott's bread and butter pudding made especially for Nathan, they sat in the sitting room drinking coffee. Heavy curtains shielded much of the daylight, but enough got through to highlight paintings glimmering darkly on the walls and, Vivi noticed, a swathe of dust along the mantlepiece. She privately wondered if Ruby, the maid of all work, perhaps needed a little more encouragement with the feather duster.

Admiring what she could see of the paintings, she opened her mouth to ask Nathan if any of his own art was displayed in the house but he spoke first. 'We best get upstairs, Vivi, and get you unpacked. I need to repack my kit for the morning. We're in my bedroom, aren't we, Mother?'

'Ah no,' Freda said. 'We have redecorated the large guest room for you both.'

'To great and unnecessary expense,' grumbled Digby.

'Goodness, Mother.' Nathan laughed. 'What were you thinking? That sort of money rarely gets spent in this house.'

'I was inspired by visiting the Miles' house on Grosvenor Street earlier this year. Your mother, Vivi, has exceptional taste.'

'That is awfully nice of you to say,' she offered and received a brief smile in return.

Moments later, she opened the door on to a pleasant bedroom with a square bay window and a view of the garden, floral wallpaper and a green rug as delicious as a summer lawn. She felt mildly surprised and touched at the effort made on her behalf.

Standing at the window and gazing at the view, while Nathan unpacked, she realised that Farthing Hall stood on the edge of a line of hills, with its garden and stables at the back overlooking the flat land that stretched eastwards all the way to Margate and the sea. At the front lay rolling countryside, clothed in ancient woodland, with Canterbury nearly half an hour away by car. Genna's home in Sussex was a good two hours. Vivi decided that she must learn to drive.

'Happy, darling?'

She turned to answer, but Nathan continued to count his shirts, squinting at a cuff and testing a button, and she grasped that this may be a typical and rather meaningless question of his, and that he did not necessarily expect an answer. As well as whether he took tea with sugar or not, there seemed to be many other nuggets about her husband waiting to be uncovered.

'Yes, darling, I am,' she replied anyway.

He continued to fuss with his shirts.

She sighed, turned back to the view and resolved to try to be, as Nathan so often asked of her, happy.

* * *

Nathan came down the stairs in uniform, alien in a dark-blue naval coat, yellow insignia on his shoulders, cap under his arm. Vivi, waiting in the hallway, took a step back, as if confronted by a stranger.

Freda sighed. 'Ah, look at my boy.'

'He'll do,' Digby said.

'Remember, Mother and Father, short, sharp farewells,' said Nathan. 'That's what we do in this family.'

He shook Digby's hand and kissed Freda lightly on the cheek, at which she fumbled up her sleeve for a handkerchief and pressed it over her eyes.

Nathan led Vivi out of the front door where his car waited on the gravel, newly polished by Mr Buckley for the occasion, filled with his petrol ration, his kit pack stowed on the back. He took her in his arms, his coat forming such a barrier between them that Vivi knew he would not be able to feel her body shaking.

He placed a kiss on her forehead.

'I will write every day like I did before.'

'Every day?'

'Well, as much as I can.'

'But where will you be?' Her voice sounded small and frightened against his shoulder. 'I won't know where you are.'

He drew back and placed a finger over her lips. 'Possibly patrolling the Channel, but I haven't told you that.'

They turned at the sound of his parents' footfalls on the steps where they stood and watched: Freda wet-eyed and grimacing, Digby appearing as gruff and as nonchalant as ever.

Vivi held on to Nathan, her quiet tears soaking his sleeve, her heart crumbling. Their farewell no longer seemed private, spontaneous, or particularly honest, for Nathan released himself from her embrace, put on his cap low down over his eyes and, in that moment, appeared not to be Nathan any more.

* * *

Freda made her excuses and went to bed early, leaving Vivi to sit through the nine o'clock evening news with Digby, pretending to listen, but not wanting to hear. Although, truth be told, not a great deal was going on anyway. Digby commented as such and got up to switch off the radio, his bad leg dragging a little, which often happened, he said, when he was tired. He offered her a nightcap.

'No, thank you, Digby. I'm off to bed, too, now.'

'Suit yourself.' He shrugged, sipped at a tot of whisky, and opened his broadsheet.

She stood up to leave, but he stopped her with, 'That horse of yours arriving tomorrow?'

'Ah yes,' she said brightly. 'Such a shame that Nathan won't be here. But even so, I have to say, I am excited.'

'Good for you, Vivienne,' he said. 'Not that we need another nag to feed and look after. Not sure what my son was thinking, to be honest.'

Vivi wanted to say that perhaps Nathan had been thinking of something for his new wife, to see her through troubling times, with war declared and him away at sea. But when her gaze rested on the threadbare carpet, the Victorian furniture, the general unkempt shabbiness of the place, she bit her tongue. Apart from her and Nathan's bedroom, not much money had been spent in this house, it seemed.

'I will of course contribute to her upkeep,' she said. 'In fact, leave her entirely to me.'

'That's very generous of you,' Digby said, sounding like he did not know how to deal with a feisty American girl. He shook his paper and peered at her over the top of it. His sharp moustache and sagging jowls gave his face a severe, critical look. 'You're quite the independent young woman, aren't you?'

'It is certainly what my parents had in mind for me.'

His gaze lingered on her for a long uncomfortable moment.

'My, you have turned out well.' His expression lifted into a strange, satisfied smile. 'And we are certainly pleased to have you as part of the Calloway family.'

'As am I, happy, to be here, with you and Freda.' She floundered through the mild mistruth, his comment unsettling her. 'Good-night, Digby.'

She hurried up the stairs, her breath juddering as if she were in flight, frantic to shake off the strange churning feeling. But she slowed when she reached the landing, telling herself not to be so darn ridiculous about a cantankerous man who evidently spent far too much time alone, and liked to speak his mind.

'Is that you, Vivi?' Freda's voice drifted through her open bedroom door.

Vivi halted and poked her head in, grateful for a distraction.

Freda sat in an armchair in her dressing gown, holding a steaming mug. Oil lamps on the bedside and dressing tables offered pools of yellow light, making the corners of the room murky. An enormous wardrobe loomed, its carved edges casting nightmarish shadows and the velvet cover on the bed looked like a deep red lake.

'I like to have my cocoa up here alone every evening. Shall I ring down for one for you? I expect you'd like a little company? I know I do sometimes.'

Freda's kind tone touched her, but the uneasy feeling had returned.

'But what about Digby?' she asked. 'Won't he be up soon?'

'Oh, we are an old married couple. He sleeps in his dressing room these days.'

Vivi ventured in, smelling soap and violets and, underneath, another less pleasant smell of mothballs and musty clothes.

'Excuse the state of me,' Freda said, wiping at her red-rimmed eyes. 'Just having a little weep, you know. I ought to be used to it now. My boy going off to sea. You'll get used to it too, in time, my dear. Let me ring down to Ruby...'

She reached for the button by the fireplace.

'No cocoa for me, thank you. I'm ready for bed.'

'Ah, but would you mind giving me a hand? I feel embarrassed these days asking Ruby to help.' Freda stuck out one foot. 'I'm utterly done in and my shoes, they're so blessed tight.'

Vivi hesitated for a moment, then knelt on the carpet in front of her mother-in-law and gingerly took hold of her shoe by the heel. Puffy flesh bulged painfully around the sides. She braced herself before tugging and coaxing, wondering why Freda could order the redecoration of her and Nathan's room but not stretch to new footwear.

With her shoes off at last, Freda groaned and flexed her damp stockinged feet, the ends of her toes blunt from being crammed inside.

'Thank you, Vivi. Of course, in the old days back in the twenties, when I was first married, I had a lady's maid who'd do all this for me.'

Vivi got up. 'I'm sure we can stretch to a maid for you,' she said chirpily.

Freda stared at her.

'We?'

'I mean, me. If you want one. After all, I have my allowance.'

Freda tilted her chin, compressed her mouth, pride paining her face.

Vivi blushed, hearing her father's voice in her head: *no good ever came from talking about money in polite society. The English hate it.*

'Although I don't suppose *I'll* need a maid,' Vivi blundered on. 'I found it hard to get used to the butler at Grosvenor Street. And anyway, servants are difficult to come by these days, aren't they? They've all gone into the factories. Goodness, imagine working in munitions. I'm sure that's not for me, but I think I will need to find something to occupy me while Nathan is away.'

Freda continued to stare, before speaking evenly.

'It would be very generous of you to pay for a lady's maid's wages, Vivi,' she said. 'But there is no need. And I hope you don't think that we'd expect such a thing.'

'Not at all. I'm sorry,' she said, mortified. 'I guess living here with you is all very new for me. For all of us.'

'Not to worry. We are all upset by Nathan going.'

'But I'm afraid I've offended you. And I think I have upset Digby too.'

'You leave Digby to me.'

The sharp, painful look on Freda's face made Vivi's scalp

prickle.

But then her expression softened, as if at the click of her fingers.

'Well, dear, I'm ready for bed. One more thing. Would you fetch that box over there for me? Yes, that's it, there on the dressing table.'

Vivi brought over the rosewood box and rested it on Freda's lap.

'Thank you, dear. I won't keep you any longer.'

Freda dipped her head, pushed her fingers into the depths of her hair. Her coiffure moved in an odd way, and she lifted it clean off her head.

Vivi suppressed a gasp, struggling to contain her shock at seeing the true nature of Freda's hair: grey strands as threadbare as the carpets downstairs.

'Oh, Freda.'

Freda laid her wig inside the silk-lined box carefully as if handling an injured animal. She shut the lid.

'If you wouldn't mind, my cap is on the hook.'

Vivi handed it to her.

'Our secret.' Freda looked up at her only after she'd covered her head, her eyes moist and plaintive. Her dressing gown sleeves had slipped back and Vivi could see a bruise blossoming over Freda's wrist, like an ink stain. It looked sore, and empathy coiled inside Vivi's chest.

Freda plucked at her sleeve to hide it, wincing as she did so. As well as having thinning hair, Freda must bruise easily too.

'Goodnight, Freda.' Vivi planted a tender kiss on her dry, powdery cheek, sensing a new and bizarre strain of intimacy. 'See you in the morning.'

Vivi slipped away, shut the door, and turned towards her own room. Digby lingered outside his dressing room next door, a bulky shadow on the landing.

'I hope you sleep well,' he slurred, his whisky nightcap working already. 'Going to bed alone as a bride seems an almighty shame.'

'Never mind, Digby,' she said with forced cheer as she slipped past him. 'Nathan will be back before we know it. Goodnight.'

She shut her bedroom door and leant against it, dizzy with relief at being alone, at last, exhaustion threatening to floor her.

Ruby had earlier drawn the blackout and curtains, lit the lamps. Vivi's trunk had arrived from London and her clothes were already away in the wardrobe, her writing case sitting on the bureau in front of the window. But the room, however beautiful, remained empty and lifeless, a pretty kind of cell.

Tears pricked Vivi's eyes. A line of bleak, drawn-out days opened before her. Her mother had taught her that a lady only ever cries in private, so here in her room she finally let herself sob, pressing the heels of her hand into her eyes.

But at least the first dreadful day without Nathan was over. In the morning she would write to him on his ship, to Genna and to her parents. She would tell them about Margate, Nathan's present, and how electric light, like at Grosvenor Street, had, unsurprisingly, not reached Farthing Hall either. She hoped they'd be having a fine old time on their journey back to America. Her mother's second rule was never to laugh in public but, of course, never stuck to it. And remembering this, Vivi smiled.

* * *

The mare waited on the cobbles, her hooves shifting tenderly, her dark eyes soft and trusting. Mr Buckley held her head as Vivi pulled herself up into the saddle.

'Ah, Mrs Calloway, isn't she a beauty?' he said. 'Lieutenant Calloway knows his horses.'

And it seemed Nathan knew her too.

'She is, oh my, she is.' Vivi lifted the coarse white mane and let it fall through her fingers. She felt the solid warm potency of the animal beneath her. The horse's silver freckled coat gleamed in the sun. 'I do love a grey. They seem charmed, special.'

Robin moved the mounting block away and stood back, as he'd evidently been taught to. 'Weren't white horses Mama's favourite kind too?'

'That they were, son. Now go open the gate for Mrs Calloway, there's a good lad. I'm sure she'll want a good ride out.' Mr Buckley stroked the mare's whiskery muzzle, glancing after the boy as he ran to the gate. 'Mrs Buckley died having Robin, Mrs Calloway,' he said. 'Not sure if you were aware.'

'I wasn't. I am sorry.'

'He's like her. It's almost...' Mr Buckley trailed off, concentrating on adjusting the bridle.

He looked up at the sound of engines droning across the sky. A squadron was flying over.

'It's our boys, don't worry,' he said.

'I know. I'm getting used to it.'

'Who would have thought, eh, that we're in it all over again? Hardly seems like yesterday,' he said, a darkness crossing his face.

Robin darted back to his father's side and announced, 'That's done for you, New Mrs Calloway, ready for your ride.'

'That's right, Robin. Lieutenant Calloway's mother is Mrs Calloway. And I am the New one.' Vivi smiled down at the boy from the saddle and patted the horse's neck. 'What shall we call this lovely creature, Robin? What do you think?'

'Well, I think she looks like snow,' he said. 'She's all white and speckled in places. A little bit like a snowdrop?'

'There we are,' said Vivi. She secured her headscarf tightly under her chin, took the reins and squeezed her knees. Father and son stepped back as she urged the horse forward. 'Let's see how Miss Snowdrop likes to ride.'

She went through the gate and followed the track along the side of the Hall, leaving behind Freda's jumbled gloomy rooms, her spirits lifting with her new sense of freedom. On the lane, an old wooden sign pointed with a finger *To Farthing Hall* and on the other side of the road the milestone said:

Farthing 1/4 mile
Canterbury 10 miles

Behind it, and all along the side of the road, as far as Vivi could see, rose woodland in misty layers of green, tinged with the gold of turning leaves. Further down, a bridleway opened between the trees, and Vivi kicked Snowdrop on, turning her head towards it.

'Let's have a gentle stroll through the woods, my girl.'

She entered the embrace of gilded oak, hawthorn and birch, the canopy chattering with birds, Snowdrop's hooves a small rustling in the huge cathedral-like space.

'My, this is wonderful.' She inhaled the clean, earth-mould smell. The woods near the farmhouse on the Hudson were darker, primeval and truly wild, while this English setting, with its dappled shade and sun-lit glades, banks of nettle and fern, seemed innocent and friendly, as if the trees had been waiting for her. On the cusp of autumn, the English woods would possibly never match the brazen colours of fall in New England, but they simply and quietly got on with it.

Snowdrop's silvery ears turned with curiosity as they plunged deeper through the trees. Vivi occasionally glanced behind with a notion to check which way they'd come, but after a fashion, gave up, enjoying the sense of being lost, of being away from the confines of Farthing Hall. Nathan had warned her about Digby being difficult and Freda, hard work, but Vivi, after yesterday's awkward exchanges, decided to work hard in return; pull her socks up, as her ninth-grade teacher had often put it.

Ducking under low-slung branches, reaching out to touch the rough bark with her fingertips, she wondered whether she should ask Mr Buckley's advice about buying a car. She'd like to visit Genna in Sussex, take Freda for days out, and generally live up to her independent spirit. But in the next breath, she stamped on the idea: far too showy. She'd come across as the vulgar American they all probably secretly thought she might be. She imagined Freda's proud sunken face, Digby's blistering pent-up fury.

She must speak to Freda's parish ladies, volunteer for the war effort, do everything she could to fit in. She would create a comforting world for Nathan to come home to. She allowed herself a secret smile, feeling the ferns brushing against her knees as Snowdrop plodded on.

After their short honeymoon in Margate, there may well be a baby to look after, too.

Snowdrop stomped her way out of the trees, following her nose into a clearing. As they emerged, Vivi could feel the sun on her face and she squinted in the dazzling patchwork of light and shade. She pulled Snowdrop up in surprise.

'Well, what do you know.'

There, deep in the woods, beyond a high garden wall, Vivi spied the top of a dwelling: a chimney stack and the roof with slipping-down tiles. In the centre of the wall sat an arched wooden door, shut fast. Something about the deep silence of the place made it feel abandoned. Yet a great peace surrounded it, like a watchful presence.

'My, Snowdrop, it's like we've stepped into the middle of a fairy tale.'

Vivi reined the horse in alongside the wall, the top colonised by tangled creeper. She stood up in the stirrups and peered over. There stood an astonishing little cottage. She wondered whether she was still on Calloway land; whether this old house might be part of the estate. A derelict workman's cottage, or a woodman's lodge, perhaps.

The garden had been left to grow wild, rose bushes rampant, dandelions choking the broken-down vegetable patch. The windows of the ground floor looked dark, cobwebbed and blank. No sign of life.

She listened. Not a sound.

'Hello?' she called, her voice cutting the stillness. 'Hello? Anyone home? It's Mrs Calloway.' She smiled, thinking of how Robin had addressed her. 'The New Mrs Calloway.'

Sunlight streamed through the woodland canopy, and the upper stained-glass windows tucked under the eaves shimmered like amber jewels. A breeze drew itself through the tops of the trees, and no one answered.

Vivi dismounted Snowdrop and pushed at the wooden door, feeling resistance from a mass of weeds. Inside the walled garden, beyond the beds of white roses, some at their sweetest, some decayed, sat the cottage, with pigeons on the chimney the only visible tenants. She walked along the mossy terracotta path and called again, 'Hello?' but the house only seemed to look at her in startled welcome, as if woken from sleep.

Curling her hand around her eye, Vivi peered through a murky window. Sticks of dusty furniture loomed out of the dim interior. She glanced again up at the glinting, stained-glass windows, as if to make sure, grasped the doorknob and turned it.

The door would not shift, was locked fast. And Vivi felt an odd wave of relief for it felt wrong to trespass, to disturb the slumbering house. She turned on her heel and hurried back to Snowdrop, shutting the garden door behind her.

4

After settling Snowdrop back in her stall, brushed down and watered, Vivi went back into the Hall in time for lunch with Freda.

While her mother-in-law toyed with Mrs Scott's midweek fish pie, Vivi listened to her recount of her morning – supervising the arrival of evacuee children, taken in by Doctor and Mrs Willis, and other folks in the village.

'Little unwashed Bermondsey urchins,' she said. 'And Digby is not best pleased by the shortage of beefsteak. Apparently, there is none to be had at the butcher's.'

Vivi felt another sense of relief, for it appeared that Digby and Freda never had lunch together, and she could do without her father-in-law's displeasure for an hour or two. As Freda reached for the parsley sauce, Vivi kept her eyes firmly away from her hairline, desperate not to stare, and noticed another bruise had bloomed under her cuff.

Vivi scratched around for a conversation point, something for distraction. The cottage traced through her mind and sat on the tip of her tongue, but something made her want to keep it her own secret, for now. She managed to hold off long enough for Freda to excuse herself for her afternoon nap and for Vivi to escape up to her bedroom to write her letters.

The sunny morning had folded down into drizzle and the colour of the woods, the edge of which she could see if she tucked herself into her rain-spattered window, had become a dull sulky brown. The perfect opportunity to attend to her correspondence, like any English countrywoman, or like an officer's wife, might.

Relishing her task, Vivi wrote out each of the three envelopes in readiness.

To Genna she dashed off a few vibrant lines to tell her the latest and beg her to come and visit her as soon as possible. Brief and snappy.

Nathan next, but she felt stifled. How easy it was to demonstrate feelings through touch and expression, laughter and kisses, being able to see his response, him testing her words. On paper, her sentences sounded diluted and formal. She wanted to show him how strong she could be in his absence. Dealing with his parents. A proper Navy wife. But this felt like a downright fib. Instead, she babbled about Snowdrop, and added far too many kisses.

To her parents, she relaxed, describing their seaside honeymoon town, life at the Hall, Snowdrop. She begged for a letter back as soon as they arrived at the farmhouse – for her mother never liked to miss New England in the fall – longing for a photograph or two of her old home. For when she left it and headed to New York to embark for Southampton, she had thought it would only be a matter of time before she saw it again.

The rain eased. She opened the window to listen to the birds reviving themselves and heard a strange hissing sound from the front of the house, as if something had come in over the gravel. Not a car, for she heard no engine. The postman, perhaps. In a snap of excitement, she hurried down the stairs to see Ruby opening the front door to a teenage boy, his bicycle sideways on the ground behind him, a wheel still spinning, a sheen of sweat on his face from negotiating the long hill up from Canterbury.

Ruby took what he mutely offered her: a plain brown envelope. She spun around and held it out to Vivi.

'A telegram? Is it for me?'

'Oh,' Ruby faltered. 'It's addressed to Mrs Calloway. I'm not sure which one, ma'am.'

'Mrs Calloway is napping, so I will take it.' Vivi thanked Ruby, who hurried off to the back of the house and to whatever task she had been doing there.

Vivi tucked her thumbnail under the envelope edge and began to climb the stairs, a cold fear for Nathan's safety gripping her, making her light-headed. As she pulled out the chit of paper, she could hear the birds singing in the garden, the faint plod of the boy's feet over the gravel, the whirring of bicycle wheels.

But as soon as the words printed on the telegram came into focus, a sudden thunderous rushing sound obliterated everything, and she felt herself falling through screaming darkness. Her hand found the smooth surface of the banister and she swung around, sat down with a thump on the stairs.

Her parents' ship had been torpedoed. Not far beyond the coast of Ireland. All 357 souls on board missing, presumed drowned. The uneven type on the official ticker tape stated this, and so Vivi must believe it. And yet how could she believe and function through this dreadful plummeting sickness?

She groped her way upstairs, the birds absurdly still singing outside, and along the landing, passing her mother-in-law's shut bedroom door. She stumbled into her room, her sweating hand clutching and screwing up the telegram, and sat at her desk, where she dropped it into the wastepaper basket. A flimsy, ridiculous piece of paper to bear such impact. She stared out of the window at the day that had started with joy and promise, her body numb and curiously still, a barrier forming itself like a skin around her. The rushing in her head grew louder, became physical, began to grind like an insistent machine. Her shoulders slumped under the weight of it. She closed her eyes. Her parents, those bright laughing sparks, were at the centre of the noise, but she could not hear them over another voice, her ninth-grade teacher, coaxing her:

'Miss Vivienne Miles, sit up straight and pull your socks up.'

Taking a shuddering breath against the churning cold, she sucked her stomach in, sat erect and loaded her pen with ink, pulled her parents' unfinished letter towards her and continued to write. She ensured her handwriting appeared as copperplate as her teacher had once admired, signing off as usual with *your Vivi*.

Her hands seemed to work automatically as she slotted all three letters into their envelopes and sealed the edges. The address on her parents' letter, to the farmhouse on the Hudson, blurred and faded, but she fought her dizziness, stared at the words, to pull them into focus, to bring them back to life. She groped for the stamps that Ruby had given her earlier from Mrs Scott's little stash, and stuck them on.

Reaching down into the wastepaper basket for the screwed-up telegram, she smoothed it out, daring herself to look at it again. But the words, stark and official, still held no meaning for her and the chaos inside her made her body shake.

Vivi fixed her eyes on the window and longed for Nathan, to hear his steady voice, his familiar observation that it looked like it might well rain again. She stood abruptly and hauled on her mackintosh, tying the belt far too tightly at her waist so she could feel *something*, something normal, and slotted the letters into her pocket. Downstairs, she left the crushed telegram on the hall table next to the clock for Freda or Digby to find, and walked out of the house.

The rain had given the gravel, the trees and the hedgerows a painful layer of brightness, creating a false backdrop to her brand-new unrecognisable world.

In the distance, she spotted a lithe little figure, jumping in the puddles along the lane.

'Robin,' she called, the effort of doing so making her weak. She plodded towards him, her legs barely working. 'Do you know where the postbox is?'

He stopped, waited for her to catch up.

'Hello New Mrs Calloway. It's along this way. I'll show you. Come with me.'

The boy fell into step, and trotted beside her, glancing up at her face every other step as if to check something.

'Are they your letters? Can I post them please?'

Her voice drifted like air through her lips: 'Yes, yes, you may.'

She handed them over and Robin fixed his clear-eyed stare on her face.

'You sound different, Mrs Calloway, and you don't look like you at all,' he said. 'But I hope that you are still the same?'

Vivi watched the boy reach up and slip the envelopes into the postbox, the letters for Genna and for Nathan, and the letter that would eventually arrive at the old catslide-roof farmhouse on the Hudson, never to be opened.

'No, Robin,' she said. 'I don't think I can ever be the same.'

5

ELISE, JUNE 1940

Inside the hospital, the appalling noise of confined bedlam seemed to gather above and fill the high ceiling. It settled briefly when the men spotted Elise bearing a tray of tea. She went from one soldier to the next. Dirty hands with blackened fingernails grabbed the delicate china cups, the contents gulped in one go. She caught whiffs of dank clothing, engine oil and blood, and the smell of incapacitation.

She ran out of tea far too quickly; her back ached, her feet tight with pain.

'I'm going back for more,' she announced to the room.

They'd come from the boats, down at Margate harbour since daybreak. All manner of classes, crammed against the harbour arm, waiting to dock and unload their human cargo, conscious or unconscious, the worse slammed straight into ambulances. Ragged gangs of soldiers, wind- and salt-battered, soaked, they waited with supreme patience, eyes wide in smoke-blackened faces, cigarettes in trembling fingers. Not, thought Elise as she steadied her heavy tray, how the British army left our shores.

Harassed doctors scanned the line, pulling out the worse. One of the soldiers took his cup of tea, called out: 'Aye, here's a pretty face. I feel better now, doctor. Can't I go home now?'

Elise hardly dared glance his way. What a coward she felt, blinkered for far too long, hunkering down with her mother in the little cottage on King Street.

Someone sitting on the floor grabbed at her leg.

'Whatever you do, don't go into the next room, darling, it's far worse in there,' he said.

She looked him in the eye. 'I will do if I'm needed.'

Nurses bobbed in and out, eyes down in dedication. Over by the door, Elise heard one of them speaking in escalating phrases of authority.

'Oh no sir, you should be reporting to Westgate Ward. That is the ward for the Naval officers.'

'I told you. I'm not leaving my man, here. He's in a bad way.'

Elise handed her last cup of tea to a young soldier bent double in his church-hall chair.

'Can you help me send word to my mother?' he asked, peering up at her. 'Can't write, see.'

She put her hand on his shoulder. 'I will. Give me five minutes.'

She put down her tray, walked towards the door, with a mind to find pen and paper from somewhere, but the man who should be in the Westgate Ward lingered in the doorway, the nurse chiding him. He had his back to Elise: tall and lean and broad shouldered, the fabric of his naval jacket singed down one arm. He was bending down to speak to another man, a seaman, on the floor, who crouched, head on his knees, weeping.

'He's my Petty Officer, was in my shore patrol, nurse, nearly got left behind,' the officer said. 'Germans strafed us. The sea was burning. He saw his best mate drown. I'm not leaving him behind now.'

'But, sir, your burns. You're injured,' argued the nurse. 'The doctor needs to see you in the ward where he can make a better assessment. I think you need morphine.'

'But he needs something too.'

Elise stepped forward.

'I will take care of him, sir. What's his name?'

'McVie. Harry McVie.'

The officer turned to look at her.

She flinched, tried to disguise it, forcing herself not to react. The officer's hair on one side of his face looked like it had been shorn badly, his left ear charred black. A ruddy raw line snaked down his jaw. His uncompromising eyes appraised her, and something jarred in her memory.

On the floor, McVie began to wail.

Elise knelt down beside the seaman and took his hand, his rough skin chaffing her palm.

The nurse barked above her, 'What's your name, girl?'

'Elise.'

'No. Your surname.'

'Drake.'

'Get that man some tea, Drake. Talk to him, try to calm him down. He's upsetting the others, for goodness sake. Sir, come this way.'

'In a moment, nurse,' the officer said, wearily, on the edge of fury.

He squatted down beside Elise and spoke earnestly to McVie. He glanced at Elise sideways and she saw his expression soften.

'I never knew your name. All these years. I forgot to ask,' he said to her.

'What?' She wondered what he saw, something in her beyond the chaos and the noise and the pain around him. Again, his face swam through her memory.

'How arrogant of me,' he said. 'I would have hoped I have changed in all these years. How is your knee?'

Goodness, she thought in confusion, his burns have made him delirious.

'I helped you, remember?' he said. 'You fell on the rocks.'

She stared at him. Something about him stung her, shifted her mind to a day long ago, a breezy wild day on the beach, the rock pools, her old summer dress, collecting seaweed for her mother. And the boy.

McVie began to call for his mother. His pain bellowed from his gut as he folded himself up. The pitch of his voice frightened Elise.

The officer spoke with authority, straight into her ear. 'And now, you can help me by looking after my man here.'

Elise nodded, muted with shock, her thoughts tumbling.

'Sir. If you will,' pressed the nurse, 'it is vital you see a doctor right now.'

A sigh rattled through the officer's body and he got to his feet, allowed himself to be led away by the nurse, throwing a glance back over his shoulder, which Elise barely caught, for McVie began to vomit in her lap.

Later, as evening fell, Elise opened the back door into the kitchen and the sound of her mother's music box drifted through from the front room: 'Für Elise' playing in the soft yellow lamplight.

'You're home,' her mother said. 'What time is it? My goodness, how are you?'

Elise had no idea how to answer her. She sat down in the armchair by the hearth, peeled her shoes off her feet, slumped back against the cushions.

The comforting scent of the herbs in her mother's kitchen, the shelves lined with bottles and jars filled with her remedies, made her want to cry.

'I feel like I need to burn this blouse,' she said after some moments, surfacing through a well of exhaustion. 'As for my skirt.'

'You look worn out, my dear.' Her mother poured her tea. The tune on the music box came to an end. It had been a present from Elise's father when Elise was born. She watched Elise sip her tea. 'You look like you've seen a ghost.'

'You might say that I did.' Elise managed a smile. 'A living breathing ghost from summer past.'

Her mother threw her a puzzled glance.

Elise gave a light-headed laugh. 'Do you remember years ago, I came home from the beach with a bandaged knee?'

Her mother put her head to one side. 'That sounds like something you would do.'

'Bandaged with someone else's handkerchief? I have it, still, upstairs somewhere. And today I bumped into the boy – the man – who gave me that handkerchief, who helped me because I hurt myself, and who, oh Ma, he's so badly injured.' She took a breath. 'Burns.'

Her mother leant forward, her eyes widening, her large-knuckled hands clasped on her lap. 'He was at Dunkirk?'

'He remembered me, from all that time ago. In all that commotion, despite his pain, he knew who I was. But of course, his face... half his face, you see. I couldn't... and yet his eyes. I recognised his eyes.' A bright light pierced her chest when she thought of the way he looked at her. She shook herself. 'How silly is that? All those years ago. We were children.'

Upstairs in her bedroom, her stomach warm with her mother's stew, she robotically pulled on her nightgown. Numb with exhaustion, she slipped under the covers, and caught the moist fragrance of the sea as her mother steeped seaweed downstairs on the range.

But as she lay her head on the pillow, seeking sleep, her mind became flooded with the noise from the hospital: the cries and groans, and the agonised silences in between. She'd forgotten to help the boy who couldn't write.

On the armchair downstairs, her mother's folded newspaper had showed photographs of soldiers disembarking from the Little Ships, their dirty faces grinning, eyes bright, raising cups of tea as a toast. But that was not what she'd seen at all.

And beneath it all lingered the man she only knew as Nathaniel – and only because she had heard his father yell his name across the sand. She thought of his voice, calm and measured, and kind, despite his terrible injuries, as he said: 'I never knew your name.'

She turned over and sent out a plea that he could sleep tonight, that he did not feel too much pain. And that she might see him tomorrow.

6

VIVI, JULY 1940

When the news came through about Nathan, the rushing cold shock blew another hole inside her.

Nearly nine months had passed since her parents' death and Vivi had lived through a dark, gruelling winter and experienced her first true English spring. Plum orchards had bloomed on hillsides and yellow anemones winked under hedgerows. Against the quiet blue sky, she had noticed planes, like tiny crosses, so high up to be almost invisible. Luftwaffe reconnaissance, Digby informed her, keeping an eye on things. With each day that passed, she had awoken earlier and earlier to the chorus of birdsong rising from the woods. Each day another to spend alone, wandering like a shadow against an exquisite pastoral backdrop, worrying about Nathan doing his naval duties 'somewhere in the Channel', or walking the rooms of the house in the dreary wake of her mother-in-law.

'We need to keep you busy, Vivienne,' Freda had said, with a vigour that didn't quite ring true. 'Whenever Nathan is away, that's what I do, and I think it's the antidote for many ills. A full diary always helps me buck up.'

But Vivi had wanted to argue that she wasn't unwell. She didn't know what she was. Grief for her parents kept its distance, pushed to the outer reaches of her consciousness. In its place, a drifting darkness.

Freda took her silence as acquiescence and rattled off a list: the Farthing fete to organise, knitting socks and jumpers for soldiers, persuading the housewives and cooks of the village to give up their pots and pans to be made into Spitfires. But Vivi couldn't bear to think of all that needed to be done; despair made her exhausted. She knocked on cottage doors and attended meetings in genteel parlours, smiled at people she didn't know, those who never knew what to say to her in return.

Spring melted into early summer and Vivi would take Snowdrop for long, slow walks through the woods where bluebells spread beneath the trees. She would lose her way deliberately, breaking through banks of emerald ferns, skirting the old cottage on horseback, peering over the high wall. Bees stirred in the unkempt flowers, oblivious to the world beyond. Watching them, and gazing at the sleeping little house, felt like a remedy; Vivi's secret, standing silent and steady within the chaos. The radio bulletins kept getting worse.

And news from the hospital in Margate about Nathan thundered down through it all.

'We'll nurse him here,' said Freda, with queenly resolution. 'Best place for him. As soon as the doctors sign him off, we'll bring him home where he is meant to be.'

Vivi visited Nathan, taking the train from Canterbury to their honeymoon seaside town with Freda perched on the edge of the seat opposite her, wringing her hands. She had wanted to go alone at least once but, with one look at Freda's fraught and glassy-eyed agony, she had conceded that Freda must accompany her. Digby, meanwhile, seemed to be always engaged in some business matter or another to be bothered to take them in the car.

But when, at last, they were able to collect Nathan, Digby insisted on driving, at which Freda offered a flurry of gratitude, ordering her husband's favourites from Mrs Scott, and insisting on pouring him the finest whisky.

At the hospital, Digby parked the car, stared straight through the windscreen, and said, 'I'll wait here.'

They found Nathan waiting for them outside the ward, sitting upright on a hard chair, his head bowed, the bandage not as bulky as it had been the last time that they'd seen him, not covering his right eye any more. But it still looked as if it weighed him down.

The nurse bustled along and went through the list of require-ments for Nathan's convalescence. They stood in a semi-circle around him, speaking as if he were not there, or at least he were still a child. Freda lapped up every detail.

Vivi moved closer to Nathan and rested her hand on his shoul-der. At her touch, he looked up at her momentarily, before mutely shifting his wary gaze from the nurse to his mother and back again.

Freda and Vivi shuffled back to the car, each linking Nathan's arm, with Freda's non-stop commentary rattling between them. Digby got out of the driver's seat and stood aloof and watchful, puzzled, as if he didn't recognise his son. Freda guided Nathan into the back, slipping in after him, leaving Vivi to the passenger seat. There was a brief sting of hurt that she could not sit with her husband, making her feel pathetic and childlike, but she resolved to be patient. Her husband simply needed to be home safe and sound. The rest could wait.

'We've set up your own room for you, dear,' Freda said, contin-uing the one-sided conversation as Digby fired the engine. 'And Mrs Scott is on standby with her restorative recipes. Looks like we have a bottle of analgesics here in your kit bag, good. Oh, what's this here?'

'I'll look after that, Mother,' Nathan said.

Vivi glanced behind her to see him take a glass jar from his mother's hands.

'But what is it?' asked Vivi. 'Some sort of green chutney? Or pickle? Looks intriguing.'

'It looks rather odd, if you ask me,' said Freda. 'Doesn't look edible.'

'It's just something from the hospital,' Nathan said.

'The nurse who discharged you didn't mention it?' Vivi said.

Nathan appeared not to have heard her.

'Well, I must say, I think you have improved.' Freda rattled on. 'From the look of you. You seem more yourself. Don't you think so, Vivienne? Of course, Nathan, your father is none the wiser, as he did not see you at your worse. But you're glad he is on the mend aren't you, dear?'

Digby concentrated on the road ahead, his moustache moving with indistinct words of agreement.

'What's the plan, son?' he asked. 'Has your commanding officer been in touch?'

At the sound of his father's voice Nathan sat himself up. 'Yes, he has. I got the charge through yesterday. There's a job waiting for me at the Admiralty,' he said, his voice small against the sound of the engine.

'Pah, you're going to see out the war behind a desk in White-hall? Thought you'd be better than that, son. Didn't you insist on a return to active duty?'

'None of this is what I wanted or expected, Father.'

'Oh, but it means he will be safe, Digby, and on dry land,' Freda sang out. 'So exactly what I wanted.'

Vivi turned in her seat, tried to catch Nathan's eye. 'You will be extremely useful, darling. You've been through an awful lot, and we are very proud of you.'

'But your injuries, they're only superficial. Surely you can get back on a ship?' Digby said, his voice thundering. 'In the last lot, they'd call that a Blighty.'

'Well, that's what happened to you, dear,' said Freda. 'You were sent home, injured. And soon after that we met. Remember?'

Digby harrumphed. 'That's as may be, but I could barely walk. Still can't get far these days, as well you know. And driving this car is a blessed nightmare.'

Freda's chin reeled back. 'Yes, dear, of course.'

'You know, Digby, that when Mr Buckley starts giving me lessons, I can do all the driving,' Vivi said. She felt incensed by his dismissal of Nathan's injuries: '*only* superficial'.

Without turning her head, she sensed his dark stare, which lingered longer than it ought, burning her right cheek while the car skirted the length of Manston airfield. She kept her gaze on the standing planes and men waiting around in the sunshine, ready to take off when the bell rang.

'Now what would you like to do, Nathan, the moment we get home?' Freda said as if chiding a child. 'Go straight upstairs and get into bed or take a short walk for a little fresh air? I must say, that hospital was fuggy beyond words. I'll come with you if you like. I could do with stretching my legs.'

'Mother, I'm going to close my eyes now.'

And on they drove, in silence, heading along the country roads.

Vivi turned again to look at her husband. Around the edge of the bandage, his skin appeared puckered, and his jaw red and pockmarked as if he'd been afflicted with measles. Watching his eyelids flickering in the sun that streamed through the trees overhead, she felt relief drench her like a warm shower. He looked better than expected, and he would now be safe in an ordinary office somewhere, with telephones ringing and paperwork piling high. And working in Whitehall meant he could stay during the week at Grosvenor Street and be at the Hall for weekends. He'd been away too long. All she wanted was to be alone with him, and be his wife. Soon, very soon, he would be home. And they could start living.

Digby made a low grumbling noise, and, at the corner of her eye, Vivi saw him move his hand from the steering wheel and reach over to her. She felt his palm press firmly over her knee.

She froze, gave a sharp glance at his profile, pulled her legs to the other side of the seat. Had he made a mistake? Had he forgotten himself? Did he mean to do that? Or was he simply trying to comfort her, realising what a strain it was, with Nathan injured so badly? But Digby offered nothing else, no kind words or fatherly gesture, nor even any eye contact, staring at the road ahead. He did not explain himself. Just a peculiar liquid smile on his face.

Vivi's father-in-law remained mute all the way back to Farthing Hall, his hand back on the wheel, while Vivi's repulsion stayed with her.

Digby took himself into his study and Freda, having read a message left for her in the hallway, announced that the parish committee were urgently expecting her, and went off in a flurry of angst and apology, leaving Vivi to walk alone with Nathan, slowly, carefully, up the stairs.

'Your mother prepared this room for you,' she said, opening the door. 'But wouldn't you prefer to be in our bedroom?'

'I'm not sleeping at all well, Vivi,' he said, dropping his kit bag onto the floor. 'I don't want to disturb you. This will do until I'm better. Must keep Mother happy, mustn't we. After all, she has gone to all this trouble.'

He sat on the edge of the bed, catching sight of himself in the mirror. He winced and turned his head to stare out of the window.

'Vivi, I'm exhausted. I'm not sure you'll want to look at me like this, let alone share a bedroom.'

'What baloney,' she said. 'I'm your wife.'

She found him fresh pyjamas, and busied herself with his kit bag, pulling out his sponge bag, socks, a soiled shirt.

'Leave that,' he snapped. 'I can deal with it. Most of it should be in the bin.'

Vivi stiffened. She set her face with a light, nonchalant smile, and sat next to him on the bed. The silence rolled on for some moments, and the room grew heavy with it. She followed his gaze out of the window overlooking the woods, the frame filled with layers of green. A blackbird sang his charming song.

She thought again of the abandoned cottage, deep among the trees, its secrecy spinning pictures in her mind.

'Nathan, I meant to tell you, ages ago, last autumn, after you left, I was riding in the woods, when—'

She felt him move closer, touch her hair and an aching tenderness, the same as the time they'd been caught in the rain on their honeymoon, spun in her belly.

'I'm sorry I spoke to you like that.'

He dropped his hand. Vivi closed her eyes, willing him to continue.

'I'm desperately tired, knocked for six. I cannot sleep. When I close my eyes, all I see is Harry McVie's face. The burning waves. His mate's blackened head sinking. I cannot remember his name. For the life of me, I cannot remember. And Harry didn't make it either.'

Nathan rested his hand over his face. Vivi watched a solitary tear run beneath his fingers.

'Nathan, darling.'

He flinched at her voice, shook himself.

'I'm sorry, Vivi. Enough self-pity. All of this has made me a major grouch.' He gave her a weak smile. 'But we'll get there.'

'Shall I leave you to your own devices?' she asked, longing for him to put his arms around her.

'I must do things for myself, Vivi. I need to have some semblance of dignity, of independence,' he said, 'or I will be a complete goner. You understand, don't you?'

Vivi nodded, thinking of the way Freda fussed, and not wanting to be like that. But this didn't stop her wanting to understand what had happened to him out there in the Channel.

'But one thing you can do,' he said, suddenly playful, a glimpse of his old self, 'is help me by keeping Mother at bay as best you can.'

She caught his eye in the mirror, delighted to see a little sparkle remained. Their smiles matched.

'Tell me, am I to suffer steamed white fish and coddled eggs and nursery puddings for months on end?' he asked.

'You must do as you are told,' she laughed. 'Doctor's orders. That said, I will leave you to get some peace.' She glanced into his kit bag. 'What *is* in this jar? A prescription from the hospital?'

Nathan hesitated.

'It's a seaweed poultice. I've been easing up my bandages and applying it underneath – after lights out, when the nurses aren't looking, of course. It's smooth and cooling. Doing me good, I hope.'

'Well, what do you know.' She turned the jar in her hand. It had no label, or instructions. 'But how do you come to have it?'

'A volunteer at the hospital gave it to me.'

'A volunteer? Not a nurse? That was good of her,' Vivi said carefully. She pictured the girls in their VAD uniforms, dipping in and out of the ward, bearing tea and comfort to the injured. 'But is she allowed?'

'I expect not,' Nathan said, 'but, you know, I'd do anything to get myself better. Seaweed has special properties, this person... she said. It will help heal my burns. She said to give it time and it will work its magic. Is it doing the job?' He began to peel the end of his bandage away from his head, not taking his eyes from Vivi's face. 'What do you think?'

Vivi's heart turned over. How vulnerable his naked scalp and damaged ear looked, the tightening skin around it, crumpled, red and raw. But this odd-looking poultice must be doing some good, for she did not feel as shocked as she expected to. Even so, Nathan having to apply it without the nursing staff knowing seemed rather strange. And, anyway, who was this volunteer? Perhaps the done thing would be to write and thank her.

'Are you in pain?' she whispered. If only he'd tell her, perhaps she could help him, too.

He rattled his pill box. 'Not as long as I have these beauties.'

Vivi felt a curious quickening of joy rising through the bedrock of distress. She realised how tense she'd been, all this time, bracing herself against the bad things that might happen. But, she realised, they already had. And Nathan was by her side for the first time in months and she would take care of him. Time would move on; his scars would heal, with or without the old-fashioned remedy in the jar.

And one day, Vivi thought, as Nathan had promised after their honeymoon, they would get there.

She unscrewed the lid, dipped her finger into the cool green paste. Standing in front of him, she slotted herself between his knees and began to smooth it over his forehead.

Nathan winced, braced against pain, but after some moments

she sensed him relax and give in, his features softening. Perhaps, she thought, their moment to start again.

'But what happened to you?' she whispered, planting a light kiss on his hair. 'Out there?'

He flicked his head back away from her touch, put his hands on her hips, pushed her away.

'Stop that now,' he uttered with high-pitched despair. 'That's enough.'

'Nathan, I only—'

He shook his head, took the jar from her hands, screwed on the lid, his eyes widening with a look that frightened her.

'How can I, my dear Vivi,' he said, 'how can I possibly tell *you*?'

7

While Nathan napped, Vivi rode Snowdrop down the hill behind the house and along the narrow droves, skirting the flat wide water meadows. The horse's legs swished through long, burnished end-of-summer grass, and cloud reflections glimmered in the still, marshy water. Birds dived and scooted, too quick to catch her eye. High above, somewhere over the sea, Vivi saw the tangled vapour trails of men battling it out in their machines.

She ran her fingers through Snowdrop's silvery mane, feeling the steadying rhythm of plodding hooves, remembering how she'd ride for hours when they stayed at their Hudson farmhouse, and how comforted and exhilarated she'd felt, how like herself she had been. A tear splashed down on to her glove.

'It's not your fault, Snowdrop,' she whispered. 'It's that you arrived at the same time as the telegram, and everything is all mixed up inside me.'

She'd tried her hardest to be brave. In the months since her parents' deaths, she'd craved the solace of Nathan's touch, his physical presence. The few letters that got through from him had been stilted and formal, as had hers in return; the words reflecting nowhere near the people they were. And when she saw him lying on his hospital bed, desperately injured, she wondered how she could ever lay her burden on him.

Oh, he had been well looked after. The Westgate Ward had had a precarious sense of calm, backed by bustling and hushed voices, guarded by the Sister at her desk by the door. Vivi would walk past rows of anonymous figures, bandaged in all manner of ways, propped up or sleeping, or staring at the wall. And Nathan, with an alarming amount of gauze taped over one side of his face, his hair matted against the white pillow, fluid flowing from a suspended bag into his elbow, a stranger to her. Her whispered greeting had made his eyelid flutter. She'd dared not touch him. And yet, someone else had been able to, to give him the poultice remedy.

Vivi halted Snowdrop, watched the sky. The planes had disappeared, the vapour fading; lives lost, or saved, she had no idea. And this, then, seemed the way of it for now. If Nathan didn't even want to talk about what happened to him, and she could not express herself, what possible chance did they have?

On the telephone the other day, Genna had sensed her frustration, offered her distant words of comfort, distracting her with stories of Dornie's jaunts out of Biggin Hill. But Vivi could not say what she wanted because the telephone, set up in the nook under the staircase, meant her voice echoed throughout the house, with Digby listening in his study.

She turned Snowdrop's head to start back, choosing the bridleway that would bring her out by the church, the thin grey spire visible through the trees on the ridge. It felt as good a place as any to aim for. Gazing at the countryside around her, she realised how much her life in New York now seemed as if it were just a play she'd once seen on Broadway: a dazzling, brightly lit stage of fun and laughter. Such naive and childish fun. How spoilt she had been, but she was paying for it now, as she sank into her new, terrifying, grown-up life.

She emerged through a hedgerow on to the Farthing Road, crossed over and dismounted and tied Snowdrop's reins to the post by the church wall.

On this quiet mid-week afternoon, Farthing appeared deserted. A solitary delivery van rumbled past. Way along the street, she spotted two of Freda's parish ladies chatting outside a cottage. She walked into the churchyard, the silence and solitude growing profound.

The gravestones were in varying stages of decay: some crooked, keeling over, the inscriptions vanishing, others scrubbed and pristine. The carved marble tomb of Nathan's grandfather – the sailor Calloway and builder of Farthing Hall – glowed in the sunlight, commanding attention. Vivi contemplated it, remembering one of the first things Nathan had told her, back in the drawing room at Grosvenor Street: that he had wanted to be an artist, had been pressed into the Navy to please his family. But, knowing him, he would have enlisted anyway when war broke out; nothing could change what had happened.

Over in the corner was a tiny pale headstone, a short narrow grave, alone in the shadow of an ancient spreading yew. A baby's grave. A single date, May 1928, had been carved into the stone.

'How sad for you, little one,' she said. 'You don't even have a name.'

She imagined the suffering contained in that faded lettering, but could not get far, for she was struggling to contain her own despair, let alone someone else's.

As she walked back to collect Snowdrop, she stopped by the verge and gathered a handful of wildflowers: ox-eye daisies, cornflowers, and blood-red poppies. She returned to lay them by the headstone, compassion switching to desire. An impulse for new life, tentative and precarious, streamed through her mind.

A child, yes, a child: the remedy for both her and Nathan.

* * *

She left Snowdrop at the stables with Mr Buckley and headed to the kitchen, seeking Mrs Scott's earthy company. The cook, a broad-beamed titan dressed in white with a cap pinned over her gleaming forehead, had laid out the family's rations for the week on the kitchen table, and was busy concocting recipes for each day, tapping a stub of a pencil against her chin.

'Afternoon, Mrs Vivienne,' she said. 'The tea in the pot might be a bit stewed, so I will make you another.'

Vivi pulled out a chair and sat down at the table. Lingering in the warm, fragrant kitchen for an afternoon cup of tea with Mrs Scott had become tonic for her, a little ritual which had Freda rolling her eyes in confusion, compressing her lips and tutting. And somehow, Vivi thought as Mrs Scott poured her tea, that made it rather enjoyable.

'Now we have three eggs left over from last week, which seems to me like one small miracle. And we have this haddock from the fish man.' Mrs Scott bent down to sniff it. 'I think it will go another day. Ah, and have you seen the haul of plums that Mr Buckley brought over from the farm? He repaired a window for them, so now I can make another batch of jam. You know how much Mr Nathan likes plums, so I'll save the best for his pudding tonight.'

Vivi did not know how much her husband liked plums but could hardly admit it.

Robin burst through the back door. 'Hello New Mrs Calloway. I'm to report that Snowdrop is settled, she is eating some hay and possibly having a sleep now.'

'Ah, thank you, Robin,' said Vivi, smiling at the boy's grubby knees and fallen-down socks.

A child, yes. Boy or girl?

She carried on listening to Mrs Scott's suggestions for Sunday dinner, watching, amused, as Robin stalked along the wall on tiptoes towards the sideboard. He slid a drawer open, keeping one eye on Mrs Scott, and plucked out a teaspoon. In a flash, he dipped it into a jar labelled tapioca and slipped it into his mouth.

'I've told you before, boy,' screeched Mrs Scott. 'I have eyes in the back of my head. That's our precious sugar. And all your teeth will fall out if you're not careful.'

Robin gave her a sunny smile to prove that it had yet to happen.

'But the jar says that it's tapioca,' said Vivi, peering at the ceramic lettering. 'Is that to fool Robin, I wonder? Obviously, it has not worked.'

'Ha, no, we've had that jar for years,' said Mrs Scott. 'It belonged to Mrs Hoodless, she was the housekeeper when I was a young kitchen maid, when old Mr Calloway was alive, and Mr and Mrs Digby newly married. After the last war. It's a silly thing: Mrs Hoodless dropped and broke the original sugar jar. She felt so bad about it, that she saved up to buy a new one, out of her own money. She came back with this – the tapioca jar – because it was all they had, and all she could afford. I remember the conversation, right where you're sitting. She was a good woman, Mrs Hoodless. She taught me everything I know. She didn't want to feel obliged to the family. A dear woman...' Mrs Scott's eyes turned glassy.

'Why didn't she take the jar with her when she left?' asked Vivi. 'After all, it belonged to her.'

'Oh, Mrs Hoodless died,' she said and then turned to Robin, forcing herself to perk up. 'Here, little thief, make yourself useful and take the last of the jam to your father. Tell him to remember to scrape the mould off the top first.'

Robin snatched up the jam, with a triumphant war-cry, and dashed off back to the stables.

'She died in service?'

Mrs Scott turned to her and nodded. 'Twenty-six years old, she was. Hardly an age.'

Vivi felt that she could pry no further. 'When you used the title Mrs, I imagined a much older woman.'

'Housekeepers take that title. I'm not married. Neither was Mrs Hoodless.' She paused, and closed her mouth with finality. She picked up Vivi's cup, even though she had not finished, and ferried it over to the sink. 'If you'll excuse me, Mrs Vivienne, I need the table. I need to press on with Mr Nathan's pudding. This blessed war has put paid to me having the kitchen staff I used to.'

* * *

Vivi rose early as usual and went along to Nathan's room to see what he might like for breakfast. Her tap on the door drew no answer. She went into the darkened room. Usually, he was awake and reading in the early-morning light in the chair by the window. She pulled back the curtains.

'Nathan? Are you awake?'

He lay in a tangle of bedclothes, his head turning from side to side on the pillow. He could not answer.

'Nathan, darling!'

She reached for his hands to steady them, where they were up by his face, plucking at his bandage.

He looked blankly at her, his eyes peering into the near distance, wide and vacant, his mind travelling somewhere else. She rested her palm on his forehead and quickly drew it away as if he'd burnt her. She hurried down to the telephone to call the doctor.

'A high fever,' Doctor Willis said, an hour later, glancing at his thermometer. 'Not surprising. He's been in hospital for a month or more. They can be filthy places.'

'Is it to do with this dreadful poultice he's been using?' Freda said, fussing round the bedside. 'I never liked the look of it.'

The doctor barely glanced at the jar that Freda was showing him and Vivi wished in that moment that she'd insisted on throwing it away when Nathan came home, instead of believing herself to have overreacted.

'It certainly wouldn't help matters, Mrs Calloway,' said the doctor, rummaging in his bag, 'and it isn't useful enough to do any good anyway. Get rid of it if I were you. I'll increase his dose of analgesics. Good old laudanum. Keep him cool, plenty of liquids. Is he eating much? No, I suspected not. Ensure that he does. I'll be back later this evening to check on him, maybe up his dose.'

Vivi went to Nathan's bedside. He seemed unaware of her touch, nor the voices in the room. His eyes were squeezed shut, his skin taut over his cheekbones.

'Don't look so frightened, Mrs Vivienne,' the doctor said, brandishing a phial of medication. 'I'm prescribing laudanum for your husband to calm him down, help him sleep. Not because he is in pain.' He shut his doctor's bag with a snap.

Vivi glanced at him, thinking, you stupid man, it might not be physical pain he is raging with, but it is still pain.

The doctor went, leaving behind a whiff of stale tobacco.

Freda paced the room, wringing her hands.

'Why was he using that filthy seaweed thing?' she uttered, darting to Nathan's bedside. 'What if it has done him harm? Nathan, what have you done to yourself?'

'Shall I fetch Digby?' Vivi asked reluctantly. She didn't want to go anywhere near him.

'No, leave him. He certainly won't want to be involved with any of *this*.'

'I'll go speak to Mrs Scott and Ruby. Get something organised for Nathan to eat.' Vivi looked at her husband, at the mess of sheets, at his jerking chin, his glazed expression. 'This bed needs changing, for a start.'

'Take this disgusting thing. Get Ruby to throw it away,' Freda said, giving her the poultice jar. It felt heavy, the glass slimy in her hands.

Downstairs, on her way back across the hall from the kitchen, after dealing with the ghastly poultice, anger, like a spasm of pain, snapped in Vivi's head. She tapped on the study door, waited, tapped again. No answer. She opened the door. Digby sat behind his desk, a tumbler of whisky cradled in his hand.

'I've come to tell you how Nathan is,' she said.

Digby swirled his glass. 'Willis filled me in on his way out,' he said. 'Sounds like my son is fit to be tied.'

She opened her mouth, but immediately clamped it down. The words seared her tongue.

'Oh, don't look like that, Vivienne. I can see you don't approve of me, sitting here, pouring whisky when it's not yet noon. All while Nathan lies up there on his sick bed.'

'I've got other things on my mind,' she said. 'And I need to get back upstairs to my husband.'

'You've got five minutes to listen to me, though, haven't you?'

Vivi said nothing.

'Whisky?'

She shook her head. 'Of course not.'

He studied her, ran his fingertips over his bristly grey moustache. Seemed to admire her.

'You know about my leg, don't you? Even if no one has told you all the details, my disability is obvious.'

Vivi lifted her chin in acknowledgement.

'It was the most appalling moment of my life when they told

me I could no longer fight. Ferried back from the Front to the nursing station, strapped to a stretcher, loaded on to a train home like a piece of baggage. A Blighty, some said. Do you realise what that does to a man?'

'I can't imagine.' Vivi said, wondering why this man was choosing to relay his own injuries to her, while his son lay upstairs, seriously ill.

'No, I don't suppose you can.' Digby's eyes shifted over her. 'Oh yes, I got my service medal, but folks talk, you know. They see me coming with my shuffling leg and I can almost hear it. Around here. In the village, after church, in the kitchen, no doubt.'

'I'm sure that's not the case, Digby.' Vivi turned, her hand on the door handle.

'They all think I'm a money-making coward. Because the injury was lower leg, you see. My father pulled down the old manor house to build this monstrosity, as my dear wife calls it. Didn't sit well with the born-and-breds, I can tell you.'

Vivi glanced at the ceiling. 'Look, Digby. I don't know what all this has to do with Nathan right now, but I—'

'Burns, scars, disfigurement, yes, I can deal with that. But not *weakness*,' Digby roared. 'They'll think he's a shirker, too. That's why I want him over this and back out there. It's as simple as that.'

Vivi inhaled, her blood seething. 'And I simply want him to be safe, like any wife would.' She opened the door.

Digby drained his tumbler, set it down with a hard knock on the desk. 'Wait. Hear me out. You don't understand. I couldn't continue in the Navy like my father wanted. For reasons I won't go in to here. That was before 1914. And when war broke out, all I could be was a Brown Job. A Tommy. Poor bloody infantry. Now look at me.'

'But why did you leave the Navy?'

'Never mind that.'

He stood up and hobbled over to her, the drag of his leg more pronounced after he'd been drinking. He stood close to her, his breath sour in her face.

'Look at me.'

She wanted to peel herself away from him, her disgust coiling like a spring.

She shot him a glance. 'It is a shame that you could not have had a Naval career like your own father,' she said, evenly. 'But Nathan does. And that surely must please you.'

'But look at him now!' Digby placed his hand heavily onto her shoulder, began to grope the fabric of her blouse. This, like the time in the car, no accident, making her stomach churn. He leaned in close, inhaling over her ear, the door post pressed hard into her back. 'And look at the state of me. Drummed out of the Navy. Sent home from the Front with a so-called Blighty. You will hear rumours about me, Vivienne. Usual tittle-tattle. And you will choose to ignore them.'

She dipped down, removing herself from his grasp.

'Your affairs are none of my business, Digby,' she said. 'Matter of fact, I feel sorry for you.'

She darted out the door and stopped short in the hallway. Freda stood in her way, her eyes sharp and seeking.

'Freda, your husband has been drinking,' she uttered, and then skirted past her, making for the stairs.

She glimpsed Freda going into the study, caught the timid tone of her question, could hear Digby's contemptuous laugh, like a rabid bark, even as she hurried along the landing.

* * *

That evening, the stars looked close enough to touch. The doctor had left, and Vivi sat by Nathan's open window in the darkness, mindful of the blackout, letting the cooling night air flood in, washing over her face and throat. Somewhere in the wood, an owl called, regularly, insistently, while the clock downstairs in the hallway struck the quarter hours. A single plane out there somewhere drew a shuddering line across the sky.

Freda opened the door, making the light from the landing shoot around the walls.

Vivi leapt up to shut the curtains. The room immediately felt clogged and stuffy.

'Can Nathaniel hear that plane, do you think?' Freda asked in a whisper fierce with anxiety. She set down a fresh bowl of water and lit the lamp. 'Did you see those planes earlier? Sounded like a whole squadron of them. I had to close the window in case they disturbed him.'

Vivi glanced at Nathan. The opiate Doctor Willis had administered had barely done the job. His hands flinched over to his face, as if he could hear gunfire, bombs, and explosions within the silence. Sweat soaked his pillow; his hair tufted and damp.

Vivi took the bowl, sat by the bed, and dipped the cloth in the water, patting his forehead, following his jerking movements with patience, tears stinging her eyes. Whatever miserable world her father-in-law wanted to drag her into, however he tried to shock or pester her, she would resist. She had to focus on Nathan. She would pour all her time, all of her strength into her husband.

Ruby knocked on the door and came in carrying fresh sheets and pyjamas.

'Mrs Scott is preparing more chicken soup,' she said. 'Shall I change the bed now, Mrs Calloway?'

'Leave it, Ruby,' said Freda, her face pale, her mouth disappearing in a line of misery. She came to the bed, indicating that Vivi must rise and give her the seat. Vivi took the bundle of linen from Ruby and told her she could go.

'Leave the bed, Vivienne. We can't keep disturbing you, can we Nathaniel?' Freda said, leaning over him. 'You need your rest, you need quiet, you need your mother.' She reached for Nathan's hands and clutched his fist, as if fighting with him. 'Now, now, Nathaniel, it's Mother. We must stop all this nonsense now, and rest.'

His eyes drifted open. Fixed on Freda.

Vivi felt a sudden, enormous relief. He seemed to be emerging through his fever, battling his way out.

'Mother, is that really you?' he said. 'Mother, what's under your wig?'

Freda dropped his hand, her fingertips fluttering up to her hairline.

'Freda, he doesn't realise, he can't mean it...'

Nathan reared up in bed, staring around the room, staring at nothing. 'I damn well couldn't save him!' he cried. 'His head black. Burning. Drowning.'

He crashed back on to his pillow, his breathing demented, his hands frantic, twisting the sheet.

Tears streaming, Freda cried, 'What happened, Nathaniel, what happened?'

Vivi put her arm around Freda's bony shoulder. 'He is trying to tell us,' she said. 'But perhaps it's best we don't know.'

Nathan's breathing eased and he soon seemed to settle, his face smoother. He opened his eyes and stared straight at Vivi.

'Elise,' he said. 'I remembered your name.'

She flinched.

'Elise, you helped me.'

'He doesn't know us, Freda,' Vivi whispered. Her voice sounded thin and calm, quite the authority, but her blood seemed to be beating in the wrong direction. 'He doesn't know where he is. He thinks he is still in the hospital. She must have been his nurse, or someone. Nathan, Nathan...?'

Freda recoiled visibly. 'A nurse? But why would he know her first name? And we don't know any Elise.'

Vivi drew up a chair on the other side of the bed and watched as Freda stroked Nathan's shoulder, her mouth gaping. Nathan shifted on the pillow, caught sight of Freda and his expression altered, like that of a child seeing its mother for the first time. He drifted away again, eyelids fluttering into sleep.

In the dim lamplight, Freda looked as fragile as Vivi felt. The clock struck another quarter hour and an odd sort of truce, a bond, a meeting of wills, settled between them, radiating across Nathan's sleeping form.

Later, not long after midnight, Freda left Vivi alone with him, and at the sound of the door clicking shut, Nathan woke and turned to face her. He gazed at her with a look coloured by recognition, and fired by love. She felt a scratching in her chest, a desire for him. Perhaps the drugs had chipped off his veneer to reveal the soul she had been seeking all this time, the Nathan she could never quite put her finger on. The elusive man she loved.

'Nathan my darling, I'm here,' she whispered, 'and you're home, and soon you will be well.'

But Nathan's face fell flat, disappointed, as if he had been expecting someone else.

8

'Come on then, Robin, if you want to live dangerously,' said Vivi, pulling on her driving gloves and tying her headscarf, wishing she'd put on her fur-lined jacket. The heater in Nathan's car did not seem to be working properly and the day felt truly autumnal: damp and grey, with the only visible brightness from the trees where leaves turned yellow and gold. 'That's it, climb in the back seat, Robin, if I were you. You will be safer there.'

'Don't listen to her, son,' Mr Buckley said, settling himself into the passenger seat. 'Mrs Vivienne is a fine driver.'

'Fine, you say?' she said, pressing the starter button. 'I guess so, for a learner.'

The engine spluttered and broke into a roar.

'Easy on the accelerator, madam,' Mr Buckley said. 'Or should I say, *gas*.'

Vivi lifted her foot, engaged the clutch, and smiled to herself as the car made its tentative way across the gravel with a series of gentle lurches, each one causing Robin to burst with giggles.

'No laughing at the back, young man,' Vivi said, slowing at the entrance onto the lane and flicking the indicator to turn right at Mr Buckley's direction.

The windscreen wiper swished fallen leaves from the windscreen.

'Wrong lever, madam, this one. That's it. Now we're off.'

Vivi made steady progress, trundling carefully through puddles, and feeling thankful that no vehicles came at her from the other direction. And she never got used to being on the wrong side of the road, whether as a passenger, or now, actually driving the car.

'We won't go far,' she said, as they approached the village. 'I'm mindful of the ration.'

In all honesty, she would rather not have to take her lessons under the curious and amused gazes of the Farthing folk, until she felt a little more competent behind the wheel. But she could not have gone the other way, on the road down to Canterbury, in case of having to do a hill-start, the thought of which, with the unpredictable state of Nathan's brakes, unsettled her.

His car had seen better days and Vivi longed to buy a new one. She knew exactly what her father would have said: *Just throw money at the problem, Vivi.* But in this case, his money would not be able to talk, or if it did, would say the wrong things.

Trundling tentatively past the first row of cottages on the village lane, Vivi knew, an American girl reincarnated as an English countrywoman, she had to tread carefully and find a way to fit in. And having a flash new car would not help matters. She glanced down at her skirt, which emulated her mother-in-law's drab tweeds. Her Fifth Avenue outfits would stay firmly shut away in her wardrobe for the duration.

Vivi flicked the indicator, and caught Mr Buckley's smile of approval as she eased up beside the brick-and-flint wall of the church.

'As far as I am concerned, Mr Buckley,' she said, 'This driving caper, as convenient as it is, does not beat a good ride out on Snowdrop.'

'I bet it's still as bumpy,' Robin piped up from the back seat.

Mr Buckley turned to look at his son. 'Hop it, Robin. Mrs Vivienne is about to negotiate a three-point turn, and you, my lad, can make your way back home on foot. She doesn't need you as the cheeky Greek Chorus in the background. Off you scarper.'

'Right-o,' said the boy. He set his cap on his head and cheerfully clambered out of the car.

Vivi gave the steward a grateful smile and, carefully, meditatively, she completed the turn, starting off back the way they came.

'Perfection,' said Mr Buckley, responding to Robin's wave as they passed him.

Vivi felt a satisfied warmth settle inside her, her confidence blooming as she continued down the lane without incident, and safely drove them back through the gate in the hedges and across the gravel. She felt buoyant with success and seeing the Hall appear, swiftly ticked off all manner of improvements she wanted to make to it. New roof, bathrooms, fix the floors. But in an instant, she remembered Digby's warning words about the villagers, their mistrust of the family, the legacy of the Sailor Calloway. And in wartime, she realised, her plans may appear extravagant, and not at all appropriate. She needed to tread carefully in all aspects of her life. After all, she was a Calloway, now.

As she wrenched on the handbrake, Nathan stepped through the front door, a cautious smile pinching his tight, scarred face. He found it hard to smile these days, he told Vivi, as if his face had shrunk around his jaw. And he stood there, a little less proud than he had been, his shoulders not so square. But something about him seemed brighter. It had been a good few months since he'd come home from the hospital, his fever a thankfully short-lived episode. Vivi had put his confusion, his not recognising her firmly to the back of her mind. He had been incredibly ill then, and his strength now returned in small but noticeable stages.

But his recovery meant that, once again, he would be heading into danger, going to London to start his desk job at the Admiralty. He'd be away for the working week, staying at Grosvenor Street, returning home on Fridays for the weekend. And Vivi couldn't bear to think of it. The battle in the skies over Southern England had been won; but now war rained down as bombs on the ordinary folk on the city streets, right onto their doorsteps.

Vivi got out of the car, thanked Mr Buckley, who drove the car around to the back of the Hall, and she hurried up to Nathan, her heart turning over as he greeted her.

'Well done, Vivi,' he said, his eyes bright, despite his faltering smile. 'I expect you're going great guns.'

'Not doing *too* badly,' she said. 'Ha, listen to me. I seem to be speaking like an English person.'

'I wouldn't expect anything less from you. I'm proud of you,' he said. 'Mother has just ordered tea. Although, quite frankly, looking at that greying afternoon sky, I think it's time for a G and It instead. It must be nearly five. What do you say?'

Optimism rose inside her, on the back of her driving triumph.

'I say, that's the spirit.' She linked his arm to stop him walking back into the house. 'I was wondering, Nathan,' she said, resting her head on his shoulder, softening her voice, 'if you thought it might be time to give up your sick room. That you might prefer to have G and It by the fire, in our own bedroom? What do you say? It does feel so empty in there these days.'

He gazed at her, puzzled, his own questions circling his face. Vivi wondered if she sounded frivolous and unfeeling for asking, after everything he had been through. Was she pushing too far, too soon? Really, could this brave, damaged man really love such a spoiled Park Avenue princess? She shuddered, remembering the dreadful moment when Freda's voice rang out in the drawing room at Grosvenor Street.

'Are you cold, darling?' he said, putting his arm around her, holding her tight. Vivi closed her eyes, daring to relish this new warmth, the feel of his solid embrace a balm to her doubts. 'And may I say, what a suggestion, Mrs Calloway.' He planted a kiss on top of her hair. 'How about you ask Ruby to lay the fire, I collect my stuff from Sick Bay, settle in, and you fix the drinks?'

Vivi smiled at him, sensing her own igniting flame, daring to imagine that they could get there, at least, could be starting again. She caressed the back of his neck. He reached for her hand and pulled it away.

'But one step at a time, Vivi,' he said. He kissed her hand, but his lowered voice held a chilled edge of conviction. 'It's just that, I'm not sure about... I'm sorry.'

She felt the barrier form again, wider than before; her hopes stalling. Had she wished for too much, too soon? She felt herself shrink a little inside.

'You're shaking. Must be cold standing around out here,' he said, cheerfully, as if none of this had passed between them. 'Let's get back inside.'

Shutting the front door, Vivi took a deep breath and resolved to put on her sunniest smile, fix the best G and It her husband had ever tasted, and stop trying so hard. Nathan went upstairs, passing his mother on the way down. Freda barely acknowledged either of them. She stood outside Digby's closed study door and raised her fist tentatively to knock, the sound of it small and timorous across the hallway. She waited, her head bowed, neck stringy with tension, her mouth pinched, listening for the gruff rumbling command to enter.

Vivi, realising they didn't have any ice on the drinks tray in the sitting room, went back to the kitchen to see where Ruby was, and to ask Mrs Scott for some. She returned with the full bucket, wondering how she'd ever be able to fix a good drink when there were never any lemons, when a sound from inside the study made her freeze. Standing in the middle of the hallway, she cocked her head, but whatever it had been – a single, odd, low thump – did not repeat. In the past, she had heard her parents-in-law argue in that room: Digby's barking of disapproval, laced with anger, and Freda's plucky response. But this dreadful silence from behind the closed door, an appalling acceptance of whatever seemed to be taking place, felt more terrifying than their regular fiery quarrels.

Vivi made the drinks, hurried upstairs. Ruby had lit the fire in their bedroom and drawn the blackout. The soft lamplight and pulsing flames warmed the space, making cosy shadows around the walls. Nathan had left his shaving kit on the washstand, had hung his dressing gown on the hook behind the door, and now lay stretched out on their bed, hands behind the back of his head, gently snoring.

She set the drinks down, sat in the chair by the hearth, and softly called his name. Sipping from her tumbler, she waited. Her husband looked rested and peaceful, such a contrast to how he'd appeared, even the week before. He continued to sleep, and Vivi stoked the fire, drained her glass. She called out again, louder this time, gave up, and passed the time working her slow way down Nathan's drink.

* * *

A week later, Nathan departed for London, leaving Vivi without the car – she wouldn't dream of asking to borrow Digby's – and with Freda's brittle company. They listened to the radio news in the sitting room, the bulletins about the bombing raids, night after night, the devastation of the East End docks, and now, Coventry, their combined unspeakable fear for Nathan at his desk on White-hall sparking the air between them.

'Don't you think, Vivienne,' Freda said, getting up to switch off the radio, and wincing as if in pain as she sat back down, 'that hearing all of this, about people sleeping in the Underground; their homes destroyed; the firefighters saving St Paul's at all costs. It makes ones' own troubles, stuck out here in relative safety, seem insignificant really.'

'It does, and it is truly horrific,' Vivi agreed. 'I feel so helpless, really. But we each have our own feelings, our own small lives, our own reasons for sadness.'

Freda dipped her head in acquiescence.

'Which we of course, have to accept.' Vivi pondered her situation, how she resolved to try hard to be happy. 'We can only do the best we can. Do our best to help others, within our own limitations.'

'But sometimes, Vivienne,' said Freda, in sudden compressed fury, 'there comes to a point when there is nothing else for it.'

Vivi glanced in surprise at her mother-in-law, noticing for the first time a bruise on the side of her neck, marking the tender skin under her ear. She wanted to ask about it, wondering if there may be something she could do. She'd heard arnica was good for that sort of thing. And it seemed Freda bruised so very easily. Vivi had recently spotted a small advertisement in Freda's local newspaper, from a woman over in Margate who provided such remedies, herbal and such. Perhaps she, too, purveyed treatments for bruises. Vivi tried to recall the address.

'Freda, I was wondering about arnica, if you may be able to...' she began, lifting her hand to gesture at her own neck, but felt stunted by the intensity in her mother-in-law's caged fury, the grip of her fists on the arms of her chair.

In a sudden clear moment, Vivi realised that Freda's anger had never been directed at her – even though she may have often thought so – and it seemed to be released in full fury, ricocheting every which way around the room.

'Vivienne, dear,' Freda said, her voice grating. 'Has Digby ever been inappropriate with you?'

Vivi sat forward in her chair. 'Goodness, Freda, what?' she cried in shock, her racing thoughts skirting around the time in the car, and in the study during Nathan's illness. Digby's loathsome proximity. But to reveal this now, when Freda looked so pained and utterly done in, felt like compliance, that she'd accepted his repugnant behaviour. 'I don't know what you mean, really.' She felt the lie spiking her tongue.

Freda scrutinised her with a grim set to her mouth, reading something on Vivi's face.

Vivi lowered her voice, glanced at the closed sitting room door, thankful for their privacy.

'Freda, if you don't mind, I find this rather an odd turn in conversation. You may have noticed, I tend to keep a polite distance from your husband.' She did not wish to give the hateful subject any more time than it deserved. 'Shall we leave it at that?'

* * *

Winter plodded on, the days slow and gloomy. Christmas came almost without comment, with Nathan barely at home for more than a brief snatched respite, the action moving into the North Africa desert taking up his energy and his time. Two rabbits, shot by Mr Buckley, ended up baked into a pie for Christmas dinner, for there wasn't a turkey in the village to be had – or at least not for the Calloways – and New Year passed without so much of a pop of Champagne cork. Freda appeared worn down, watching Digby,

Vivi noticed, with a silent wariness, and sometimes fury, but most often looking as revolted by him as Vivi felt.

One bleak and unremarkable January morning, Vivi rose early and alone to a cold bedroom, the grate heaped with ash and her hot water bottle like a slab of stone under her feet. She wrapped up and went downstairs for a scoop of coal, so she could at least light the fire and stay in bed longer to keep warm.

In the scarce grey daylight limping through the hallway windows, she noticed the door to Digby's study ajar. It struck her as odd, for he tended to be a stickler for all doors to remain shut, especially in winter, to counter the icy draughts.

She reluctantly tapped and poked her head around, wondering why he, of all people, would be up and working at this hour.

Digby lay stiff and slumped over his desk, among scattered papers and leaking ink pens, his fingers clamped around a half-empty tumbler of whisky. His jowls were squashed flat into the blotter and for days later, Vivi imagined the long-ago inked words impressing themselves onto his dead cold skin, to be read later when Doctor Willis hauled his body up for the mortuary men to carry him away.

9

VIVI, FEBRUARY 1941

Digby's death changed everything. The house felt stifled, tired, sinking into decline, and Ruby struggled even more to keep on top of her work, evidently only able to deal with what was on the surface. Vivi longed to throw open all the windows, renew the air and start afresh, but it was far too cold outside.

Nathan brought the cold in with him when he got home late after visiting the solicitor's office in Margate. He came into their bedroom, the chill of the winter's night clinging to him. Vivi had been sleeping but his entrance woke her. She sat up in bed. The coal fire in the grate had disintegrated into ruby embers. Shivering, she reached for her shawl, while Nathan busied himself in his dressing room. Cufflinks rattled into the dish, his tie swished as he hauled it off, his belt buckle clinked.

'Did you check in on your mother?' she asked, turning up the lamp by the bed.

In the half-light in crumpled striped pyjamas Nathan looked young and pale, and distracted, as if Vivi's question had been ridiculous.

He pulled back the covers, shuffled down. 'I do not have the energy for her tonight.'

'I don't blame you,' Vivi said. 'Today has been difficult all round. I tapped on her bedroom door earlier and when I told her I had no news from the coroner's office she sent me away with a flea in my ear.'

The day had spun out much the same as all the days since Vivi had found Digby. Her mother-in-law kept to her room, being taken soup and steamed fish at regular intervals by herself, Mrs Scott or Ruby. Convalescence food that she toyed with and left on the plate. She would sit upright in her bedroom armchair, with tearless eyes and a fixed grim expression.

'She wants to get it over with,' said Nathan. 'The funeral will be a step towards acceptance, once the coroner releases him.' He hesitated on the last word, as if unsure how to form it.

Vivi rested her hand on his arm. 'You look worn out. You must have had a day of it too. How was the solicitor?'

This had been the second meeting since his father's death. He'd been frustrated after the first; now he seemed entirely deflated.

Nathan thumped his pillow into a more acceptable shape.

'Vivi, I can't talk tonight.'

She switched off the lamp and ran her hand over to him through the warmth under the covers. She found his hand, and entwined her fingers in his, wondering if he might want her to comfort him. It never seemed to be the right time, but perhaps the wrong moment would, on this occasion, be right.

He let her kiss him for a couple of breaths and then pushed her gently back by the shoulders onto her pillow. For a second, she thought that he wanted her as much as she wanted him. But he stopped, pulled away, turned onto his side.

'But, what happened at the solicitors?' she asked, drawing air into her lungs in a rush of anger.

His voice in the dark sounded too loud, angry almost, like Digby's.

'It's a mess, Vivi, an utter unmitigated mess. Now go to sleep.'

But how could she sleep?

Vivi stared into the dark, hearing Nathan's breath eventually slow into gentle snoring.

Lying next to her husband, her jaw set and the tone of his voice still ringing in her ears, dread began to draw lines around her body. The feeling melded into guilt, and it prodded her, wanting her to admit that when the private ambulance rumbled away across the gravel, carrying its stiffening cargo, she had felt utter relief.

* * *

The sound of the piano downstairs early the next morning woke Vivi. Freda. She had never heard her play. Apparently, Digby always dissuaded her, and Freda said she was not the most accomplished of players, but a fairly competent Beethoven's 'Moonlight Sonata' drifted up through the floor, something not heard at Farthing Hall for a whole generation. Digby had hated anything German.

'My goodness,' Nathan said sleepily next to her. A thin light edged the curtains and the cold air smelt of coal smoke. 'What is Mother up to? She hasn't played for years. And now she'll have us shot as traitors.'

'It sounds like she must be feeling a little better.'

'That's not *better*,' Nathan said. 'Sounds more like a rebellion to me.'

The sonata stopped on a duff note and Vivi leaned over to ring for some tea. Silence, followed by sketchy notes tinkling like a musical joke, and then, after a pause, 'Für Elise' began to cascade upwards.

'Oh, I love this tune,' Vivi said, and turned to tuck herself against Nathan's back, her arm circling his hip. But something ticked in her mind: Nathan, in the depths of fever, uttering the name. *Elise.*

He pushed her hand away, extracted himself, hauled back the covers and trudged towards his dressing room, leaving Vivi in the warm pit he'd left behind.

'Nathan, won't you stay?' she said. 'Can't we lay here a while? Listen to the music?'

He turned at the door to look at her. Vivi realised how much a part of him his scars were. How much she had got used to them. The hospital, or rather the volunteer person with that strange concoction – despite Dr Willis's and Freda's objections, and her own quiet mistrust of it – had done a good job, helped him heal. But she knew such a potion could never work for her own scars. They sat deep inside her, unseen, and only felt by her. She wanted Nathan. She needed him to help her own recovery.

'Nathan?' She reached out her hand.

'No, darling. I'm not... not now.'

She felt her jaw wobble, tears pool, dipped her face to hide them.

He sighed and sat by her on the bed. He touched her hair like he might a child, ruffling it.

'Vivi, did I demand that you go to bed with me when your parents died?'

She sat up, shuffled to the other side of the bed. He'd spoken gently, but the words felt like bullets. She stood, tying her dressing gown belt in a ragged knot.

'You weren't here, Nathan.'

He gaped at her, astounded. How could she accuse him of not being here for her, when he was away serving his country, half-drowning, losing his men, having the skin on his face scorched? Her throat ached with guilt.

'Darling, I have to sort out a great many things,' he said, his patience elongating his words. 'My father's estate. My mother. I'm worried about her. This is odd.' He looked at the floor. The music continued. 'But what do I know? None of us know what to do, do we? She won't talk about it.' He gave a minute shake of his head. 'Plus, there may be an inquest.'

'I was alone.' Vivi felt petulant, having to explain herself. 'But you are not alone now. I am with you, beside you, through all that you must do. And I am sorry about your father.' She paused, took a ragged breath. 'When my parents... I needed you. Is that too awful to admit?' Another sob rose, a traitor on the back of a dark memory.

'But I am here now.'

She wiped her hand over her face, her frustration grinding like machinery, her shout of laughter surprising them both.

'Oh, Nathan, no you're not.'

'Vivi please...'

The piano downstairs stopped.

'I think you best go and see your mother,' she said.

Vivi opened her wardrobe door and ran her hands over her dresses, most of which had travelled with her across the ocean. She thought of herself at seventeen with Genna, riding cross-town in the back of a cab, draped in furs and wearing satin shoes, snug between their mothers, among stacks of hat boxes, on their way to a soiree or lunch or back from a shopping spree on Fifth Avenue. She remembered the giggles, like euphoric springs inside, coiling and shooting out of her. She longed for the simplicity of the past, wishing she had known that she must savour moments of happiness, for they were fleeting, burning bright, gone. But in that, she guessed, lay the essence of joy.

She dressed in black Chanel wool – thinking to hell with it, and what anyone thought – fixed her own hair, for Ruby proved nowhere to be seen, and went downstairs to telephone Genna. Curled up on the stool under the stairs, free to speak without worrying about Digby overhearing, listening to the lilt of her dearest friend's voice, for three minutes only, Vivi felt her young self re-shaping in her mind.

She put down the receiver and walked to the study door, knocking as she turned the handle. Nathan sat hunched at his father's desk, head down, shielded by stacks of paperwork. The memory of Digby hunched there sent a shiver of nausea over her skin, chased by contorted empathy for Nathan. He glanced up at her, said nothing, and pointed his gaze firmly back at the documents before him.

'Nathan, I'm sorry about earlier,' Vivi said. 'I seem to be a bit uppity at the moment.'

He said nothing.

'Can I do anything for you?'

He sighed, the sound of it wrenching from his body. He rested his elbows on the table, his head cradled in his hands.

'There's nothing that can be done, except try not to panic, try not to take flight, try not to throw myself off the top of the Widow's Watch.'

'Nathan.'

'I won't do that. But there is no money left, Vivi. Absolutely none. The solicitor yesterday didn't mince his words. Bad investments, ill-advised share schemes, gambling. Christ, the gambling. Farthing Hall is mortgaged to the rafters.' He shifted some papers. 'The horses will have to go. The staff. What is Mother going to say?'

'The horses? Even Snowdrop?'

Nathan looked at her. She clapped her hand over her mouth. How self-absorbed she sounded. She pulled up a chair, sat down opposite him.

'But darling.' She sighed, waiting for his attention. 'Aren't you forgetting something?'

Nathan blushed. 'I know, Vivi. Your money.'

'It's a dirty word to the English, isn't it.' She smiled hesitantly, trying to stay bright. 'But let's talk this through, Nathan. Something we've never done. For goodness sake, I am sitting on a fortune. Granted, it is tied up in property and bonds, and what-all and may take months to unravel. But there's the house on Grosvenor Street, the New England farmhouse. Daddy also had a yacht on the Hudson. I've not done anything with any of it. The war put paid to making decisions like that.'

That, and the enormous shock through which she found herself still tumbling. Nathan began to shuffle a ream of letters, his eyes wet and unfocused. She sat still for many moments, watching her husband's dignity draining away.

'This is an odd one,' he said, clearing his throat. His voice deepened. 'Your father's name appears on these leases and bonds. On quite a few, truth be told. Joint ownership, joint investment. Thrown me a bit, Vivi. I don't understand.'

Nathan continued to speak. Vivi watched his mouth, but heard her father's voice, low and earnest, as they sat in the hall at Grosvenor Street on the morning of her wedding. She could recall the scent of orange blossom and the image of the white satin shimmering.

Old Digby may be an odd fish, but I feel he is pretty sound, business wise.

A crystalline moment, poised between two segments of her life. Her father's gaze, on her like a spotlight. Regret now, for not telling him, for not expressing what it felt like to bear its restorative force.

Digby and I go back years. You will be fine.

She sat back in her chair and watched her husband leaf through papers, turning them over, shifting into different piles. She remembered the letters he had written her that first heady summer; the letter in which he had proposed, his words wet and drifting off the page into nothing as she fished the notepaper out of scented bathwater. How she had found it difficult to picture his face. Looking at him now, in grave concentration, the life she had imagined seemed non-sensical; Nathan was further away than he had ever been.

'Nathan.' She swallowed down the dryness. The back of her neck went rigid, feeling cold, felt exposed. 'Was this marriage arranged between our fathers?'

Her husband's head jerked up, his features warping into confusion, brushed by a shadow of guilt, so brief that it could have been the idea of it, coming to him, to be rejected instantly.

'Come now, Vivi, surely that's not what you're thinking?'

She could not answer him. His expression stayed fixed in disbelief, widening with shock. And yet, he would not tell her what he might be thinking.

When she couldn't bear to look at him any longer, she let her eyes fall onto the documents on the desk, the scattered paper trail of deceit, coercion, lies, the legacy of Digby, and felt her world crumbling once again, her bones turning into ash.

* * *

Nathan went back to the Admiralty a few days later, and not long after that, telephoned from his office to speak to Vivi. He asked her to pull out a certain document that he'd found in Digby's papers and post it to the solicitors in Margate. The conversation could only be brief, the regulation three minutes, and Vivi felt relieved. She said she'd do what he asked, at once.

'I only remembered I'd forgotten to deal with the dammed thing this morning, Vivi,' he said. 'Listen, are you all right? You sound a little... peaky.'

He sounded further away than ever, not a matter of fifty miles.

'It must be the line,' she said. A little peaky? Did he not realise that the ground shook beneath her feet, and he did nothing to steady it? 'I'll say goodbye. You must be busy.'

Vivi went into the study and quickly unearthed the paperwork from one of the piles, not wishing to stay long. The scent of Digby's tobacco, stale and fuggy, lingered. She opened a drawer to find an envelope and noticed, under a sheaf of writing paper, the tip of a large old-fashioned key. It did not resemble any she had ever seen around the Hall, either on Mrs Scott's belt, or on the hooks by the front door. Her thread of curiosity knotted and twisted back on itself. She picked it up, turned it in the light, and slipped it into her pocket.

That afternoon a pale sun came out to brighten the cold blue winter sky, and Vivi rode Snowdrop her usual route, down the lane a way before turning into the woods. The horse's breath blew in clouds of vapour and twigs snapped loudly beneath her hooves, echoing in the stillness between the trees. Vivi's fingertips began to feel chilled and numb, but she turned her collar up and pressed on. The cottage in its clearing looked despondent, the ivy along its wall bedraggled, as if yet another year of neglect had put paid to its previous luminosity. Vivi dismounted and opened the wooden garden door, feeling she ought to apologise for not having been back sooner.

The rose garden, in wintry sleep, appeared brown, spiky and dishevelled. She stood on the mossy doorstep, and tried the key. It fitted. It protested a little, grated against rust in the keyhole's throat, and, as she knew deep down it would, it turned. She opened the door, and the cottage exhaled a dusty scent, herbal and ancient, and on the edge of decay, but not entirely unpleasant.

Her boot crunched on dried-out leaves, blown in under the door, and the corners of the room melted into dark shadows, the scant afternoon light failing to reach far enough through the trees. The place seemed dull and inconsequential. No one had lived here for many years, and Vivi sensed disappointment, a blunt feeling that the house had not met her expectation, or its side of their understanding.

Mindful of Snowdrop waiting outside in the cold, of the deepening gloom of the woods, that she needed to get back, for Freda would expect her for tea, she turned to go. But her boot knocked against a box, an old crate imprinted with the name of an orchard in Blean, tucked under the cupboard by the door. It gave a rattle when she gently nudged it again with her toe.

Vivi knelt on the dusty floor and pulled the box out. Again, disappointment. It contained some old crocks, shattered bits of china squirrelled away for sentimentality perhaps or to be used at the bottom of plant pots. Edwardian, she guessed, from the scrolling design of the broken lettering: blue on creamy ceramic glaze. It must have been a storage vessel, the sort Mrs Scott might keep on the kitchen shelves at the Hall. She tapped with her fingertips, rearranging the shards, piecing them together like a jigsaw. They spelt out the word *sugar*. She'd found nothing more than a broken old sugar jar.

10

Genna parked her car at a chaotic angle on the gravel and, emerging in a waft of ginger fox fur and Chanel Number Five, she passed the keys to Mr Buckley, asking if he'd kindly deal with both the motor and her suitcase. He saluted two fingers to his brow and cheerfully fired the engine.

Vivi embraced her in the hallway, breathing in her scent, feeling her voice vibrate inside her as she uttered her hellos.

'Come through and have coffee,' she said, relief crushing her words. 'Except it isn't coffee, but chicory, I'm afraid. Something Mrs Scott has rustled up.'

Ruby dipped into the sitting room with the tray and curtsied in Genna's direction. It wouldn't be long before the girl handed her notice in and headed off to the war effort, Vivi thought: a better job with a better uniform.

Ruby flashed her dimples and closed the door behind her.

'That girl doesn't curtsy for me,' Vivi said, pouring the drinks.

'It's the title,' said Genna. 'I'm still getting used to it. Dornie teases me no end.' She watched Vivi closely. 'My goodness, Miss Vivienne Miles, you're a sorry sight.'

'It's lovely to see you too, Lady Dornford. How is Dornie? And by the way, have you forgotten? I'm Mrs Calloway these days. The *New* Mrs Calloway.'

'You'd hate me if I didn't tell you. I am concerned about you. You have lost your spark.'

'I was going to say haven't we all, these days, but not when I look at you, Genna, darling.'

Genna waved the compliment away. 'Dornie is well. When I see him, he tells me he is well, anyhow. We've both been worrying about you. It has been one thing after another for you, ever since you landed in this blessed country.'

Vivi's hand shook as she handed Genna a cup of dubious brown liquid.

'Some good, some bad,' she said.

Genna kept her eyes on Vivi as she took a sip.

'The good being you marrying Nathan,' Genna stated. She set the cup down, puckering her lips, and lifted the lid on Freda's sugar bowl. 'Not sure why your maid bothers to bring this in. There's nothing in it.'

'I'll mention it to Mrs Scott,' said Vivi, but knew it wouldn't make any difference. The tapioca jar in the kitchen had been empty for a week or more. 'But you must know, we haven't had sugar in a good while.'

Her mind switched to the cottage, and the broken crocks in the box. She felt unsettled, as if suddenly losing her seat on Snowdrop.

'Oh heavens, it doesn't matter. I'm still the fussy old gal I've always been,' Genna said. 'God, I thought I might make you laugh. Vivi darling, whatever is the matter? I want to help make things feel a bit better for you, honey. Or at least start trying.'

Gazing at her dearest friend, Vivi tried to clear her mind, dismiss the confusion.

'There's one good thing...' she started.

'There we are.'

'The coroner has released the... has released Digby, and so the funeral can take place.'

Genna winced. 'Yes, a good thing. Listen, honey, please tell me what I can do to help you. I do not want to see that look on your face a moment longer.'

Vivi said, 'Genna, I...'

The door opened and Freda came in, dressed in crow-black, her thin grey hair coiled into a French pleat. Genna rose to her feet.

'Lady Dornford,' Freda said, clutching Genna's offered hand in both of hers, her large knuckles protruding and her voice light with welcome. 'It feels like years.'

'Not since the wedding, in actual fact, Mrs Calloway. I'm so sorry for your loss.'

Freda flapped her hand as if to cut off the sentiment. 'So good of you to come. We have been at sixes and sevens, I'm afraid, haven't we Vivi? But events are moving on.'

Freda sat down, her sigh pumping out of her as a breath of tangible relief. She clutched a handkerchief as if it were a prop, rolling it over in her hand. Vivi noticed a smoothness to her skin, as if she'd slept for a hundred years, her tearless eyes looked bright.

'My, if I may say so, I do like your new look, Mrs Calloway,' Genna said.

'Yes indeed. And so do I.' Freda patted the nape of her neck. 'I felt it was high time for a change. Had one of the village ladies style it for me. Got rid of that God-awful wig.'

At this, she gave Vivi a whisper of a wink.

'Well, isn't that just the thing,' Genna cried, her voice rounded with tact. 'I did wonder.'

'So old fashioned,' Freda said. 'I don't know what I was thinking, all these years. I never liked... well, Digby never liked my premature grey hair and so I...' Her voice drifted down to regret.

'How is Nathan?' Genna said, changing the subject. She looked around the room as if expecting to see him.

'He's been in London these past few days,' said Vivi. 'They gave him permission for a week's leave, but he would not take it.'

Genna shot Vivi a horrified look. Vivi nodded.

Her mother-in-law bristled. 'He will be home in time for the funeral.'

'Freda,' said Genna, 'you must tell me if there is anything I can do.'

'We don't expect many mourners,' she replied. 'Digby was quite friendless, you see. And you don't exactly send invitations, do you? People just come. We'll see who turns up from Farthing.'

'No business associates?' Genna pressed.

'Not that we know of.'

'His one true business associate, it seems, was my father,' said Vivi.

Her comment thinned the air between them, elongated it until it snapped.

They crunched over the gravel, on an errand for Freda to give the vicar the final run-through of the service: hymns, prayers, eulogy. They turned the corner onto the lane, and as soon as they were out of sight, Vivi linked her arm into Genna's.

'You've got to help me,' Vivi whispered, her hoarse words bursting into clouds in the cold air. 'I think I'm going mad.'

'I can see it, honey.' Genna's face drew close, her eyes wide. 'What's the matter?'

Something twisted inside Vivi: innocence and hope, an entitlement to happiness that she and Genna had both worn back home like the latest fashions in the plate-glass windows of Fifth Avenue. All of it, now, dashed to the ground.

'Did he marry me for my money?' She blocked her mouth with her hand, as if she'd just cursed. 'There, that's it, Genna. That's where I am. Going over and over it like a damn stupid fool.'

Genna quickened her pace, propelling Vivi further away from the Hall. White hoar frost sparkled on evergreen hedges; trees stood out against the flat grey sky, their branches like dark veins. Genna steered them into the churchyard.

'Deep breaths, Vivi, come on. That's it. What in the world has made you say that?'

The long grass lay brown and broken, the frosted gravestones serene and lonely. They sat on a bench, their breath ballooning into vapour. Vivi peered around, trying to spot the tiny baby's headstone, but had lost her bearings, could not remember which forlorn corner the child had been hidden in. A robin sang in the yew, his bright tune peeling out. It seemed a shame to spoil his efforts.

'Inside the church is a brass plaque for my parents,' Vivi said, eventually. 'Did I not tell you? I had it commissioned last year. I go in there and polish it, once in a while.'

'You did tell me.' Genna pressed her felt-gloved hand over Vivi's, offering a layer of warmth. 'Show me.'

But Vivi sat still, found she did not want to get up, walk another step, take another breath.

'Has he ever loved me?'

She watched as Genna's mouth moved over unformed words of protest and then felt her give in, her shoulders collapsing next to her.

Genna sighed. 'I cannot say.'

Vivi, aware that her question may not relate solely to Nathan but may include her father too, said, 'Perhaps you will be able to answer, when I tell you what I know.'

The cold churchyard seemed to echo and expand around them as Vivi told Genna about Digby, the way he had looked at her, touched her. The things he'd said to her. She faltered over what her father alluded to on the morning of her wedding. He, the one true business associate of Digby. This felt far more painful than anything to do with Digby, the double-edged question of *did he ever love me* resting on this memory. She told Genna about the documents that Nathan had uncovered, the bonding of Digby and Edwin that stretched back years. All the fragments of her life since she met her husband, a meeting engineered who knew when, pulled together into a messy scribbled picture. The chaos and the falling away of everything.

'Vivi, from what you tell me, Nathan was surprised, and is as puzzled as you are about the business stuff,' Genna said. 'And as for your dear father. Surely not to goodness. On your wedding morning, it sounds like he was reassuring you about the business dealings. Digby is the crook here. What your father said was nothing to do with you and Nathan getting married. I could see how happy he was for you. And your mother too. You were a bag of nerves that morning, Vivi. I cannot believe it of him. He wanted you to be in safe hands, surely?'

'Safe!' Vivi cried, a startled sound within the quiet. 'I can't see a way through it.'

Genna's hand on hers felt heavy, restrictive.

'I am as baffled as you are, honey. What a hullabaloo,' she said. She looked her square in the face, the sassy girl again. 'But you've got what it takes. I know you are strong, and I will stay here with you, through the funeral, while you need me, and make you even stronger. Or you come and stay with me if you like. A change of scene. Dornie would love to see you.'

Vivi thought of escaping Farthing Hall and the watchful eye of Freda, and the nasty remnants of Digby. She wanted to be in a place away from this mess, where the vague oddness of a simple abandoned cottage and what it contained would lift from her mind, and leave her in peace. Where she could breathe and be herself. But she knew that she, herself, would still be with her, wherever she ran to. *Different sky, same soul*, as her father would say.

'No.' Vivi removed her hand, patted Genna's in thanks. She felt a weakening in her body. 'I must stay here for Nathan. He doesn't realise it, I don't think he'll ever know this, but he needs me.'

11

The hearse's tyres whispered as it crawled up the drive, a low-slung menace of a vehicle bearing its load, strewn with lilies. Digby's coffin appeared huge and boastful. Even in death he intimidated her, she thought as she watched from the sitting room window, the pane distorted by tape to stop the glass shattering if bombs should fall.

'It's here. Where is he?' Freda asked at her shoulder.

Vivi knew she meant Nathan, although on reflex, she nodded at the hearse, wanting to say, *he's in there.*

She rested her hand on Freda's arm.

'I'll go and fetch him.'

Touching her mother-in-law, albeit fleetingly, Vivi felt an intimacy that no longer disgusted her, or at least, no longer felt as uncomfortable as when she'd helped her remove her shoes and stow her wig all that time ago. Freda wore her natural, although thinning hair well. She held her shoulders straight and looked lighter on her feet, as if her shoes no longer pinched. Vivi had insisted on ordering her a new pair, handmade specifically for her, and sent directly from Bond Street. They must be helping, although something far less tangible emanated from Freda now. She wore grief like an outfit, widowhood as a disguise.

Vivi could not find Nathan in the study, nor the morning room, or the bedroom. She stood in their empty room for a moment, listening to the muffled busyness of the house below, then walked along the landing, opened the door at the end and climbed the wooden spiral stairs. The last set, wrought iron this time, curved as a tight spiral rising into near darkness. Her heels made hollow clanging sounds on the metal. She paused in front of the narrow door at the top. A little lightheaded, her breath high in her chest, she turned the handle and shielded her eyes, instantly dazzled by daylight as she entered the glass room perched on the roof.

Nathan, a lean figure in black, stood with his hands on the window ledge. He turned so swiftly, shaken by her intrusion, that he blurred and melded momentarily with the brilliant light. A blush tinged his forehead and his eyes darkened, arresting her. She let go of the handle, letting the door close gently, shutting out the world behind it.

'Nathan, the hearse is here.' Her voice sounded ridiculously loud in the small glass box. She expected to see guilt or anger from him at being found, but instead, all she could read was a shot of pain.

'I noticed,' he said. 'You can see everything from up here.' A sweep of his arm embraced the view. 'Old Grandpa Calloway had it right, didn't he? Building this look-out, setting up the telescope, keeping an eye out on proceedings, surveying his land, the people below.'

Vivi had remembered the telescope from when Ruby first showed her the Widow's Watch and had wondered fleetingly if it still worked. It took up most of the floor space, riveted to the polished wood floor. She felt light-footed in this teetering perch on the roof, as if the boards were swaying, falling away from her.

Down below, the hamlet of Farthing and the church lay tiny and unreal, like scattered toys. Walking around the instrument, she sat on the window seat, holding the edges with her hands, feeling it solid beneath her body. She picked up Nathan's jet-black hat and turned it in her hands, admiring the quality of the fabric. The motion of her fear settled. Up through the glass roof, the weather-vane with its metal ship in full sail waited, immobile.

She glanced at her watch. 'Nathan, the time—'

'I'm half glad you found me,' he said, his twist of a smile like a punished schoolboy. He looked at her smartly, to get the measure of her. 'Because you can save me the bother of telling my mother. I'm not going.'

Vivi gave a little cry. 'Nathan, you must!'

He glanced at her, on the edge of amusement. 'You did not know my father.'

'I knew enough.'

Nathaniel nodded his acknowledgement and leaned his arm on the telescope. How attractive he looked, with his well-cut suit draped smoothly across his shoulders; the whiteness of his shirt brightened his face, and the faint shadow of stubble defined his jaw, the scarring no longer a blemish, now a part of him. She remembered why she had fallen in love with him and yet her skin prickled as if she had barbs growing on her, defending herself at all costs.

He ran a finger over the lens, collecting a ridge of grey dust, and examined it, as if he had all the time in the world. Reaching into his top pocket, he drew out a slim silver flask. He gestured with it to her, and she shook her head. She'd read somewhere in Freda's *The Lady* that women wanting to start a baby must avoid strong spirits.

Nathan took three sips and slipped the flask back into his pocket. Vivi imagined Freda pacing below, wringing her hands, and felt frustration squirming inside her.

'Nathan, really—'

'Everyone is expecting me,' he said. 'Everyone is *expectant* of me.'

'But you know that you should do the right thing. I can't believe for a minute that you won't go.'

He grasped the handles of the telescope, twirled it around and dipped his head to peer through the lens.

'There they are, trooping into the church already,' he said, singsong and bitter. 'Not that many, must be said. The doctor and his wife I suppose feel they must show their faces. Some of the tenants from the village. But we both know my father was an awful bastard. And me too, by association I expect.'

His helplessness stung Vivi.

She tried another tack.

'Can you see the sea through that thing?'

'No,' he laughed, dryly, 'and that's the blinding folly of it. Of everything. Traditionally, this room is supposed to be for lonely wives waiting for their husbands away at sea, keeping watch for returning ships.' His words snagged at her, seemed to sum her up. 'But we cannot see the coast from here. Even on the clearest of days. What folly. Still, if we can't see the sea, we can at least keep watch on other things.'

A well of hope filled inside her.

'Remember, Nathan, our honeymoon. I want to go back there, to Margate, to find that beach you told me about, where you went when you were younger. I want to walk by the sea.' She sounded plaintive, like a child asking for an ice cream. 'And I, Nathan, wish that I had been able to go to my parents' funeral.'

'Ah, you see. You are always able to trounce me.'

She looked at him, daring him.

'Believe me, Vivi, I can't begin to imagine what you went through, and I am so terribly sorry I was not here by your side. As you are now.' His recognition filled her chest with fire. 'But, here, now, I'm not sure I feel *able*—'

'But that's why you must,' she cried.

He shook his head. 'You said that you knew *enough* about Digby.'

The use of his father's first name startled her. She sat up straight, attentive.

'I did.'

'But you don't know half of it, Vivi,' he said. 'If I tell you, I think you will understand. I don't want to go to my father's funeral because he is disgusting to me.'

He sat next to her on the seat. He whipped out his pocket watch, checked the time, and clicked it away again.

'You know about his debts, his scandalous and somewhat immoral business decisions. Even his war record was not great, with rumours of a self-inflicted injury, his stupid lame leg, and there he was berating me for being signed off to desk duties having had half my face burned off. But that's not the worse of it.'

'It's not?'

Nathan sighed and took her hands in his. The gesture, unexpected, and riven with meaning, made her crumble. She enjoyed the weight of his hands, could feel a pulling sensation through her blood.

'You heard about his short-lived naval career? Yes, well. He was drummed out. Immoral behaviour. That's why he ended up in the trenches.'

'I can understand that some sailors do get a reputation,' Vivi said, ponderously.

'Not all of them for seducing their commanding officer's wife.'

'Good heavens. I can see why you feel ashamed of him. I am so sorry.'

'But even that...' Nathan's words broke up, trembling out of his mouth. 'Even that wasn't the worse.'

Vivi held his hands tighter. 'There's more?'

'When I was a child, we had a housekeeper.' Nathan's gaze flicked to the window as if he could see through it into his past. 'She came here soon after the Great War, when my parents were newly married. Mrs Hoodless. She wasn't married. Housekeepers take that title, you see. Did you know that?'

Vivi simply nodded, not wanting to say she'd already heard of Mrs Hoodless. She didn't want to interrupt his flow. And they both needed him to speak.

'She was young and had this exquisite face, such delicate features. I loved her, like a boy can love a grown woman. A reverence, you see. A pure love. Her hair was very fair.' He glanced at Vivi. 'A little like yours.'

Vivi held his stare, observing his sudden realisation of the association.

'I was seven or eight. And I thought she was a fairy. I believed she was a fairy, or a princess. You know, unobtainable and perfect. She drifted around the house, making everything work, and she made everything right. She must have had a solid core around all that beauty to do the job she did. Everyone loved her. Even my mother, who you'd think might have not taken to her.'

'Mrs Scott has mentioned Mrs Hoodless,' Vivi admitted.

'What did she say?'

'She said that she died.'

'Her downfall was her beauty.' Nathan looked at Vivi, as if it might be the case for her. 'She caught Digby's eye. Such an old cliché, but there we go. That's my father. One wonders if she had been employed in the first place because he'd taken a fancy to her. Fact of the matter is he ruined her. He had his way with her. And she had to leave. I don't remember her going. From then on, there was an absence, an emptiness in the rooms that I, the young boy, slowly became aware of. I asked about her every day for a week, or so Mrs Scott tells me, for I had forgotten I did that. I was, after all, very young. And again a month or two later, only of course, to be fobbed off. Time had moved on. Before I properly realised what had happened, she was long gone.'

'Where did she go?'

'She went away to have her child. I only heard all of this later, much later, a few years ago, when I was a naval cadet. Mrs Scott sat me down and told me. At the time, my mother had arranged for Mrs Hoodless to go to some house for unmarried mothers, or some such place. Remember, this was in the late twenties, and things hadn't much improved since Victorian times. It must have been like a poor house, some terrible institution.'

'Oh, my goodness, I see.' But Vivi did not *see*. It felt so desperately unimaginable.

'But before that could be arranged,' Nathan said, 'she apparently stayed at the gamekeeper's cottage on the estate, for a week or so. It seemed Digby needed her out of his sight. But my mother insisted she was housed somewhere, Mrs Scott said. Or else she would have been on the street.'

Vivi's understanding began to piece together, like Mrs Hoodless's shattered sugar jar. She must have taken the shards with her to the cottage, after replacing it with the tapioca jar. A keepsake, perhaps, from happier, settled times?

'Nathan,' she said, 'this is appalling. What happened?'

'She ended up at the institution. The child died at birth.'

Vivi pressed her hand to her breastbone. She thought of Mrs Hoodless, picturing grace and magnificence, waiting pregnant and alone in the cottage for someone to decide her next move. And how she'd fretted over breaking the Farthing Hall crockery.

'And Mrs... the housekeeper?'

'She hung herself.'

Vivi gasped, rested her palm over Nathan's juddering hand.

'She is buried here in the churchyard. Again, Mother stepped in and arranged for her to be brought back. Although the headstone only states that it's her baby's grave.'

Vivi closed her eyes, the image of the lonely little plot in the corner of the churchyard shuddered in her mind.

'The vicar at the time agreed to have them buried together.' Nathan said. 'And agreed that no one would acknowledge Charlotte. Something to do with suicide.'

Vivi recoiled. 'Charlotte?'

'Yes, Charlotte.'

Vivi watched the colour seep from Nathan's skin, liquid pooling in his eyes. He clasped his hands together, felt blindly for the flask in his pocket. Then he stood, took a nip, and marched to the window. He kept his back to her as he announced brightly, 'Vicar's waiting outside the church now. Must be nearly time.'

But another name came to Vivi, like a blown leaf bowling along in front of her; a leaf that she wanted to chase and snatch from the ground. She heard musical notes. The tune played by Freda one recent cold morning, and Nathan's reaction.

I thought her name was Elise. Vivi stopped herself saying it, for that would force something else bewildering to be true, another riddle to unravel. She looked at Nathan, and knew that he needed her.

She thought of her father talking on her wedding morning about the revolving door where he'd bumped into her mother. Had been bowled over by her. How, coming from two different worlds, they had met in the middle.

Vivi walked over to Nathan and rested her hand on his arm. He stared down at it.

'It is all so very sad,' she said. 'Such awful things for you to have lived through, and to not understand. Only to find out all those years later. That poor woman.'

'And still, it goes on,' he said, his eyes seeming to carve up the space around Vivi's head. He sounded haunted. 'I don't want to end up like my father. I don't want to be him, or anything like him.'

'But you're not, Nathan, you are nothing like him.'

He looked down at her. His mouth opened but all that came out was a ragged sigh.

'Is that your mother's brooch?' he asked, eventually.

The diamonds sparkled like ice on the bosom of her black dress. She nodded. He touched the gems lightly.

'My brave Vivi.'

She wrapped her arms around him, rested her face against his chest. His embrace felt like a pleasant memory.

'Remember how we danced, like this, on the night we met?' she said. 'The world may be at war, and it feels like everything is all falling apart, but we can still dance.'

She felt him press his head against hers. How easily she could break down; how easily she could demand that he admit their love was teetering on the edge, their marriage a sham. That there was too much buried beneath its surface. But all that was left in the world for her was Nathan, and she clung onto him as if he were a life raft in a burning sea.

'I will do everything I can for you, Nathan, for you and Freda,' she whispered into the cloth of his suit. 'For you are my family now. This is my home. And, after all, I am an officer's wife.'

He kissed the top of her head.

'Come on' he said. 'We are going to be excruciatingly late, and we can't have that, can we? Let's go and bury Digby.'

12

ELISE, MARCH 1941

Someone knocked on the front door. Elise, sitting in the dim front parlour, glanced in surprise at her mother, wondering who on earth it could be. For when the postman delivered letters or the townspeople came to the cottage on King Street, to ask for tinctures for stomach trouble, bee stings, corns, 'too much wine', or 'lack of baby', they knew to come to the kitchen door.

'Go round the back!' Elise's mother called.

Due to lack of space, or more likely, Elise thought, knowing her mother, as a barrier to the outside world, the dresser stood in front of the door that opened onto the street. And the one small window, partially blocked by it, meant the parlour always had a twilight feel, and that her mother must have the eyes of an owl.

'I'll see who it is,' said Elise, as footsteps rang along the cobbles in the passageway.

She walked out to the kitchen and her stomach flipped. The tall figure waiting behind the panels of frosted glass in the back door struck a profound note inside her: the set of the shoulders, the line of his jaw, the way he cocked his head.

Nathan. She opened the door, questions spinning in her head,

Why? What? How?, but they missed her mouth on every orbit. She hadn't seen him since the day before he'd been discharged from hospital last summer. She'd gone to his ward to say goodbye, but he'd already left.

'I hope you don't mind the intrusion, dropping by like this,' Nathan said. 'I wanted to thank you and your mother, for your care, and your kindness last June. Sorry it has taken so long, but events seem to have overtaken us. I happened to have business in the town here, and couldn't leave without paying my respects.'

Elise kept her gaze on his eyes, on his expectant smile. His injury flickered at the corner of her vision, a mild distraction, the scaring taut and pockmarked, a little red, like a permanent blush. His coat smelt of cold sea spray; he must have taken a walk along the harbour arm.

'My goodness,' she managed to say, surfacing through tumbling thoughts. 'I didn't expect to see you again.'

But she'd often thought of him, and also of his wife, that attractive creature she'd spotted visiting his bedside, her hat vibrant against the dull hospital walls, freckles cascading over alabaster skin, the blue of her eyes brightened and wet, her voice dulcet and American. Immaculate taste. Of course, she'd thought, a man like Nathan would have a wife like that. Elise had tried not to gape at Mrs Calloway, had slipped away; she wasn't meant to be in Westgate Ward anyway.

'Is that the sailor I hear? Don't leave him standing there, Elise,' called her mother. 'Bring him through and put the kettle on.'

Elise gestured for him to come in. Nathan slipped off his hat and stepped through to the parlour.

'Ah, I can see my poultice worked a treat,' Elise's mother said, indicating that he sit in the fireside armchair. 'It's such a joy to see the results of my handywork. Just looks like you've had a mild case of the measles, sir.'

'Ma, really!' Elise laughed, her nerves jittering. She touched her hair. She hadn't bothered to roll it that morning; after all, she was only home for a few days. She hadn't been expecting visitors, especially not *this* visitor. Her hair must look like rats rats' tails.

'Your mother is right, Elise, and it is fine handywork indeed,' said Nathan. 'It's a pleasure to meet you.' He shook the older woman's offered hand. 'I am surprised as everyone how well it has healed, despite everything. I had a bad fever at one point while I was convalescing. But I got through it. It could have been so much worse.'

Elise's question surfaced at last. 'But why... how did you find us?'

'I asked at the corner shop,' Nathan said, sitting down and looking perfectly at ease, it seemed, in Elise's home. 'They soon pointed me in the right direction.'

'Everyone knows us round here, for one reason or another,' said Elise's mother with triumph, and went out to the kitchen to make the tea.

Elise and Nathan sat without speaking, while her mother clattered teacups in the kitchen. The kettle sang on the range. Elise tried not to stare at him, but he found her gaze, squinted, and lifted his hand flat over his brow as if to peer at her through the gloom.

'Sorry, it's so dim in here,' she said, feeling shy, the urge to explain.

But Nathan laughed. 'I'm teasing. It's comfortable and cosy. My home is somewhat chillier, especially on a day like today.'

Elise imagined the country house he'd mentioned on the beach all those years ago: large and surrounded by gardens, she decided, way out of her reach. She imagined his wife gracing a grand staircase.

'I'm glad to see you looking so well,' Elise said, hurriedly. 'I mean, last time I saw you... I can't lie. It was a shock. To meet you again, and your injuries. Only my first week volunteering, you see. In fact, my whole experience at the hospital last summer was traumatic. But it made me determined to do something. You are lucky to have caught me today. I am usually at St Thomas' in London. I'm training to be a nurse. If I can make one small difference, I will be happy. And I often wonder about your man, Harry McVie.'

'You made a big difference to me,' Nathan said. He leant forward, his hands clasped. 'Harry passed away, I'm afraid.'

Elise flinched. A good nurse, or not, she would lose patients.

Her mother came in with her hat and coat on bearing the tea tray and announcing that she was popping out to the baker's, even though the queue was a mile long and they didn't need bread.

As her mother's footsteps echoed away along the passage, Elise stoked the fire, adding another shovel of coal. The strange silence in the snug parlour stretched to fill the corners. Nathan's teacup rattled, and flames hissed and popped.

'It's all change for me, too,' said Nathan, conversationally. 'I have been given a desk job at the Admiralty on Whitehall, so I will be shuffling piles of paperwork instead of commanding sailors onboard ship, much to my mother and my wife's relief. I still get to wear the uniform, though.'

'Well then,' Elise said tentatively, 'it sounds like they will be happy about it.'

'Life at home has been difficult. God, I feel odd even mentioning it, seeing as we are all of us struggling one way or another. The war seems to drain joy from everything, doesn't it, and one doesn't like to complain one little bit.' He stirred his tea, pondering. 'But somehow, I feel able to tell you.' He caught her eye. 'And you, in a way, are a stranger. Perhaps that's why it is easier.'

Elise wondered at this: why he had bothered to seek her out. Surely, he could talk to his friends, his wife?

'My father passed away last month.'

'Oh goodness, I'm so sorry.' She pictured the bellowing angry man in a bowler hat on the beach.

'The funeral was last week and I'm back here in Margate to see the family solicitor in Cecil Square. For the umpteenth time, it seems. Blessed paperwork to deal with.'

He sounded weary, his voice shattered, but equally as if a weight lifted from him, as if speaking to her eased a tangle inside him. He glanced at her, and she felt he allowed her in.

'Was it sudden?' she asked.

'It did not come as a surprise. My father was never happy with the world. Never happy with any of us. Blotted it all out with whisky.' His dismissal sounded brutal. 'Died at his desk, tumbler in his hand.'

His confiding in her felt like an honour, as an encouragement. 'And how is your mother coping?' In her mind, the lady sat on the beach in a straw hat, battered by the breeze.

'Not so good, as you might expect, but getting better,' he said. 'The funeral was delayed. The coroner was involved. A sudden death, you see. So much to sort out. My wife has been steady and wonderful.' His face hardened, as if he needed to shield himself. 'She lost both her parents soon after we married, and I wasn't there for her. Her bereavement and my injury changed us both.'

'But that's simply awful,' said Elise.

Nathan looked at her over the top of his teacup, as if she distracted him: puzzled him. His presence seemed to nurture her. It felt honest and liberating. And she felt a key turning inside her, turning against something vibrant and golden, whether locking it away, or unleashing it, she could not say.

Nathan shook himself, put his cup down, looked at his watch. 'Listen to me, I do apologise. I seem to be spilling it all out today. I wanted to drop by and thank you and your mother, but I must go. As I said, so much to do.'

Fighting disappointment, Elise said, 'Of course. I mustn't keep you.'

He paused. 'I hope you don't mind me confiding in you.'

'Not at all,' Elise said, and tried for a laugh. 'What are strangers for?'

* * *

Two months later, she found his letter in her pigeonhole at the nurses' home, on Admiralty-headed notepaper, asking her if she might like to meet him for tea. The surprise felt like a shiver, and it shadowed her for days.

The following week, as Elise hurried across Westminster Bridge, Nathan's request felt curious and pleasant to her. A friend from her childhood, wanting her company, to share a little time. It opened a window for her: a breathing space from the back-aching work, the stench, and the blood and the cries of helpless patients. But more than that, she thought, as she clipped along in her nurse's cape, it gave her a burst of joy, of unexpected confidence.

The bridge afforded the best view of the city, even today as a pall of smoke lingered over the East End, still burning from the raid two nights earlier. Cherry blossom tumbled through the air on Embankment where bombed buildings gaped their most private innards. And uniformed men and suited women bustled along Whitehall, hollow-eyed from lack of sleep.

Nathan had already secured a table at the small café on Piccadilly.

'Elise, my goodness, how well you look,' he said, standing as she came in.

'I look like a nurse,' she said, taking in his dark naval uniform. 'Whereas you, you look...'

'Like someone who knows what he is doing? Gets the job done? It's nice of you to say so,' he laughed.

The café had a sweet, steamy aroma. They ordered tea and buns and Elise relaxed amid the murmuring conversation and tinkling of china.

'What a show we had the other night,' he said. 'How are you bearing up at the hospital?'

'We have a system,' she said. 'As soon as we hear the siren, we help the porters deposit our patients in the cellar, wheeling the beds along corridors, the walking wounded helping *us*. And then we go down to the air raid shelter. It's so regimented, it can't go wrong. Until it does. It is hard to leave the patients. I hate that bit.'

Nathan stopped stirring his tea.

'It is a bit of a muddle, isn't it?' he said. 'No one has done this before. The best thing, in my book, is to do as you are told, and hope for the best.'

'But don't you think that sounds inconsequential? It doesn't seem sincere enough.' Elise sipped her tea, felt his gaze on her. 'Especially when it is so very awful.'

The end of her sentence cracked on her tongue, and she quickly drained her cup.

'Yes, let's admit it,' he said, the look in his eyes deepening. 'Awful.'

She smiled at his understanding. She noticed how well his face had healed, even since February.

He touched his fingertips to his cheek.

'My mark of service,' he said. 'I try not to wear it like a medal, but even so... it is certainly a conversation starter. But I want to tell people. I'm no hero.'

Elise wanted to tell him otherwise, but the words died inside her head. She must not reveal that part of her to him.

'Where are you staying?' she asked. 'I take it you don't travel home to Kent every day. Do you have digs?'

Nathan laughed. 'Digs? Yes. My wife's house on Grosvenor Street.'

Elise's eyes widened, a blush burnt her cheeks. Of course, such a woman would own such a place: a place Elise struggled to conjure in her mind.

'Most of the rooms are shut up,' he said. 'Valuables, of which there are many and are nothing to do with me, packed away, the furniture covered. I stay on the ground floor. And the kitchen is in the basement. I spend a lot of time down there. Seems safest. I have a char three times a week. Bit of a bachelor's mess, you might think, but remember I am in the Navy, and there is no such thing as untidy with me. Well...' He lifted an eyebrow. 'Not really.'

'But it must be good to get home, out of London, for the weekends,' she said, slowly spreading butter on her bun.

'Is that real or is it marg?' he asked, as if buying time to consider his answer. 'Ah, yes, it looks real. And, yes, the weekends.'

She looked up from her plate, remembering Nathan's father. 'How are your family?'

'As you know, my father died in February,' he said, as if this settled the matter.

He bit into his bun, polished it off in two mouthfuls. His expression switched, and Elise saw a blankness harden over his eyes.

She wanted to distract him.

'I meant to give this to you, when you dropped by.' She opened her handbag and pulled out the handkerchief he had lent her on the beach, all those years ago. Something about the enormity of it all turning full circle, coming to fruition, made her light-headed. 'I can return it at last,' she said. 'Properly laundered.'

Nathan took the handkerchief and turned it over in his hands as if he had never seen such a thing before, his monogram bright against the white.

'My God, Elise. After all this time,' he uttered, his face still, his eyes glittering at her.

She leant forward, confused by his tone. 'You can see how well I kept it. All laundered and pressed.'

'But you should not have done.'

'Done what?'

'Given it back to me. It was a gift to you. How many gifts do you return?'

'I didn't realise it was a gift,' she said.

Nathan looked as if he didn't believe her.

'I haven't received many *gifts* over the years,' she said, feeling hurt. 'And evidently, I don't know what to do with them when I do.'

His cheeks coloured, and his scar flamed deeper.

'Elise,' he said, shaking his head. 'I'm sorry. I thought that perhaps you had not treasured it.'

'And I felt sure that you would want it back,' she said. 'Had regretted giving it to me in the first place. A slip of a girl you happened to bump into on holiday.'

'Elise, really, that's not what...'

The waitress leaned between them to clear the cups.

When she withdrew, Elise snatched up the chit left on the table. 'Although, I am going to pay for our tea,' she said. 'There's a gift, right there. Are you going to be picky about that?'

She slipped out her purse and made a little stack of shillings.

'The look on your face,' said Nathan, putting the handkerchief into his pocket. 'I'm not going to argue with you. Thank you for the handkerchief. I insist on leaving the tip.'

Elise and Nathan laughed softly together as, in unison, they bundled their napkins and pushed back their chairs.

Out on the street, back into the reality, the end of the afternoon, Elise's spirits tumbled.

'I ought to be getting back to the nursing home,' she said, tying her cape.

Nathan appeared to be standing taller than ever, attractive in his dark-blue naval jacket.

'Perhaps one evening you would care to dine with me?' He sounded formal, and distant, as if it was something he felt ought to be said, from time to time, at certain moments.

Elise shook her head. 'I'm not sure. My shifts, you see.'

She felt as if Nathan's wife stood right beside her. She didn't even know her name.

'I understand,' he said. 'But I could do with the company. It is nice to see a friendly face among all of this... and, after all, I still owe you.'

Elise opened her mouth to protest, for surely after everything, they were even now. The air raid siren began its ominous wail.

Nathan looked up at the sky between the chimney pots.

'What now? In day light?'

'I better go,' Elise said, sudden fear making her turn as if to run.

He caught her arm. 'I'm not waving you off into this, Elise. Come with me. We'll go to the Underground.'

They hurried towards Piccadilly Circus, bumping shoulders with people, some sprinting, others nonchalantly continuing to window shop or hop on the back of buses. Taxis deposited folk seeking shelter. An ARP stood guard at the entrance to the station.

'No entry, sir. It's rush hour and packed down there. The platforms are too narrow for all these extra folks.'

'We'll find another.'

Nathan led Elise down a side lane, and they emerged into an enclave of quiet cobbled elegance, the Mayfair streets lined with flat-fronted mansions in dark London brick. Darting along Saville

Row, Elise glanced through iron railings, down to the basement workrooms of the tailor's shops.

'Grosvenor Street is not far from here,' said Nathan. 'And, as I said, it has a decent cellar.'

The siren continued its ghastly uneven drone, its whining voice conjuring terror. The streets by now had emptied but the sky above the roofline remained passive and clear.

'Here?' blurted Elise, as Nathan guided her up a short flight of steps outside one of the mansions and opened an enormous green door.

Nathan nodded and stood aside for her to walk in. Elise gasped. Marble stairs swept upwards from the hallway, inside which the footprint of the cottage on King Street could easily sit. All appeared grand and magnificent, and yet Elise sensed the house felt untended, and unlived in, and no longer a home. The air smelt still and unbreathed; oblong ghost marks on the walls indicating where mirrors and paintings used to hang.

Nathan settled Elise on a sofa in the drawing room, a sofa so comfortable, it felt like being cradled in heaven. She eased off her shoes, let her toes curl into the deep carpet and felt like weeping. She had never in her life been stockinged foot in a carpeted room before. A massive fireplace held the remnants of a small fire. Folded, thumbed newspapers lay on the coffee table, empty cups of tea, a plate with crumbs on.

'I'm slacking,' Nathan said. 'What would my CO say?' He busied himself, clearing them away. 'So,' he said, conversationally, 'Vivienne inherited this house from her parents.'

He placed a brandy in Elise's hand. Her fingertips felt cold, her insides gently shook. Now she knew his wife's name and it made her real, and, oddly, made Elise feel more connected to Nathan, for he had shared something intimate.

'Everything you see was her parents', and hers now,' he said.

She'd never had anything stronger than her mother's black-berry wine but she sipped the brandy and felt the warm vapours circle her heart. She glanced behind her, out of the window at the slice of sky.

'Shouldn't we go down to the kitchen? The cellar?'

'Would you rather go to a shelter?'

Elise shook her head, for that would mean having other people around them, and she liked the solid silence here inside this house, its old elegance defiant in the face of possible destruction. She liked Nathan's soothing presence, like a shield against the approaching storm.

'We'll go downstairs,' he said. 'I can make you supper. Bring your drink.'

Elise followed him across the hallway, through a green baize door and down a flight of stairs. She sat at the corner of the large kitchen table, while Nathan took off his jacket and began to slice bread.

'It's a bit stale,' he said. 'We can have toast.'

The range under the mantlepiece was unlit but the small cooker next to it had been pressed into service for heating soup and frying bacon and eggs. The enormous kitchen felt welcoming and safe, with its ranks of chinaware on the dresser, the battery of copper saucepans.

Nathan turned a can of soup into a pan. She found a spoon, lit a flame under it and stirred, while he filled the kettle. Upstairs, in the splendour of the drawing room, they had both seemed out of place. But down here in the kitchen, as Nathan set out the toast and Elise buttered it, they fell into step with each other. They ate without speaking and the siren continued.

Nathan looked up at one of the arched windows under the ceiling.

'It's getting darker,' he said, quite cheerfully, 'but seems like nothing's happening. Might be a false alarm. They sound the siren if anything is spotted over the Channel. We might be in luck.'

The siren stopped. The windows had no blackout and so they sat without a light on. The room began to fill with evening shadows. They waited for the All Clear. None came. This meant, Elise knew, there was no turning back, and the bombers were coming.

Nathan made tea and they drank it at the table.

'Last summer when I was tucked away in Kent convalescing, recovering from this,' he drew a circle in the air around his face. 'When our boys were fighting battles in the sky, I could only sit and watch, while death played out overhead. I appreciated the delicate balance of life, of what we have, and what we will lose.'

Elise's mind drifted home, to her mother sitting in their dim parlour, hearing about the raid on the wireless, playing the music box that her father had given her when Elise had been born. She thought of how his health had failed, the consequence of gas in the trenches; how he'd died when she was so very young. How Elise did not know him, did not feel his love. How Nathan spoke to that empty part of her.

'I was so sorry to hear about your father,' she said.

'That's not what I meant. Don't be sorry.'

'No, I...'

'He is not worth your sorrow.'

Elise wanted to protest, but the look in Nathan's eyes, a sort of smouldering revulsion directed backwards, against himself, stopped her.

Nathan patted the table. 'Good job this is solid. We'll make ourselves comfortable. Then let them do their worst.'

He went upstairs to collect pillows and blankets. Elise sat alone, sensing a precipice opening before her, of not being able to stop herself stepping into it. An ominous droning began, high above, rolling across the sky.

She wanted to call out for Nathan. He seemed to have been gone for such a long time. He was probably telephoning Vivienne, to reassure her, wishing he had put Elise in a taxi back to St Thomas's. She glanced again at the kitchen doorway. What if he didn't come back?

In Hyde Park, the anti-aircraft guns began to fire, but the bombs fell anyway. A pounding volley, striding down the street towards her. She heard a screaming whistle arcing through the air. She pressed her hands to her ears and found herself on her knees beneath the table, Nathan pulling her down, his voice calm and low in her ear, the softness of a blanket beneath her.

'They will wonder where I am,' she uttered, bewildered. 'The nurses' home.'

'They will understand,' he said.

He settled behind her, wrapped his arms over her, covered her with his body, held the pillows around their heads. The portion of night through the windows rained an unearthly red. The building shuddered and explosions thundered. Elise felt the crump of bombs injuring the earth, the sensation, more than the noise, vibrating through her core. Living through the previous raids seemed to make the next one worse. She knew what to expect. There'll be no need to bury us, she thought.

'Don't think that because I wear this uniform that I'm a courageous man,' Nathan said, his words clear and low, behind her. 'I made a mistake, at Dunkirk, Elise. And you saw the consequences. You saw McVie.'

From the sound of his voice, almost a sob in his throat, she felt he had never told anyone that before. She found his hand in the darkness and pressed it with hers. She felt his embrace tighten.

'We all make mistakes,' she whispered and shut her eyes. 'And we'll also know that this, then, will pass.'

She felt Nathan press his lips to the top of her head. The stench of smoke drifted down, and time stretched like a dark corridor filled with nauseating terror.

'I feel I know you, Elise,' Nathan whispered in the dark. 'You are from my past, that moment of freedom when I saw you on the beach. Only you and me, no one else around.'

She wanted to say, *until your father arrived and started shouting*, but she said nothing, too frightened to breathe.

'It is as if I have always known you,' he said. 'You were the one who knew me then, you saw the best of me. So briefly.'

'And I still have the scar on my knee,' she said, and memories of sunshine and rock pools filtered through. The sound of the sea, the calling seagulls. She smiled to herself. 'Remember, I fell on the rocks. My battle wound. You helped me.'

'We are equal, now Elise. We're even. But why now?' he asked, his words grating in wonder. 'Why are you here now?'

His voice seemed to tap on a door deep inside her. Why indeed, should she be here, with Nathan Calloway, cowering under a table in the basement of a fine Mayfair mansion, while hell rained down above the rooftop? An ambulance bell clanged as it drove past, into the danger of the outside world. And yet here they were, the boy and the girl on the beach, sheltering, and seeking safety. Finding each other again. She turned, felt for his scarred and damaged face, cradled it in her palms and kissed him.

13

VIVI, JUNE 1941

As the taxi from Victoria turned off Park Lane and headed into Mayfair, Vivi asked the driver if he wouldn't mind diverting past St George's church where she and Nathan had married. She hadn't been in town since then. She felt curious to see if it was still standing.

Someone had left a folded newspaper on the back seat of the taxi, but she kept her gaze through the window, fixed on the passing streets. Nathan was right about the general shabbiness, everything covered in a film of brick dust, and people with heads down, simply carrying on. Purple buddleia bushes colonised bomb sites and the plane trees showed off their summer green, scattering sunlight, as if war did not exist. She did all she could to stop herself reading the headlines.

On his days home at Farthing Hall, Nathan remained vague about what it might be like for the sailors on the convoys, the sitting ducks for U-boats, bringing supplies across the Atlantic from America. He spared her from any detail, nothing more than she might read in the newspaper, but her imagination rotted with images of her own making. Of tight iron-clad passages deep below decks and the dreadful pitching and rolling. Of battleships stalking like shadows, engaging, exploding, sinking; their men taken by icy black waves, swallowing a cocktail of seawater and oil.

Vivi nudged the newspaper onto the taxi floor as it trundled over the cobbles of St George's Street. Two years had passed since she married Nathan here; nearly two years since she lost her parents, and now she returned to the place she'd last seen them alive. For Vivi, as her life moved on, the reality of what happened to them could only deteriorate into the honest and permanent truth. But there St George's church stood, portico intact and classical pillars defiant, if not a little unkempt. Immemorial and blessed, Vivi decided. And perhaps, she hoped, a good omen.

'Berkeley Square got it a good one,' the driver said. 'The last big show, back in May. And did you see? All along Bruton Street, too. Smithereens. Not just the East End; it's posh people too. Been quiet since then, though, you'll be pleased to know. Perhaps he's done with it. Giving us a breather. Come up to the Smoke much, ma'am?'

'No, thankfully, not since the start of it all,' Vivi said, and felt like a traitor. She saw him glance at her into his rear-view mirror. He had obviously registered her accent.

'We need your lot,' he said. 'If you don't mind me saying. What does Churchill have to do. Beg?'

Two years ago, as the girl fresh off the boat at Southampton, a remark like that would have stung, and had her floundering for a response.

Vivi caught his eye in the mirror, and said, 'Do you think I have a hotline to Mr Roosevelt, sir?'

He shut up and the taxi passed the end of Grosvenor Street. Vivi craned her neck for a glimpse of her house. Her train had been delayed – damage to the tracks somewhere around Canterbury – and so she thought that instead of dropping off there as originally planned, she'd better go straight to Claridges on Brook

Street to meet Genna and Dornie. Yes, her old home, still standing, despite the near miss Nathan said he'd had in May.

'And here she is,' Genna said, as the waiter showed Vivi to their table in the salon at the hotel. 'A sight for sore eyes.'

Claridges had not suffered, it seemed, had retained a certain glamour, despite the low-wattage bulbs. Waiters zipped about within its mutedly gleaming interior, and someone played a piano softly in the corner. Genna leapt up and wrapped Vivi in her scented arms, and Vivi caught her breath, feeling suddenly, overwhelmingly, that she'd come home.

'She most certainly is a morale-booster,' Dornie said, rising to kiss her cheek, and indicating to the waiter that he'd like the Champagne poured as Vivi settled in her seat. 'It's been too long, Mrs Calloway. Gracious, what a great deal of water has passed under all our bridges since we last met.'

Far too much, Vivi thought. How young she'd been, how starry-eyed, the last time they'd been together; dinner at Grosvenor Street, dancing at the Velvet Rose, a taxi home at dawn. Time seemed to have ripped a layer off them all.

'Isn't there something delicious about a tipple in the afternoon,' Genna beamed, as their glasses clinked, and the sandwiches were uncovered. Vivi admired her friend, the shine in her green eyes, her ruddy hair like a glorious beacon.

'Tipple?' Vivi said. 'Oh Lady Dornford, you do sound so awfully British.'

Genna laughed. 'Perhaps I've been here too long?' She winked at her husband. 'But gee, I think it sounds kinda wonderful.'

'I've missed seeing you two together,' Dornie said, settling into his chair. His RAF uniform fitted well, suited him. The blue, smart and distinctive. 'So entertaining. I like to sit back and let you get on with it. Take it all in. One person missing though.' His tone suddenly tempered the mood. 'How is Nathan? He is joining us later, I take it?'

'Yes, and he's looking forward to it,' said Vivi, although she really had no idea. 'He'll see us at the house after work. And yes, my taxi came past it on my way. It appears to be intact.'

'But I hear the Velvet Rose isn't,' Genna said. 'So, no dancing for us tonight.'

Just as well, thought Vivi, for she felt unsure about trying to re-enact everything from the past, from that first sparkling evening. She feared that she would no longer feel the same about anything, and that Nathan certainly wouldn't. That it best not to tempt the memory; that it was all best left behind.

'I'm selling the house on Grosvenor Street,' she said, and both her companions raised their eyebrows. 'At least, it is listed for sale. Will be impossible, I know, for who in their right mind... and also, the Park Avenue apartment, and Daddy's yacht. I wired a New York realtor last week.'

Dornie gave a soft whistle.

Genna pressed her hand over hers. 'Are you sure, honey?'

'The funds will help Nathan secure Farthing Hall. And so will help Freda,' she said. 'God knows, it may help me.' She stopped herself adding that it felt like a way of severing ties with her past, of a way to look forward, seeking a brighter future. Relinquishing her family's assets, yes, but something she must do, or her marriage would fail.

Dornie, ever the gentleman and sensing the conversation changing tack, excused himself, and Genna leaned in, her eyes wide.

'Vivi, really, are you sure?'

'Genna, really. I am trying everything.' She took a fortifying glug of Champagne.

During Nathan's short visits home these last couple of months, he had seemed a sketch of himself, not quite whole. And she had circled him as if trying to find another way in. Before the funeral, up there in the Widow's Watch, she felt she'd reached across the void between them, found their connection again within the grimness of Digby's death. But that new feeling had soon trickled away, lost in the enormity of everything else. Now, Vivi constantly returned to him calling her his 'brave Vivi'. She must be that person. Whatever made him turn from her, then she must follow.

'Remember, Genna,' she said, 'when we chatted in the churchyard, before Digby's funeral, I worried that Nathan may never have loved me, had married me for my money. I see things differently now. Something seems to have shifted in me, and in him. I can't explain whether it's for better or worse. But this is how I see it. I am simply going to release that money, give it to him, for then the balance between us will be better. I don't like having that hold over him. I mean, the money is his anyway, according to English law, but I want to do this, to make this gesture, to show him that I support him. That I love him.'

She saw the doubt in Genna's expression.

'Honey, are you sure? Should you not take legal advice?'

Vivi waved the notion away; it felt too much of an encumbrance to contemplate.

'Oh, he had a wretched childhood,' she said, as if that made everything crystal clear. 'That ogre Digby. I can't tell you the half of it. The legacy of that man. It's too awful to speak of – it taints me, it taints the Calloways. But, these days, Genna, you saw it when you visited: Freda seems better. And I feel that we can all be better now.'

Genna signalled for their glasses to be topped up and Vivi sat back, her confession exhausting her, although she felt that she had only scratched the surface. She did not want to worry her friend any more than necessary. Give her all the confounding mess in her head. She did not want to tell her that Nathan had told her, up in the Widow's Watch on the morning of the funeral, that he did not want to end up like his father. The way that his father had treated Charlotte Hoodless. And that, despite this, deep inside her head chimed the name *Elise*. That a year on, she still found it hard to reconcile it. Nathan, gripped by fever, had called out for Elise. And no one had ever heard of her.

* * *

They took the short walk back to the house on Grosvenor Street, Vivi and Genna linking arms, giggling softly as the Champagne settled, with Dornie teasingly reassuring them, following behind, that he kept a close eye on them.

The grand façade and the green door struck Vivi as familiar, but not necessarily comforting. Bricks and mortar, she told herself. An asset to be liquidised. She opened the door and stepped in, feeling not so much the chatelaine, but as a visitor, passing through.

'There you all are.' Nathan came out from the drawing room to greet them, looking tired, rather pale, like he did these days. 'Welcome to the naval officer's digs. Not necessarily shipshape, I'm afraid. I must be losing my touch.'

Vivi laughed with relief; he seemed more himself, despite appearing weary. Nathan, no longer the rough outline; his mood light and playful. She threw her arms around him, held him tight. He gently eased her away. 'And I see tea at Claridges has done you all the world of good,' he said.

'Not so much tea was drunk,' Vivi said. 'Look, I've brought you a doggy bag of sandwiches and cakes.'

'And Lord and Lady Dornford,' Nathan said, shaking their hands. 'Lovely to see you again after so long.'

'Oh, for goodness sake, Lieutenant Calloway,' Genna giggled and gave him a sassy hug. 'Call me Genna or I'll walk out that door.'

As Nathan settled their guests in the drawing room – promising tea, or more Champagne if required, plus he had a particularly nice bottle of whisky for Dornie – Vivi skirted the stripped-back downstairs rooms. She willed the empty walls and naked floorboards of the dining room, where they'd held that fine dinner, to echo from a time past, and to be best forgotten. But as she heard a cork pop and Genna's exclaim of delight from across the hall, memories of happiness flooded her. Her mother's taste and her presence, and her father's energy and his will, lingered.

But not in this house, Vivi told herself, firmly shutting the dining room door. *Only inside myself.*

They left the drawing room curtains open to the summer evening, enjoying the long dusk as it filled the space with soft speckled light. Nathan would not allow Vivi to lift a finger; he darted around as host, bringing trays of tea up from the kitchen and a re-heated stew that the char lady had prepared.

'Better than anything Claridges can offer, I'll wager,' Dornie said, tucking in.

Genna wound up the gramophone and found some old jazz recordings. As the music played, she danced gently by herself over the deep-pile rug and Vivi settled back into the armchair next to Nathan, half listening to his conversation with Dornie.

'...how quickly the tables turn. A vengeful chase, I hear,' Dornie said, 'Hunting down the *Bismark*.'

'The reports said we rescued about a hundred German sailors, out of over two thousand,' said Nathan. 'Pulled them up on ropes and treated them like shipmates. You know this, Dornie, when we come eye to eye with the enemy, we understand that they are the same as us. As bloody frightened as us.'

Dornie glanced out the window at the peaceful evening sky. 'Seems like you have had a reprieve in London since May. Vivi, your beautiful house stands to live another day. Let's hope that's the last of that. Was there much damage here, Nathan?'

'No, not to this property. I was lucky that night.' Nathan caught Vivi's eye, looked quickly away. 'I set up camp under the kitchen table. Stayed there until dawn.'

'Best place for you, darling,' she said.

'But I felt such a useless coward. Not doing my duty,' said Nathan. 'I'm such a—'

Genna sashayed over and hauled her husband out of his armchair. 'Let's bring the Velvet Rose here. Let's dance to the music, Dornie,' she said, 'Like we did before.'

Watching her friends waltz around the darkening room, Vivi reached out for Nathan's hand and squeezed it. She wanted to reassure him, for she felt him retreating once again from her, coiling in on himself, on his fears. And he was right: they all had them, each and every one.

Nathan returned her gaze, and his eyes glimmered in the evening twilight. She couldn't read his expression and knew it best not to ask.

Vivi titled her head, smiled softly at her husband, to encourage him, let him know it was fine with her if he felt stunted: a naval officer stuck behind his desk, or sheltering under a kitchen table. Let him be constrained and drowning under paperwork. Rather that, than losing him into the freezing waters of the North Atlantic.

14

ELISE, AUGUST 1941

The end of summer Bank Holiday in the seaside town did not have quite the same ring to it as it usually did, with barbed wire scarring the beaches, the seafront peppered with craters and day trippers staying at home. Despite this, Elise felt relieved to be away from the hospital, from smoky old London, delighted to walk along the passageway and into the little cottage on King Street. Able to take a couple of days leave and, for a moment, to pretend to be the girl she once had been.

'My goodness, Elise, you do look well,' said her mother. 'Which surprises me. In your letters you always tell me you are run ragged.'

'I am, Ma, it doesn't let up. But they feed us well, perhaps that's it,' said Elise. 'And hard work must suit me, I suppose.'

'Glad to hear it. I have some competition, then, with the canteen staff.' Her mother chewed her lip, pondered something, her gaze knifelike. 'Although I'm not sure that's it. I think you are only telling me half the story.'

Elise lifted her hand in protest, but her mother continued, 'Now you go and sit in the courtyard, I am going to make us a pot of tea, and you can tell me what the matter is.'

She went back outside to sit in a patch of sunshine, stumped momentarily by her mother's gift of being able to read her. But, she realised, she never had been able to hide her thoughts and her troubles from her for long. She really should be used to it by now.

Her shoes bruised the thyme that filled the gaps in the cobbles, releasing its astringent fragrance. Lavender fizzed with bees and the windowsill overflowed with scarlet geraniums. Her mother made use of every square inch of the garden. In the far corner grew the dark weeds: nightshade, henbane and foxglove. A blackbird piped from the wall, sounding a little off key, and seagulls dived and wheeled overhead. Elise listened to the cups tinkling inside the kitchen and the kettle singing, and wished she could simply curl up and hide here at home, and ignore her prowling fears.

Her mother came out with the tray and set it on the upturned barrel that served as a table. 'I bet you won't taste a cake as good as this one in the nurse's dining room, Elise,' she said, slicing her apple sponge. 'And as for my tea, well. It is fresh from the grocer's. I was first in the queue this morning.'

'Well, that all goes without saying,' Elise said, lightly, milking the cups. Being home with her mother, she hoped, would help her forget the night of the raid, what happened between her and Nathan. But the truth of it could not be shaken off; it followed her around. 'Ma, you never let me down.'

'No, you are right, there, Elise.' Her mother settled down beside her and turned her face up to the sun, and closed her eyes to its warmth.

As the moments passed, Elise hoped that her mother had changed her mind, had decided to bottle up her thoughts, and not challenge her again. But she swivelled in her seat, reached out and held Elise's cheek delicately in her hand, hard adoration sparking in her gaze.

'From the look of you, my dear,' she said. 'I think we are a little too late for clary sage.'

Elise set the milk jug down, and concentrated on the blue Willow pattern, the trees, the bridge, the pagoda, not daring to meet her mother's stare.

She knew about clary sage. Her mother wrote many an entry detailing it in her journal. Elise had always been wary of its power: its woody sweetness, its potent musk. And her mother would say, there is nothing to fear from clary sage, in the right situation. It was a nurturer, a master healer for women. The ladies of Margate and the surrounding villages who came down the passageway and knocked on the back door never asked for it by name, but her mother may subtly steer them towards it. The ancient art, she'd say, proved to be the simplest of things in our troubled times.

'But Ma, how do you know?' Elise said, feeling young and rather absurd, tears stinging her eyes.

Her mother laughed kindly, reached down, and rested her warm hand on Elise's belly.

'Oh, my dear Elise. I always know.'

BOOK TWO

1944–1945

15

VIVI, JUNE 1944

For a change – for she knew she ought to change something – Vivi rode Snowdrop along the banks of the water meadows behind Farthing Hall, trailing through the long grass and scaring rabbits, which disappeared into the hawthorn like silken ghosts. She felt, like everyone else she suspected, a weariness that made her bones cold. The soldiers had landed on the beaches across the Channel, and she simply wanted it to be over. But she had been in this place before. She'd sensed a shift, when America had come into the war, a movement of hope and of rising pride. She hoped her taxi driver had felt satisfied. But two and half years had passed since Pearl Harbour. Was it too much to ask to hope that things would be better by now?

Vivi gazed over the marshy land, at the wide sky, at the clouds reflected in the still, reed-lined water. The empty, open space seemed to hollow out her insides and she realised, after five years in England, she still wanted to go home. Perhaps, she thought, being back in her childhood house on the Hudson, somewhere familiar, would mend the scars.

She'd sold the New York apartment and the yacht, but had held onto the farmhouse, kept it running with tenants. What sort of state it was in, who knew. What did it matter anyway? When she felt so at a loss, wealth and property proved meaningless.

When the war was done, perhaps Nathan would sail back with her. But it seemed such an impossible obstacle, running through her hands like water. And, of course, what about Freda? She felt ridiculous even thinking about it, escaping this life when she'd only take her troubles with her. Different sky, same soul, indeed.

She ought to be getting back to the Hall. Her mother-in-law would be wondering where she'd got to and she wanted to reply to Genna's latest letter. And Nathan had telephoned that morning, left a message with Ruby, to say he would be home later, which seemed odd, as it was a Wednesday, and he rarely appeared midweek. She wanted to be ready to rewind the spool of wool that unravelled each time he left, to mend the things she had no means of identifying. She kicked Snowdrop on.

The church spire rose from a new and refreshing angle against the horizon and Vivi headed towards it. Riding down the village lane, the sound of Snowdrop's hooves drew glances her way. She lifted her hand in greeting at the ladies outside the village shop, the man who ran the bakery. He lifted his cap, the ladies nodded politely. None of them spoke to her.

She pulled the horse up near the churchyard wall, dismounted and tied the reins to the post. She needed a rest, a moment to delay returning to the Hall, to adjust her spiralling thoughts. She must present her good-wife strength, as always, to Freda. Put on her brave face for Nathan.

A small group of people had gathered in the churchyard, heads bowed around a newly dug grave. The vicar, his white robe battered by the breeze, intoned from his open book. The soil looked dark and fresh. Vivi had no idea who had passed away and felt she ought to, as one of the principal women at Farthing, as Freda often liked to remind her.

A young woman stood by the open grave, her pale hands clasped against her black coat. Vivi recognised the stiff grief in her face, the sorrow plaguing her. Next to her stood Mr Buckley, his hat held in tight fists. He must know this stranger; he must be her friend. Realising how much she stared, Vivi turned to leave, but found herself drawn back to the girl, taking in her slight frame, her dark, sloppily clipped hair, her hat worse for wear.

She spotted a child, a tiny thing with a good coating of baby-fat, peering out from behind the girl's coat, paying no heed whatsoever to the vicar. And why should she? She wouldn't understand. The child seemed to be in her own pretty world, her eyes darting between butterflies dancing over the long grasses and the birds diving in and out of the yew. Her tiny hands clutched wildflowers plucked from unkempt graves. Vivi watched, fascinated by the pain threading through her heart.

A child, she thought. If only, a child.

And then, suddenly, the little girl broke away, unnoticed and, tottering along the path and through the church gate, fast on her feet. She beamed up at Vivi. Her button-sized face, her pinprick dimples in buttery cheeks made something inside Vivi snap. The child offered her the ragged bouquet.

'My goodness,' Vivi whispered, bending down to her, her breath short. 'What adorable flowers. As adorable as you are.'

'You. Lady. Flowers.'

'They are not for me.' Vivi tried to smile, fighting a flood of misery. 'Keep them for your mother. She would like them, I am sure. She will wonder where you are.'

The child flicked her little shoulder, pulling at her bottom lip with her tiny front teeth. Her dress was patched but clean, her eyes, clear green, her plaited hair like a dark rope, tied with a red ribbon.

Go, Vivi thought. Go before I steal you away.

She heard thuds of earth thrown down onto the coffin. The final dreadful moment.

The child clucked and hummed, offered Vivi a smile like sunshine. Not daring to take the girl's hand, for a touch would seal her fate, Vivi gently gestured that she should go back through the gate, back into the churchyard where she would be safe. Where her mother would be waiting. But the child used her delicate fingertip to break the spider webs lacing the bars on the gate, her voice singsong and bright: 'Nanny's gone to the moon. Up to the moon. See, my flowers.'

'Who's gone where?'

'Nanny's gone to the moon.'

The vicar finished. The tiny congregation rippled with movement. Vivi saw the young woman jerk as if woken and glance down at the empty space beside her, before turning sharply, her face blanching.

'You need to go back to your mother,' Vivi said.

She heard a hoof clomp. Snowdrop's reins must have slipped the post. The horse came up behind her, looming and gigantic. The little girl looked up, screamed, and fell back hard onto her bottom.

Vivi bent down to the child. 'No, dear, no, it's all right. Snowdrop won't hurt you. She inquisitive, like you.'

'Kate, Little Kate!'

The young woman darted through the gate, her call shrill with fear, her face twisting in terror. She stopped, as if someone had hit her, her eyes wide, chest rising, staring at Vivi. She held out her arms and said the child's name again, a thin whisper: 'Kate, come here, now.'

The little girl scrambled to her feet and the woman lifted her greedily, pressing her possessively into her shoulder, her eyes glazing with tears as she turned her back, shielding her child from Vivi and hurried away.

'I'm sorry!' Vivi called, and knew she hadn't heard her.

The people melted away. Vivi looked for Mr Buckley, but he had gone. Digby's grave stood out, the granite sparkling audaciously in the sunlight. Beyond it, in the dark forgotten corner, lay Charlotte Hoodless and her unnamed baby. Vivi looked down at the bedraggled flowers that the child had dropped on the floor, making her realise she must soon replenish the pewter vase on her parents' memorial.

'Goodness me, Mrs Calloway, what a to-do.'

She turned to see Mrs Willis, the doctor's wife, by her side, her narrow face pecking the air in search of information.

'Was that the Drake child I heard crying?'

'I don't know,' she replied. 'I have never seen her before. I hope she is all right. Drake you say?'

'The evacuees. They came up from Margate a few years ago. Keep themselves to themselves, they do. Hardly ever see them. That child, she's not used to being out beyond her own four walls. Has probably never seen a horse before, or indeed a lady such as yourself.'

'Oh, of course, the Drakes,' said Vivi, her cheeks colouring.

'Yes, poor Annie Drake. The curious Mrs Drake. It's her daughter I feel sorry for, and of course there's the child. A dead sweetheart, or something. Lost to the war. Unmarried, though, as far as we can tell.' Mrs Willis stopped, as if her own tongue might trip her. 'Ah, but I'm not one to gossip.'

'No, Mrs Willis, we can't have that.'

The doctor's wife fluttered her hand and trilled, 'Good afternoon.'

Vivi waited, leaning on the church wall, and watched as a man with a spade began to fill in the hole, sealing the woman, Annie Drake, whoever she was, into her grave.

Something in the young woman's face switched on a memory, taking her back to those long fretful days by Nathan's bedside at the Seabathing Hospital. The way she did not quite catch her eye. Or perhaps it was simply her anxiety, that pulling around her mouth, misshaping it as she cried out for her daughter, that reminded Vivi of her own pain.

* * *

Back at the stable yard, Robin appeared, lugging a basket. He put it down on the cobbles and as Vivi dismounted, he scooted over to steady Snowdrop's head. She thanked him and asked where his father was. He pointed towards the closed door of Mr Buckley's office.

'He said he wanted a nap.'

'And what have you there?' Vivi asked, stripping off her gloves and nodding at the basket. 'Errands for Mrs Scott?'

The boy's eyes smarted. 'Mrs Scott, yes, ma'am, yes.'

A loaf and a jar of jam protruded from under a linen cloth.

The stable clock chimed. Vivi pictured Freda rising from her chair in the morning room to head upstairs to her boudoir to change for lunch, possibly glancing at her watch, wondering where Vivi could have got to.

'Will you help me take care of Snowdrop first, Robin?' she asked, moving to lead the horse into the stall. 'I'm in no rush to go anywhere.'

Robin stole a glance at the basket, then busied himself, skirting around her, collecting combs and brushes, and drawing fresh water from the trough.

'Let's rub her legs with straw first,' Vivi said. 'It's a trick I learnt as a girl. Gets the mud off a treat. Come on, here you are.' She held out a fistful of straw.

Robin dithered for a moment, seemed to be holding on to something inside him. He took the straw, without catching Vivi's eye, and began to rub the horse's foreleg.

'You love the horses, don't you?' she asked, wanting to draw him out of this new shyness with her. Perhaps he had begun to grow up, the inhibitions of his younger years vanishing.

'I do, ma'am. When I'm older, I want to have horses. Lots of horses. And breed foals.' Robin's words speeded up, catching up with his dreams. He carefully cleaned Snowdrop's forelegs. 'Have beautiful mares like Snowdrop. My own stables like this.'

'Why?'

'They make me feel at home.'

Vivi smiled, understanding. Robin should be eight or nine now, still young, but quite a lot older than the little girl in the churchyard.

'Do you know what happened today, at the church?' she asked thoughtfully, teasing a piece of grass from Snowdrop's mane.

'It is very sad.' Robin's cheeks coloured, his eyes widening in confusion.

She wanted to stay chatting to the boy, letting their conversation eat up her time before she had to report to the dining room for luncheon with Freda.

'Who was the lady who died, Robin?' she asked. 'The lady whose funeral it was?'

The boy shook his head, but something bubbled below the surface.

Vivi pictured the young woman's face and the little girl, and her bones moved in an uncomfortable way.

'You knew her?' she asked tentatively. 'The lady? Your father must have done, for I saw him standing by the graveside. It is very sad, Robin. I'd like to pay my respects if I can. She was one of the villagers, after all.'

Robin continued his work, his brows lowered as he groomed Snowdrop, his gloomy concentration radiating impressively for such a young lad.

Vivi, feeling rather wretched, asked, 'Robin, are you sad?'

His pale face appeared around the silvery curve of Snowdrop's rump.

'Yes. She was the nice lady who lived at the Amber House.'

'Where? The what?'

Robin's eagerness erupted, like the flare from a match, his sadness fickle, forgotten.

'I named it! The cottage in the woods. No one else knows its name. Apart from the others. And no one is supposed to know about... apart from Mrs Scott, because she gives me the basket. And Pa, of course.' He pressed his fingertips over his mouth and whispered. 'But the Annie lady died.'

Vivi stared at the boy, pressed her fingertips to her cheek. The old gamekeeper's cottage, the tumbledown place hidden in its walled garden in the middle of the woods. The glowing stained-glass windows, the colour of amber. She had not been back there in a good long while but now it rose through her mind as if she'd just opened a picture-book. The property belonged to the estate, to Nathan. And yet it now had occupants. She had no idea. For goodness sake, even Mrs Willis knew about *the curious Mrs Drake*.

Robin jigged his leg, eager to escape this interrogation, waiting to be dismissed.

'Off you go,' Vivi said lightly, 'don't forget your basket.'

She walked across the yard to Mr Buckley's office and raised her hand to knock on his door, questions racing through her mind. Questions about the evacuees, about Mrs Drake, about the young woman, about little Kate. She hesitated, cocked her head to peer through the front window. Mr Buckley lay back in the armchair by his stove, legs stretched, head back, eyes closed, an empty tumbler on his lap. His usually placid face, with neat beard and wide ready smile, looked ravaged. A frown cut his brow in two. Vivi saw him lift a hand and press it over his squeezed-shut eyes, and she turned away.

In Nathan's study, she pulled out the accounts ledgers, turning the pages, scanning figures. She found records for Cringle Cottage and the Moat House over the other side of Farthing, the row of cottages by the church, all payments entered, present and correct. She ran her fingertip up and down the columns, but could find no entry for the cottage in the woods. No wonder the estate had been in such disarray if Nathan, following his father's tendency for waste, did not take rent from its tenants.

But then, she decided, Nathan surely knew best. He would have come to an arrangement, however needy these evacuees may be, for the estate had to prosper to provide homes and a living for everyone. But it was as if the old gamekeeper's cottage did not exist.

The sound of tyres came in over the gravel. It was Nathan parking his car. She heard the creak of the handbrake and went to the window. Usually, his arrival made her weak, silly like an absurd child on her birthday, but something in the way he sat frozen in the driver's seat, his hands clutching the wheel, staring into the middle distance, the line of his jaw grim and defeated, triggered her unease. Watching him, she remembered the same feeling she'd had on the liner crossing the Atlantic, the almost indiscernible and yet sickening sway of the ship beneath her feet; her perspective constantly shifting.

Vivi gazed at him through the window as he sat in his car for what seemed a ludicrous amount of time for someone having driven all the way from London. She gasped, swallowing a nauseating trickle of outrage, as Nathan got out of the car and walked away from the house, off down the drive, and turned the corner onto the lane.

16

Later that evening, sitting at her dressing table, brushing her hair, Vivi asked, 'Where did you go?'

She stole a glance in the mirror. Nathan stood on the other side of the bed, undoing his shirt, his face pale, distracted, not properly hearing her.

'When? Earlier?'

'Yes, of course, *earlier*. You didn't come straight into the house. You were gone for hours.'

He sighed, thinking it over, his eyes wary as they shone in the lamplight.

'I needed a walk. Stretch my legs, fresh air. I can't breathe for brick dust in London. And it's pretty much like hell at the Admiralty these days.'

'I can well imagine,' she said, evenly. 'It must be frantic up there, with the invasion only a week or so in. I was wondering how you managed to get away to come down here, in the middle of the week.'

Nathan flung his shirt onto the bed, grabbed his pyjamas.

'In actual fact, I was due some leave...' he said, lightly.

Vivi watched his face. 'There was a funeral today at the church,' she said. 'Seems we have tenants in the old gamekeeper's cottage. A family. A young child. Apparently, the older woman has died. They are evacuees, so Mrs Willis tells me. I felt rather foolish not being aware of who was living in one of our cottages. I was going to ask Mr Buckley what he knew about it, but—'

'Don't bother him with it,' Nathan countered. 'It's nothing to do with him.'

Vivi wanted to beg to differ. She said, 'But I checked the ledgers. We aren't taking rent from them. Not that that is my main concern, Nathan. But it isn't good practice, is it? We need to be fair to all our tenants and treat them equally. I understand that this family may be in need. In fact, by the look of the young woman...'

'I'm extremely tired.' Nathan's face seemed to darken with misery. 'Can't we discuss it in the morning?'

Vivi got up from her stool and walked over to him, laid her hand on his bare shoulder. His face clouded in that usual way it did when she drew close to him, a sort of swimming of his eyes, a jerk of his chin, as if he were floundering within the scent of her perfume, the very essence of her.

'Nathan, of course we can. But what's wrong? You seem incredibly...' Vivi wanted to say *sad*, but that sounded in her mind too whimsical an expression. She thought he looked like he had splintered in two. 'You are really not yourself.'

He rested his hand over hers, his touch surprising her. He sighed and tilted his head back, as if to appraise her, daring to catch her eye.

'Vivi, the army are fighting their way into France, a long, drawn-out battle for every mile of land. Our ships are still in danger of being torpedoed in the Channel. And I have responsibilities.'

His retort stung her. Of course, how utterly selfish, how utterly

Park Avenue Princess, of her. Despite this, frustration continued to pucker inside her.

'But it has been like this between us for years, Nathan,' she uttered. 'It just never seems to get any better.'

He gave her an astonished glance. 'And you don't seem yourself either,' he said, his voice tight and weary. He balled up his pyjamas, tossed them on the chair. 'You don't seem at all happy, Vivi.'

'I'm not terribly happy,' she admitted, 'but I want to be.'

A huge sigh dragged itself out of him. He made her sit down with him on the end of the bed, rested his hands on her shoulders, his face expressionless, as if he could not wrap his feelings up into words.

'Listen, Vivi. Have you any idea of your beauty and your grace and your worth? As a person?'

'Nathan, really...'

'No, please listen to me. Let me speak. Look at us. You are stuck with me in this backwater, when you should be cruising down Fifth Avenue in the back of a limousine, going to parties, having a ball. The New Yorkers, I understand, are still living it up. And yet here you are knitting socks and attending WVS meetings, listening to small talk, trailing in the sad shadow of my mother.'

'Nathan, that's unfair.'

'You should have married a Wall Street broker, Vivi. Should be residing in some Upper East Side mansion. Not chained to a worthless half-rate sailor like me, with a disfigured face and a hopeless family.'

Vivi recoiled, fear battering her like an ice storm. She felt as if Nathan was holding up a shield and using it to push her away. Cutting down their marriage with every syllable.

'But what is all that but trappings of a so-called happy life?' she uttered, her mouth clogged and dry, feeling as if she fought for her life. 'Rich, yes, entitled, yes. My life is here quiet and simple, and thank God for that. I know sometimes I sound like I don't under-stand or appreciate you. That I am a little self-absorbed. But believe me, every day of my life, I am aware of what is going out there. I think about you all the time, and what you are having to deal with.'

Sitting in her lamplit bedroom, feeling her husband's pain as keenly as her own, she could not see this other existence that he imagined for her. Noisy, brash, sticky Manhattan had vanished, no longer important, the farmhouse upstate a fairy tale of her young imagination.

'My life here is with you,' she said, reaching for his hand. 'I want to be with *you*, Nathan.'

'But, Vivi. I cannot seem to give you what you want or need.' Nathan wavered, his shoulders shifted, his eyes flicked to the window. The cooler night air flowed in around the blackout. 'I try. I try so very hard.'

She watched his face soften with despair.

'Nathan,' she said, 'I know you do. We both do.' She moved closer to him and slipped her hand around the back of his neck. 'Please, let us try again.' She needed him, had to admit it, knowing it would demean her, break her down, make her small and vulnerable. How touching his skin made her body vibrate, that his presence, his attentions felt raw and necessary to her. She rested her head on his shoulder and felt his arms move heavily around her, gradually, as if getting used to holding her again.

'I keep thinking that when all this is over, you will leave me,' he said into her hair, his voice hoarse. 'When it is safe to cross the Atlantic, back you will go. And how can I blame you?'

His words trembled in his throat. She sensed a change in him, sensed his desire.

'Why should I leave you, Nathan? You are all I have,' she whispered, turning her head to kiss him, slipping her nightgown straps from her shoulders. 'You are all that I want.'

'Vivi, believe me, I don't deserve you.'

'Believe me,' she said, 'you do.'

Later, in the darkness, lying beside Nathan, Vivi heard an owl calling from deep in the wood, melancholy and comforting in the wide silence. And the young woman from the cottage stalked through her mind: the woman's stricken face, and the catch in her voice as she called for her daughter.

She listened to Nathan's soft breathing as he fell asleep, and thanked God she no longer found herself in the place that the young woman did: in a mess of raw and enraged mourning.

Vivi sighed, felt hopeful. She reached out her hand and nestled her fingers into Nathan's hair.

* * *

She waved Nathan off in his car the next morning, as he headed off back to London, and then strolled around the corner of the house and over the lawns, towards the stables. The summer's day had a celebratory feel: a certain glory in the air. Vivi felt exhausted but in a tender, oddly euphoric way. Last night, she'd surprised herself how well she'd articulated her feelings, vented her frustration, and how Nathan, after a slow and quite unsettling start, had met her in the middle. He had revealed much more of himself than she ever imagined. It had been cathartic, and momentous, for them both. And yes, she loved him more.

Snowdrop must have heard her footsteps ringing on the cobbles, for she stomped around in her stall and presented her white face over her stable door. Vivi went to say hello, stroking her velvet-soft nose, feeling her comforting hot breath on her hand.

'Good morning, Mrs Calloway.' Mr Buckley emerged from the adjacent stall, not looking quite himself. 'I thought I heard you.'

His neat waistcoat and clipped beard appeared as always, his usual smartly turned-out self, but his face looked as if sleep last night had been a stranger.

'I didn't realise you wanted to ride this morning, ma'am,' he said, pushing for courtesy and yet sounding so utterly tired. 'Robin is off on an errand, but give me a moment, and I'll get Snowdrop ready.'

'Oh, no, that's fine, Mr Buckley,' Vivi said brightly, to show him she hadn't noticed how dreadful he looked, that she hadn't spotted him yesterday, shut in his office, clearly weeping. 'You certainly keep that boy busy throughout his school holidays. But I feel like taking a walk instead. Isn't it a lovely day?'

The steward's face stiffened, and she countered her blunder. 'But before that, would you be so kind as to make me one of your lovely cups of tea. Do you have the time?'

He gave her a doubtful half-smile and led the way into his office, making a fuss of plumping the cushions in his armchair before he offered her a seat, and busied himself with the tea caddy and kettle.

Usually, Vivi felt at ease in Mr Buckley's office: its brown interior, good solid desk, the fresh earthy smell of hay and leather, equestrian books lining the shelves, and point-to-point trophies gleaming. But today the air here felt taut, the atmosphere raw and, as he passed her a steaming cup, he would not look her in the eye.

'That's lovely, thank you,' said Vivi, taking a sip.

Mr Buckley sat down, and concentrated on the view from the window, as if he wished he could be getting on with something else, somewhere else.

Feeling the need to break the silence, she said, 'As a matter of fact, Mr Buckley, I dropped by yesterday...'

'Ah yes, Robin mentioned it. I am sorry, ma'am. Yesterday was quite a day.' He straightened his tie and offered half a smile, but his eyes told her something different.

'And I am sorry, Mr Buckley,' she said gently. 'I saw that there was a funeral yesterday. Was Mrs Drake a friend of yours?'

He nodded, glanced away from her, cleared his throat. 'She was indeed, Mrs Calloway. A dear friend.'

'How awful for you.'

Vivi knew that the steward had lost his wife when Robin was born and she sensed, from the look on his face, that Mrs Drake perhaps had been more than an acquaintance to him. He had found another companion, someone he clearly cared for, and had lost them. What else could she say? She'd never felt this barrier of manners between them before. She'd always had a good rapport with Mr Buckley, enjoyed passing the time of day with him. In the past, it had never been merely the lady of the house conversing with her employee. She felt concerned for him, and equally she did not want to pry into his grief.

However, curiosity drove her on. 'I didn't know Mrs Drake at all, but I am sure she will be missed,' she said, thinking of the young woman at the graveside, guessing her to be Mrs Drake's daughter, and the little girl. Little Kate. 'In actual fact, Mr Buckley, I didn't know we had tenants at the gamekeeper's cottage. Or,' she tried to lighten the mood, '"the Amber House," as Robin likes to call it. Is that where Robin is now, I wonder? Another errand? Another basket of goodies for the Amber House?'

Mr Buckley looked at her. 'I can understand your confusion, ma'am.'

'But you don't seem confused, Mr Buckley,' Vivi said, evenly. 'As steward of the estate, it appears that you knew all about them.' She felt awful for pressing him, but could not help herself. 'Yes, I am confused. There is nothing in our ledgers listing the existence of the Drake family.'

'Ma'am, I wonder if perhaps,' he said brusquely, 'you should talk to Lieutenant Calloway about this. It's not really for me to say.'

Vivi drained her cup, set it down. His unusual manner gave her the cue to leave.

'I am sorry, I will leave you in peace. I can see you are busy, or need to be busy.'

He seemed to sink with relief.

'I do feel that I should pay my respects, however, to the folks at the Amber House,' Vivi said. 'I understand that the little girl is called Kate. Annie Drake's granddaughter? Such a sweetie pie, isn't she?'

A whimsical smile lit up Mr Buckley's face as he stood to open the door for her.

'Yes, ma'am. An absolute poppet of a maid,' he said. 'And so like Elise.'

Vivi felt a sickening hard blow to her chest, gripped the door handle to hold herself upright.

'Elise?' She swallowed. The name ringing like a cold bell in her head. 'Such a pretty name. Like the tune.'

Vivi thought she heard Mr Buckley agree, but didn't want to listen. She blundered out of the steward's office and across the stable yard cobbles, turning her ankle on the uneven ground. She kept on going, back around the house and down the lane. Breathless already, she turned into the woods.

The trees embraced her, the air bright with birdsong, sunlight flickering through the canopy. How different it felt, not being on horseback. How at a loss she felt as she brushed through towering ferns overspilling the pathways, edged past stinging nettles, her thoughts colliding, sending themselves in all directions.

The cottage emerged from the haze of green, the brick russet red, and the flint like silver. Its serene friendliness was lost on her now despite, in the upstairs windows, the stained glass catching the sun. The Amber House, indeed.

Vivi sat down, exhausted, behind a great oak, and leant against its trunk, the huge roots forming a chair for her. Peering around the tree, at the closed wooden door in the garden wall, she gave a wry smile; if she were on Snowdrop, she'd be able to see over the top. She rested her head back, and tried to calm her breathing. Watching the fragments of blue sky between the branches, she realised what a fool she'd look if someone spotted her here, the New Mrs Calloway, late of Manhattan, hiding behind a tree. Why didn't she simply go up and knock on the door, say good morning, offer the young woman her condolences? After all, the property by rights belonged to her. But Elise, her elusive name, and her sad eyes, dragged herself through the muddle in Vivi's head. And Vivi could not trust that she would conduct herself as her mother had taught her.

She made up her mind she ought to slip away before anyone saw her, when through the wood, beneath the rustling of leaves and piping birds, came a voice, a soft lilting song.

'Katie, K-K-K-Katie, I will meet you by the k-k-k-kitchen door...'

Vivi craned her neck. Robin dawdled along from the other direction, lugging his basket, and tapping at the undergrowth with a stick he'd found. He must have been dilly-dallying, as boys on their school holidays with the countryside their playground are inclined to do. Robin slung the stick away, set the basket down, turned the iron ring and opened the door in the wall, finishing his song with a flourish. He left the door wide open.

Pressing herself against the tree, her heart thumping, Vivi held her breath. The tended roses, now a glorious, glimmering white; the vegetable patch thrived, bean frames blazing with scarlet flowers, tomato vines warming in the sun. Beds of fragrant, unruly herbs clustered along the terracotta path and Elise came out of her kitchen door with the little girl, who unlatched herself from her mother and ran up to Robin, squealing his name.

Something black and vile opened inside Vivi: a terrible, bitter rage. She clutched at the gnarled tree trunk, clinging to its earthy, solid mass. She stared, her eyes widening, although she did not want to see. Elise and her child: the truth before her, if only she would allow herself to acknowledge what it meant. And in her mind, Nathan saying, over and over, how he did not want to end up like his father. But what was this, if not mirroring Digby?

Oh, Elise was no poor Charlotte Hoodless, confined to the cottage for a matter of days, with her pitiful souvenir of the broken sugar jar, before being sent off to her fate. No, Elise and her family had made their home here. Mr Buckley had struck a bond with Annie Drake, young Robin the go-between. And Elise had been around for a long while; Elise had been there when Nathan had needed her.

Vivi gripped the trunk and hauled herself up, her mind flaming with jealousy, and the awful mortifying embarrassment of being tricked. Who else knew about this cosy family at the Amber House, about the Drake child? Mrs Willis, clearly, and, Vivi suspected, Mrs Scott, for who else sent Robin off with the basket of provisions? And what about Freda?

Vivi turned and crashed her way back through the ferns and nettles, finding the path, her way back to the Hall. She had no idea if she went the right way, but the glowering rage inside her propelled her on.

The only person she wanted the truth from, the only person she needed to ask: Nathan. And, yes, once again. He was not here.

* * *

Vivi let herself in the front door, and stood in the quiet hallway, shattered and on the edge of absurdity. She looked down at the rents in her trousers made by brambles, the rash of stings from nettles on her hands, at the scuffs on her shoes.

She heard the chime of the telephone inside Nathan's study, as someone put the receiver down. Freda opened the door and came out into the hall, her face stricken and blanched with shock.

'Vivienne, ah Vivienne,' she said, her eyes brimming.

'What on earth? What has happened?' A clot of terror congealed inside Vivi's throat. She swallowed hard, her stomach twisted.

Freda came towards her with outstretched hands, clutching for Vivi's, squeezing them so hard it made Vivi wince.

'Freda, what?'

'That was Genna. That was Lady Dornford, your friend,' Freda's words stumbled. 'I am so terribly sorry. It's her husband. It's the lord.'

'Dornie?'

'He's gone.'

'Gone where?' Even as Vivi asked, she knew.

'I couldn't get much detail. In three minutes, she could barely speak to tell me properly. She's at home in Sussex, that much I know. Vivi, I am so sorry. Vivi, what are you doing? What shall we do?'

Vivi had no way of answering her. She rushed out of the door to the garden, across the lawn and down to the stables. She hammered on Mr Buckley's office door.

'Drive me to the station, please Mr Buckley. Do you have petrol? I will pay for petrol. I need to get to Genna's. Genna needs me. I don't think I can drive. It's too far. I need to get a train. A train to London, I suppose, then I can change. I can get another to where she is. Sussex, somewhere. Oh God, you know, it's.... Can you drive me to Canterbury? I need to catch a train to London. Please, Mr Buckley, please.'

The steward leapt to his feet, came out from behind his desk.

'Mrs Calloway, of course I will. I will do anything you ask.'

Vivi gazed at him, saw his grieving for Annie Drake; his face taut, his eyes sunken, and smeared with tears. But he, in an instant, slipped on his jacket, did up his top button and tie.

'In fact, Mrs Calloway, I will drive you all the way to Lady Dornford's home, and drop you at her door myself. All you need to do is tell me where you want to go, and I will take you there.'

17

ELISE, APRIL 1945

Standing in front of the mirror, Elise brushed her hair, pinned it in a Victory roll. She found good stockings in the drawer and, as she pulled them on, remembered Nathan caressing her on the night of the air raid. She put on her best shoes, smoothed down her dress, wondered if she was presentable, wanted to ask her mother if that might be the case.

Nathan's note, sent over with Robin the day before, had been to the point: he would visit today, if convenient for her. She'd felt confused, a rush of anger. Nathan had seen his daughter only a handful of times and had last stepped through her door on the day of her mother's funeral. Elise had not been able to bear his concern. All she'd wanted was to be left in peace to cry.

Downstairs, Elise poured out a teacup of milk and brought it back up for Kate. Sitting on the bed next to her, she touched her daughter's cheek.

'Wake up now, darling, and you can have your morning drink.'

The child snuffled to the surface of her dream, opened her eyes.

'We have a visitor today,' Elise said, rearranging her daughter's dark fringe. 'I want you to get up and dressed, and I will brush out your plaits.'

The child protested and reached for Elise, tucking herself under her arm. Elise pressed the cup into her hands. Kate's smile twitched, and she drank.

'Play the tune, Ma-ma,' she said, a white ring around her lips.

Elise wound the key on the music box, and they listened to the plucked off-key tune, the scent of the spring garden coming through the window.

'For *you*, Ma-ma,' Kate said. 'It's for you.' She leant over the side of the bed, touching her finger to the tiny buttons on Elise's shoes. 'Why shoes, Ma-ma? I've got bare feet. Wriggly bare toes.'

'I've decided to be nice and smart for the visitor today,' said Elise. 'And I've brushed my hair, see? I need to do yours.'

The music box wheezed to a stop.

'What is the visitor?' Kate asked.

Elise swallowed, gaining time, making space for the words. She wiped her daughter's face. 'It's your Daddy, Little Kate.'

* * *

Elise pulled out her mother's journal from the recess in the fireplace and turned the pages to her last entry, nearly a year before:

June 1944. Tonight is the full moon, and I pray for the men landing on that foreign shore. Walking into danger, into uncertainty. I pray to keep them safe. And that their souls, and my own, will make room for all that is to come.

She'd found her mother sitting in bed when she came up with her morning cup of tea, as she had done every day as soon as she was old enough to work the stove, all those years at the cottage in King Street. Her mother had been writing in her journal, propped up against the pillows, the pages open on her lap. Elise had offered her a sunny, 'Good morning' and went to the window to draw the curtains. She turned at the silence, noticing the ink from her mother's dropped pen seeping into the sheet and her fingers, clenched, marking the page she'd got up to.

Her mother had loved her new home tucked away in the woods. She had accepted Elise's situation with utter composure, had insisted on coming with her on the train up to London, quite a feat for someone who never left Margate, to sit with her and Nathan on an Embarkment bench overlooking the Thames, while Elise told him her news. She had witnessed Nathan's distress, and his remorse, and his willingness to do what he could. She had eagerly packed up their King Street cottage in readiness for when Mr Buckley drove down in his van to collect them and bring them to their new home. She'd projected great harvests of beans and tomatoes for the years ahead.

Sitting at the kitchen table, Elise flicked backwards through her mother's journal. It read as if her life had ebbed and flowed, as if time had not moved in one direction.

Ah yes, the remedy when Kate had a bad cough: goose fat rubbed liberally on chest and back. Protests. Persuasion needed. And stern notes in the margin:

Remember, always save your string. Remember, when storing your broom, place with bristles upwards.

Elise glanced at her broom propped in the corner and loss bolted through her, new and fresh, a different slant on an old, old feeling.

An entry early in 1941: a woman from out of town had visited the cottage on King Street. Even though she had not been at home, Elise remembered that the money paid for the concoction her mother had prepared had been a princely sum.

Mistletoe: seven berries is all that's required.

Her mother had written.

Easy to come by at this quiet, sleeping time of the year, thriving in clusters, like ragged nests, at the top of bare winter trees. The mysterious parasite, with its luminous white fruit, has a will to survive the hardest of frosts, not needing to link with the earth. Heart medicine. Make a tea, boil for a quarter hour.

Elise wondered why this brew might be so costly, with mistletoe so common in the depths of winter.

Keep on top shelf, mark as deadly. Wash pan thoroughly after use.

Her mother, she realised, had been making poison.

Elise heard the door into the garden open and his step along the path, his shadow at her open door. A year or more ago, she might have wanted to fall into his embrace, melt into him. But her body stiffened, and she turned only when he said her name.

Nathan hesitated on the threshold. He looked older, harried, as if he'd been years at sea.

'How are you?' he asked.

'We're fine. Tea?'

She walked over to the stove and clanged the kettle on the hob, pulling mismatched cups from the dresser shelf. Elise wanted her mother to be here, sitting at the kitchen table, offering her counsel that always seemed to come from the most unexpected of angles.

Kate tottered in on bare feet. She tugged at Elise's skirt.

'Here she is,' Nathan said, a strange twist in his voice, taking a step or two across the floor. 'My goodness, all grown up.'

The child looked up at him. 'Are you the visitor?'

He squatted and reached both hands to her, delighting in her. Elise watched, enchanted. Kate held out her arms to be scooped up.

'Are you the daddy?' Kate asked.

Nathan held his daughter perched high in his arms. He nodded, his chin brushing her hair. He caught Elise's eye over the top of Kate's head, brightness sweeping his face. Kate's finger began to trace a curious line along his scarred cheek. Elise felt it cut to the quick.

'Come out to the gar-gen, Daddy,' Kate said.

Elise held Nathan's querying gaze and nodded her assent.

'Yes, come on, show your mother and me what flowers you've been growing,' he said.

'And the veg-ables. And 'erbs. Come on Ma-ma.'

'In a minute, Kate. Go with your... go with the visitor.'

Elise watched from the doorway as Kate tugged Nathan by the hand around the garden, saying hello to the flowers. He responded with curiosity and pleasure, as if he had never seen tulips before. His delight in their child felt like the only crumb of comfort Elise had ever tasted. He gestured for her to join them, but she shook her head.

She retreated, waited for the steam to start screaming through the kettle spout. Nathan lifted Kate, their identical dark heads against the cherry blossom. He told her about the bees and the honey flies and gave the butterfly a name. Elise tapped on the window, and they both turned to her and waved. The garden shimmered as if under water.

'So, you were able to get away from the Hall?' she asked as she served bread and butter and thick slices of ham that Robin had brought over in his basket.

Nathan spoke carefully, feeling his way. 'Vivi is away, visiting her friend. Genna, Lady Dornford, lost her husband last year. Vivi spends a great deal of time there these days.'

Kate, unable to keep still, trailed around outside to find things to bring to Nathan: a clover head, a pebble, a little pink worm.

'And so,' Elise said, 'you thought you'd better come and see me?'

Nathan rested his cup back, his posture strained, as if in pain. 'Believe me, Elise, if only I was able to split myself in half.'

'Forget it,' she said. 'I know that.'

'How can I forget it?' he uttered, his mouth tight. 'How can either of us forget it?'

She stood to clear the table, to occupy herself, wondering how this conversation could even continue. How, now, he would regret bothering to visit, regret ever meeting her.

'Guilt does terrible things to a person,' Nathan said, his voice low as if he had to scrape his thoughts from deep inside. 'I cannot forget my obligation to you. I cannot ignore how our paths have crossed. And what we have together.'

Elise kept her back turned to him, stacking plates. 'You mean, you being at the Seabathing Hospital where I was a volunteer?'

'Even further back. On the beach.'

Elise closed her eyes briefly. She remembered seeing him with his parents. She could have gone left, or right, and she turned right and walked past them. If she had gone left, he would never have seen her. But there were no rock pools to the left; it was never quite as interesting.

'I could have stayed put and finished my sandcastle,' he said, warming to the memory. 'But I followed you.'

They both waited, allowed the memories to form, the beginnings of possibility.

'Elise,' he said, 'when you came to tell me about... to tell me your news, I buckled. And I have been trying to surface ever since. All I can think about, all I can do is my best, to atone for it, my behaviour. To help you and Kate lead a happy life.' He dipped his head as if the weight of it still sat there. He studied his hands. 'I feel as if I am constantly on the edge of something wonderful, or something disastrous. From the outside, it seems I chose disaster, but look at Kate, look at her.'

Elise heard their daughter's chatter, and felt her defences rise, prickly and petulant.

'And yet, Nathan, it feels it is truly impossible, to live like this.'

He stared at her, swallowed hard.

Kate slipped into the kitchen, laid a flower head by his plate, and darted back out. Her daughter seemed to remember him, from when he visited after her mother's funeral. She seemed trusting, as if she knew him.

'Why not stay the afternoon, stay to read Kate a bedtime story?' Elise said, feeling expansive. She sat back down at the table. 'Tell me about Vivienne's poor friend. The husband, was he in France?'

Nathan picked up the flower, he shook his head, lips compressed.

'No, based here. RAF. It was the worse of luck. He's... he was Wing Commander at Biggin Hill. A quiet day. Routine, really. He was helping his men clear out an old munition store. There must have been an unexploded German shell from a raid, from back in Forty. Blew him up, and one of his lads, too. Terrible thing was, he always insisted on being part of the team, never stood back and commanded. Hands-on, you know. He was one of the boys.'

'There is always someone worse off than you,' Elise said, with compassion for this stranger, for all the strangers. 'Ma always insisted on that.'

'Elise,' he said, leaning forward. He wrapped his hand around her forearm. 'This cottage will always be your home.'

She pulled gently away.

'And Kate, she will go to school,' he said. 'We'll find a good one. She'll succeed at whatever she does, we can be sure of it.'

Elise cut two slices of Mrs Scott's cake, letting his reckless confidence drift.

'I thought my mother would grow old here,' she said. 'She was fifty, fifty-one. That's all.' Something tightened in her throat and she carried on, to ease it out. 'She was traumatised by my father's death, and she locked it inside. I know nothing about him. All I have is the music box. Ma did not trust the world, so she controlled it. She barred the front door of our old home. It was a bit of a joke, but you can see the serious side. And still they sought her out for what she could do for them. A remedy here, a concoction there. She didn't like *people*. But here...' Elise glanced around the room. 'She bloomed. She fell in love with Mr Buckley.' She smiled. 'And when she shut the garden door, we were protected.'

'I wanted you to feel that way. I wanted you to be safe,' he said. 'You miss her...'

'Oh, she's still here.' Elise's own assurance startled her. 'When someone sees fifty-one summers, they want to see a few more.'

* * *

Later, Elise stood at the bedroom door, while Nathan settled Kate down for bed. Her daughter asked for the music box. Elise wound it up and it played, tinkling into the soft dusk, while Nathan told Kate a story, straight out of this head, about the sea, a tale of Fastnet and the Fair Isles, and tempestuous Biscay, lulling her to sleep.

They went downstairs together and outside to fetch in the wood for the fire. Evening had fallen and the house looked sleepy, done with the day. Elise sensed a delicate movement in the air. Rain, on its way. Nathan fixed the blackout over the windows, stacked the wood for the fire and sat, stretching his legs out across the rug in front of the hearth like the man of the house.

'But do you miss living by the sea?' he asked, looking younger in the lamplight, not so tired.

'I do.' Elise poured Mrs Scott's cherry wine into teacups. 'This place is lovely, the air here sweet and earthy, but by the sea it's so clean, I get heady with it. And I miss those raucous seagulls. Their crying way up there used to ground me, settled me. But also, I'm happy here. Despite *this*.'

'*This*?'

'When you said "we" earlier. Nathan, we can never be "we".' Loneliness assaulted her; a sense of being alone. Always, naturally, alone. She breathed slowly to ease the tightening in her chest. 'You talk about Kate's education as if we are husband and wife. But the reality is something else entirely.'

'Elise, Elise,' he said. 'I will always...'

She stopped him. 'But Vivienne.' The name dropped from her mouth, like a foreign word.

At the church, at her mother's funeral, Vivienne had dazzled her, breathed her beauty out all over her. It had cut like a bright sword through Elise's grief, her panic at losing Kate for a handful of moments. What chance did Elise have, in the face of that?

'Vivienne is yours and I am not.'

His face clouded, something turning under the surface. He

struggled to speak. 'Elise, if you... is it possible, do you think, to love two people?'

Elise shook her head. The first time he'd used the word 'love' for her, and it stung, as if it had been the opposite.

'Vivienne was right in front of me,' said Elise, 'I was in such a state but she looked so very wretched. More than sad. She looked like she had given up. Nathan, Vivienne needs you. And it seems to me, despite everything, that I don't, as much as she does.'

Nathan inhaled, as if burnt. He went to say something, but seemed to fold back into his chair, exhausted. A crisp pattering of rain hit the window.

Elise got up to fetch yesterday's newspaper sent over in the basket and sat back down opposite him, turning the pages. She read about the progress of the Allies in France and the Low Countries, the advance on Berlin.

The rain grew heavy, in for the night. Everyone must be able to hear it: Robin, Mr Buckley, Mrs Scott, and Freda Calloway, and all the people of Farthing. Perhaps even Vivienne Calloway, wherever she was, visiting her friend. In the churchyard, her mother's headstone would be soaked and running. Life is precious, Elise thought; life can be gone in a matter of moments.

For one evening, they could pretend. Nathan sitting by her fire as if he'd always been there, their daughter sleeping upstairs. But Nathan was right. The reality spelt both wonder and disaster.

'I see that we have crossed the Rhine,' she said.

'Yes, we heard. It may only be a matter of time. Perhaps, we are near the end? Thank God for that.'

Nathan rested his head against the back of the chair and closed his eyes. He slept and the evening ticked on, his presence natural, a part of her.

When the clock struck ten, she folded the newspaper and fetched his hat and coat. Before she woke him, she took his hand.

He remained deep in sleep, riding the waves of his sailor's dream. She remembered, at the height of the raid in London, beneath the table at Grosvenor Street, when the world tore apart around them, Nathan had whispered to her, 'We are equal now, Elise. We're even.'

She woke him, and asked him to leave, to walk back alone to the Hall through the rain.

18

VIVI, MAY 1945

'I think there may be some sore heads in the village this morning,' Vivi said, as Freda came into the breakfast room.

The French windows stood open, the smell of cut grass freshened the air and mist lingered low around the clipped box trees. An unbearably beautiful May day, although Freda looked rather fragile and jaded, didn't seem to notice. Vivi had never known her mother-in-law to come downstairs to breakfast in her dressing gown.

Vivi had been sitting with Freda yesterday, a quiet and usual morning, when Ruby had burst in without knocking, and without the tea tray.

'Mr Buckley says, you must switch on the radio, ma'am,' she'd shouted, as Vivi, on reflex, reached for the dial. 'Switch it on, switch it on, you don't want to miss it.'

And Ruby had plumped herself down on the sofa beside Vivi as the announcer on the World Service assured them that the war in Europe was over.

'My good God,' Freda had sighed. 'At long last.'

Ruby clapped her hands, bounced in her seat. Mrs Scott

bustled through with Mr Buckley, who seemed to have found a bottle of Champagne from somewhere, and a joyful noise had filled the room. Vivi had heard a rising cheer in the distance, as the children from the village school, Robin among them, spilled out down the lane, followed by a bright ringing sound.

'The bells, it's the church bells,' Freda had said, sitting very still, tears rolling down her cheeks.

Mr Buckley said, 'The vicar said he couldn't find anyone to do it. Said he's going to ring them himself.'

Vivi had taken the brimming glass that the steward offered her. Nathan would be in the thick of it, at the Admiralty; what must it be like in London, she'd thought, what celebrations and parties, and drinking? She'd sipped the Champagne and felt a little sick. What did it all matter, she'd thought. Her parents and Dornie were still dead.

'The fireworks on the village green were a nice surprise, weren't they, Freda?' she said as her mother-in-law slipped gingerly into her seat at the breakfast table. 'Who organised that? I can guess Doctor Willis.'

'Mrs Scott's punch was another surprise,' said Freda, resting her chin on her hand and staring into her teacup. She picked up a slice of toast, buttered it slowly, bit it, then put it down. 'My goodness, I suppose one is allowed a cup or two on VE day, but really...'

'Nathan telephoned first thing,' Vivi said, to distract Freda from her indisposition. 'He's coming home. He's sorry he missed it all here. He said the crowds in London were extraordinary, as you can imagine. They descended on the Palace, shouting for the King.'

'I think I'd better go back to bed,' said Freda, her voice pinched. 'I am feeling particularly peculiar.'

'I'll bring you something up a bit later.'

Sitting alone, Vivi caught the faint whiff of a spent firework. One must have landed on the terrace. She'd watched from the garden last night, alone, as they burst in the sky over Farthing, the church bells still ringing, the spire luminous under transient stars, flickering and falling into darkness: friendly explosions, friendly fire. The metallic smell of gunpowder smoke evermore a reminder of relief and a sense of loss, that there was no going back. Her life, many lives, changed forever.

Vivi gazed out now at the garden, her mind blossoming with the thought of Nathan. They had spent a great deal of time apart, this last year; she had put space and distance between them. Genna had needed her, and Vivi had needed to be away from him, the Hall, and the secret she had uncovered at the cottage: Elise Drake and her little girl. The secret she had yet to confess to knowing. But her rage and her confusion that day had melted in the face of her friend's grief; it had become something she could not trust within herself. Had she over-reacted, she wondered, while she sat with Genna, and held her while she wept. Had it all been one almighty coincidence?

And the most surprising thing of all: she still held a bright longing for Nathan. She stared out the window, at another glorious spring day. Perhaps, now, a trip back to New York. Perhaps, now, a child.

She must telephone Genna, she thought, for her friend's grief would resurface, perhaps be even worse now, for Dornie had died without seeing this day.

Something moved at the corner of her eye, a shadow against sunlit haze. Someone small, stumbling around the edge of the lawn.

'Robin?' she said out loud.

The boy appeared to be struggling with a heavy, awkward bundle. He made his determined way past the dark hedges as if seeking cover, heading for the stable yard or perhaps the kitchen. Vivi watched his progress, fascinated for a moment, wondering what jape he was up to this morning. And yet the load he carried reformed itself into something wriggling and human. He seemed to be speaking to it, his head dipped, his tender cradling of it giving Vivi the creeping sense that something in fact may be very wrong.

She stood, and hurried across the hall, through the baize door. She heard, before she reached it: a commotion simmering along the back corridor. Mrs Scott's booming exclamation, Ruby's fired question cut short, Robin's high-pitched plea. The two women looked around as Vivi burst into the kitchen and Mrs Scott stepped forward, her wide frame shielding Robin and whatever he'd brought into the house.

'We are dealing with it, Mrs Calloway.'

'Dealing with what, exactly? Robin? I saw him in the garden. Robin, there you are, what in the world?'

'Mrs Calloway, we can sort this out.'

The boy seemed smaller than usual, his face older and rigid with terror, his cheeks fiery, his eyes leaking. And on the floor by his feet, seeking shelter behind his legs crouched the bundle he'd been carrying: a child. The Drake child.

Vivi could see she had grown a little since the last time she had seen her: her limbs plump and smooth, her narrow shoulders shivering, her terrified stare, bright through her dark fringe. Curling her body around Robin's ankles, the little girl plucked at his socks with dirty fingers. Her hair lay unbraided and ragged, her nightgown bunched, the hem crusted with mud, her feet naked and wet with dew.

Vivi squatted, and grasped for her hands. She inhaled with shock.

'Whatever is the matter, little one?'

The child wriggled free from her, turning her face upwards, seeking Robin. Vivi looked around at blank faces.

'She is so cold. What has happened?' she asked. 'Why is she so cold?'

'We're trying to get it out of Robin,' Mrs Scott said. 'We think there's been an accident, ma'am.'

'Where? At the gamekeeper's cottage?'

Ruby and Mrs Scott recoiled, drew in a collective breath, a sharp look darting between them.

'That we don't know. But the child needs warm milk, soup or tea. Beef tea.' Mrs Scott marched over to the stove. 'It looks like she has been outside all night. It's spring, but it is still chilly. Look at her feet, my goodness. Ruby, fetch a blanket.'

'She needs a warm bath, poor little maid,' said Ruby.

Vivi turned back to the boy. 'Whatever has happened? Why have you brought Kate... this little girl here?'

He stared at her, struggling to find words and the permission to use them.

'What's the matter? It is all right to tell me.'

Robin began to cry, shiveringly, holding his arm over his mouth. The child hid her face against his shins.

'She's in the garden.' Robin sobbed into his sleeve. 'She's asleep. Fast asleep. I could not wake her.'

Questions ricocheted from the women around the kitchen.

'Speak up, boy.'

'What's that you say?'

Vivi placed a gentle finger under his wobbling chin.

Quietly, she said, 'Who is asleep, Robin?'

'The lady at the Amber House.'

'He means Miss Drake,' Mrs Scott said, by the stove. She glanced at Vivi for one second.

Elise Drake. Vivi pictured her dressed in her mourning black, rigid with grief, her horror that she had, briefly, lost her child. And then, standing at her kitchen door, cradling her daughter, while Vivi spied on her.

'We need to telephone Doctor Willis,' Vivi said. 'Mrs Scott, please do that. Ruby, find Mr Buckley. Ask him to go over there, to the cottage, straight away.'

She squatted down by Robin and gently tried to persuade the little girl to come to her, coaxing her, calling her 'my darling'. Eventually, she managed to lever her into her arms.

'I will take her upstairs with me. We have a warm fire in the bedroom. I can tuck her into bed.'

Kate felt stiff and unyielding in her arms, and was offering frightened sobs. She clutched at Vivi's collar, her fingertips burrowing and tugging her hair.

'Ma-ma,' she uttered near her ear, and Vivi felt the surface of her heart peel away.

Mrs Scott and Ruby remained still, mouths open, staring at Vivi.

'Did you not hear me?' she said over the top of the girl's tangled head. 'Miss Drake needs our help.'

'Straight away, ma'am,' uttered Mrs Scott, aghast, her lips loose with shock as she followed Vivi out of the kitchen.

Crossing the hall, Vivi heard the telephone tinkle as Mrs Scott lifted the receiver in Nathan's study. Outside, a car door slammed, and footsteps crunched the gravel. She paused, squeezed the child tighter, sensing the terrified pulse in her chest, cupping tiny icy feet in her hands.

Nathan opened the front door and saw Vivi, holding the child. His step faltered. His jaw jerked, and his eyes, unblinking, darted from face to face. The girl twisted in Vivi's arms, reached out for him, squealed 'Daddy.'

Nathan walked straight over and gathered the girl into his arms. His purpose, his intent, sent a slithering sensation up Vivi's back. The child fell onto his shoulder, pressed her cheek to his neck. Vivi saw more than joy in the little girl; she saw instinctive trust.

She opened her mouth in question. Blunt fear made her words fall away. The whispers inside her mind, the dormant suspicions, that this last year had kept her sleepless and had greeted her each morning, focused into a piercing, blinding light.

'You're fine, Little Kate,' Nathan said, his words elongating with uncertainty as he caught Vivi's eye around the child's head, his stare laced with panic. Vivi looked away, did not want to witness it. 'Tell me, Kate,' he whispered to the child. 'Whatever has happened?'

The child would not, could not say.

A grating sick feeling shifted around Vivi's skin, tingling cold over her scalp.

'It appears her mother has had some sort of accident at the cottage,' Vivi said, her tongue clotting. 'I've asked for Mr Buckley to go over. Mrs Scott is telephoning the doctor. I am taking the child upstairs to bed.'

Nathan looked up the stairs, shook his head in wonder.

'But how, Vivi... will you... are you able to...?' he uttered, his distress tearing his face.

Vivi nodded and Nathan exhaled, as if he'd been holding his soul inside. He spoke delicately into the little girl's ear.

'Stay with the nice lady, Little Kate. I will be back soon.'

The child nodded, her eyes wide and bright with tears. As her gaze reached Vivi's, a snippet of trust smoothed out her features. Nathan eased her back into Vivi's arms, her body spooning against hers easily. Kate needed Nathan, needed both of them.

Vivi steeled her body, resisting the girl's tenderness.

Nathan stepped back as if to look at Vivi anew. He had never seen her hold a child before; it felt like a new sensation for them both. She saw his eyes deepen, gratitude softening the agony inside him.

'Nathan, do what you need to do,' she said, coolly.

He touched his fingertip to Kate's cheek, kept his gaze on Vivi. As he turned for the door, the reality of now being responsible for this child burst inside her mind.

* * *

Vivi drew the curtains so that the bedroom was filled with tranquil light, as if it lay deep within the wood, and lowered the child down into her bed. Kate slumped, whimpering and exhausted into the rumpled sheets. Her eyes fluttered on the knife-edge of sleep, giving herself up to the comfort of the bed, and to Vivi. Primeval trust in a stranger.

Vivi smoothed Kate's hair, dark against the pillow, as sleep claimed her, and felt a tiny thrill of triumph that she'd settled so quickly. She drew the armchair close to the bed and sat, exhausted. Darts of shock pulsed through her blood.

'What do you know, little one?' she whispered. 'Why in the world are you here?'

Her temples fizzed and her mind turned back on itself. After all, perhaps for the child, Nathan as landlord had been the only father figure she'd ever known. Didn't Mrs Willis say that there had been a sweetheart of Miss Drake's, lost to the war? And who was Miss Drake to Nathan, anyway: a poor evacuee, pregnant when she arrived here at Farthing with her mother, by all accounts. And yet the truth came at Vivi from dark places. Nathan had called out her name during his fever, long before Elise arrived at the cottage. There were no records of the Drakes in the estate ledgers. Why would Nathan hide them? The child resembled Miss Drake, and yet around the eyes, Vivi saw Nathan. And how old was Little Kate?

Vivi gazed at the sleeping child and the facts gnawed at her, lingered like the smell of smoke after a fire.

If only her father were here, he'd tell her what to do. Her mother, she'd know best.

Vivi caught sight of her own reflection in the dressing table mirror, and recognised suddenly, her mother. Her throat contracted. How alike they had been. The woman in the mirror looked strong on some days, not so much on others. She felt laced together with appearances.

'I wanted a baby,' she said aloud, the admission blowing cooling wind around her ears. 'Isn't it the natural course of life for many people?'

She rested against the back of the chair, closed her eyes, not wishing to see any more of herself. What could she do but wait for Nathan's return?

Kate slept on, like a convalescent recovering from illness, a trauma she had no words yet to describe. She turned in her sleep, her small hand lifted from the covers, opening like a flower, as if searching for someone.

Vivi heard Freda's bedroom door open and the sound of her tread along the landing outside, followed by her irritable shout down the stairs for Ruby. A hurrying of the maid's footsteps and a mumbled apology. Mrs Scott's voice in the bowels of the house. The telephone ringing. Car tyres over the gravel.

Eventually, someone tapped at the door and before Vivi had a chance to call out, they entered. Nathan stood on the threshold, pinpoints of red on his cheeks. Why her husband felt he had to knock on his own bedroom door, she had no idea.

'I need to talk to you, Vivi.'

His eyes did not meet hers and she felt her core tighten. After everything they had been through together, he surely could not be about to tell her it was over?

He closed the door behind him and sat on the edge of the bed, leaning forward to gaze at the sleeping child. Vivi stared at her husband's profile.

'Kate has been drowsing on and off, but once or twice has cried out,' she said, needing to fill the silence. She faltered. 'Will Doctor Willis come and see her, do you think?'

'He will. He is on his way. He's seen...' Nathan exhaled hard, his head sagging between his shoulders. He kept his eyes fixed on Kate. 'He has seen Elise.'

Elise. He tenderly eased the name out into the room. She remembered Freda playing the tune on the piano, that cold morning after Digby's death. And how Nathan had hauled back the covers and left their bed.

'She was still unconscious when I left the hospital,' Nathan continued. 'Doctor Willis helped me take her there, Mr Buckley drove us. The Seabathing Hospital at Margate, where I was with my face.' His hand moved to his mouth. 'It looks very grave indeed.'

'Is she going to be all right?' Vivi asked, automatically.

'He doesn't think so.'

She flinched, remembering her confusion, in the Widow's Watch, when she'd assumed Elise was Mrs Hoodless's first name. She glanced at the bed, and the sleeping child.

Vivi sucked in her breath, forced herself to remain still.

'Nathan, what has happened?'

He folded his arms.

'Elise must have slipped on the path in the cottage garden, knocked her head. Robin said...' A sob bubbled in his throat. 'Robin said that Kate was huddled beside her, must have wandered out in the night looking for her. Must have woken and not known where her mother was.'

He reached out to the child, his hand finding her little foot under the covers.

'From the look of it,' he said, 'Elise had not moved. Had been there all night. The doctor thinks a stroke. Her mother died last year, the same thing. There was blood from her head...' His finger-tips touched his own temple. 'Her blood, soaking the ground.' His mouth moved oddly. 'She may have gone out to watch the fireworks, last night. She'd be able to see them, from the garden. Or at least, hear them, I don't know...'

His voice drifted like a faint brushstroke painting a picture only he could see.

'Nathan,' said Vivi, 'The child?'

'Robin was taking the basket down...'

'I don't mean Robin.'

Nathan rubbed his hand around the back of his neck.

'Vivi.' He dropped her a small glance. 'Elise and Kate have been living in my old gamekeeper's cottage in the woods these last few years or so.'

'I know,' she said, prompting him, not wanting him to, but needing him to tell her, to come out with it, once and for all. 'They're your tenants. The evacuees? What are they to you?'

He did not respond. Instead, he stood up and went to the window, his back turned.

His silence confirmed the truth, the poison spreading through Vivi's body. Kate's glee at seeing Nathan downstairs in the hallway, her outstretched arms, his agonised expression. The little mew of 'Daddy' haunted the space between them.

Nathan turned towards her, his face in half-silhouette, the brighter window behind him. But she could read his expression. He didn't have to say it. The brutal meaning of Little Kate, sleeping in their bed, and who Elise Drake had been, who she remained, to him, shattered like glass in the space around her.

They both jumped at the single hard knock on the door.

'Your mother?' Vivi asked, barely able to speak.

He nodded.

'Tell her to go away.'

'Vivi, I can't do that.'

Fury surged through Vivi, burning away her frustration and the constraints she'd lived with since setting foot in Farthing Hall. A new fire inside her made her want to wriggle free, to be herself, to be the Vivi her parents raised.

She stood, her legs like liquid and marched to the door.

She opened it a crack.

'Are you feeling better, Freda?' she asked, her words clipping around her tongue.

'I am a little, yes, thank you,' Freda replied. 'I was wondering where everyone was. Ah, Nathan, there you are. I thought I heard the car earlier but wasn't sure. There's all manner of lowered voices downstairs between Mrs Scott and Ruby. Whispering. You know I hate whispering. Some sort of to-do from last night, I wonder, they were all rather enjoying themselves...' Her head bobbed to look past them. 'It must be time for tea. I shall ring the bell and we can have it together in the sitting room. Now you are home, Nathan, dear, we can have our own celebration. Get Ruby to fetch a bottle. Raise a toast to Churchill. I might be able to manage a tot. What do you say?'

'We won't have time for tea today, Freda,' Vivi said quietly.

'What? Why not? What is going on?' Freda stopped, her gaze flicking deeper into the room.

Vivi watched her slow realisation as she noticed the small form sleeping in the bed: a furrowing across her brow, a flinching of the loose skin around her mouth. A shaft of anger, no, fear, in her eyes.

'Is that the Drake child? What is she doing here?'

Nathan opened his mouth, but Vivi spoke first.

'Not in here.' She ushered them both on to the landing and shut the bedroom door. 'Freda, we must tell you. I'm afraid that

Miss Drake, the tenant at the old gamekeeper's cottage, had an accident last night in the garden.' She was surprised by how easily she spoke, how calm she sounded. 'She is in hospital...'

She looked at Nathan.

'The Seabathing at Margate,' he said. 'We drove her there this morning.'

Freda took a breath, ignored Nathan and stared at Vivi, her mouth narrowing. 'And who is paying for *that*?'

'I am,' Vivi said confidently.

She felt Nathan's surprised glance more than she was able to see it.

'That's very commendable, Vivi. But it doesn't explain the child.' Freda glanced over Vivi's shoulder at the closed bedroom door. 'Is there not someone in the village who can take her in? One of the mothers perhaps? Mrs Willis? She always seems to be involved in things like this. We're not a charity. I don't want her here under my roof.'

Nathan recoiled. Vivi could see his hands flexing at his sides, loathing in his eyes fired at his mother. Vivi stepped closer to him, and gently touched his sleeve. She took his hand, holding it low, by their sides. The wordless touch only they knew, formed back in the early days of their marriage, when, for so long they had not been able to share a physical space. The forty-four letters he'd sent her, as they'd courted love over long distances. What were all those promises, their declarations worth, Vivi wondered, as she looked at Freda's angry face, if she did not step in and prove that she at least meant her side of it? If she did not speak up now, the whole thing would amount to nothing.

'The little girl's mother is gravely ill, Freda,' Vivi said, her words ringing like a clear bell. 'The child, Kate, is staying here at Farthing Hall where she can be looked after properly. Where she belongs.'

Freda's mouth dropped open. She gawped at Vivi.

From the corner of her eye, Vivi saw Nathan turn his head to her in slow astonishment as she said, 'Where she belongs.' She sensed his body shift closer to her, his limbs restless with gratitude. His stare lanced the side of her face, their bond sealed. She caught his eye, and saw that he understood her. She felt the goodness that he was made of. She hoped he could feel in return her acceptance of him, of his flaws, of his humanity.

The baize door on the landing banged open and Ruby scooted through with a bucket of coal, then bobbed and uttered a, 'Begging your pardon,' before hurrying off.

Freda shuddered. 'Why are we talking out here where anyone could hear us?'

Vivi rested her palm on the banister, to ground herself, give herself strength.

'It doesn't matter. Everyone will have to know sooner or later,' she said, speaking of a future that she had no idea how to picture, but one that she must carve out for herself, and for Nathan.

She felt his hand squeeze hers.

'They will have to know what?' Freda fired at her son. 'They'll certainly wonder what that child is doing here.'

Nathan inhaled, seemingly to draw deep from a cold well of patience.

'We will discuss this later, Mother,' he said. 'Now I haven't the time.'

Freda sank. She ran a fingertip around her compressed lips, her eyes sharp, evaluating.

'I want to get back to the hospital,' he said, 'and take Elise whatever she might need, speak to the doctors again. I hope to God...' His gaze fell on the closed bedroom door.

Freda roused herself, bristling. 'This is most inconvenient. All of this. How are we to explain the child? The Drake child? Living here at Farthing Hall?' Freda's stare fixed on Vivi like a searchlight. 'And what do you mean by "where she belongs"?'

'Strange and upsetting things happen in wartime, Freda,' said Vivi. 'Children are left as orphans. We will take care of her.' Nathan's grip on her hand tightened. 'If Miss Drake doesn't pull through, we will adopt her.'

'Why on earth would you do that?' Freda asked, below her breath, 'Nathan, speak to me. Don't just stand there. Say something, why don't you? Adopting a stranger's child? What will people say? We simply *cannot* have another scandal in this house.'

'If you are that concerned about it, Freda, we will change her name,' said Vivi. 'We will call her Isobel. After my mother.'

'But this is ridiculous,' cried Freda. 'What difference will that make?'

Vivi turned and walked back towards her bedroom.

'Vivienne,' Freda hissed, horror seeming to gag her voice, 'I'm talking to you. Where do you think you're going?'

Vivi ignored her, saw only her life expanding, the image running ahead of her. Her and Nathan, starting all over again. A dash of hope.

'Hush now, Freda. Keep your voice down,' Vivi said, turning to look at Freda. 'Your granddaughter Isobel is asleep in there. And I don't want you to wake her up and make her cry.'

BOOK THREE

1959–1962

19

BELLA, JUNE 1959

The telegram arrived while she was packing. Short and to the point, but the message lingered with her, like a headache she could not shift.

```
Very sorry I cannot meet you off boat-train
this time. Busy at the Admiralty. All
love, Dad.
```

Bella threw her thickest jumper on top of the bulging trunk and shut the lid with a thump. What did he mean, 'this time'? This was the last time.

Tomorrow, she would leave the boarding school in the mountains of Le Chable. Tomorrow, the long journey home.

Five years she had been here. The lush springtime meadows, the peaks of a land in its infancy, were at first as luminous as a fairy tale, inspiring the artist inside her. But they'd quickly dulled into a fake theatre backcloth. How she longed to escape. The smell of Thursday's cassoulet and used gym kits, footsteps ringing along corridors, the nudging of elbows and the clockwork of timetables.

Indecipherable algebra. Girls chattering in Italian and French, rarely in English to her. She struck a lonely figure.

She checked the chest of drawers. Ha, she'd missed an ugly set of regulation woollen undies, a necessity to stave off the Swiss Alpine chill. But they'd never done a good enough job for her; the cold seemed an unshakeable part of her. Not that she complained like some of the girls, who twittered and rubbed their mittened fingers, declaring that they were not born for this sort of weather and would go off to sip cups of hot chocolate in the village café and recount their summers in Monte Carlo.

How could Bella talk about the chill sitting inside her? She could barely explain it to herself: this yearning for something unseen, and it had nothing to do with the snowy mountains. It had first crept into her when her parents told her they were sending her away to school. In a foreign country. Twelve years old. And she did not have the tools to articulate her distress, although a squalid instinct told her it had all been Grannie's idea.

She shut the drawer on the underwear, leaving it behind.

The next morning, Bella went down the stairs for the last time, and watched as her trunk was loaded into the school charabanc, serenaded as always by the perpetual off-beat clanging of cowbells in the Alpine meadows. She said goodbye to the mistresses and the girls, who waved her off enthusiastically, seemingly pleased to see her go.

Her train pulled lazily through summer mountain passes, leaving Le Chable's formidable beauty behind, and she waited for the coldness to disappear. Surely it would, for the distance between Bella and home, between Bella and her parents, closed with every mile. But then she remembered. *Busy at the Admiralty.*

Other times, she'd disembark the train at Victoria to find her father waiting for her: their glorious end-of-school ritual. Straight on for tea somewhere glamorous – 'just we two,' he'd say – before browsing two rooms at the National Gallery, one her choice, one his, or a small artist's salon he'd discovered along a cobbled Mayfair lane near Mama's old house.

This time, she stepped down on to the platform, into the clanging, grainy fug of smoke, feeling the good old sooty London air around her, and spotted a familiar figure down by the ticket barrier. She gave a gasp of disbelief. The porter thumped her trunk at her feet with a, 'Won't be a moment, madam,' and went off to find his trolley.

Madam, indeed!

She wondered how she looked through his eyes. In her couture linen coat, which had been ordered for her by her mother from Paris, Dior no less, and her hair knotted like the French girls at school, beret at the perfect angle over her forehead, dark fringe peeking out, she knew she looked different. Perhaps the child had disappeared, and a young woman emerged. But one glimpse of her bewildered face reflected in the murky train window, and she became the schoolgirl again.

'Bella!'

The figure approached. Her astonishment knocked the breath out of her.

'Good grief, what a year has done,' Robin called, approaching fast. 'You're quite the lady now. Gloves and handbag and everything – oops. I am being too familiar, Miss Isobel Calloway!'

The same easy, clear-eyed smile, that exhalation as he laughed. But no tweed jacket and country boots; only a shirt and tie this time. High-waisted, smart trousers. His hair shorter, cropped at the back. A grown-up man about town.

She laughed, blushing. 'I'm catching you up, Rob. Don't forget I'm seventeen now, though sometimes I feel seven. What does it matter? You have always said what you wanted to me.'

'That I have,' he said. 'Within reason. Now where's that porter gone? We have another train to catch.'

'What are you doing here?' she asked. 'You're here to take me home?'

'Don't look so surprised. Your mother asked my father. I understand *your* father is busy, and I was planning to head home this weekend to see my old Dad. It's a good job he caught me – telephoned the payphone in the hall, left a message with my landlady – or you would have struggled on your own. It's always horrible trying to make a connection. You might have missed it. And we can't have that, can we?'

'No, I suppose we can't.' Bella let her words drift into the echoing din of the station, and followed Rob as he instructed the porter to take her trunk to the Canterbury train. The six or seven years he had on her laid out a trusted and reliable path for her to follow. The years made him a man. She trotted beside him, sending him little glances, reassuring herself. Class did not come into it – he the son of the steward, she the daughter of the house – for they'd both, privately, implicitly, had none of it. After all, she'd known him forever.

Settling herself beside him in the brown and burgundy carriage as the train picked up steam, his comforting presence, his familiarity settled inside her. Even his scent – his own fragrance – was the essence of home. She stole a glance at his face, and the cold melted.

'What has a year done to you, Rob? Have you finished your National Service? Can you fire a gun? What was Woolwich like? Have you got a taste for London, then?'

'I can verify that it was all a monumental waste of time. Polishing boots, square bashing, getting barked at, re-making your bed because the sheet is not straight. If it's stationary, paint it white; if it's moving, salute it. And see this?' He ran his hand through his fringe, making his quiff bounce free. 'I got away with it all this time. I greased it back, put my cap on, and they were none the wiser.'

'And square shoulders to boot,' Bella laughed.

'Thank God, I've done my time. Discharged at last.'

She pulled down the window and as the suburbs faded and the countryside streaked by, the breeze lapped her face. Like a baby gulping her inaugural lungful, she took her first breath of Kentish air in a long time. She smelt cut grass, earth, sweet May hawthorn, England. Riverbanks and cottages, red-roofed oast houses, everything tender and softening in old age. She wiped the stray tears from her cheeks, hoping Rob had not noticed.

She sat back and they started talking, their conversation filling the carriage with layers of questions and laughter.

The train rumbled across the points outside Canterbury and the cathedral's faded-gold towers rose against blue sky, a dappled vignette already forming in her artist's mind.

'What will you be doing now?' Robin asked, as they stepped off the train. 'Now you are no longer a schoolgirl, and have the world at your feet?'

'Paint,' she said. 'This summer I am going to paint the cathedral, the hop gardens, the orchards, everything.'

'I knew it.'

'Dad wanted to be an artist, but he was never allowed. I blame Grannie, and dead old grandpa Digby. For surely, you should do what you want in life?'

'It depends,' said Robin, snatching a glance at her. 'Sometimes you must do what is right.'

They got into a taxi at Canterbury station and let it take them up the long hill to Farthing.

'It's been a while for me, too,' Rob said, peering out at the countryside. 'Being here. Being home.'

'Of course, you have already flown the nest,' Bella said, and for a moment had a brief wondering about his London digs, his job, girlfriends, perhaps, someone special.

'I have,' he said. 'Exchanged the army for a job in the bank. But I see it as a hiatus. Getting it out of my system. Eventually, I will come back. I love this place too much.'

The woods crept thickly into the side of the road, the church spire pricking the horizon and Bella had to wonder. Farthing had its charm. But the village folk kept a polite distance, as if she made them terribly shy, their greetings tripping over their tongues. She, the daughter of the Big House; she, the posh girl who came home from her Swiss school each summer, a little taller, if possible a tad more sophisticated. Only Rob ever seemed to breach the gap between her and the rest of the world outside the Hall.

As the taxi pulled in over the gravel, the familiar long windows glinting in sunlight, she felt a strong sense of arrival, of having done this before, which of course she had. But more from being with Rob. From being frightened but also being looked after. The feeling puzzled her, like a dream she could not quite remember when day broke. She smiled at him in open, honest gratitude, wanting to say something, but not knowing how.

'This summer, now you are home,' he said cheerily, 'I will get down as much as I can, and how about we continue with your riding? What do you say? You can try for a trot. We can try you on Snowdrop.'

'Ah, you know I cannot ride for toffee,' she said, getting out of the car. 'So unlike my mother, who looks like she was born in a saddle. But there's something about horses that has always scared me. Can't explain it, really. Even dear gentle old Snowdrop.'

'We can do something about that.' He looked at her through uncommon shyness.

Before she could respond, Bella heard her mother's voice. She glanced up to see her pattering down the front steps, trilling her name, waving her hand, her fair hair all iridescent beauty, and Bella felt like a child again, awkward and tiny, Snowdrop's long white face looming over her.

Her mother paid the driver, thanked Rob, and took her arm, leading her back up the steps.

'Look at you, all grown up.' Her mother's beautiful smile shined bright enough, but concern deepened the blue in her wide wolf-stare eyes. 'We are sorry that Dad was not able to meet you,' she said, gazing hard as if trying to reacquaint herself with her face. 'I always think it's such a long way to come on your own, my darling. All the way across France, the Channel. How very brave you are.'

'I enjoyed it,' Bella said, looking for Rob and realising he had gone around the back, presumably to seek out Mr Buckley. 'And I wasn't on my own for the last bit.'

She stood in the hallway and felt her shoulders drop. Like the clock chimes that punctuated its days and nights, the Hall had always been the same. Bella knew her way around in the dark. She knew every creaking board, every varying smell. Her parents' bedroom, lily of the valley; her grandmother's more savoury; the boot room, damp earth. All manner of aromas emanated from the kitchen corridor, depending on what Mrs Scott rustled up. A cold hyacinth scent in the new upstairs bathroom, with its gold taps and marble tiles. The hall smelt of beeswax with the parquet floor polished to dangerous degree on her grandmother's instruction. The door to her father's study closed, as usual. The great window at the top of the stairs draped in swathes of golden cloth.

'What have you done now, Mama?' Bella laughed, admiring everything around her, remembering how her mother would complain about the time they had no electricity. And now, opaline lamps adorned walls and tables, the landing no longer dim and treacherous.

'Ha, this is not the half of it,' she replied and then lowered her voice. 'Grannie is not best pleased with my revamp, but then when is she ever?'

Bella stripped off her gloves, threw them on the hallway table next to the photographs of her parents' wedding, and of the grandparents she had never met. The tragic ones who drowned in the Atlantic, captured in the twenties, cloche hat and pin-stripe suit, their energy vibrating through time. Eyes gleaming with American corn-fed joy, and so distant from Bella in more ways than she could muster. In his studio portrait, Grandpa Digby looked almost Victorian, with a lustrous moustache and steeled eyes. His picture terrified her.

'Where is Grannie?' Bella asked.

'Ah, taken to her bed. She's resting. Feeling a bit peaky.'

This came as no surprise; her grandmother often took off to her bedroom, 'Having another funny turn', as her father would say.

'Anyway, let's get you some tea. I bet you haven't had a decent cup in ages. Mrs Scott has baked especially.'

Her mother opened the door to the sitting room with a flourish, and Bella walked into a space she hardly recognised: new sofas and chairs in pale-blue silk, with cushions she could sink into, the windows open to the day and no longer shrouded in heavy tapestry. Voiles pooled on the floor and danced ethereally in the light breeze that touched the fronds of silver-green potted ferns. The room seemed to suit Vivienne's colouring: ice-blue and rose-gold, a freshness and sparkle.

'Mama, it is beautiful, like something from *House and Garden*. But where are Grannie's dusty old plants?'

'Relegated to the back corridor, with all manner of other trash. Don't tell Grannie I said that.' She gave a giggle. 'I am mighty glad you like it.'

Perhaps because she had not heard her mother's voice in a while; her accent sang with stronger tones, her Americanness shining through, setting her apart. It had often come to Bella, in dreams on cold winter nights, that she would return from school to find her parents, or more likely, her mother, gone back to the States where she belonged.

She listened while her mother regaled her with the pitfalls of getting this room 'just so', and told herself not to pay attention to her dreams, in case they became nightmares.

'There she is, home at last.' Mrs Scott bustled in, ruddy faced with pleasure at seeing her, balancing a great tray of tea.

'There she is indeed,' her mother echoed, eyes shining, 'my darling daughter.'

Bella sat back, cosseted by the brand new chair, home at last. Her mother set out the cups and poured the tea with relish, embracing the ceremony like any native-born Englishwoman might do. She arranged plates and forks, the delicate tower of cakes, as if playing with a doll's tea set. Her body seemed to have widened somewhat, her figure not faring well or flattered by this season's fashion, despite the couture she sought out on her trips to Bond Street. And her face, perhaps lined a little more, like a map of her feelings: joy, and something else less tangible. And, Bella noticed, too much make up, as if the happiness had simply been painted on that morning. Sadness was a necessary part of her demeanour, like the tatty edge of one of Grannie's discarded cushions.

20

Ever since Bella had known her own name, ever since she had recognised her face when she looked in the mirror, she knew her father would leave. Each Monday, he would pack his bag for his important job in smoky old London at the equally smoky, mysterious Admiralty. She hated the sight of his suitcase waiting in the hallway, but she would place his shoes ready for him because he asked her to, yet longing to hide them so that he couldn't go. But, after the achingly long dismal week without him, he'd be home again for the gleaming jewel of a weekend.

When Bella herself left, or rather, had been packed off to boarding school, he would make sure he met her at Victoria when she came back for the holidays, rain or shine, waiting in his smart coat and polished shoes, a smile as wide as his hat. But this time, he happened to have been busy, had sent a telegram to explain. She understood. She should be a grown-up about it. For she was, as Rob rightly pointed out, no longer a schoolgirl. And yet, still, it stung like a blow to her cheek that he had not been there to welcome her.

That next morning she went downstairs through the quietened

house, hearing only clocks ticking, the oaks stirring outside. She crossed the hall and slipped into her father's study, closed the door, and stood perfectly still. Chunks of sunlight found their way through the shutters onto his paintings: seascapes and galleons straining against the swell and Bella's own drawing of a fishing boat in Margate harbour. The childlike outlines appeared sketchy and faded by the sun, but her memory of their trips to the seaside remained sharp and true, as if they were still happening, some-where: a recurring daylight dream. She recalled settling down on the harbour arm, the pair of them sketching, painting; her father nipping from his hip flask as the sea breeze picked up, talking about art and colour and perspective and life; waves slapping the sea wall, raining them with foam. Laughter; the seagulls joining in.

He often left her, during those afternoons, for an hour or so, while he saw to some business or other in the town, and she felt quite happy with a paper cone of salty cockles, waiting for his return. They'd always pack up and leave quickly after that, the day done with, her father silent and inward, something on his mind.

She peered at the picture. Yes, the dried drops of sea water were still visible, enhancing the sketch, her father would say. He'd framed it and tacked it up between his own canvases, its wonky lines amusing him no end.

The room proved familiar and comforting: the applewood logs in the grate, the leather chair and, faintly, the smell of oil paint. His artist's clutter had evidently been tidied away. She ran her finger-tips over book spines – weather almanacs, and ancient encyclopae-dias – and over the desk of smoothest walnut. She lifted the lid on the ink well. Yes, full to the brim for when he came home. She checked the drawer – tucked under the desk where her father's knees would go. Yes, locked fast. All as it should be.

She sat down and closed her eyes. There had been a time when she had been small and engulfed by this creaky chair, her feet drumming mid-air. She could feel sunlight through the study window burning deliciously through her closed lids. Her father used to tell her – and she would listen hard – about how the seasons changed, and how the tides turned, how the mysterious rule of twelve governed the incoming surge. He told her sea stories, tales that she'd heard before deep in the well of childhood, and yet wanted to listen to time and again. He warned her that, even though she may want it to, she should never expect life to stay the same.

Bella opened her eyes. Dollops of sun danced on the drinks trolley against the wall. Carafes filled with dark liquids sparkled. Chunky cut-glass tumblers stacked neatly. One enticingly emerald-green bottle winked at her.

She hauled herself out of the chair.

When he got home from his week's work, her father would pour from this green bottle into a tumbler. Water, clear water, he'd told her, to which he added ice, something fizzy and a lemon slice. And he'd sit in his leather chair, loosen his necktie, let himself drift off, straying far from being Lieutenant Nathaniel Calloway of the Royal Navy, his eyes wandering past her through his window, beyond the confines of the Hall.

'One for the road, Bella,' he used to say. 'Bottoms up.' Or, 'Got to get my sea legs.'

Bella unstoppered the cork and inhaled the fragrance of herbs, cut grass, thinking it an odd way for water to smell. It reminded her of her father, of walks over the water meadows behind the Hall: pools reflecting clouds, birds darting from cover, the Thanet plain shimmering towards the invisible sea.

She took a gulp and liquid fire exploded in her head. She spat, let out a horrified wail, but the dreadful sourness continued, consuming her. The pleasant scent inside the bottle had not prepared her for this poison. It turned on her, burning, would be with her for ever. She crammed her fingers against her mouth to wipe the vileness away.

The door burst open.

'What was that noise? What are you doing in here!' Her grandmother descended on her, brittle and thin, and ferocious.

The bottle slipped from her hand and shattered on the floor, chaotic and uncivilised, the glass dangerous and wet.

'Look at the mess you've made! Look at it!'

Her grandmother's furious gaze zipped from one part of the disaster to another. When it landed on Bella, she paused, twitched her head. A dribble oozed from Bella's mouth and snaked around the buttons on the front of her dress.

'Look at you...'

She flapped her hands, the part of her grandmother that bothered Bella the most. The skin wrinkled with age, but at the end of her tapering fingers, the nails were as pale and smooth as a baby's.

Dizzy and nauseous, Bella trembled. The taste in her mouth, sickening.

'That's your father's gin,' Freda seethed. 'What has that expensive boarding school taught you? Little thief.'

Bella darted past her and out the door, her grandmother's anger following her across the hallway and out of the front door.

'Isobel! Where do you think you are going!'

Bella kept running. Over the gravel, along the hedge-lined drive, through the front gate. She did not stop until she'd pounded halfway down the lane, her eyes smarting, the gin lingering sour and bitter and dreadful. But not as dreadful as her grandmother's anger.

She bent double by the sign that pointed with a finger *To Farthing Hall* and regurgitated the liquid onto the verge. Behind the milestone across the lane, trees rose in misty layers of green, the darkness, an enticing blur. For some reason or another, she had always been discouraged from going into the woods. Her mother did not want her running wild like a village urchin so her playground had been the tranquil water meadows on the other side of the house. She'd imagined that she'd get lost in the woods. She'd imagined a haunt of witches who might put little girls in a pot, or mischievous sprites who'd steal her from her parents.

She wiped her mouth on her sleeve, thinking of her grandmother's shrieking, her rudeness, her anger, which would be worse, far worse, if she could see her crossing the road, squeezing through the stile and pushing into the embrace of the trees. Bella smiled, inhaling the sweet air. At seventeen, she could do what she liked. She slipped into the wood and began to run with the free spirit of the child she once had been, her footsteps disturbing the clean earth-mould smell, she, a small noise in the vast cathedral space. The trees welcomed her, the canopy chattering with birds. She knew the trees, almost all of them, for her father had lots of nature books. She patted the trunks as she passed: hawthorn, birch, ash.

Stopping in a patch of dappled shade, she licked her lips, amazed at how a mouthful of gin could alter so much the flesh of her tongue. She peered into the dark dells, into glades beyond banks of nettle and fern, the wood deeper than she thought possible. The stillness felt like a presence, smiling at her.

She nibbled a thick blade of grass and the juice worked to ease the taste in her mouth. She plucked another and felt better. Then she plunged on. What would her grandmother say if she knew? She knew her mother would be concerned but her father wouldn't mind; he never minded about anything.

Laughing, she broke from the cover straight into sunlight and she stopped, blinking.

In a patchwork of light and shade ran a high flint wall. And above it, a chimney stack, a roof with tiles slipping: an astonishing little cottage. Sunlight caught on windows where stained glass shimmered like orange jewels. She picked her way out of the undergrowth. Any movement would shatter the spell, make everything disappear. For this house, like in a fairy tale, would vanish at any second. This house could only exist in the bedtime stories her father had perhaps once told her and that she had, perhaps, forgotten.

Bella's foot cracked a twig. She stopped. Dared not breath. But the cottage remained. She wished she'd brought her sketchbook for she wanted to draw it, instantly. In the centre of the wall sat an arched wooden door, shut fast. And next to it, the stump of a tree that had been felled long ago. Bella stepped on it, found a hold in nooks in the brickwork, her fingers deep in ivy. On tiptoes, she peered over.

Around an unruly patch of lawn bloomed snowy roses. *In need of a good prune*, her mother would say, but Bella thought them worthy of the convent garden she'd visited in the Alps. She leant on top of the wall, mesmerised; the garden looked serene, neglected, a sleeping, perfumed sanctuary. The roses cast shadows over dandelion-studded grass, and with it, little footprints through Bella's memory.

'I know this place,' she whispered. 'This is mine. This is where I am meant to be.'

She jumped down and grasped the cobwebbed hoop of iron on the door and pushed. The old wood complained, resisted her. A mass of weeds had grown to block her way. But she heaved until the gap was wide enough for her to slip through and hop her way, ankles tangled, onto the path. If a witch had ever lived here, she'd be long gone.

The garden smelt heady and damp. Dark corners, rampant and untamed. But the roses nodded, like breezy snowflakes, petals littering the earth. Around their feet grew rosemary and meadowsweet and other herbs whose scents and names tickled her mind. She looked at the cottage and felt she gazed at the face of a lonely old friend. She shook her head at a slow-approaching memory, as if it were naughty.

A blackbird sang and, following the sound, she noticed a window of milky glass next to the front door. It was open a chink. She poked her nose into the gap. Inside, the deep corners looked velvety. A memory, like sweetness, like bread and butter all rolled in to one, bowled around her head. A lady smiling down at her in the sunshine. Shoes with one darling button, and a dress with a tatty hem. Arms scooping her up and holding her close, and Bella – small, curled up, sleepy – resting her head while contemplating white roses. And, miraculously, her father stood right next to her.

She opened the door and stepped inside, inhaling the old breath of the empty kitchen: wood, ashes and spice. A tap dripped through a door in the far wall. The old range looked dead, but she could hear the chink of the kettle against it. The flagstone floor, dusty; a broom propped in the corner, bristles upwards. Stairs rose enticingly up into sunlight, but she resisted. She was trespassing and should only stay a moment. She'd allow herself to touch one thing, and one thing only.

A cubbyhole by the hearth caught her eye and she tiptoed over. A large book with a cracked spine and curling pages rested there. A stranger's life, a stranger's belongings. The dresser shelves were scattered with rock crystals, cloudy bottles of liquid, like a sorcerer's haven, everything covered with a film of dust: forgotten, preserved, as if waiting for someone to come and claim it.

Bella stepped back and her foot crunched on dried leaves, blown through in autumn storms. The noise startled her and the taste of gin returned, sour in her mouth. Confusion melted into fear. The cottage was asking her to leave.

She darted for the door, her blood thin and her lungs breathless, scooted across the ragged lawn, brushing roses, thorns tugging her sleeve. Once through the wooden door, she hauled it back behind her to shut away the strange waiting feeling, shut away the memory, the watchfulness of the place.

She ran and the wood swallowed her. Dense nettles corralled her, brambles snagged. She may never be found, lost forever. The trees, once her friends, conspired to trap her. But she must find home, she must face her punishment: for sneaking into her father's study, for smashing the bottle, her trespass, being caught.

Daylight glowed at the edge of the woods and she broke through the trees onto the lane much further up than she expected, right by the church. A stitch split her side, her breath grated in and out of her lungs but on she ran, jubilant now, through the waving grass that comforted the graves and where birds swooped in golden air, gorging on insects. She scooted past her grandfather's pristine tomb. But Bella paid no heed to old Digby, the craggy man in the photograph. No one talked about him, anyway.

21

Bella gazed down from the Widow's Watch at Farthing: the handful of houses, the church, the lane snaking through. The woods, thick with summer leaf, felt strangely closer, even from up here. She willed a line of chimney smoke to rise from the trees.

She ran her finger over the dirty windowpane. This funny little room felt perfect, with a spot for her easel next to the old telescope. She would order paints from Winsor and Newton, more brushes, canvases. She would make it perfect. Her mother often praised her for how tidy she kept her bedroom: childhood dolls in a row, her books lined up on the shelves, hairbrushes and ribbons neatly aligned, everything in place on her dressing table. And her studio would be as neat, or she else would not be able to paint.

Last night, her mother had looked her up and down and announced she'd like to take her up to Bond Street to get a whole wardrobe of grown-up clothes. But what was the point when they would only get covered in paint? Bella wondered what the ladies at the Slade wore at their easels.

She caught a flash of metal at the corner of her eye. The car turned off the lane, disappeared between the oaks. She gave a squeal, rushed down the spiral stairs, banging through the baize door, thundered down the staircase and made it through the front door before he'd even cranked the handbrake on. She scooted past her mother and grandmother who were waiting at the bottom of the steps and went clattering over the stones to hug him.

'My goodness, El... K... Bella.' Nathan's words stumbled as he got out of the car. He slipped off his hat, his grey temples bright against the patch of scarred skin, his startled eyes darkening, his gaze dancing over Bella's face.

Her grandmother made a strange, sharp noise in her throat.

Bella laughed. The girls at school often moaned about parents rattling through a line of siblings before they got to their name, especially when cross. Her father must have been thinking of a cousin, or someone.

And he didn't look cross. He looked tired.

'Let a man get out of his car, at least, my girl,' he said.

They all gathered around him.

'Hasn't Bella changed, Nathan?' Her mother sounded perky. 'We all think so. Grown up so much these last few months.'

'My goodness, so you have, young lady.' His smile was weak, his eyes darting between them all.

'It's been ages, Dad,' Bella said. 'I've got so much to tell you. About school, my painting, everything.'

'Not right now, Bella,' her mother said. 'Give him a moment to catch his breath.'

Her father shut the car door with a clunk. 'I'm sorry about not being there at Victoria this time.'

'It doesn't matter, I'm home, you're home.'

'That I am. We're all here. Vivi, darling. Mother.'

'Well, you certainly do have something to tell your father, Isobel,' said her grandmother, dressed in customary black, muttering like a disgruntled nun. 'About the *gin*.'

The word curled off her tongue, sounding as poisonous as the alcohol.

'Oh, that can wait, surely,' said her mother.

Her father looked amused. 'What have you done now, Bella?' He opened the boot and hauled out his suitcase. 'Now you mention gin, Mother, I could do with a snifter after the day I've had.'

'That can be arranged.'

The two elder ladies linked their arms either side of him, proprietorially and competitively, leaving Bella to follow the group back up the steps.

'Oh, but Dad, there's something else,' she said, wanting his attention, again. 'I didn't tell you Mama, and Grannie, but I found this dear lovely cottage in the woods!'

'What?' The question stayed behind her grandmother's teeth. She dropped her son's arm, turned, fixed Bella with her frightening stare.

Her mother looked around more slowly, as if it hurt her to do so, her face tight with pain as she glanced at Nathan, her teeth showing in a hesitant smile, as if smiling would do her harm.

'A cottage, you say?' he ventured.

'Oh, it was old and abandoned, tumbledown. You know, like from a fairy tale. But no one lives there. I checked. Is it yours, Dad?'

His face did the same thing it used to when he came to collect her from the harbour, on their day trips to Margate: stifled, as if he were seeking something far away.

Bella waited, her excitement falling flat on the ground between her and her family trio. They stood, frozen, together at the top of the steps, as if caught off guard in a photograph.

'It belongs to the estate,' her father said, at last. 'It's the old gamekeeper's cottage. My goodness...'

He puffed out his breath, his face colouring. He looked at her mother, and Bella saw that usual conspiratorial look between them, the one that she had always thought of as their private love, their bond, something she could be secure in, and proud of. But this time, they shut her out.

'Good God,' he said, rather loudly. 'I had forgotten all about it.'

* * *

Bella found her father after dinner up in the Widow's Watch, staring at the view. The swallows, darting arrows against the pale evening sky, looked an eternity away. And yet Bella heard their peeping calls. There'd be a long hot Indian summer if swallows flew high; she read it in one of her father's almanacs. He turned at the sound of her.

'I am sorry for breaking your bottle of gin, Dad. But Grannie did rather surprise me, bursting in like that.'

'I can't have you *drinking*, Bella. It's bad enough for Grannie when I do it,' he said, supressing a smile, trying to sound cross.

'But I didn't actually *like* it. It was awful.'

He gave in, began to chuckle.

'That's probably a good thing.'

She still wondered what had possessed her.

'What are you doing up here? Having some peace and quiet?' she asked. 'Grannie can be so intense sometimes, don't you think?'

She wondered, for one ridiculous moment, whether he might be looking for the cottage, seeing as he had forgotten about it.

He sighed. 'I can imagine you up here, you know, Bella,' he said, 'painting away.'

'I've been making plans. The easel can go right here. I sent off a new order for paint only this afternoon, and sable brushes. Stocking up on Lamp Black and Ultramarine. Plenty of Titanium.'

'You'll need an ocean of that. I always did,' he said. 'The light up here is wonderful. Why I never thought of using this room for painting, I don't know. It was always out of bounds when I was a boy; my grandfather's private eyrie, with the telescope and all.' He ran his fingertips over the windowsill, the creases between his eyes deepening. 'Good, you've dusted.'

'Where did you paint, then? In your bedroom?'

'Yes, Digby did not approve. Mother didn't mind so much, but I had to sketch in my room, keep myself out of sight. I had to hide away my artistic side. It was an embarrassment, and I certainly wasn't manly enough for old Digby.' His face hardened on a memory, his eyes caressing the light-filled space.

It struck Bella, then, that he always used his father's first name and yet it did the opposite of what she thought it should. It distanced him, sounded more formal than *Father*, as if he hadn't known him at all.

'Thank goodness for my art teacher at Le Chable,' she said. 'Such care and encouragement, which I didn't appreciate at the time. She was lovely but always had such private sadness, you know?'

'One of those middle-aged ladies whose face reveals their lovely youth?'

'Exactly. I used to think that perhaps she had lost a sweetheart in the war. But then the girls told me she was Jewish. Lost her entire family.'

Her father flinched. 'When terrible things happen... This is why you should grasp life, Bella, and do what you want to do. I know you want to go to art school. To the Slade. And I think you should apply. I couldn't do any of that. Lots of things got in the way. The war for one...'

'But you found Mama, didn't you?'

'Found? Your mother does think that it was rather as if it had been pre-ordained, cooked up by our parents. But I think it was pure luck. I was always surprised, and grateful, that she agreed to marry me. I mean, look at her. And she had it tough too. Remember, she lost her parents, and I was injured at the start of it all. She was stuck here with *my* parents.' He looked at her. 'Don't tell Grannie I said that.'

'Poor Mama,' Bella said. 'But at least she had you, and then she had me. And all the money.'

'*Bella*,' he said, and yet his indulgence sliced through the short-lived anger. 'With an expensive education in Switzerland, my girl, you should know better than to say something like that. As for the money, your mother's inheritance, it saved Farthing Hall.'

'*Saved* it?'

'Yes, when Digby died. Look, there were years, for most of the war, when we, when Farthing Hall, went through a torrid time. And that is putting it mildly.'

'And Mama saved you all?'

Nathan lifted one shoulder defensively and thrust his hands into his pockets. He turned to the window, peered out towards the wood.

'This is a discussion for later. Much later. When you turn eighteen.'

That seemed a lifetime away.

'I don't care about the money, Dad. I am sorry that I said that.'

He had his back to her. She noticed his shoulders drooping. She wanted to ask again what he thought of the Slade, of her going to London, to live in the city, become an artist, *be* an artist. But, looking at the back of her father's head, the way he held himself, something told her that that, also, needed to be a discussion for another time.

He had been quiet for some minutes and she went to stand beside him, her eyes hooked on the horizon of wooded hills, feeling time pressing in on her, an urgency to get on with her life. She wanted to ask him about the cottage, the white roses, the lady with the buttoned shoes. He *must* remember for he had been there. Perhaps they had visited a tenant in the cottage, or had simply walked past and had been invited in for tea. The elusive joy of being in a beautiful place with a beautiful lady drifted at the corner of her mind.

Surely, he would recall it better than she could, for it happened in a time before she had any memory.

She glanced sideways, opened her mouth to speak, but saw that her father's cheeks were washed with tears, which dripped silently off his chin. She moved away, hoping he hadn't seen her notice.

* * *

The following day, Bella made it to the stable yard as Rob was loading his suitcase into the back of his father's car. Her mother emerged from the stall, her face flushed, her eyes bright from her morning ride, though her outfit was otherwise immaculate. She lingered to chat with Mr Buckley.

'Oh yes, old lady Snowdrop had quite a canter. She's doing well...'

Bella walked over to the car.

'Off so soon?' she asked Rob.

'Back to the smoke,' he said, shutting the boot.

'Where in the smoke do you live?' she asked, light and breezy.

'It's a house in Hammersmith. With the quintessential dragon landlady. But at least I have a bathroom to myself. And a door that locks.'

She tried to picture Hammersmith, wondered now far west it lay.

'Did you know I am applying for art college? It will be nice to be in the city,' she said, not quite believing herself. 'Nice' didn't sound like the appropriate word. 'Away from this backwater.'

Rob flicked his eyes to the treetops, to the woods billowing on the horizon.

'Not much wrong with Farthing,' he said. 'I often miss it.' He caught her eye. 'But you will be fine, Bella. In fact, you will be wonderful.'

She had to look away from his face and her cheeks burnt, as if she had been staring at the sun.

'Not sure about *wonderful*.'

'Now, stop that, Bella.' He lowered his voice, 'I'll have none of that.'

She caught a tenderness in the way he said her name. She had not had much of a chance to chat with him this weekend, ask him about his job, his life in London.

'Perhaps, if I get a place at the Slade,' she said, 'and I make it to—'

'Well, goodbye, Rob.' Her mother approached, interrupting them. She unstrapped her hat and her fair hair sprang free, cut these days into a glorious, thick bob.

The breeze whipped the straggly ends of Bella's dark hair over her eyes, and she felt she should not stand next to her mother, for the comparison, the difference, would be far too great.

'This was short but sweet. Thank you again for collecting Bella for us.'

'Not a problem at all, Mrs Calloway. It was important to get her home.'

Her mother gave a little wave of her fingers and set off back to the house, while Mr Buckley climbed into the driver's seat and fired the engine.

'All set, son.'

He looked out of the car window, from Rob to Bella and back again, his eyes opaque with speculation.

'Bye then, Bella,' Rob said.

He hurried around the car, got in, shut the door, and before she knew it, the vehicle was trundling off over the cobbles, so achingly slowly that Bella felt she could easily sprint, overtake it, put her hand up to halt it as if she were a traffic policeman.

She stayed rooted to the spot, split in two by urge and loss, and an instinct to follow.

22

VIVI

At last, Freda was going up to bed. Vivi watched her mother-in-law haul herself out of her chair and walk slowly to the door, wondering how long it would be before they would need to hire a live-in nurse to help her. She also wondered when Freda might finally give up wearing widow's black. Perhaps nearly two decades could not be sufficient time to mourn an odd-fish, hateful husband?

Nathan didn't seem to notice his mother leave the room. He poured himself a gin and tonic, then offered Vivi one. She declined.

The French windows stood open to the summer evening. She admired the room lavished with silks and fine wallpaper, palpable symbols of her wealth, glimmering in the sinking sun. As always, she hoped she did not come across as too flash, too American. As a nod of appeasement, she had kept the old, foxed mirror belonging to Freda and had hung it behind the drinks table, a contrast to her modern refinements.

Through the war years, Vivi had been stifled, a dutiful daughter-in-law. But when Digby died, her money had spoken, the old bones of the house finally repaired and watertight. Forgiving Nathan and taking on Kate, naming her Isobel, calling her Bella, had shocked Freda.

But not Genna.

'Isn't this exactly what Park Avenue princesses do?' Genna had laughed, something Vivi had not seen her do in a while. 'Show a bit of guts, and look mighty fine while they do it?'

More than that, bringing up Bella, caring for her had helped Vivi break free from her own grief. Prove something; show them all.

'Did you notice, this weekend?' Vivi said, wakening Nathan from his musings. 'Bella and Robin? They seem to have gotten rather soft on each other.'

'I've always thought it. I've seen the signs,' he said. 'And I am not entirely happy about it.'

'What, because he is the son of our employee? He is a fine young man. There is a certain confidence about him. That's the thing about the English.' She gave a light laugh, still self-conscious about their differences after all this time. 'The class thing. We Americans seem to have broken that down these days.'

'Ah, but, as we know,' said Nathan, switching his gaze to her. 'Class in this case doesn't fully come into it.'

She flinched. Isobel, Bella, the child from a different world, another class. But when she'd entered Vivi's life, the barriers had broken down. Vivi had become herself and the child her own.

'Then you being unhappy about it, Nathan,' she said cautiously, 'doesn't entirely make sense.'

'All I know is it won't please Mother.'

Vivi stood up to switch on the lamp to distract herself from a flash of annoyance. The pool of light in the corner made the rest of the room suddenly seem darker, the evening sky outside a limpid blue.

'Bella asked me, again, this evening why I wasn't able to meet her from Victoria,' Nathan said. 'She was teasing, but I knew she was disappointed.'

'She must realise you had something very important to do instead, needing to break your little tradition. And she seemed mighty pleased that Rob was there to step in.'

Vivi waited for him to respond, and the silence filled with the same-old thought, banked away like a smouldering coal under ashes, a presence, glowing at the back of her mind. The secret they kept from Bella.

'How is Elise then?' she asked.

Nathan shot her a look. 'Where is Bella, Vivi?' he mouthed.

'Upstairs in the Widow's Watch, sorting out her studio. She has her transistor on. She won't hear us.'

He glanced at the closed door. 'If you say so,' he uttered, warily. 'Elise is much the same, I expect. I did not have time to see her on this visit. I simply signed the papers necessary with the matron for the new treatment by the doctor. That's all I can tell you.'

Something in his passive stance irritated her.

'You can perhaps tell me how you feel now that Bella has discovered the cottage,' Vivi said. 'That was a shock. Did you see Freda's face? Bella was going to stumble on it at some point. It was inevitable. It is all inevitable. We said that we would approach the whole matter when she turns eighteen. Let her know about her mother. But perhaps now is the time.'

'Mother is not at all keen,' he said. 'She is concerned that when word gets out, which as you say, will be inevitable, that people – the good folk of Farthing – will say it is history repeating itself. People have long memories around here. They will remember what happened to Charlotte Hoodless.'

'None of us can forget Charlotte Hoodless,' said Vivi.

'The gossip raged then. It has been a long dark shadow over

our family. Mother suffered badly with it, with the shame. Of course, Digby, well, it seemed he didn't care less.'

'Can't you see, then, how the consequences here are clearly different?' Vivi said.

She walked over to the drinks table and decanted a tot of red wine.

'Nathan, you cannot keep comparing yourself to Digby. And Freda should not either. If you were truly like him, I'd have packed my bags years ago. Would be back in America. You have taken good care of Elise all this time.' She had tried to sound assertive, but it came out resentful. 'And, frankly, it is no one else's business, but ours.'

She caught sight of herself in Freda's mirror; her reflection appeared tired, anger and unhappiness simmering below the surface of her skin. Behind her, she could see Nathan's silent, stricken face, staring at her back, the looking glass showing her a distorted image, presenting two entirely different people.

'And I mean that business is *ours*,' she said.

* * *

Vivi hadn't been back to Margate since her honeymoon but had lived for a long time inside the memory of the shower of rain, she and Nathan sheltering together, her wet shoes and stockings, urgent happiness back in their room.

She drove along the seafront past the Sands Hotel, past the golden beach peppered with bodies, swimmers bobbing in white-crested waves. Clamouring voices and children's shrieks, the jingling music from a seaside organ filled her open car window like a puff of candied joy. How different it all seemed; how busy with laughter, balloons and funfair sounds. What contrast to the bleak, wartime summer of their honeymoon, the beaches hemmed in by barbed wire, and planes patrolling the skies.

On the curved road along the clifftop, she wondered how many buildings had air-raid scars papered over them, jollied up for the new generation, the teenage girls and Teddy boys posing outside the arcades who, rightly so, had distanced themselves from the troubled past. She stopped the car by the railings along the esplanade on the clifftop and cranked on the handbrake.

Vivi peered through the car window at the nursing home. She had memorised the address years before, after finding the paperwork in Nathan's locked drawer in his desk. She, of course, knew exactly where he kept the key. She had often envisaged this very terrace of white stucco buildings where Elise resided but had not seen Elise, that slender, fragile creature, since she spied on her at the cottage in the woods. It proved hard to picture her now.

She climbed the steps of Edgar House, and pressed the doorbell, a rod of nerves hardening in her middle. When she'd telephoned to arrange this visit – one day last week when she had the Hall to herself – the nurse on the other end of the line had asked for her reason. What could she tell her? That she wanted to see for herself where her money had been going these past fourteen years? That she wanted to check up on the blood mother of her beloved adopted daughter? That she felt curious? In the end she'd lied and said she would be attending in place of Mr Calloway, as he had been indisposed.

A nurse opened the door, showed her across a polished parquet floor into a waiting room with armchairs, vases of flowers, well-thumbed magazines. Vivi caught the vague smell of luncheon having been served and sensed a subdued air, as if everyone there, including the staff, had been anaesthetised for their own good. Tea was offered but before she had time to take a sip, Matron slipped in, sat at the desk in the corner, and indicated that Vivi should take a seat opposite her.

She moved some paperwork in front of her, looked at Vivi, tilted her head to one side.

'And how may we help you today, madam?'

'I'm Mrs Nathaniel Calloway. I telephoned for a visitation request last week, and I have my husband's paperwork concerning Miss Drake here.' She rummaged in her handbag and pulled out a buff envelope.

'Ah yes, Mr Calloway.'

Matron's eyes softened, remembering perhaps Nathan's handsome but ravaged face. The woman's gaze fixed on the buckle of Vivi's Dior handbag, and Vivi could tell that the woman was grasping her status. She looked far too young to be a matron, and Vivi supposed *her* status had been accelerated by nursing during the war.

She wondered whether her couture suit with its nipped-in waist, worn as armour, made her look matronly instead.

'Does it include the document of incarceration? We always need to see that.'

'Incarceration?' Vivi felt her chest tighten, willed her face to stay straight. 'Do you mean this? This form is signed and dated back in 1945 by my husband, who, as I explained on the telephone, is somewhat indisposed at present.'

Vivi waited as Matron leafed through the papers, concentrating on the sound of the pages moving against one another so she did not have to think about the information they contained.

'I see, Mrs Calloway, yes that all seems in order. We do have to check, you understand. I will take you up to Miss Drake. Please, do come this way.'

That self-assured smile again. A sharpness in her face, efficiency glittering in her eyes, her surprising youth making Vivi feel entirely dull and middle-aged.

Vivi stood, her legs weak with dread, and followed Matron out of the room and across the hallway to the grand staircase, almost feeling her way, her heels silent on the thick carpet. The place felt pleasant enough, and she pictured Nathan making this same ascent during his monthly visits, the times he left young Bella down by the harbour with her pad and pencils while he went to see her mother. Vivi had never asked about the visits, or asked about Elise, for she had never wanted to pry. But, she realised, that made her appear as if she didn't care. She should have asked, for then she would know, and have more to be able to tell Bella, when the time came.

'I'm afraid Miss Drake will not know me,' said Vivi, as they reached the landing. 'For we have never met before.'

'There is no need to worry on that account,' Matron said in a professional half-whisper as she led the way along a landing. 'I'm afraid Miss Drake doesn't know anyone at all.'

She stopped in front of a closed door with a number on it, like a hotel, and pulled out a ring of keys.

'Are you ready, Mrs Calloway?'

Vivi swallowed, a hard lump in her throat. The real reason for her visit hit her: the love she had for Bella that had grown inside her from the moment she took her in her arms in the kitchen at Farthing Hall. She and Nathan had agreed, a long while ago, Freda reluctantly, to tell Bella everything when she turned eighteen, next year. But Vivi already felt Bella's suffering, as if it were a stitch going through her skin. Bella's pain would be inevitable, and Vivi never wanted it to happen today or tomorrow, ever. If Vivi could see Elise, speak to her, lay the ghosts and the conjecture to the past, extinguish the mystery for herself, then perhaps she could do so for Bella.

She gave a hesitant nod. Matron turned the key and opened the door.

Hazy light shimmered through tall double-aspect windows, the view filtered by something Vivi could not make out, the sea-horizon a suggestion beyond. The room seemed darker than it should on such a sunny day and Vivi's mind whirled to keep up as her eyes darted against sharp beams and patches of shadow, alighting on hunks of driftwood, shells and all manner of beach-combed treasures spilling out of dishes and teacups, scattered on tables and shelves. Embroidered naïve waves, fish and mermaids colonised cushions and quilts. A bed lay in the corner. A breeze danced through open sashes, bringing in salt-fresh air, filling the room with the sea and a clacking, clicking sound.

Over the headrest of the armchair, facing the window, lay a blanket, decorated with seaweed patterns. Above it, the back of its occupant's head, dark hair striped with strands of grey, the nape of her neck pale as she bent to her needle and thread.

Vivi squinted against the light. Over the windows, top to bottom, dangled shells and chalk-pebbles, like beaded curtains, threaded onto knotted string, offering their clacking chorus.

'Elise?' Matron cleared her throat. 'Mrs Calloway is here to see you.'

The woman in the chair looked around and struck Vivi with a surprising, trusting smile, her eyes luminous, lively. She bundled her sewing into the corner of the chair, stood and offered Vivi her hand, as weightless and as tender as a bird's wing. Elise's angles appeared sharp, her joints jutting, not quite filling her clothes. The skin on her face too tight for her bones. She retracted at Vivi's touch, folding her hands at her waist, drumming large knuckles against her side. Vivi stared at her hair, which was arranged clumsily over her forehead to disguise the indent in her temple, the injury from her fall in the cottage garden after her seizure.

Elise's gaze flicked beyond Vivi to Matron and her eyes widened with fear.

'It's Mrs Calloway,' Matron soothed her. 'Your visitor. We told you about it this morning.'

Elise cocked her head as if following the name as it echoed around the room.

Vivi glanced at Matron, who gave a curt nod.

'Do you mind if I sit, Elise?' she asked.

Elise fluttered her fingers towards the other armchair.

'Are we having tea?' Elise asked, settling herself down, like a child expecting candy floss. 'We always have tea here. It's the thing I like the most.'

'I will ring for it,' Matron said. She pressed a bell by the fireplace, and sat in another chair by the window.

Vivi glanced down at the view of the seafront, then at another over the top of the music hall set into the cliff, her head empty, her words, and her reason for being there, failing. Seagulls wheeled against the blue.

'I see you have lovely views here, Elise, on the corner of the house. And right on the esplanade.'

Elise seemed to be listening to something inside herself.

'I see the sea, I taste the sea. I smell it,' she said, her words a light song, scattering notes. 'I like to hear it in my room at night. All night. There's a sound that comes off the water, like music, like voices, like breathing, always there. I sleep with my window open.' She peered at Vivi's face as if in recognition. She recoiled. 'I don't care how cold I get. They take me to the sea sometimes.'

'That must be nice.'

'Oh no, not that sea.' Elise prodded her finger in the air. 'They can't fool me. That's the wrong sea out there. Not the place I know. It should be the cove with the chalk stack. Where the waves nearly caught us.' She exhaled a ragged giggling sigh. She pressed her fingertips to her shin. 'I fell on the rocks and hurt my leg. It still hurts sometimes. Botany Bay, they call it. But I call it our bay. Where I am happy. Oh, but he's not there any more,' said Elise. 'The boy on the beach. Well, anyway, he is not here today.'

Vivi glanced at Matron. 'Who does she mean?'

Matron shook her head.

Vivi prickled. She'd heard of the bay. Was it the beach Nathan had wanted to take them to on their honeymoon, their jaunt curtailed by the pouring rain?

Elise stood, went over to the fireplace.

'Don't you love a good fire, madam? I do,' she said. 'They allow it sometimes. This ash here, see?' She prodded the hearth with a poker. 'I like to burn seaweed.'

She knelt by the bucket set on the hearthstone and pulled out strands of bladderwrack, wet and oily looking. Vivi breathed in the strong briny fragrance, watching as Elise scooped dripping stacks of it into the hearth.

'The boy.' Matron leant towards Vivi and whispered. 'She means, of course, Mr Calloway. She calls him the boy on the beach. We find it quite charming. She is always so much calmer when he is here. But after he leaves, she is bereft.'

Vivi's eyes blurred with tears. Freda, in one of her angrier moments, had once called Elise a fallen woman. And as she watched Elise try to untangle the seaweed, chattering to herself, Vivi felt that indeed she could be, but in an entirely unexpected way.

Falling in love with Nathan had been easy for Vivi, and she could see how easy it would have been for Elise too. Elise had nursed Nathan at the hospital, or at least helped him, that much he'd told her, and at the time it had been all she wanted to hear. Elise had been the volunteer who had provided the seaweed poultice, or at least her mother had: the curious Mrs Drake. The strands of the truth unravelled occasionally, revealing to Vivi a little bit more. But most of it could stay in other people's memories; she did not want it in hers.

And now, watching Elise searching the mantelpiece for the matches, which Vivi assumed Matron kept locked away elsewhere, she decided that Elise could be forgiven; that she did not deserve any form of punishment. Wasn't this enough?

Outside the bizarre little room, more shell grotto than living chamber, Vivi sensed the lively summer's day. Laughter and holiday mood. Gulls calling, a motor car or two passing by. Someone must have their windows open, the radio up high. Vivi heard a snatch, a jumpy, vibrant tune, the sound of America. Buddy Holly singing that he guessed it didn't matter any more. That poor tragic boy, she thought, dead at twenty-two.

Why, she wondered, had Elise referred to Nathan as a boy? Had they known each other as children? Anger and mistrust flared, a heat under her hairline. Everything she and Nathan had been through: their personal trauma, through the war years, together and alone, and all the while, Elise had been at the back of his mind.

Elise abandoned her hunt along the mantelpiece, slinked back to her chair and curled herself up in it, languid like a cat. Vivi, with a flash of bitter fascination, felt reminded of Bella, the way Bella moved her body. Nathan could have done what his father had done to Charlotte Hoodless and cut Elise off completely. Abandoned her, thrown her to the mercy of the outside world. And, in a similar way, Freda had ensured Mrs Hoodless and her baby had a place to rest, though somewhere anonymous and forlorn.

Vivi felt proud of Nathan for proving himself and providing care for this vulnerable creature. A flame of respect for Freda ignited, and Vivi's anger finally gave up the ghost. Her love for Nathan rose and expanded to fill another empty space inside her.

Elise laughed, wiping her wet hands down her dress.

'I'm waiting for Ma to visit,' she said. 'She hasn't been in a long time. Probably off gallivanting with her beau. She lost my father but found Mr Buckley, you know, and he found her. They love each other.'

Vivi thought of the steward's stricken face, his silence, on the day of Annie Drake's funeral.

Elise sprang back up and took an old music box from the mantel. She set it on her lap and began to wind the key.

Matron leaned towards Vivi, her voice low, professional and cold beneath the tinkling music: 'Don't look so worried, Mrs Calloway. The papers your husband signed the other week were to agree to some new treatment, some therapy, to help her memory. It's a pioneering regime. Rather experimental if you ask me.'

'Not working, is it?'

'Give it time, madam.'

'Time?' Elise jerked, focusing on Vivi. 'Ma will explain to you, madam, when she gets here. Time is not linear. Time goes round in circles, she said so. In her journal. Have you seen it? Now, where is it? I thought it was here. Nothing goes forward or backward, you see. Oh no, madam, don't see time as one long endless tunnel. Everything is happening, all at once. All of it. Good things and bad things. All at the same time. Ma will explain. When will she be coming again?'

The tune wheezed out of the music box and sent a shivering memory through her. Beethoven. The song Freda used to play.

'What a lovely tune,' Vivi blurted out, struggling for something to say.

'Ah, you seem like a nice lady.' Elise's face softened, the worries of where her mother might be vanished. 'Would you like it? Here, please take it.'

She snapped the lid shut, snuffing the music, and handed the box to Vivi.

'This is most unusual,' Matron said. 'She never lets it out of her sight.'

'Thank you, Elise,' Vivi said. 'If you are sure?'

'Yes. Ma loves it too. If you see her, will you be sure to tell her?'

'Elise,' Vivi said, leaning forward in her chair to snare her flickering expression. 'I'm afraid to say that I have bad news.'

Her mouth dried. She inhaled, could taste the seaweed brine in the air, a damp, brackish tang.

'Your mother. Your Ma. Annie. I'm so dreadfully sorry. She has passed away.'

Elise's eyes darted to Matron, back to Vivi. 'Passed away?' Her lips smacked together. 'What does she mean?'

Matron stood and rested her hand on Elise's shoulder.

'We've been here before, haven't we, Elise?'

Elise smiled up at Matron, then threw Vivi a confused flicker.

'Passed away.' She mused on the expression, savouring it. She lifted her hand to the damaged part of her head and tenderly drummed her fingers over it. 'I see. Yes. Oh, I see. Is that so?'

Vivi leant over, wanting to take Elise's agitated hands and steady them, but Elise flicked her away, bent double in the chair, and covered her face with her palms. She rocked back and forth. A moan spiralled from her mouth, a dreadful wailing from the deepest part of her, muffled by her fingers pressed hard over her lips.

'Oh, honey, we are so sorry,' Vivi uttered, fighting her own surging grief. Her own Mama and Daddy. The unspeakable reality of her parents, swallowed by the sea.

Elise gulped as if drowning. 'How can she be? How can she be?' she uttered into her hands, her face streaming with tears. 'She was here only the other day.'

The door opened, making Vivi jump: an orderly bringing in a tray of tea, the cups clattering. Elise lifted her head, sniffing, and set her shoulders back as if a teacher had come into a classroom. She wiped the back of her hands over her face.

'Is it time for tea?' she asked, her face bright and pale, her fingertips returning to her waist, tapping rhythmically at her ribs. 'It is always time for tea here. Can you see, madam, that I have the best room? I am lucky. The lucky one. I have all my things here: my sewing and my shells. My music box. Have you heard it? Have you seen my shells? I have a view all year round, not only the summer. Winter too. I can see the sea. I don't care how cold I am. And look at the fireplace. Don't you love a nice fire, madam?'

Vivi stared. Under Elise's dishevelled hair, the skin over the crater in the side of her skull looked pitted and pale.

She asked Elise if she should pour.

'Please do, madam. I like it when visitors pour,' said Elise, and let out a strange little laugh. She glanced down at her hands, fingering her soggy sleeves, a frown carving into her forehead. 'But tell me. Why are my cuffs so wet? Look at them. What a fright. They're soaking.' She took a great breath in. 'Why am I crying?

23

BELLA, JUNE 1960

The double-decker crawled up the Charing Cross road, a red beacon in the rain, lurching from stop to stop, doing battle with other buses, taxis, people. Bella swayed among steaming mackintoshes, her arm throbbing from hanging on, her portfolio resting on the floor between her wet shoes. She peered through fogged-up windows, and strained to hear which stop the conductor called, his bell clanging, urging passengers to move along, hold tight.

Rain had been her companion since she left the Hall that morning, dripping down the windows of her delayed train from Canterbury and soaking her while she waited for the bus at Victoria, watching worrying chunks of minutes eaten by the station clock. She glanced at her wristwatch, her eighteenth birthday present from her parents. The time told by the tiny hands, so delicate and feminine, seemed to laugh at her.

She stepped off the bus with a grinding sense of alarm, her damp raincoat impeding her, her fringe a line of drops, her hair, limp and sodden. The artist in her ought to find beauty in Bloomsbury in summer rain: exquisite dark-brick terraces, wet pavements, plane trees against a sullen sky. But the artist escaped her.

She took a ragged breath, peered through the drizzle, her leather portfolio unwieldy, slippery. The enormous university building loomed ahead, a formidable temple of learning and, to its left, the refined, symmetrical façade of the Slade. Two girls pattered arm in arm down the art school steps, each holding an umbrella, doe eyes, black tights and white shoes, fashionable plastic macs, laughing at the rain. They scooted past Bella, and off around the corner.

Bella hoisted her portfolio higher, wishing she hadn't let her mother dress her. Harvey Nichols seemed all very well, but her suit's weight and formality struck odd notes inside her. A frightened feeling reminded her that she must go inside; she must speak to the man on reception and tell him she had arrived; she must have her interview, if they'd still let her. She must watch them leaf through her work, and prove herself worthy, however late and soaked she may be. But the paintings inside her sopping portfolio would never match the ideas and the execution of whatever the two girls had produced that morning.

Bella fumbled for the letter confirming her appointment. Rain ruined it in seconds so she scrunched it back into her pocket. Pointless. She was an amateur, only dabbling. She turned away.

Her decision, the burst of relief, made her shudder. She wanted to be home. She wanted sanctuary. Her portfolio slipped and thumped down into a puddle. She wanted to laugh but knew she would weep. She left it lying there, her artwork soaking, her reprieve permanent.

As a fleet of buses surged towards the bus stop, the lists of destinations jangling in Bella's mind, she caught sight of 'Hammersmith Broadway' on one. And so, unincumbered by her portfolio and pipedream ambitions, she grasped the pole and leapt up onto the back step, letting the bus take her where she wanted to go.

* * *

Rob found her sitting on the steps, sheltering under the porch, her raincoat a cape over her head to shield her from the rain.

'My goodness, Bella, didn't you knock on the door?'

'She wouldn't let me in. House rules, she said.'

'I told you. Dragon landlady.'

He furled his umbrella, opened the front door into a dark hallway and led her straight up the stairs to his room.

'I'm so very sorry to barge in like this...'

An old oak dresser held a stack of teacups and crockery, tea caddy and sugar bowl, the cupboards below doubling as a wardrobe. His gramophone on a side table, with a stack of records. The bed, single, narrow. He turned, his finger to his lips, his eyes wide and laughing. Bella heard a radio playing below behind a closed door.

She watched him move some clothes from an armchair, straighten the bedspread, set a kettle onto the stove in the corner, efficient in professional white shirt and a tie, and smart suit under his raincoat.

'Sit,' he said. 'Perhaps you will one day remember your umbrella. Or have you lost it?'

'I couldn't carry one as well as my portfolio.'

He looked at her empty hands.

'I will get you a towel.'

Bella eased off her mac and hung it over the back of a kitchen chair by the stove, leaving drips of rain on the floor. She sat in the wing-back threadbare armchair and remembered how he'd taken charge when he'd met her at Victoria last year. How easy it felt to be in his company; how he seemed to know without asking too many questions.

He came back in and handed her a towel. 'It's nice and clean. I went to the launderette at the weekend.'

'I've never seen you in such a smart suit before,' she said. She dabbed at her hair, feeling drips sneak behind her collar.

'It's not me, is it?' he said. 'Clerk in the local high-street branch of the bank.'

She tugged at the damp neck of her blouse. 'I don't think this is me, either. As expensive an outfit it is, I feel it is more like something Grannie would wear. I really think I should be wearing blue jeans.'

His eyes skimmed her, rested on her feet.

'You look fine, Bella. But take those off, you'll catch your death.'

She slipped off her shoes and he set them by the stove. She felt its warmth edging closer as she wriggled her stockinged toes into the rug, and another more specific sensation, a murmur of longing, a comforting desire, as she watched Rob pour the tea from a brown teapot.

'The bank must be better than National Service though,' she said, cupping the mug in her palms, sipping through the steam.

'Marginally,' he said, settling into the chair opposite her. 'I can't see myself sticking it out. I want to be a gamekeeper, or steward, like my father, but those opportunities seem to be on the wane these days.'

'You could take over at Farthing Hall when your father retires? Dad said the other day that he only had a couple of years left. How perfect would that be? I thought that the other day, and I was going to put it in my next letter.'

Rob looked at her.

'Or a horse breeder,' she said, grasping ideas from a life that didn't belong to her. 'I know how you love horses.'

'Funnily enough, those buildings you can see out the back window are the old mews for these houses.' They both watched the rain run down the misted pane. 'I look at them every morning when I have my breakfast. Perhaps fate is trying to tell me something.'

He fetched a tin of biscuits. Bella let her eyes wander around the bedsit. Rob had described his digs in his letters, but he had never let on about its shabbiness. The landlady must be rather mean, for the furniture had seen better days, the bed surely Victorian. She saw woodworm holes. The street had once been grand, but long ago. Perhaps he didn't notice it. She spotted the darn in the toe of Rob's sock.

Her mind shifted to her mother's mansion in Mayfair, sold to save Farthing Hall, and the Calloway fortune. It seemed like a myth from her mother's youth: a glistening place from times long past. She felt sad that she never got to see inside it, and experience the splendour that had created her comfortable life. She felt herself shrink a little inside her expensive clothing.

'I feel I should offer you a plate and a napkin, Miss Bella,' he said. 'Alas, I have no napkins.'

She laughed, as if to snuff out their differences, the way he used to call her that when they were children. 'It doesn't matter,' she said. 'Nothing like that matters.'

And the root of her desire switched into recognition. The feeling seemed not to be about Rob being older – six years older – and attractive, for he had always been those things, but that she herself had grown. And the decision she made outside the Slade had formed itself into a new beginning for her. But of what, she was uncertain. She glanced at her watch. Time ticked on. Perhaps she would make the six-thirty train.

'Some things matter, Bella,' Rob said. 'Perhaps why you are here.'

She felt her throat contract. She drained her mug.

'I couldn't go in. I couldn't do it. My parents will be cross. Dad especially. He'll think I have thrown away my chance. Wasted everything. The fact that I'd been invited for interview in the first place. But I got there, stood outside and it didn't feel right.'

She couldn't explain everything. Her sense of losing herself, being washed away by the rain. Dropping a year's worth of work onto the pavement. Seeing the girls who breezed past her, the sort of girls surely Rob would know, would meet at work, or in the coffee bars, and would take to the pictures. Bring back to the bedsit, his finger on his lips as they climbed the stairs.

'You know that feeling, Rob. When something isn't right.'

He nodded. 'Will your parents be so very cross? I know they might be disappointed. But they will understand, surely. If you were not happy.'

'Not Grannie,' she said. 'She wasn't that keen to start with, me going to art school, going to London. But then there is always something she doesn't like. Always an edge to her. She will turn this into something else entirely. Use it against me: my fickleness, my ungratefulness. I can hear her saying it. Mother will be fine. Worried, but fine. And Dad, well, yes, disappointed. He wanted to go to art college but was never allowed by odious Grandpa Digby.'

She glanced at her watch again, felt crushing disappointment at the time.

'Is that new?' he asked.

'Yes, my birthday present.'

'Of course, you're eighteen now...' He trailed off.

'My birthday was a bit of a disaster actually.'

Rob jerked forward, a searching, fearful expression on his face.

'Of course, having been packed off to boarding school, and encouraged not to mix with the local children, I have no friends,' she said. 'Apart from you.' Her cheeks went a treacherous red. 'So, my party was a bit flat. Aunt Genna came. Not my real aunt. You remember her? Lady Dornford? She brought Champagne. Mother and Dad gave me this watch. Lovely, isn't it?'

'Yes, it is,' he said, not looking at the watch.

'We had a little Champagne. Shame you weren't there. I pretended it was the first time I'd ever tasted it, but a girl had sneaked some into our dorm one night at school. Gave me the hiccups, which lasted all night. Painful. Dad joked about better not let me have a gin and tonic, which was fine as I hate the stuff... Oh, Rob, I haven't told you. The gin reminds me... Oh my goodness, I have something to tell you.'

Rob's forehead contracted. His eyes watered.

'When I came back last summer, home from school, I discovered this mysterious, wonderful little cottage in the woods.'

He sat back in his chair. 'Is that so?' He got up to fill the kettle again, set it with a clang on the hob.

'It was very strange. Because I felt as if I recognised it. That I had been there before. Do you know what I mean? Like it was meant to be found. Waiting for me. I'd never been into those woods. Had always been discouraged from going there. I was rebelling. Thought I'd show them. Or show Grannie at least, but that's another story. It was deep in the trees, in this lovely clearing. All overgrown, but beautiful; faded but enchanting. Like a gingerbread house. Inside, it seemed to me, as if the family had upped and gone, although everything was covered in years of dust.'

'You went inside?' Rob's face turned pale. He gave a minute shake of his head.

'There was this lovely smell. Like herbs and flowers and spice. Cinnamon and lavender. It felt intimate. Does that make sense?'

'No, Bella. It is simply an old estate cottage. Probably needs knocking down.'

She smarted. Never mind his bank clerk suit; this did not feel like Rob at all.

She ploughed on, wanting him to understand. 'If I had been there before, it now seemed different. Before, everything was larger, as if I had been looking up at the windows, the table, the mantel-piece. Rob, it was as if I was looking at it from a new perspective. I must have been there, sometime, when I was very young, when the world, to me, was huge.'

The way he looked at her, aghast, she felt naive, as if she were absurd and ridiculous.

'Anyway, that's how I felt.'

'I assume you told your parents?' He hesitated. 'What did they say?'

'Not a lot. But this is the thing. There is always something they don't say. Even at my party, which was supposed to be a celebration, there seemed to be some undercurrent, especially from Grannie. Although Aunt Genna tried to break the ice. She's good at that sort of thing. But it was like there was something itching, something unsaid. It drives me mad.'

'That's old folks for you,' Rob said, lightly. He loosened his tie, stripped it off, and rolled up his shirt sleeves.

Bella caught herself staring at his arms; the way his shoulders filled his shirt.

'But that's the thing.' She took a breath. 'Some of our parents' generation, you can't shut them up about the war. There is always some story of hardship and sacrifice, you know, which we young-sters need to take on board, learn from. But my parents skirt around it. It's as if the war did not happen to them. But of course it did. Dad's injury, Mother losing her own parents. Grandpa Digby dying. And yet the war itself seems to be the least of their worries. Everything else is bottled up.'

'But some people can't talk about it. It is still raw. Think about it: rationing only ended five years ago. And take my neighbours. This row was hit in the Blitz. There's still a bomb site down at the end, you know. My landlady is surprisingly unforthcoming about the war. Not about a lot of other things, mind.'

'You're right; at school, it was a taboo subject,' Bella said. 'Only my art teacher – she told me what happened to her family.'

'That doesn't surprise me, Bella. There in the Alps – people might have taken sides; collaborated or helped smuggle people over the borders. The Resistance, right there, in the heart of it.'

'And there was such a coldness there,' she said, and shivered at the memory. 'And I don't mean the winters in the mountains.' She remembered how the feeling had changed when she saw him at Victoria. 'Thing is, I know I am missing something.'

Rob stole a look at his own watch.

'What are you going to do about the Slade?'

'Nothing.'

'But I thought you'd want to try again. I think you'd like London. Perhaps it will be the tonic you need. To get away from Farthing. Live a different kind of life.'

She glanced out the window at the grey skyline; could hear a rumble from the streets. Rush hour, the clanging trains. She imagined people hurrying, surging, could see the lit-up tube stations, pubs and cafes, galleries and record shops, a glittering, hard-edged world.

'No, I want to be home,' she said, seeing the look on Rob's face, and feeling a twist of rebellion, 'And when I mean home, I mean the cottage. Don't ask me why. I can't stop thinking about it. It felt like a place where I simply wanted to be.' She stopped. She wanted to say, *as is sitting here with you*. She swallowed hard on the sentiment. 'I don't understand why.'

She watched his face, saw the darkness shut down. The cottage, her memory, seemed linked to Rob, and it tore at her. She could not articulate it.

Another memory: being carried by Rob, around a lawn in morning light. Arriving at the Hall, frightened, so terribly frightened, but being looked after at the same time. It felt ridiculous.

Why would he be carrying her? It felt like a dream. Ready to disintegrate, and yet lingering, even now, a sore inside her.

'I want to do up the cottage and live there. Do my art there. No one ever needs to see it. I don't need to prove myself to my peers, to art teachers, to anyone. I simply want to do it.'

'But the Slade. It is such an opportunity. Write to them and explain.'

Bella felt confused, breathless. Why would he be encouraging her to live in London, if he himself wanted to leave?

'That is not what I am going to do. You don't understand. That is the last thing I will do.'

'Come on, Bella, don't write it off. You are stronger than you feel. Braver than you believe. I think it will be good for you. I know you. I've known you ever since I can remember.'

'Don't tell me what I am. Or what to do. You have no right to.' Her voice grew high, stinging, upper class. She wanted him to understand her. Why did he not agree?

He stood and went to the back window, gazing out at the mews houses at the end of the garden. The rain had cleared, the evening sky above chimney pots turning a crystalline deep blue. Lights in other people's windows began to prick the dusk.

'I was surprised to see you here, Bella. Perhaps you shouldn't have come.' He sounded strange, an indifference deepening his voice. 'Perhaps you should have gone straight back home. I mean, look at me, at this place.' He sighed, turned round. 'I'm not sure why you came here. It is clear that I cannot help you.'

'Oh, no but you can. You do.' An odd little panic began to tick inside her. She had come here because, standing outside the Slade, he had been all she could think of. The one person who could make it right. 'You always help me. Coming home from boarding school last summer, it was wonderful to see you waiting for me.'

'I did that as a favour to your mother. I did it for my employer.'

Her panic stiffened inside her; it felt dangerous.

'But you are such a friend to me, Rob.' She wanted to tell him, she felt more at home with him than anyone else. She wanted to change the look on his face. He seemed to be slipping into anger, slipping away.

'What time is your train?' he asked.

The struggle inside her began to deflate, replaced by a wavering reality, a crushing pressure to leave, get herself to Victoria, to do the sensible thing.

'There's another one just after seven.' She heard her voice, weakening and thin at the back of her throat. 'Sorry again, to turn up like this. Thank you for letting me dry off. The rain has stopped. If I get a move on, I can catch my train. I'll get a cab.'

He took her raincoat from the chair.

'This is dry.' He watched her put it on. He picked up her shoes. 'You'll be travelling back late... Are you sure?'

He turned the shoes over in his hands, examining them.

'Yes, I must,' she said and tightened the belt on her raincoat. 'It won't get properly dark until nine at least. I will telephone from a call box at Canterbury. Dad is home this week. He'll come and pick me up.'

She held out her hand for her shoes, but Rob held them to his chest.

'They are dry, but you could stay? I will sleep on the floor. You haven't had your supper.'

'Rob, I—' She fixed her eyes on the shoes, wanting him to ask her again, wanting to make sure.

'No, you're right.' He laughed. 'What am I thinking? Never mind my landlady, what on earth would your parents say?'

He set her shoes carefully at her feet.

24

VIVI

The news programme came to an end and Vivi switched off the radio.

Through the French windows, she spotted Freda in the garden, snipping at the topiary. The day felt ordinary in a pleasant, settled way. Vivi realised that she no longer looked around herself, at the house she'd fixed up, at the rooms she had decorated, at the life she'd created, and thought, how did she get here?

Across the Atlantic, bulletins described young Kennedy doing battle with Nixon for the presidency, shown on people's own television sets, hinting at a young new leader for her homeland. In the early days, when she'd lost her parents, isolated by war and grief, she'd found solace imagining old New York and her young, charmed life. Such innocent times now appeared like a faded old-fashioned slideshow, irrelevant in this world of colour and change.

The Hall felt like home and her marriage to Nathan, finally, her lot. Here, despite everything, the place she was meant to be. And, Vivi decided, it all came down to Bella, and her imprecise, misshapen love for her.

She took a basket upstairs to the guest bedroom, opened the

drawer. Right at the back, wrapped in a shawl, lay Elise's music box. She nestled it at the bottom of the basket, and tucked the shawl to hide it in case Freda should come back in.

Downstairs, as she sifted through the post on the hall table, it struck Vivi that there had been no letter for Bella from Robin in a long while, not since her abandoned visit to the Slade early in the summer.

Ah, but Genna had written, about her intended visit, she hoped. She left her letter unopened, to savour later, knowing exactly how her friend would counsel her: *leave the kids alone and stop with all your meddling, Mrs Vivienne Miles Calloway!*

She picked up newly delivered parcels for Bella, laid them carefully on top of the music box, then put on her jacket and went out into the morning.

A breeze stirred the leaves in the wood, the colours turning, the scent of damp earth and loam, a freshening in her nostrils. A new season, and yet nothing much had changed in the last year. Nathan still busy at the Admiralty, away for most of the week, fitting in his visits to Elise, and when he arrived back from Margate met with acquiescence from Vivi and tutting and lingering silences from Freda.

Vivi's excursion last summer remained a secret, for she had no way of explaining herself, of forming her experience into words. Her visit had wound itself into a knot inside her: a mess of pity, empathy, and guilt, tainted by her inability to know, as ever, how she felt about Elise.

The music box grew heavier in her basket.

The walk to the cottage seemed to take longer every time; perhaps she habitually lost her bearings, misplaced a little of herself along the way. When she pushed open the door in the wall and stepped into the garden, she heard Bella's transistor radio playing softly. 'Only The Lonely', a solemn tune for such a bright morning, eased its way through the open windows.

'Hello, Mama,' Bella called, getting down from her step ladder in the kitchen and sliding her brush back in the pot of whitewash. She wore narrow jeans, turned up at the ankles, and an old shirt of Nathan's, sleeves rolled to her elbows. Dabs of paint peppered her arms and a light spray of snowy drops highlighted her fringe. Her dark hair bounced in a cute high ponytail.

'What do you think? I've been up since first light. I've swept and cleaned, and done two walls already. It's going to be bright and lovely when it's finished. I've been shifting what furniture was left, and got the stove going after a fashion. Is that a flask of tea from Mrs Scott, I hope? I'm parched already.'

'How did you sleep? I was thinking of you.'

'Fine, absolutely. So peaceful. I felt I was among the birds and the trees. I felt perfectly safe, perfectly at home.' Her smile widened. 'Ah, are they my acrylics from the art shop? And sandwiches? Wonderful.'

Vivi put Bella's parcels down, fetched some crockery from the dresser shelf and poured tea. As she handed Bella her own grandmother's china cup, she pondered the twisted, unspoken truths. Vivi admired the naïve energy bursting from Bella as she unwrapped her delivery of artist's materials, her expression brightening, holding each tube of paint up as if it were the first time she'd ever laid eyes on one.

'All as it should be, thank you. Everything on the list,' she said. 'Go and have a look at my studio, Mama, in the other bedroom upstairs. The light this morning is beautiful through the windows. I can't wait to get the decorating finished, then I can settle down to my painting.'

'Ah, that reminds me,' said Vivi. 'Some huge canvases have also arrived, but I wouldn't attempt to carry them myself. I'll ask Mr Buckley to drive them over some time.'

'Mr Buckley, yes...' Bella's eyes glazed with private thoughts. She inhaled, as if to ask a question, then fell silent and began to rearrange her tubes of paint.

'Is the bed up there comfortable?' Vivi asked. 'You must be chilly. What about in winter? I always thought you'd use the Widow's Watch for a studio. Do you want to be here on your own, Bella? In the middle of the woods. It's like you are camping.'

Bella laughed but her momentum seemed to waiver, and her face, animated the moment before, faltered into fragility.

'It's a feeling I have, Mama, so hard to explain. I tried to tell Rob about it when I saw him in London... but yes. I want to be here. I don't mind being alone. After the disaster with the Slade, I want to do my own thing. And this is the right place for me to do it. I hope you and Dad aren't too cross about it all, still. I know Grannie is.'

'We're not cross, darling,' she said, though she could not vouch for Freda.

Bella fell quiet. She sat in the other armchair, sipped her tea, her eyes moving around the room. She was drawn to the place for reasons more real than she knew: a connection more profound. Vivi felt prickly with discomfort, that old familiar dragging shame. Bella had created a bubble of hope and optimism around herself, here in the cottage, and Vivi knew all too well that one day, and one day soon, she and Nathan would burst it.

'Was there any other post for me?' Bella asked, tapping her fingers absently against her thigh. 'Any letters?'

'No, darling,' she replied, hoping she did not convey that she had already deliberated the fact herself.

Bella looked away sharply, hiding her disappointment.

'Well, that's that then.'

Vivi stood. 'Show me upstairs.'

Bella's smile returned, and she led the way. The bedroom contained her easel, her materials, brushes to attention in a jar, tubes of colour aligned. Even on dull days, Vivi could tell the room would be milky with light, warmed by the amber-stained glass at the top of the windows, the whole space extraordinary. Vivi smiled, remembering the neatness of Bella's bedroom, her arranging of things. And she thought of Elise, her shells and beachcombed treasures.

'I know what you are thinking, Mama,' she said. 'You're not sure about all this, are you?'

'It's that—'

'But I feel at home here, Mama. I grew up in the Hall, yes, but spent years away at boarding school, and I couldn't bear to go away to London. I think my flop at the Slade proved that. Everything was so unsettled. But here...' She opened the casement and the woods, their smell and their sound seeming to fill the room. 'When I discovered this cottage, something changed inside me. Like I had found a place I could be me. I said to Rob, it's so hard to explain.'

Vivi nodded, wondering how many times Bella would drop Robin's name into conversation. She kept her gaze on the shimmering leaves beyond the garden wall, tears prickling her eyelids. Perhaps telling her about Elise would be a blessing, help her begin to understand. But Nathan kept saying it was not the right time, let's not spoil her birthday or distract her from her interview at the art school. Nathan was terrified. It would never be the right time. Bella would hate them, reject them: her whole life, a lie. But, surely, Vivi told herself, the truth is better.

'I have something that might interest you. Wait here.' She went downstairs, and returned with the music box.

'Goodness, what's this?'

'I found it.' Vivi faltered. She had promised Nathan that they'd tell her together, but it wouldn't do any harm, she decided, to give her this. 'I thought you might like it. It's a bit old and cranky.'

Bella laughed. 'A little like Grannie.'

'Bella!' Their giggles blended together.

'But how lovely.'

'That's it, turn the key.'

'Für Elise' tinkled into the morning, accompanying the bird-song from the wood.

'I shall play it while I paint,' she said.

'The tune only lasts a few minutes.'

'That's good enough for me.' Bella sighed. 'Mama, I must get something out of my system. Shake off school, the Slade, every-thing... and this, everything here, is helping. Ah, now look what I found downstairs.' She picked up an old book from the windowsill and handed it to her. 'I've been leafing through it. It is fascinating. Annie Drake must have been the old tenant here. Did you know her?'

'No, I...' Vivi's scalp contracted, chilled and tight. Perhaps the music box had been a step too far. She turned the book over in her hands, smelling musk, a papery smell. It felt heavy, the weight of someone's life, the leather cover soft with age, the corners rounded, the front worn in patches by a stranger's fingertips like a map of their hours and days. Nathan must have missed it when he packed away Elise's things.

Vivi set the journal back on the windowsill as if it made her arms ache.

'Have a look, Mama,' Bella urged her. 'It's a peek into another world, another time. It shows such a different way of life. She has written all about herbs, fungus, and flowers and how they can help you. What can cure, what to avoid. Do you think she may have been a *wise woman*? You know, a *witch*? Some bits sound like spells. Some make me laugh. She was pithy, this

Annie Drake. There was a bit about wishing she could find a cure for nosiness, never mind a man's balding head. She certainly paints a picture.'

Vivi hesitated, opened the book. In Annie's own hand, with quirky ticks on rounded letters, recipes for cures for all manner of complaints were written: ingredients listed, methods described, conclusions decreed. Her clients' requests, from neighbours, townswomen, country folk, ordered and noted, comments asterisked in the margins, a jest here, an observation there. Vivi turned the pages. That scent, a lingering greenness, ashes and spice, caught at her throat. Occasionally, another hand would appear on the pages, the writing smaller and more schooled, laying out paragraphs of lore on botanicals, their physic, and spiritual remedies. It seemed Elise had also written in the book, her handwriting proving to be the image of Bella's.

Vivi wondered if Bella had noticed. She felt her daughter's eyes on her, closely watching as she browsed. She found herself drawn to the dates that Annie Drake had annotated at the top of each page, the years spanning from the early thirties through to the war. The year 1940 sprang out, and Vivi felt like she dare not look. But a masochistic fascination, some strange urge to damage part of herself, pulled her in.

End of summer: recipe, seaweed poultice for facial burns.

And later, Annie's exuberant report on how well it had worked for the anonymous patient. How well he had recovered.

'Fascinating it is, Bella. Can I borrow it?' she asked. 'I'd like to read more.'

'That you may,' she replied, pleasure sparking from their exchange of gifts. Until a frown shot between her eyebrows. 'There have been times, Mama, when I thought we had absolutely nothing in common. I mean, look at you, and look at me! But these days I no longer feel that way. Things have changed, somewhat.'

'Perhaps,' said Vivi, her voice deep in her chest, 'it is because you are growing up.'

Bella laughed. 'Annie must have been quite a character, don't you think?' She gazed at her for a moment too long for comfort. 'I am glad to see you are wearing one of last year's outfits, Mama, for you need to tie your scarf over your hair, roll up your sleeves and help me with the whitewash.'

Vivi laughed. 'Well, it's a good job I brought the largest flask Mrs Scott could find.'

Bella took Vivi's arm, and they went back down the stairs.

25

VIVI

The weather turned and the first autumn storm threw rain against the windows, the air peppered with blowing leaves. Vivi switched on the lamps in the sitting room, even though the clock hands pointed to a moment after two, feeling glad she'd managed a good ride on Snowdrop the day before, for going out in the rain proved to be no fun for either of them these days.

Yesterday, she had tied the horse to the post outside the church and strolled over to Annie Drake's headstone, a new habit, sparked by reading the journal, another way of trying to align the pictures inside her head, imagining the conversation that she and Nathan must soon have with Bella.

Bella appeared to be *just fine*. But for Vivi, everything felt wrong. In fact, it was growing worse as time moved on, dishonesty stifling her and anger not far beneath.

Sitting listening to the drumming on the windows, Vivi remembered one of Annie's sayings from her journal – *Rain from the East, will last three days at least* – and wondered whether she might light the fire this afternoon to take the chill off. She thought about the cottage roof and how well it might be holding up in all this rain, telling herself not to worry about Bella, though it was all she did.

Mr Buckley stood at the open sitting room door, conscious, Vivi could tell, that his boots had made wet prints across the parquet. He slipped off his dripping cap.

'Excuse me, Mrs Calloway.'

'Hello, Mr Buckley, how are you?'

'Would you please come out to the stables? I don't wish to alarm you, but Snowdrop doesn't seem too well.'

Vivi was baffled, her understanding turning corners around Mr Buckley's understated, English way of speaking.

'Not too well?'

'I think we need to call the veterinary.'

She leapt to her feet, buttoning her mac as she followed Mr Buckley out of the back door and through the rain. Snowdrop lay on her side in her stall, her breathing laboured, her potency diminished. Her head twitched at the sound of Vivi's voice. She tried to haul herself up.

'No, no, lie still.' She knelt in the hay and stroked the horse's silvery mane away from her eyes. Snowdrop's pupils looked contracted and saliva drooled from her whiskery mouth. Her nostrils flared, catching Vivi's scent. A groan rumbled at the base of her long throat.

'I thought it might be colic. She may have eaten something,' Mr Buckley said. 'This isn't like her at all.'

'Telephone the vet. Tell him it's urgent.'

She rested her head against Snowdrop's smooth, solid neck. The rain drummed on the stable roof; a chill crept around the door.

Alone with her horse, the reality of her death clouted her in the face. An encroaching loss wrenched inside her, pulling her inside out. She whispered into Snowdrop's ears, inhaling the earthy fragrance, Vivi's comfort for all these years.

'He'll be here soon. Stay with me until then.'

The horse whimpered, exhaled, her stare snaring Vivi beneath her white lashes. As Vivi gazed into Snowdrop's eyes, the light inside them ceased, and became sudden unseeing blankness. She recoiled, sat back against the wall, and Mr Buckley appeared at the stable door, brought back across the yard by the sound of her wailing.

* * *

The next day, Nathan and Mr Buckley finished smoothing over the earth in Snowdrop's favourite corner of the paddock. From here, the land sloped away through hawthorn copses, down to the water meadows where Vivi and Snowdrop had walked the droves high above the ditches, scaring birds and rabbits from the grass, watching seasons melt from one into the other. Today, the view was obscured by low drifting cloud, and the rain continued to fall, coming in from the east, drenching her and soaking the broken turf.

Mr Buckley put his cap back on, picked up the spades and nodded to them both before leaving.

Nathan wiped his palm down his coat and took Vivi's hand. They stood side by side at the horse's grave, a neatly cut scar in the ground.

'Thank you,' she said. 'Thank you for coming back.'

'I couldn't not be here. I couldn't let you cope with this alone.' He glanced at her. 'Not like last time.'

She squeezed his hand. 'I remember how much having Snow-drop helped me in those early days. You away at sea, the battles in the sky, the threat of invasion, the uncertainty. Possibly the worse time of my life. But you gave me Snowdrop. And she saw me through it. Thank you.'

Nathan turned her towards him, held her shoulders. He lifted the peak of her hat and kissed her forehead. Rain pattered down and ran in channels over their arms as he held her, his grip long and tight.

'And you gave me Bella,' she uttered, her words muffled against his coat.

His embrace intensified, his mouth by her ear. She heard his intake of breath, his muted sigh.

'You let me give her to you, Vivi. You took such care of her when you could have, quite rightly, ended everything. And walked away.'

'Where else would I have gone?' she asked. 'I wanted *us*. I wanted a child.' Never managing to have a baby of their own had sat as a blank and puzzling space inside her. But now, as she held Nathan, she realised the feeling had disappeared. 'And you gave me one.'

'You forgave me.' The sound of his words cracked with contrition, and wonder. 'What person does that? What person puts themselves in such a situation? I cannot imagine your pain.'

He pulled back and gazed down at her, his eyes flickering over her face, fighting bewilderment, his expression framed with joy.

The years Vivi had spent circling Nathan, finding a way into him, seeking his love compounded into one moment.

'What person? A person who loves, and loves deeply,' she said, with a clarity she had not felt in years. Telling him so, she felt cleansed. 'On that awful morning, when Robin carried Bella – Kate – into our house, I made the decision. In my horror and confusion, it seemed easy.'

She gave an astonished laugh, realising that may not be the whole truth. It had been like clinging onto a life raft, a way to salvage an unbearable situation into something for the better, turning it on its head. And inside it all, a shade of self-sacrifice.

'The hard bit, I will confess, came later, as Bella grew, became the girl we know. I learnt. I went through a process, a realisation.' She saw tears forming in his eyes. 'But, at the top and bottom of it all, is love. For what else is there?'

Nathan smoothed his hands down to her elbows. 'Do you understand why I had to help Elise? I could not abandon her. Do you understand me?'

'Yes, I do,' she said, placing her hand on his cheek. 'Right from the beginning.'

Nathan's sigh sounded like a bellow of relief.

'I should be thanking you, Vivi. For what you have given all of us.'

'All?'

'Mother included. I know you don't always see eye to eye, in many things, but I believe she is incredibly grateful to you, for how you supported her, ensured she was able to stay in her home. I know she doesn't demonstrate it. I'm assuming her pride doesn't let her. But believe it. Things looked bad for Farthing Hall when Digby died. And, as you know, she had suffered his indiscretions, the scandal, the tragedy he brought to her door. And the shame seemed to be locked away inside the Hall for years.'

The thought of Digby formed an unsavoury taste in Vivi's mouth. But the idea of Freda's frozen life being liberated by his death gave her an entirely different feeling.

'Do you think deep down, your mother has a soft spot for Bella?' she asked.

'Yes, yes, I do.'

And yet Nathan did not sound like he believed himself.

'My own error, Vivi,' he sighed, 'I could not bear to have history repeating itself.'

'Stop that now,' Vivi said, placing her finger over his lips. 'For we would not have Bella.'

They began to walk back to the Hall, across the paddock, around the stables, through the garden, holding hands, something Vivi realised they had not done in a long while.

'Taking in Bella at the end of the war certainly knocked Mother, and us all, for six,' said Nathan. He paused, ruminated. 'And now, Vivi? What about now?'

'Now we continue, as we have always done. That's all we can do. And, I guess, right now you have to get yourself back to the Admiralty,' she said, realising that, even after all these years, she'd never quite got used to him working away. 'But I shall look forward to the weekend when you come home again.' She brightened. 'Remember, Genna will be here this afternoon.'

'No, I mean, now, Vivi, what shall we do about Bella? You want to tell her, and I think we should. We need to. It will be tough; it will be heartbreaking. But I know we must.'

Vivi tugged at his hand to stop him, dread circling inside her.

'Not right now,' she said. 'With Snowdrop, and what all, I'm feeling shattered. How about when Genna has gone home, we do it?' She swallowed the dryness in her throat.

'If you're sure.'

'Spending time with Genna will help me. She always sets me straight. She is the tonic I need.'

'We will be doing the right thing,' he said. 'However hard it will be.'

He took her hand, pulled her closer, his frame shielding her from the rain. Vivi felt herself bracing, knowing that in the next few days, she would need to be stronger than she'd ever been before.

Nathan rested his forehead against hers, sealing their promise.

* * *

Genna arrived in her little sporty car, its red chassis glistening with raindrops.

'Goodness me, getting out of this seat in this skirt is no cakewalk,' Genna said, laughing. She wore her hair, russet silvered with grey, in a smooth bouffant. Her face froze when she saw Vivi's. 'Oh honey, what has happened?'

'Come in, get out of this deluge. I'll fix us both a drink and I will tell you.'

'I know something's wrong,' said Genna, as they hurried through the front door. 'Apart from you looking bedraggled and soaked, that is. Never forget how well I can read your face, Vivienne Miles Calloway.'

Vivi told Genna about Snowdrop as she poured them gin and tonics.

'The vet thinks it may have been a poisonous plant,' she said, handing Genna her drink. 'That she ate something by mistake when we were out on our usual ride. It happened so quickly. She took a rapid turn for the worse, before the vet even got here. There was nothing we could do. I am still in shock.'

'That's no surprise, honey. I am so desperately sorry. What do you think it was? Aren't foxgloves toxic?'

'Yes, but not in season. Nathan thought perhaps yew. It seems most likely. I have taken to stopping by the church more often these days.' She could not explain the visiting of Annie Drake's grave, even to her best friend. 'There's a huge old tree in the graveyard. Some berries or leaves might have blown onto the road. I didn't notice. I should have done. It is the simplest thing, the stupidest thing, and yet so awful.'

'Honey, this is so miserable. You mustn't blame yourself. I know what your mare meant to you.'

Vivi leaned forward. 'Listen, Freda will be down to join us soon, so let me take you up to the guest room. Bring your drink. I want to show you something.'

'Not for Freda's eyes?'

'Not at all.'

Upstairs, inside the bedroom, Vivi closed the door, switched on the lamps and pulled the curtains over the rain-battered windows. She opened the drawer in the dressing table and unearthed Annie Drake's journal from where she'd hidden it under a stack of spare linen.

'Bella found this in the cottage,' she whispered, handing the book to Genna. 'It belonged to her grandmother.'

'What? To Freda?' Genna immediately shook her head in realisation. 'Oh no, I see.'

Vivi waited as her friend sat on the bed, set down her drink and carefully turned the old, crackling pages. She gasped, here and there, her eyes widening in fascination at the nuggets and insights, a stranger's voice from the past.

'My, Vivienne, isn't this something?'

'I knew you'd find it interesting.'

'Was she some sort of apothecary, the mysterious Annie Drake?' Genna caught her eye. 'And Bella still doesn't know? About Elise?'

'No. But Nathan and I, we have vowed to tell her soon. And I mean, very soon. We meant to on her birthday, back in February, but that seemed far too mean, what with everything else going on.'

Genna reached out to grip her hand, her face contracting in empathy.

'You're a tough gal, Vivienne. But you know where I am if you need me. Always.'

'And I have Nathan,' said Vivi.

Her throat tightened at this, her head swimming in confusion, for she had never been able to believe it before.

She went over to the fireplace and knelt to light the fire. Genna continued to leaf through the book.

'I wonder what Annie Drake has to say about poisoning,' Vivi said as she stacked the coals and kindling. 'I did see something about mushrooms and toadstools, a long list of the ones you can eat, ones to avoid. Perhaps she will tell us about yew?'

'Possibly,' said Genna. 'My, she was a colourful character. Ah, a proud professional woman too. She must have decided to take out a newspaper advert to promote her wares. She's snipped it out and pasted it in here.'

'Good for her.' Vivi paused, wondered why a small ad in a newspaper chimed with her. 'Anyway, there will be hot water later, for a bath if you like.' Vivi struck a match, watched the flames blossom. 'I thought we'd have an early supper, cocktails to start. Four of us ladies tonight. Nathan won't be home until Friday.'

'Oh, wonderful, Bella will be here.'

'Yes, in your honour. She rarely sets foot these days.'

'I imagine all this rain won't put her off.'

'No, she is quite the independent girl. She has grown so since you last saw her. Something changed for her this year. And not only the issue with the art school and moving into the cottage. I'm pretty sure she has a thing for Robin Buckley. She seems wilder, but more herself. Does that make sense?'

'She's got your fire, all right, Vivi. Must have rubbed off on her. Nature and nurture, and all that.'

Vivi relished her friend's presence, her sound counsel.

'I'm so glad you are here, Genna. But oh, I am always worried about Bella—'

Vivi heard her friend gasp.

'Found something interesting?'

'Well, yes.' Genna ran her finger thoughtfully down one of Annie's long passages. 'Not yew, but mistletoe. I didn't know it was poisonous.'

'But out of season for Snowdrop to come in contact with it.' She sat down next to Genna. 'Isn't it usually out around the holidays?'

'Ah, I think it is there in the trees all year round, but it's that we see it more in winter when the leaves have fallen. Dornie and I... I have it in my beeches down in Sussex. Do you have it in the trees by the churchyard?'

'But it's too high up, surely, for Snowdrop to have eaten any.'

'The sad bit is we will probably never know. Poor Snowdrop. But listen to what Annie has written: "Seven berries are all that is required. Make a tea, boil for a quarter hour. Keep on top shelf, mark as deadly. Wash pan thoroughly after use." Sounds like Annie Drake was about to do someone in.'

'I expect some of her tinctures were toxic, and she was being careful about it.'

'Ah, yes she was a thorough lady,' said Genna. 'She has marked the date, "January 1941". My, what a time we were all having then. And her customer's order is detailed below, but all she has written is "a countrywoman" – look – who seemingly went all the way down to Margate for this special mistletoe draft. Paid well for it, according to Annie.'

'Let me see that.' Vivi took the book, forcing her memory back to the war, with Nathan recovering from his injuries, the enemy prowling the French coast, her parents swallowed by the sea. The image of Digby slumped lifeless over his desk; the sickening realisation that had washed through her when she found him, his stiffening fingers around the tumbler, his face squashed into the ink blotter. When she had stumbled into his study, she had teetered on the edge of terrible understanding, numbed by shock, resisting the reality of what her eyes were telling her. The same sensation gnawed at her now.

Annie's description suddenly spiralled into a recognisable form.

Surely, something like this could not be true?

'Whatever Annie brewed up with mistletoe would certainly harm someone,' she said cautiously, tiptoeing over her words. 'Poison them.'

Genna's eyes widened, staring at Vivi. 'But who is the countrywoman?'

'I don't want to think about it.'

Genna shuffled around on the bed to face her, the look on her face telling Vivi that she was not going to let this go 'But, Vivi, do you remember Freda, after Digby died? I was here. You saw the change in her? And not just getting rid of that God-awful wig. The look on her face when the coroner finally released his body for burial?'

'Relief, I think. Digby was a beast. He was nasty to her.' Vivi flinched, thinking of the bruises Freda had tried to cover up, the dead-blood fingerprint marks on her wrists, the marks on her neck. Of the small ad that Vivi had spotted in Freda's local paper. 'Freda must have felt glad, on some level, that he had gone. The way he spoke to her, Genna, the way she pussyfooted around him. Always careful what she said. Her constant shifting, adapting to his every mood. When he—'

The memory of Digby's hand pawing her own shoulder, his hot breath on her face snuffed out her words. Inappropriate, indeed.

'I remember how Freda reinvented herself,' said Genna,

warming to the thought. 'The merry widow. Still rather prickly, though.'

Vivi's surprised laugh burst out. 'How can we say such things?' she said. 'She was simply relieved the old dog was dead.'

'I can imagine—'

'She didn't poison him. She wouldn't do that, Genna.'

Genna's gaze pinned itself on Vivi, that look she gave her when they were both thinking the same thing. Those times in the back of a cab on Fifth Avenue, or a soiree in a Sixty-First Street mansion, across the room in the salon at Grosvenor Street when they first met the Calloways, her Manhattan bedroom, when they didn't need to speak, had been likely to burst into giggles, or on occasion, tears.

Genna shut the book and handed it back to her. 'Annie Drake knows the truth.'

Vivi did not say a word. The fire pulsed and crackled in the silence.

Genna swallowed her gin and tonic, and Vivi slipped the journal back into its hiding place.

* * *

Bella arrived in the chill of the early evening, a little too late for cocktails.

'Sorry, Mama,' she said, peeling off her raincoat in the hall, leaving drips in her wake. Her hair was coiled up on top of her head, charming and dishevelled, her fringe coquettish over her eyes. 'I was deep into my painting, forgot the time. Then I knew I better run, and I am soaked.'

'We should have sent Mr Buckley to pick you up. Or I would have driven over.'

'Oh no, you would have been too busy, and I wouldn't ask it of him. But I have forgotten my shoes to change into. Not sure wellies are appropriate for our ladies' supper. I hope we will be raising a toast to dear old Snowdrop?'

'I'll find you some shoes.'

'Oh no, I am all right in stockinged feet.' She opened her arms, hugged Vivi. 'Mama, I am so sorry about Snowdrop.'

Bella's damp and angular slightness, her chippy way of bouncing around subjects, took Vivi back to Elise's strange half-lit room on the seafront. That same sensation was twisting in her chest.

Bella kicked off her rubber boots, depositing sodden leaves on the floor, and padded towards the sitting room.

'Where is Aunt Genna? I can't wait to see her,' she said, opening the door. 'And Grannie, of course.'

'Here she is.' Genna leapt up to embrace Bella. 'My, my, look at you.'

Freda stayed seated, only offering her cheek for Bella's peck. 'Hello, Isobel.' She gave her a beady look, up and down. 'So, is this the latest fashion?'

Bella smoothed her hands down the green brocade of her shift dress, the neck high, the sleeves ballooning in medieval fashion. 'I made it, Grannie, from your old curtains. Remember? They used to hang on the landing.'

'Goodness me, of course I do. Whatever next! Rather short, isn't it?'

'Oh, come on, Freda,' Genna laughed. 'If I can go above the knee, surely Bella can.'

'On the knee is as far as I will go,' said Vivi. 'But I think it looks rather wonderful.'

Bella did a pirouette, her giggle tinkling. 'But I thought you'd approve, Grannie. I am being immensely frugal. I am not earning

any money from my painting, or anything else, and I don't
expect to—'

'Yet,' said Genna.

'And Dad told me ages ago that I mustn't even consider Mama's
money.'

Freda tutted. Vivi caught her mother-in-law's glare, but ignored
it. Bella should know better than to bring that up.

'I want to support myself,' Bella continued. 'And in the mean-
time, I thought I'd make my own clothes. I can't tell you, sewing
brings me great joy. While painting fires me up, a needle and
thread calms me down.'

'At least needlework lessons in Le Chable didn't go amiss,
then?' Freda said, on the edge of scorn.

Vivi decided to ignore Freda's mood, busied herself by pouring
wine for everyone, her mind occupied with its own thoughts: Elise
and her embroidery, the seaweed patterns, and the sea motifs.
Genna encouraged Bella to sit closest to the fire and Freda leant
forward, putting on her spectacles to scrutinise the hem of Bella's
skirt. Mrs Scott had set out covered dishes on a hostess trolley for
supper so they could all help themselves throughout the evening –
so wonderfully casual, compared to the dinner party before the
war at Grosvenor Street, when Vivi met Digby and Freda and
Nathan.

'In the old days,' Vivi said, 'I would have to wait for the butler to
pour my drink. Now we must help ourselves, but don't you
prefer it?'

'Good God, yes,' said Genna.

Bella laughed. 'It is such a curiosity, Mama, the way you all
used to live.'

'I know you have heard this before, but things changed so
much,' she said. 'Servants simply disappeared into the war. I am
only thankful that Mrs Scott and Ruby stayed on. Ruby is the

biggest surprise. I thought she'd bolt as soon as they started putting those "come into the factories" posters up.'

'And yet some servants disappear for far more terrible reasons,' Freda added.

Vivi stopped pouring.

'Oh, Grannie, that sounds like a whiff of scandal,' Bella said. 'Surely not at Farthing Hall?'

'You do not know the half of it, my girl.'

Vivi took a glass over to her mother-in-law, the first, as warranted by her status, yet could not look at her as she offered it.

'You do hear tales of girls below stairs getting themselves into trouble with the master of the house,' said Bella, settling back into her armchair, curling her legs under her. 'Isn't it a story as old as time?'

Freda took in a sharp breath. 'Don't be so flippant, Isobel.' She sounded appalled. 'It isn't a laughing matter.'

'Grannie, I am sorry. But as Mama said, time moves on.'

'Not that much.' Freda, taking the glass, looked up at Vivi. 'And consequences remain.'

Vivi felt brave, no, defiant, enough to return her stare. She wondered who Freda might be thinking of: Elise or Charlotte Hoodless. Probably both.

She threw Genna a look, asking for help.

'Freda, I do like your blouse,' said Genna, once again picking up on her silent plea.

'It's not especially new. I do have to be a little frugal, too, after all, seeing as I must ask my son and daughter-in-law for a clothes allowance.' Freda's genial smile froze her face, failed to meet her eyes.

'Well, I for one know that us ladies of a certain age must choose between our face and our figure.' Genna laughed, lightening the mood with another subject switch. 'And I have certainly chosen my figure, for my face does not bear too close a scrutiny.'

Vivi could not help but agree with her friend. Genna's tall frame held up well, while her face revealed her pinched and busy map of widowhood.

'And I, my face,' Vivi leapt in. 'My figure cannot cope with these latest looks. They are for the young girls. I shall stick with what I know. I need a waistline.'

'Mama, you look fine,' said Bella. She stretched her feet out, wriggling her toes towards the heat of the fire.

Vivi hurriedly furnished everyone else with a drink and then took a great gulp herself, hoping for yet another swing in the conversation. She perched next to Genna on the sofa, feeling her friend's supportive squeeze of her hand.

Freda took small and frequent sips of her wine in her usual queenly fashion. 'And how is your painting going, Bella?' she asked.

Bella seemed surprised at her grandmother's interest. 'I'm just getting started, getting the cottage how I want it first before I really dive in. In an odd sort of way, the cottage feels like home. It has been since I moved there. I had this feeling, you know. But I also wanted to rearrange it slightly, give it my own touch. It is a special place. I belong there.'

Vivi noticed an assertive twitch of Freda's shoulders.

'Don't you think you belong here at the Hall, Bella?'

Bella threw Freda a challenging look. 'Not always, Grannie.'

Vivi longed for Freda to shut up, and for Nathan, for his presence to curb his mother.

'Especially,' Bella pressed on, 'when I have spent more time in a foreign country, away at school, than I have here. To be honest, Grannie, Farthing Hall has never felt like home.'

Genna leant forward, trying to dissipate the rising tension. 'Do you have hot water now, Bella?'

'Yes, Dad asked Mr Buckley to install an immersion heater. And the range is beautifully warm.'

'I can see you flitting back here in the depths of midwinter,' Freda said, continuing their conversation. 'No matter what you say.'

'Not if I can help it, Grannie.'

Silence expanded into the room, seeping out into the corners. Rain dripped down the chimney, hissing into the fire. Vivi got to her feet and began to take the lids off the platters, clattering them clumsily, dropping a spoon.

'Come on, everyone, we have Mrs Scott's delicious supper to get through.'

She dared to look around and caught sight of Freda's stony face. At that moment, it hit her that, not only two hours before, she'd been toying with the idea that Freda had murdered her husband. And the thought kept returning, like the second hand on a clock, sweeping around its face.

On the mantelpiece, the clock stood at seven. Bella had only been here half an hour, and Vivi sensed the time would stretch into a long, uncomfortable evening.

That night, Vivi slept surprisingly well, but woke with a mildly thick head. She wished she hadn't drunk so much wine – it's always that last glass, isn't it, she thought to herself, with a downturned smile. She rang for Ruby to bring her a strong pot of tea, then remembered that she and Mrs Scott had the day off.

The sky through the landing window looked loaded, the air grey and three-dimensional, the trees dripping; the third day of rain. She heard the front door shut as she turned the corner on the landing. She walked downstairs and crossed the hall to peer through the window. She could see Freda tramping out across the gravel, bent under a huge umbrella, her black raincoat being tugged by the wet breeze, resembling the wings of a stalking crow. She wondered what had taken her out so early on such a dismal day. Walking in any weather never seemed to be her preference.

Alone in the kitchen, Vivi set the kettle to boil, decided a slice of Mrs Scott's plum tart would do for a breakfast and sat at the kitchen table, thinking, as she often did these quiet, empty mornings, of Bella. She spooned at the delicious pastry and cold custard, and sipped a steaming cup, feeling revived within moments. She thought back to Bella's tender gratitude to Mr Buckley last night when he had tapped on the sitting room door at ten thirty and asked if she wanted a lift back to the cottage. She wondered, as they all said goodnight and went up to bed, if perhaps Bella and Mr Buckley may talk about Robin during the car ride. That Bella would receive nice news, that Mr Buckley may drop a hint that Robin missed her, or had asked after her, and that Bella may be able to relay something as agreeable back to him, or some such fantasy.

Freda had settled down once she'd had another glass of wine. The spikey exchanges had petered out, although Freda barely glanced Bella's way as she left, her mouth pinched, the set of her shoulders, painfully braced.

Running her bowl under the hot tap, Vivi decided she'd leave Genna to her lie-in, knock on her door in an hour or so. The kitchen felt cold and dim, unpeopled, tidy and yet strangely redundant. She shivered, glanced over her shoulder as if suddenly aware of someone walking in, and yet the room remained empty; it had been a memory. A similar morning, when she had felt a little jaded from the party the night before, when Freda had taken herself back up to bed. The morning after Victory in Europe Day. The kitchen, vibrant with crisis: a terrified child. Nathan mortified, Vivi unshakable. Questions bouncing off the ceiling. Scandal on the verge of unravelling.

The bowl slipped from her hands as she realised, clattering into the sink. She knew where Freda was heading out to this morning.

Vivi raced out of the room, up the stairs, cursing that she still needed to dress, to get her car out of the garage, to drive through the rain to the cottage, to find Bella before Freda did, undoubtedly, disastrously, too late.

26

BELLA

Despite her late night, Bella woke early. In a fug of sleep, she slipped on her dressing gown and headed into the second bedroom, not wishing to think, except about her art. However, thoughts of Robin continued to bloom in her mind.

She opened the paint tubes and mixed the colours, forcing herself back to her dreaming state. She liked to see, or sense at least, the sun rising, to see her painting evolve in different lights, to watch it alter, as an imaginary viewer might in years to come, at clear dawn, at brilliant midday and drowsy evening haze.

The sound of the rain filled the room like static. It had not stopped for three days. Outside, the trees in the wood blurred, the autumn gold and bronze and yellow taking on a pewter sheen. The damp air thrilled her, made her feel alive. She wondered if there may be thunder approaching, from somewhere over the sea.

Her feet were bare. She liked to feel the boards under her toes, no matter how chilly. Standing at her easel, she felt a vibration in her bones, portentous, an animal sense. And she recognised the feeling as her imagination, her drive to create. She took a breath, relishing it.

And anyway, did thunder come at this time of year? The peculiar Annie Drake would say so in her book.

Her brush strokes scratched in discord to the rhythm of the rain on the window, the amber glass bright with it. Her painting grew in layers, one over the other, and another, the topmost layer informed by what lay beneath, appearing as it did because of its foundation, the patina building.

She did not hear the door open downstairs, or the sound of someone crossing the kitchen floor. She only heard the ring of a heel on the top step. She turned to see her grandmother standing in the doorway, the black of her coat shimmering and wet, her hat battered by the weight of water.

'Hello, Grannie.' She tried to disguise the surprise in her voice. Had her grandmother visited to apologise for her prickliness yesterday evening? It seemed strange to see her. She never came to the cottage. 'You're up early. Whatever is the matter?'

Her grandmother said nothing. She stepped into the room as if trespassing, taking in the paraphernalia of Bella's studio, puzzled. She seemed to be coiling in on herself, her wrinkled hands with their smooth fingernails twitching at her sides, which annoyed Bella. She had disturbed her at work, for no reason it seemed.

'What do you think of my studio, Grannie?' she asked, her patience stretching.

'You feel at home here.' She sounded flat, stating detail.

'I do, Grannie. Isn't it wonderful?'

Her grandmother walked to the window, stared out at the rain. She looked at the ceiling as if an answer lay there.

'Have you ever stopped to wonder why?'

'I have, I do—' Bella paused, confused by her interest.

'Do you want to know why?' Freda asked, her eyes spiking. 'Why you feel so at home? You might not want to, but I think you should. No more dilly dallying.'

'What are you talking about?' Paint dripped from the end of her brush and hit the floor. She felt it splatter, cool across her naked foot.

'You were born here.'

Bella laughed. 'Here?'

'Yes, Isobel. Here.'

'Mama came to the cottage to give birth to me?' She gave a quick glance around the room, seeing it anew. 'Well, it makes sense. Why I feel like this. But why wasn't Mama at the Hall, or in a maternity home? Why would she come here?'

'You have a lot of questions, Isobel. And yes, rightly so. And I think they should be answered.'

Bella swallowed, unnerved by her grandmother, by her rage, focusing on her.

'Grannie, what do you mean?'

'Because you're not your mother's child.'

'*What*?'

'And your real name is Kate.'

Bella wondered why her grandmother seemed so angry. How much she should dislike her, and want to punish her for her tetchy company, for never seeing eye to eye, to spin this ridiculous story.

'Your mother is not Vivienne. Your mother is someone else.' She tilted her chin. 'This was your real mother's home, this cottage. Possibly why you like it so much.'

The sound of rain filled Bella's ears, a torrent of noise, enlarging the air, and muffling her grandmother's voice as she continued to speak, words flashing like barbs and slaps. Bella wanted to duck.

'What?'

Her grandmother took a step closer. She looked terrified of Bella and Bella, appalled by her proximity, turned back to her easel. But her work did not make sense to her any more. Had it ever meant anything? No wonder she'd abandoned her paintings in the puddle outside the Slade. She must look ridiculous, standing there with paintbrush in hand, in a silly pretend studio, in front of a piece of such amateur art.

'Your real mother was locked away many years ago for her own good.'

Bella took a sharp breath, her eyes raking over her grandmother's face. The air felt dead, as if it no longer had any oxygen, could no longer give her life.

She watched as her grandmother twitched, seemed to come to. And then she heard her utter, 'Sorry, Isobel, sorry'. She felt her move in on her, her hand encircling her forearm, urging her to come downstairs, to come and sit down, a curious gesture skewed with warped purpose.

Bella pulled her arm away, skimming the table, scattering paint tubes. Her palette tipped off, landed face down on the floor. Staring at it, she felt a trace of relief, and smiled for a second. That's that then.

And yet her grandmother's words continued to knock on the walls inside her head, until she heard, and felt, something break.

She brushed past her and went down the stairs. Perhaps she would feel different in another room, another place entirely. She opened the door to the rain. She stepped out, barefoot, into it, the sensation, cold and drowning, pummelling her, making her gasp. She sucked the wet air in, but it turned raw, grating down her throat.

This house, this garden, her sanctuary: yes, it made sense; an inverted, deceitful, terrible sense. The place Bella had discovered, had been drawn to, had revived, and loved, turned on her. Water gushed down the drainpipe, overflowing, splattering. Rose bushes bent under the torrent, the herb beds beaten down. The structure would rot, the roof would cave in, the amber glass would shatter. And she would too.

Someone called her name, and the garden door swung open. Her mother, her eyes ablaze. She was heading for her, reading her expression, her arms open, but Bella pushed her away, could not bear her.

She crouched down, her back against the cottage wall.

Above her head, the shouting began. Both women in the doorway, screaming at each other. Bella peered up at them through her sopping fringe. From Farthing Hall to Le Chable, she'd always thought her feet had never felt on solid ground, her foundations loose, not quite right or belonging anywhere. Her mother, grandmother – she did not know them.

She heard her grandmother apologising. '...time she ought to know... we couldn't go on... can't take all the blame...will she be all right?'

And her mother's response: '...can't believe you'd do such a thing... with Nathan not here... couldn't you wait?!'

Her mother squatted down, her face too close to hers. Those wide-spaced eyes, the blue not belonging to Bella, the fair luscious hair a mockery, for nothing of Vivienne Miles Calloway had anything to do with her.

'My darling, would you like to talk to Dad? He will be coming home later. Come on, get inside out of the rain.'

'My *dad*?' She mouthed the word. She wanted to ask, couldn't bear to. 'Why would I want to speak to him?'

'Please, darling.' Her mother's stare, fixed on her, shifted through hope, darkened into despair. 'Freda,' she snapped, 'don't just stand there. Do as I ask and go and find Mr Buckley, and fetch Genna. Ask her to bring the book. Yes, she'll know what you mean.'

Her grandmother tramped off towards the garden door, casting a sharp glance back over her shoulder, catching Bella's eye, as she did so. Fear, and a whiff of contrition.

'Please come inside, Bella,' her mother said again, tugging at her arm. 'I will try to explain.'

Her limbs felt heavy, her strength melting. The cold made her naked feet ache; her body was shutting down, putting up a wall to stop her thinking, seeing and understanding. Her whole life, one cruel lie. Shivering, she gave in to it, allowed her mother to haul her up and back inside.

With the door shut, her mother began to stoke the fire in the range, her hands unsteady, scattering coal. Bella stood in the middle of the kitchen, trembling, and watched, seeing someone out of place here in the cottage, unpractised, out of kilter with her surroundings.

And then she saw herself, standing on the outside, looking in. She, too, out of place. The chill she'd felt all her life, within her family at the Hall and in the empty mountains, the feeling that she'd managed to dispel these few short months making her home at the cottage and painting her heart out, returned, creeping and suffocating, fastening its hold.

She wanted to speak; she knew she'd sound like someone else.

'Who am I?'

The woman turned from the stove. 'Sit down, you're freezing. Here, close to the fire.'

Bella stared at the beautiful, terrified stranger. 'And who are you?'

'Oh, darling, I wish your father was here. I've always wished he was here. He needs to tell you himself. We didn't want it to happen like this. We've been fools. I've always been your mother, but I, oh good God, what an awful mess.'

Bella flinched, steadied herself, not wanting any more answers, though she knew she had to ask.

'Is he my father?'

'Yes, yes, he is.'

'How do I know that?'

Bella heard Vivienne's answer cracking through the room but could not focus nor pick out the words. Something menacing flapped around her head, a rushing of air, the black wings of a bird, her own hands. There seemed no point to them, or to her, for she seemed not to be a real person. Bella, from nowhere, an empty being, in the shape of a girl.

Except there must be something left of her, for the pain felt savage, and she heard someone weeping, felt someone take her hand.

Her mother coaxed her upstairs, a climb in stages, a pause, and a struggle. A final acquiescence. She helped her into bed and drew the curtains, shutting out the rain-splattered morning. The mattress cradled her, the covers scooped around her body, the pillow an infinite cushioning beneath her head.

The crying, she grasped after some time, came from her mother, who was sitting by the bed, tears streaming unchecked. Bella closed her eyes, could not bear to witness it, and saw someone else, perhaps herself, or a woman quite like her. The scent of a sweet summer evening, the sound of bees on the roses outside, her father's voice, a tale of the sea, and a tinkling tune, in the far corner of the room, from a wind-up music box.

* * *

The morning, twenty-four hours later, seemed like an entirely new world to Bella: drowsy and hollow, the rain blown away. Shy sunshine filtered through the trees and into her bedroom, projecting flickering shadow-leaves across the walls.

Her mother, a fair, poised angel, remained by her bed, stiff with exhaustion. Bella turned over, to face the wall, shutting her eyes to the memory, the dream turned into a nightmare. She recalled vague movements during the long, disjointed hours. Genna's voice downstairs – warm and positive – a clattering of the stove. Being made to sit up and sip a brew. Tasting something hot, green and floral; hearing, within the filth in her mind, her mother praise Annie Drake's journal for the herbal tea, 'to make you feel better, my darling, to sleep'. And Bella, her mouth thick with despair, uttering, 'But I don't want to dream'. The liquid had coursed down her throat, filling her with a pleasant, swaying sensation. And once again, with the room dark and her father's voice by the open bedroom door, urging her to rest.

Her mother set a tray of tea on the bedside table. She poured warm water into a bowl, offered a flannel and soap.

'Bella, you have a visitor waiting downstairs,' she said, dunking the flannel, wringing it out. 'Would you like to see if you can get up?'

Bella pressed the warm cloth to her face. She nodded. She wondered fleetingly who it may be; she hoped for her father, dreaded it being Freda.

'I'll help you get up if you like, but then I will leave you.'

Bella shot her a glance, but didn't want her to go; she wanted to say so, call out, 'Mama' as she walked out of the bedroom, but did not know how to say her name.

She got dressed, or at least found her way into her clothes. She felt unhuman, a column of muscle and bone, turned inside out and numb with shock. The Bella she had been, now a tiny dot, was disappearing; she had no substance. Her life, everything, meant nothing. A great empty hole. Except Robin. She thought of him waking to another ordinary day in his bedsit, installed in his own world, a world in which she no longer featured, and all the while, time and distance grew wider between them. The realisation of this truth arranged itself in front of her, to grab her attention. She could not look at it. She tried to tidy her hair, but gave up. Dust began to settle inside her head, synchronicity whispering, and she heard his voice say, 'Goodbye' to her mother down in the kitchen.

She went to the top of the stairs, sat down on the top step, and held her knees close to her chest. October sunlight, growing richer by the moment, drenched the world beyond the cottage, seeping in across the kitchen floor below.

And down by her fireplace, flicking through Annie Drake's journal, sat Rob.

'Why?' she asked. 'Why are you here?'

He glanced up, a dash of fear in his expression, his face sharp with concern.

'Bella.'

'How did you know? To come here?'

'Your mother, she got word to my father. He called me yesterday.'

She thought of the telephone, shrill in the dim Hammersmith hallway, imagined the landlady's thunderous face.

'I caught the earliest train I could.'

Bella's throat thickened. Her eyes stung. 'Why?'

He put the book down and came to the bottom of the stairs. He sighed, long and heavy.

'Because your mother said I was the only person that she knew could help you.'

Bella flicked her head, batting the idea away.

'My mother?' Pain hissed through her teeth.

'Mrs Calloway. Vivienne, I mean. Christ, Bella, you look so pale.' He reached up and gestured to her. 'Come down here. I will make you breakfast, a cup of tea and toast. I'm good at tea.'

She clutched her knees tighter. 'No, I am quite happy here, thank you.'

He perched on the bottom step, looking so at home it seemed preposterous.

Pictures and sound edged through Bella's twilight memory: Robin's voice, a child's voice, singing a song about a girl named Katie, meeting her by the kitchen door.

'Your father came here last night, apparently,' he said. 'But you refused to see him.'

Anger rose like a pulse of flame. Hadn't her father once warned her that life would not stay the same?

'Is it any wonder?'

'Oh, Bella.'

Her childhood, a half-lit dream containing her parents, spooled backwards into darkness, incomprehensible and unsteady. She tumbled through it, lost, and grasping. The dream had ended; a cold real morning had arrived, leaving her beached and exhausted in a room where all the adults spoke with forked tongues. Except Rob. She gazed down at him; the face and the voice, and the song, that had been with her all her life.

'I knew your mother. Elise,' he said, arranging his face, fighting emotion.

Her name, to Bella, sounded like a chime. 'Elise?' she whispered.

Rob nodded. 'She lived here with her own mother, Annie Drake. This is why you feel you know the cottage, the Amber House, the time you were here. You were very young. I expect they all thought you wouldn't remember.'

'*They* all?'

'They were trying to protect you, not knowing what to say, when to say it. I couldn't tell you, of course I couldn't. It wasn't my place. But I longed for you to be happy.'

'Was I happy here?'

'You were happy.'

'Then why did I leave?'

Rob shifted on the step, his body turned fully towards her.

'Elise had an accident and never properly recovered. Annie had already died. You were tiny. Your father and Mrs Calloway, they stepped in. Of course, your father, he had always cared for you, you know, and for Elise. But we know what that generation can be like. Things brushed under the carpet, simply not talked about. The threat of scandal.'

A snap of anger. 'Is that why Grannie hates me so much?'

'Really, Bella...'

'What did all the villagers think? The staff at the Hall?'

'They were told your parents had adopted the little orphan girl from the Amber House. But they may well have thought differently. My own father sat me down, made me understand the new story. That they changed your name to Isobel. He said not to talk about the old days, about when I used to bring over the basket of groceries. I loved coming here. Seeing Elise, Annie, you. Remember, I was only a boy, so I didn't really understand. And the war, well, it made so many strange things acceptable, or at least almost understandable.'

Bella closed her eyes as layers of realisation drifted down, one on top of the other, like a stack of papers, a mesh of words, forming a picture for her.

'My name was Kate, wasn't it? Grannie told me.'

Rob looked aghast, nodded. 'Yes.'

'What did my father do?' she asked, suddenly snapping. 'Have an affair with this Elise? Why don't I remember her? Why don't I...?'

Her questions vanished before she could form them. She stared down at Robin, sitting there on the bottom stair: the only person who made sense. The kettle on the range began to sing, and she watched him go to find cups, set them out on her table, spoon tea from the caddy.

'But I do remember, Robin,' she said. 'That's why I love it here.'

She longed to go back, to see the lady, the darling button on her shoe. But the vile deceit gripped her again, shaking her, exploding little earthquakes within. Mist lingered where Elise's face should be. Even her own name, what people called her, proved to be a lie; she'd been named after Isobel, the American grandmother, yet that woman had had nothing to do with her.

She gripped the banister, clung on to the solid wood, cut and hewn in another century. She imagined all the years the cottage had stood here in its patch in the woods, the years that had been her unspeakable past.

She rested her head in her hands, raked her fingers through her hair.

'No one has spoken her name, until you,' she said.

And she remembered, the music box tune stirring eddies of memory.

She pulled herself up and walked down the stairs, sat down in the fireside chair, and picked up the journal. She could feel Robin watching her.

'Some of it is priceless, Bella,' he said, resting a steaming cup beside her, his voice light with relief that she had at least moved from the top of the stairs. 'Annie's descriptions. You as a teething toddler being made to suck cloves. Goose fat rubbed on your chest for colds, herbal remedies. Ointments and tonics. All manner of stuff. It is a work of art, really.'

'A lost art.' Bella turned the pages, windows into long ago. 'Last night they gave me some tea to help me sleep. I suspect it was something Annie Drake might have brewed. It worked. I slept, but I woke to this. What happened, Rob?' She looked at his face, searching. 'Grannie... Freda said that Elise had been taken away, locked away. What on earth—'

'The elder Mrs Calloway sounds rather troubled, doesn't she? I am not surprised,' Rob said kindly.

'Tell me why.' She took a long shuddering breath, feeding her courage. 'Please.'

Rob sat down opposite her, watching her closely, and explained Elise's accident, her collapse in the cottage garden on VE day. How he had found them both, Bella – Little Kate – and Elise, early the next morning. His urgent terror, a boy, ten years old. How he could not wake Elise, but picked Bella up and carried her to the Farthing Hall kitchen, the only thing he could possibly do. Why Elise lost her memory, and her senses. How Vivienne took Bella in, how Freda may not have been too pleased about it. And how Nathan had taken care of Elise ever since. The nursing home by the sea.

Bella listened, watched him speaking, the dust in her mind forming into solid shapes. She thought of the trips to Margate with her father. The name Kate, tolling like a bell in darkness.

'My father and Elise, they were in love?'

'That much, I don't know.'

She looked into Rob's eyes.

She knew.

'Do you remember,' her laugh sounded surprising and fresh, 'how we said our parents never talk about the old times. Is it any wonder?!'

Silently, she wept.

'Are you all right, Bella?'

'No.' She dashed her hands over her face, wiping the tears. She went to the niche by the fireplace and returned Annie Drake's journal to its hiding place. 'But one day, I may be.'

'Bella,' he said quietly, his taut expression melting into something less tangible, and private, 'when you have finished your tea, would you show me your paintings?'

Upstairs, her studio looked tidier than she'd left it, the tubes back in their place, the patch of paint on the floor from her dislodged palette wiped clean, her canvases propped against the walls, a gallery of her inner life. She waited in the doorway, a tingle of shyness coiling through her, as Robin stepped reverently from one painting to the other.

Watching him gaze at her most private expressions, she was able to see her work in a new light. She painted from imagination – elongated people, white horses, and sea creatures, and all with luminous dark eyes against a backdrop of aqua waves or a swirling green forest. A fantasy: distorted but beautiful. Once, she had wanted to paint what she saw outside: the countryside, the cathedral, the orchards. Now, she stepped inside her imagination. Her work neither modern nor avant-garde, but simply herself, an expression of Bella, Little Kate, the girl within.

'I've often wondered why I like to paint the sea so much,' she said, leaning against the door jamb, 'when I seemed to have been landlocked all my life. But now. Now I understand. You see, Dad took me to the sea. And there, I didn't know it, but I was close to my mother.'

As if he sensed her pain, Robin came over and linked his arms around her, pulled her close, a strange feeling: outlandish, new, and utterly beautiful. She laid her head on his shoulder, and he cradled her, holding her up, his head resting against hers.

'You call this place the Amber House,' she said, her mouth against his shoulder. 'Why is that?'

Rob drew back and looked down at her face, smiling on the

memory. 'I was here, waiting for them, when my father brought Elise and Annie over in his van, all the way up from Margate. Under strict instructions from Mrs Scott not to dawdle, to leave the basket, go straight back to the Hall.'

'And you didn't of course,' Bella said.

'Of course, I didn't. I wanted to show them around. Showing off, more like. I remember scooting up the stairs, with Elise following me. I came headlong into here, and the sun was streaming in through the windows. I ran up and down in the empty room like a right urchin, waving my arms through the shafts of light, all orange and warm and glorious. Elise... your mother, she must have been pregnant with you, said that the light was the colour of amber. I didn't know what that was but I told her, "you are going to live in the Amber House".'

Bella shut her eyes, relishing the strong, real solidity of him, how normal this felt, how she had never been held this way before. A feeling of being looked after, taken care of. And a link to her past. She thought she may collapse yet knew that, if she did, Robin would prop her up.

'What your mother... what Mrs Calloway said – that I am the only person who could help you – means a great deal to me,' he said. 'For you are the only person I have ever wanted to spend my time with.' His whispered voice brushed close against her ear. He leaned back so he could look at her face. 'And I haven't much to offer you, Miss Bella Calloway.'

She extracted herself, went to the windowsill, lifted the lid on the music box and wound the key. 'Für Elise' chimed around the room. Then she returned herself back into his arms, and they danced, for as long as the music played, the sweet innocent tune that had rung through Bella's young life.

'The song you used to sing, Rob. "K-K-Katie".'

'Ah, you remember that?' he said. 'My Dad used to sing it all the time. It was from the Great War.'

She felt a pang of distress refreshingly outside of her own. She took in his generous, peaceful face.

'Oh, Rob, I have two mothers and you don't even have one. I'm so sorry.'

He cradled her face, left a sweet kiss on her forehead. 'Now, now, it's all right. I have always had you.'

They danced, even though the tune had stopped.

Bella laughed and looked into his eyes. 'I always thought there was something wrong with me,' she said. 'But now I know why. I need to go to the sea. I need to see it, Rob. Will you take me there? Will you come with me? There's someone I need to visit.'

27

VIVI, TWO YEARS LATER, 1962

She thanked the doctor, saw him to the door. Once the sound of the car had faded off down the track, she took Elise out into the cottage garden to sit on the bench against the wall under the honeysuckle, planted by Robin last spring. Close by, baby Kate sat warbling in her playpen in a patch of sunlight scattered with fallen petals, her nappy a pudgy cushion, her plump arms jerking with delight at a new audience.

Vivi passed her the teddy she'd tossed out on to the lawn, seeing Nathan and Bella in her, in her dark hair, and something around the mouth: a yearning for the child never conceived. But Bella always insisted Kate looked like Robin, with a dash of Elise, somewhere inside that steady, questioning gaze.

Vivi wondered if Elise saw it too.

Elise settled herself on the seat. She didn't speak as she contemplated Kate, the little baby peering up at her through the playpen bars, but her fingers stopped tapping at her side, her limbs realigned themselves, her eyes shimmered.

Vivi pressed her hand to Elise's arm.

'You'll be all right here for a moment or two?' she asked. 'Relax in the sunshine. I'll fetch you some tea.'

'Oh, I love tea.' Elise's face widened with her smile, then rested into serious consideration. 'And I will watch over the baby.'

Vivi threw a glance over her shoulder, making sure the baby was safe, and went back inside. Rob sat at the kitchen table, balancing his accounts, jerking his head now and then to keep an eye on his baby daughter through the window. On the radio, the Light Programme played softly in the background.

'How is Elise this morning?' he asked.

'Whenever the doctor leaves, you may have noticed, she becomes a bit agitated, but not so much today,' Vivi said. 'Perhaps we will see an improvement?'

Rob put his pen down, looked up at her. 'I'm not sure how likely that will be, Vivienne.'

'We can only hope,' she said, filling the kettle and setting it on the stove.

'Morning, Mama.'

Bella came in through the back door, wearing her huge paint-splattered apron, her hair in a tangle on top of her head. Hearing her call her Mama, the one thing that had not changed through all the upheaval, and the time that had passed, sent melodic relief through her mind.

Bella bore the familiar inner spark from having had an early start in her studio. Robin, with the help of Mr Buckley, now retired, had built it for her in the garden behind the cottage. Vivi imagined that it was the spot where he had found Elise and Bella all those years ago.

'You look like you have had a good session, Bella,' she said.

'It was okay.'

'I know that look,' said Robin. 'She means it's going brilliantly.'

Bella blushed just like she'd done as a child, and jerked her shoulders cheerfully.

Vivi also admired Bella's restraint, her modesty, her not wishing to jinx anything in the run up to her exhibition that autumn in the little Canterbury gallery.

Robin glanced at the clock. 'Are you ready for the handover, Bella? Ready to take the reins? We have quite the system now, Vivi, as you can see. It runs like clockwork.'

'I don't doubt it for a minute,' she replied, pouring steaming water into the teapot and bringing it to the table. 'You two are a wonderful team.'

Before their wedding last year, a small affair at Canterbury registry office, Robin had left the bank and returned to Farthing Hall to set up a livery business, championed by both Vivi and Nathan. Now, while he spent time at the stables, Bella stayed home at the Amber House and cared for Kate; when Bella painted, he looked after their child.

Bella peered out of the window. 'And I see Little Kate is chatting away to Elise, look at that. How she entertains her. Mama...' She turned to her. It had been unexpected for Vivi, and Nathan, that Bella insisted on using Elise's first name, making Vivi's surge of happiness at being called Mama underpinned by guilt. 'I'll take her tea out to her in a moment, but I wanted you to see something first.'

Bella opened a drawer in the dresser and pulled out a sheaf of writing paper. She sifted it in her hands, the tips of her fingers a rainbow of stains in shades from blue to green. She sat down next to her at the table and passed the pages over.

'What's this?' Vivi asked.

'Elise has been writing a great deal recently,' said Bella. 'You know how we encourage her, how the doctor thinks it will do her good. She leaves scraps of paper around the place, even though I bought her that lovely leather-bound diary. Anyway, I found this whole cache of pages under her pillow yesterday. They are letters as such, that she has written to Dad and sometimes to herself. As if she is talking to herself.'

'We all do that,' said Vivi, trying to make light of it.

She held the crumpled wad at arm's length, a tatty ream of pale-blue Basildon Bond wreathed with Elise's delicate hand-writing and blotted with ink. Part of her felt as if she was overstepping a boundary.

'Then should we read them?' Robin asked.

'Exactly what I was thinking,' Vivi said.

Bella's eyes sharpened with tears.

'If anyone reads them, it should be Dad,' she said.

Vivi folded the pages in half. 'Can I take this envelope?' she asked, plucking one from Robin's stationery tray. She tucked Elise's words, Elise's world, inside it, sealed it, and secured it in her handbag.

Bella nodded at her, contemplating her, with trust, final and absolute, deep in her eyes.

Outside, the high-summer day approached noon, the sun warming the walls around the cottage, deepening the canopy of green. Vivi had not felt such peace, been aware of such solidity beneath her since, as a girl a tad younger than Bella, she had stepped off the boat onto the dock at Southampton. A lifetime ago.

Bella stood up, stretched luxuriously, hearing her daughter's chirping laughter and Elise's delighted response. She collected Elise's cup of tea and went out into the garden to join them.

* * *

As Vivi walked up the gravel drive to the Hall, Freda's pleasantly competent version of 'Für Elise' drifted towards her, the notes lingering tenderly in the air. She opened the front door, called, 'Hello'. The music stopped mid chord.

Poking her head around the sitting room door, she saw Freda at the piano, her sparse white hair bright in the sunshine, stiff-shouldered, her expression tainted with being caught doing something she shouldn't. Vivi had seen that look many times over the years since Digby's death. She'd decided not to comment on her mother-in-law's playing, let alone admit that every time she heard it, she admired her in another new and unexpected way. Of all the unspoken subjects at Farthing Hall, the playing of Beethoven's tune seemed the easiest to comment on, and yet Vivi resisted, placing it among the many other things that she would never ask.

As Genna once said: *Annie Drake knows the truth.*

'Have you seen Nathan?' she asked instead.

'He's in the garden,' Freda replied. 'All those plants he ordered from the nursery have just been delivered. Never seen so many.' The hardness, Vivi realised, had disappeared from Freda's voice long ago; her eyes no longer that of a stranger. 'Never thought that son of mine would have such green fingers.'

'People change, Freda,' she said. 'We all know that.'

Freda slowly closed the piano lid, and rested her hands there, as if longing to continue to play.

Out in the garden, Nathan stood on the lawn, puzzling over the pots of young honeysuckle and jasmine, a cluster of naked rose bushes, casting his eye around the pristine topiary as if he wanted to bring an artist's eye to the monochrome green, to paint the garden with colour.

'Happy, darling?' he said in greeting.

'I think it will be beautiful out here when you're done.' Vivi walked into his arms to kiss him. 'It'll be a lot of work though. Will Mr Buckley be helping?'

'He may, although I pretty much want to do it myself.'

'Something tells me you are gearing up for a nice, long, early retirement, Nathan.' She squeezed his hand.

He laughed. 'You're reading my mind. It's about time I gave in to middle age, isn't it?'

'But for now,' she said, 'why don't you sit in the deckchair in the shade, and I shall bring you a nice gin and tonic?'

'That sounds like an excellent idea. But only if you join me.'

'I may pass on that for the moment. I think you may be wanting some time alone.'

He looked at her askance.

She opened her handbag, drew out the envelope and pressed it into his hand.

'What's this?' He slit it open, glanced at the handwriting, his face blanching. 'Good God. Is this Elise?'

Vivi nodded, not capable of meeting the astounded look in his eyes.

He walked over to the deckchair by the hedge, and slumped into it, exhaling a great sigh. With the faintest of trembling, his hands, as he held the pages, betrayed his feelings. Vivi stood beside him for a moment, wanting to protect him, to demonstrate her care. And yet she knew the right thing to do would be to let him be.

He reached up for her hand and held it to the scarred side of his jaw. He searched her face, as if seeking her love and fearful he would not find it.

'I'll be right back, Nathan,' she said.

As she walked across the lawn, her body drenched with sunlight, she felt happiness pulsing from her toes right up to her head, as humble and as thrilling as the day she'd first met him. As perfect as the dance in the private velvet air of the London jazz club. She felt as loved as the girl she had once been.

She turned at the back door, satisfied that Nathan had begun to read Elise's letters, and went inside the house.

EPILOGUE
ELISE

Today, summer lights up the room. The walls glow, warm and heavenly. And I am safe. The feeling moves up and down inside me, disappears, reappears, waves breaking on the beach. Our little beach, Nathan, do you remember?

I miss my room on the coast. The blue horizon, the smell of the sea. The red sunsets hissing into the waves. But I packed up my things and brought them with me: my shells, my chalk pebbles, seaweed and mermaid purses. I have hundreds of them. Have you seen them? I gave you a mermaid's purse once, do you remember, to keep you safe.

I fill this place with the sea.

It is quiet here; a different sort of peace: a woodland peace. You would like it, Nathan. Trees, fern and bracken, and there are white roses in the garden. We love the scent of the roses, don't we? Everything familiar, everything strange.

All is green and light and amber.

I must keep scribbling, or the words will escape me.

They tell me I forget, and writing helps me remember. And I like to write to you. We have a secret, our very own treasure between us, don't we? Our little girl. And even though I forget, part of me always knows. Nathan, I wish I could pin it down.

Let me write this quickly: there's a nice lady, as fair as an angel, and ever so beautiful, who comes to visit. And she sometimes brings a doctor from London. He is kind and he looks after me. What will he say to me next time, I wonder? What will he prescribe? What will I say to him, Nathan?

I will say that sometimes I see you. And sometimes, I see our little girl. And yet sometimes, it all disappears.

I hear voices downstairs.

The couple who live in the amber house have an adorable baby girl like ours. I have no idea who the young lady and gentleman are, but they seem to know me. They know me very well. Listen. They're calling my name.

They want to take me on a trip to the sea, the proper sea, our sea. You remember our bay, our beach, don't you, Nathan?

Ma says time does not flow in linear fashion but goes round and round, an endless circle. And we are still there, on the beach, boy and girl, meeting for the first time.

Perhaps, one day, you will come and look for me again.

We will sit on the rocks, Nathan, paddle the pools, listen to the sound of the sea, watch the waves breaking.

And there, in the distance, is the life we are going to lead.

ACKNOWLEDGMENTS

The story of Vivi, the officer's wife, and her nemesis Elise, has taken on many forms since I first conjured it up. It took four years, three rewrites and a hefty dose of fortitude for me to create the novel you now hold in your hands.

I would like to thank my agent Judith Murdoch for her patience and belief that I could get there in the end, and Emily Yau, my fantastic editor for showing me where the true essence of the tale lay. And to everyone at Boldwood Books, thank you for your support and comradery.

My father Gerry Law served in National Service in the 1950s, and his stories – the concealed quiff and the endless saluting and whitewashing – inspired my character Robin's experiences. And his country boyhood is a continual source of inspiration, too. Thank you, Dad.

AUTHOR'S NOTE

This novel is a work of fiction, and while residents of Margate, and the Men and Maids of Kent will certainly recognise the places I mention, from the Seabathing Hospital to the Sands Hotel, King Street and Botany Bay, I have also taken a little artistic licence. The idea for the hidden cottage – the Amber House – formed while walking through the ancient woodland of East Blean, and, even though I never found a cottage, who knows, it may yet be discovered. The mansion and church in Mayfair are there for all to see, but the hamlet of Farthing and the Hall exist only in my imagination.

MORE FROM CATHERINE LAW

We hope you enjoyed reading *The Officer's Wife*. If you did, please leave a review.

If you'd like to gift a copy, this book is also available as an ebook, hardback, large print, digital audio download and audiobook CD.

Sign up to Catherine Law's mailing list for news, competitions and updates on future books:

https://bit.ly/CatherineLawNews

ABOUT THE AUTHOR

Catherine Law writes dramatic romantic novels set in the first half of the 20th century, during the First and Second World Wars. Previously published by Zaffre, her books are inspired by the tales our mothers and grandmothers tell. Originally a journalist, Catherine lives in Kent.

Visit Catherine's website: www.catherinelaw.co.uk

Follow Catherine on social media:

facebook.com/catherinelawbooks

twitter.com/authorcathlaw

instagram.com/catherinelawauthor

goodreads.com/catherinelaw

Boldw⚭d

Boldwood Books is an award-winning fiction publishing company seeking out the best stories from around the world.

Find out more at www.boldwoodbooks.com

Join our reader community for brilliant books, competitions and offers!

Follow us
@BoldwoodBooks
@BookandTonic

Sign up to our weekly deals newsletter

https://bit.ly/BoldwoodBNewsletter

Printed in Great Britain
by Amazon